WHEN HEARTS IGNITE
VICTORIA LUM

When Hearts Ignite

By Victoria Lum

Copyright © 2024 Victoria Lum

Published by Eternal Hearts Publishing

Cover Design Copyright © 2024 Y'All That Graphic

Editing by Theresa Leigh and Amy Briggs

Proofreading by Virginia Tesi Carey

ISBN (Paperback): 979-8-9876470-9-7

ISBN (E-Book): 979-8-9876470-8-0

AUTHOR'S NOTE

AUTHOR'S NOTE: PLEASE NOTE this story may contain areas that may be sensitive to some readers. For a list of potential areas of sensitive content, please visit: https://www.victorialum.com/sensitive-content-information

DEDICATION

For all the ladies who love reading about men who claim they will never fall in love...ever. This one is for you. Also, if you're a fan of bonus epilogues, don't miss out on the ones for this book. Trust me.

RELATIONSHIP TREE

THE KINGSLEYS AND EXTENDED FAMILY
(LA HEARTS SERIES)

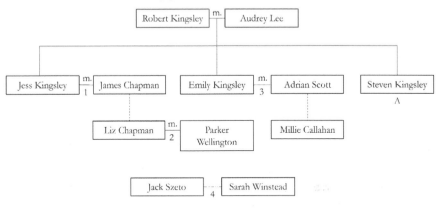

Robert Kingsley — m. — Audrey Lee

Jess Kingsley — m.1 — James Chapman   Emily Kingsley — m.3 — Adrian Scott   Steven Kingsley A

Liz Chapman — m.2 — Parker Wellington   Millie Callahan

Jack Szeto --- 4 --- Sarah Winstead

THE ANDERSONS AND FRIENDS (THE ORCHID SERIES)

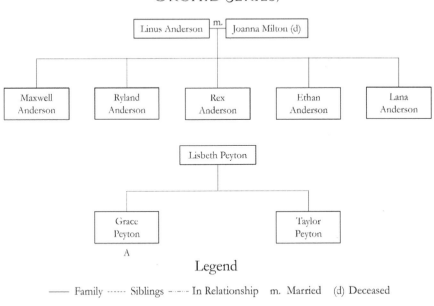

Linus Anderson — m. — Joanna Milton (d)

Maxwell Anderson   Ryland Anderson   Rex Anderson   Ethan Anderson   Lana Anderson

Lisbeth Peyton

Grace Peyton A   Taylor Peyton

Legend

——— Family ······ Siblings -·-·- In Relationship   m. Married   (d) Deceased

Books

1 – *The Sweetest Agony* 2 – *The Coldest Passion* 3 – *The Harshest Hope* 4 – *The Brightest Spark*

A – *When Hearts Ignite*

Disclaimer: Only main characters are included. Awesome side characters including children are not in this tree.

CHAPTER 1

I'M BROKEN. DEFECTIVE.

I've come to that realization a long time ago. The thumping organ in my rib cage is supposed to race and pound with emotions, the apparent signs of what makes us all human. I've never felt the agonizing want of needing another person more than I need my next breath, the crippling blow of heartbreak cutting out my knees from under me, the highs and lows waxed by poets and musicians in lofted tomes and award-winning lyrics.

Or at least, I don't think I have.

"Steven? Are you sure you don't want to stay? It's only four in the morning. I don't have any plans today," a sultry, raspy voice murmurs from the haphazard pile of sheets in the middle of the bed in one of the premium, sound-proofed suites of the Rose floors at The Orchid, the most exclusive establishment in the world for the rich and famous.

The voluptuous figure shifts on the bed, a pair of long legs with reddened handprints on the thighs peeking out from under the comforter. A pair of handcuffs is wedged by the fluffy pillows I'll never use for sleep. Her lacy black dress, bra, and thong are littered across the soft carpet. The room is dark except for the soft light filtering in from the ensuite bathroom.

The smell of sweat and sex lingers in the air. My skin is slick and damp from exertion. Three back-to-back sessions, dulling the inconvenient biological need inside me to the background once again. Unlike my love for gourmet food and fine dining, my time with women is a means to an end, the sex feeling something like the bland taste of porridge or chicken noodle soup when you're bedridden with sickness. It's necessary, but not something to be savored.

"No. You know I never do. Thank you for your time today, Liesel."

I finish buttoning up my white dress shirt, which I carefully draped across an armchair before we tumbled onto the bed, and shrug on my bespoke suit jacket, my hands straightening out the sleeves, and dusting off a few pieces of lint stuck on the fabric.

I pull out my wallet from my pocket. After taking out a few crisp hundreds, I tuck the bills into a purple, embossed linen envelope on the dresser, careful to place it so it's precisely aligned to the edge of the surface—because nothing annoys me more than things being out of order. The Orchid isn't a brothel, so we can't be too crass as to hand over money outright. The beautiful envelope represents a gift we can choose to bestow upon our women if desired.

A gift. *Not* a payment.

In this invite-only establishment for the rich and powerful, all our wants and needs are catered to, whether they're the award-winning cuisine from Michelin-rated restaurants, access to the specialty bars, lounges, gentlemen's club, or top of the line spas on-site. In addition, there's transportation to private islands for vacation, contacts to the top surgeons, or couture designers of the world, and specialty Cuban cigars flown in directly from the source at the cigar club, among other perks. But there's an unspoken, but popular service provided, which fits under the broad umbrella of companionship and straddles the lines of legality.

The men and women who choose to work on the Rose floors where adult entertainment reigns supreme, from specialty clubs to private suites separated out from the other luxury rooms for guests embarking on less amorous pursuits, are carefully vetted in a series of comprehensive background and physical checks and are also under iron-clad nondisclosure agreements even the Supreme Court couldn't break.

Nor would they want to since a few of the justices are members here.

The rustling of the bedsheets and the soft footsteps alert me to her presence behind me before the whiff of expensive floral perfume hits my nose. I pick up my watch next and flip it over to the back. Delicate arms encircle my waist as I trace the engraving with my fingers.

Mind over matter.

The watch is one of the few gifts my father gave me, a classic timepiece which has withstood the test of time. He gave it to me when I graduated from Harvard, along with a terse nod of approval. *"Son, we Kingsley men live with honor. We do things the right way even when the world doesn't."* I slip it on and carefully wipe off the thumbprints on the face.

I hate those damn smudges on the clear glass.

"Are you sure? You seem tense this time. Maybe we can move up our date to next week instead of three months from now?"

I stiffen. Goosebumps pebble on the back of my neck. The warning bells in my mind blare loud and clear.

Slowly removing her hands from my waist, I turn around, finding Liesel's blue eyes wide with a trace of hopefulness she tries her best to hide. A flush spreads over her face, half-hidden by her long locks of brown hair. She slowly bites her lip, a move normally seductive coming from her, someone who could grace the cover of magazines, but is now fraught with tension instead.

"I think it's time we part ways, Liesel," I say gently, my heart prodding along as if I'm talking about the weather outside instead of ending a long-term companionship arrangement.

They can't get attached to me. Their adoration and emotions are of no use to me. And it's something I'll never be able to reciprocate.

Nor do I want to.

My mind flits to my older sisters, Jess and Emily, both hopelessly in love with their men, James and Adrian, respectively, and I can't help but ask myself, *don't I want what they have?*

The truth is, I couldn't care less.

I know I'm not built that way. These tender emotions aren't languages I comprehend, and they're worthless to me. They are liabilities impeding common sense and logical thinking.

The closest thing to love I have for the women in the world are reserved for my sisters who've supported me all these years, with Jess being more of a mother figure than our mother ever was and Emily being the spark in the large, cold house we grew up in, and that's more than enough.

Liesel's eyes dim as she processes the meaning behind my words. She pastes a fake smile on her face, a smile no doubt trained by Sofia Kent, the manager of the Rose floors, before she unleashes the girls to work with high-net-worth clientele.

"Is it because I asked you to stay? I'm just worried about you, that's all. You seem troubled this time. You don't have to stay if you don't want to. We can see each other once a quarter like you prefer."

Liesel nervously twirls a thick lock of hair while she clutches the bedsheets around her body like a suit of armor, as if it'll soften the blow or rewind time. She swallows, her smile faltering at my silence.

My lips curve into what I hope is a sympathetic smile, and I cup her cheek with my hand. She lets out a small sigh. I know she needs tenderness and reassurance from me, but I can't give her what she's looking for. It's best to cut things off before they get worse.

"You've been wonderful to me, Liesel. But you know as well as I do this was never meant to be anything more. I was clear about that. No emotions. No relationships. Just sex every three months."

I may be an asshole most days, but I still have a conscience inside me. And this woman did nothing to earn my wrath.

Her eyes flutter shut, and she leans into my touch, her breathing coming out in short pants. She knows what I'm saying. She just doesn't want to admit it.

"I said this when we first met two years ago. If feelings get involved, we part ways before *you* get hurt, and I don't want to see you hurt. You're a wonderful person. I hope you find what you're looking for in the future. But you won't find it in me."

I'm not like my family—my father's fractured heart and my mother's equally tormented soul, ironically tied together for eternity in matrimony, or my sisters, who hold all the humanity from the Kingsley union. Pausing, I take in her trembling figure, her eyes squeezed shut as she tries her best to rein in her emotions. Looking back, perhaps I stayed with her for too long—two years, eight nights of sex and conversations, long enough for her to get attached and wish for more. Somehow, they always do.

Perhaps it's the money or the lifestyle I can afford them, because I never understand the need to be more than what we have right now. A heaviness forms in my chest, and I retrieve a blank check I carry in my pocket for unexpected situations. I scribble an amount on it and sign my name before tucking it inside the envelope.

"Go back to school. Be a nurse. That's what you wanted to do, right? That's why you worked here in the first place. This check should take care of your tuition." Releasing a deep breath, my pulse steady, I step away from her. "Go after your dreams, Liesel. Go find someone who deserves you."

Liesel's eyes flutter open, moisture clinging to the tips of her dark lashes. She wets her lips and doles out a wobbly smile. It's an expression I've seen time and time again when entanglements become complicated.

Hurt and sadness.

But I feel nothing.

Not a nagging pinch of pain, not a clench in my chest, not a flicker of regret. Only the same numbing emptiness which never seems to be filled. The world is a swath of grayscale, its palette uninspiring, the sensations muted as if I'm trapped underwater.

Does it matter if I'm broken if nothing hurts?

And this tells me what I'm doing is the right decision.

I'll be damned if I follow in my parents' footsteps.

"A kiss for goodbye?" she whispers, her voice pitchy.

I shake my head. Another one of my rules. No kisses on the lips. It's too intimate and in some ways, even more intimate than sex. The mouth is where all the words are spoken from, a direct connection to the thoughts in our minds.

And no one can have that part of me.

"Goodbye, Liesel."

With a curt nod, I leave her standing in the dim room, heartbreak bleeding out from her eyes, and exit the opulent suite, which in the daylight probably engenders awe from new members who've endured years on the waitlist, completed multiple interviews, and coughed up a six-figure annual fee to gain membership. They'd no doubt be gaping at the jewel-toned wallpaper and gilded furniture in fabrics reminiscent of Parisian parlors from bygone eras.

I hardly notice any of it. The luxury enjoyed by many is just fancy wrapping paper over an empty box. Sometimes, in moments like this, I wish I could feel an iota of excitement, of anything other than constant emptiness.

Slipping the rose-shaped keycard into my pocket, I walk to the elevators and press a button to one of the top floors housing the premium suites and apartments for overnight guests in the fifty-plus story building in the middle of Manhattan, which boasts of unparalleled views of Central Park.

A short ride later, the doors silently glide open, yielding another dark hallway of deep redwoods and wrought-iron sconces, the pathway dotted with ornate side tables and fresh blooms, scenting the air with the sweet aroma of lavender and lilies.

My phone pings. A market notification and a text message.

"Voss Industries, Notorious Blackguards, Sniffing Around TransAmerica. Will It Be Civil or Will There Be War?" My heart, which has been steady despite the dull ache in my chest, sinks as I read the headline. Father's company. The thing most important to him. An insidious thread of guilt mixes with satisfaction. I should help him save his company.

I should.

But part of me doesn't want to. Part of me wants to be the spectator watching a serial killer receive a lethal injection. But Father is not a cruel man.

I'm the cruel one. A horrible son.

Perhaps Father was right all those years ago, not loving us.

I swipe to the text message, the lead feeling heavier in my chest.

Mother

> Steven, I've tried talking to your father about retiring. His health has gotten worse and I'm worried. He says the company may be in trouble. Can you talk some sense into him?

I stare at the message and heave in a deep breath. My father works almost as much as I do and TransAmerica, an international conglomerate which has its fingers in most industries, is his swan song, his legacy. It's the company he devoted his life to, especially after Mother's family infused much needed capital back into its lifeless shell all those years ago, when the old money Kingsley name was just a name with empty coffers.

The company means so much to him, he puts up with staying with a family he doesn't care about. But now, his health is on the decline. If he doesn't take care of himself, things won't end well for him.

The earlier guilt makes a resurgence, and for the first time, uncertainty slithers in my veins.

Can I really stand by and do nothing while his company goes down in flames?

My sisters never knew what I heard all those years ago. I couldn't bear to tell them. It would break their hearts. And perhaps the truth of that night has been a slow-release poison, corrupting my insides over the years.

But I have the power to help him now. If I don't help him, no one will.

Releasing a heavy exhale, I pull up a new text to my assistant.

Steven

> Get me all the analyses we have on TransAmerica as soon as possible.

I stop in front of the towering double-doors to my suite, my home away from my actual apartment on the Upper West Side. Sometimes it's much more convenient to stay overnight here with all the amenities and waitstaff.

Furthermore, most of my friends enjoy congregating at The Orchid, a sanctuary where the paparazzi are forbidden to enter, a place for us to relax and be ourselves without worrying about an unflattering photo or an unsavory headline appearing in front of gossip rags the next day. Everything we could want in terms of food and entertainment can be found in this building. The business connections and networking are just a side bonus.

After retrieving my regular room card, I swipe the sensor before entering the grand foyer of the spacious corner penthouse.

"Welcome back, Mr. Kingsley." Jarvis, the on-site butler, materializes from the small attendant's quarters attached to the suite. His slicked-back hair, mostly white with streaks of gray, is immaculately coiffed, and his dark suit has nary a wrinkle in sight as if it's four in the afternoon, not the wee hours of the morning. "May I get you any refreshments?"

"I'm fine. Go back to sleep, Jarvis. It's still dark out."

"Have a good evening, sir."

I stride through the living room, currently cloaked in darkness, with nothing but a lonely moonbeam streaming in from the gap between the velvet curtains. My footfalls are soft on the cold marble floors but somehow still echo in the hollow space as I enter the bathroom, shrugging out of my clothes along the way.

Staring at the mirror, I exhale, watching my breath fog up the surface. The soft back light illuminates every harsh line on my face and my disheveled hair, the inky blackness of the strands a stark contrast to the white, sterile marble walls. My jaw is covered in a day's worth of scruff. Faint pink scratches mar my neck and chest, no doubt from the exertion of an hour before.

But it's my eyes that give me pause. The usual hazel appears lifeless, the green edges dulling like the falling leaves on the cusp of a barren winter. A sunken darkness gathers underneath. I crack the joints in my stiff neck and smooth a hand over my haggard face. Sleep continues to elude me, my body automatically jolting awake after a few scanty hours of shut-eye and no amount of tossing and turning gives me any reprieve. Instead, I end up staring at the dark ceiling, the bottomless nagging want in my gut threatening to swallow me whole, except I can't identify the source of the unease, the origin of the discontent.

In the past, my work has been my shelter. My distraction. My focus.

Lately, it seems like nothing I do is enough anymore, and everything is a meaningless routine. I can't help but wonder, *is this all there is to life?*

After opening the shower door, I twist the dials precisely three times, and watch the steam cloak the room into a suffocating fog. I gently step under the hot spray, my body wincing at the scalding heat, but I make no move to adjust the temperature. My clenched muscles slowly relax under the water, the pinpricks of pain fading into the background, and I inhale a deep breath of eucalyptus scented air from the diffuser on the counter.

I welcome the pain, the scorching water turning my skin pink in a matter of seconds.

Perhaps it makes me feel alive somehow.

My mind is now clear, no longer muddled with a need to fuck, and my thoughts drift to the pile of work waiting for me in the office later today, including the call with my brother-in-law, Adrian Scott, over the management of the investment holdings in his real-estate empire which will bring in quite a few more zeros to the ledger of my firm once he signs on the dotted line.

The headline of the TransAmerica troubles shoves its way to the forefront. The hot water pelts against my skin in a pounding rhythm and I close my eyes, letting the flames wash over me as the nagging guilt slithers inside me once more.

I swallow and expel a deep breath.

I'll talk to my father again. Perhaps it's time for me to let bygones be bygones and save his company for him.

CHAPTER 2
Steven

"SON, THEY'RE GOING TO take everything away from me. Everything I've worked so hard for, and I can't stop them." My father's anguished voice breaks as he swipes a frail hand over his face and the weariness he's not bothering to hide anymore.

I stare at the monitor, taking in the man I've looked up to my entire life, and suddenly, I'm hit with the realization he isn't invincible. He's flesh and blood like the rest of us.

Now, as he sits in his office and I'm in mine on opposite sides of the country, I finally notice how his cheeks are sunken in, how his gray hair is finally beginning to thin at the top, how his complexion appears sallower than the last time I saw him. He looks like he's shed some weight as well, as his dress shirt hangs loosely on his thin body almost like clothing on a dress hanger.

I don't remember the last time I've seen him smile. Surely, he must have when I told him I got promoted to the head of the investments department in the biggest investment bank on the East Coast? Or last Thanksgiving when I flew back home for the obligatory dinner where Mother had the chef prepare Father's favorite pan seared foie gras with caramelized figs and tender filet mignon with a side of garden salad, as if that'd offset the clogged-up arteries from the meal?

I wrack my brain for the details, but I come up empty. I don't even remember if there was laughter at the table or if we all sat around the formal dining room with three dozen forks and spoons, eating in silence, waiting for the meal to be over so we could go back to our regular lives, or at least, I could spend time with my siblings and their families, where the actual festivities began.

Father dissolves into a fit of coughing and my chest clenches. I want to tell him everything will be okay. I want to see the glint of admiration in his gaze as he doles out a terse nod of approval. Perhaps the little boy hiding behind the window that fateful rainy night long ago has never disappeared. He's only been in hiding, waiting for the right time to step into the light.

Twirling my pen with my fingers, I swallow. "Father, I've been following their actions. Voss Industries are unscrupulous, but they aren't invincible. We both know they've been sniffing around TransAmerica for the last few years, so the fact it took them this long to make a move tells us something. They don't have the strongest case, or they'd have convinced the board to sell a long time ago. A hostile takeover is the last resort. I think they'll continue to circle the company for a while, attempt to buy out smaller shareholders, and won't do anything drastic until they see a better opening."

Father's eyes flutter shut, and he leans back in his office chair. He looks like he hasn't slept in ages. "All these years, all the sacrifices. I can't keep fighting anymore."

A burning fire begins at the base of my spine and slowly travels up to my chest at his despondence. Has he ever fought for his family the way he fought for TransAmerica? I tamp down the rising anger inside me. If there's one thing I hate more than failure, it's regret. And I can't let the past become a catalyst for more regrets in the future.

I clench my jaw and take a deep breath of eucalyptus scented air from the office diffuser, the scent forever reminding me of Nana, who never changed her perfume in over fifty years before she passed away. Sitting up, I exhale and lean forward. Despite whatever faults Father has had, no one is allowed to make him feel this way. No one is permitted to topple a Kingsley without repercussions.

I won't allow it.

"I've been monitoring the situation in case Voss goes forward with the takeover later. Pietra is keen on my idea as well," I begin, watching my father's eyes slowly drift open, the dying spark inside them flaring at my words.

A few months ago when TransAmerica issues started appearing more serious, I came up with a plan, but until last night, I couldn't bring myself to step in, to save the one thing that mattered more than us to him.

"We both know Voss is good at purchasing companies and selling them for parts later. But we at Pietra Capital believe TransAmerica is better as a whole. If they proceed with a hostile takeover, we'll join the proxy fight, and if we win, TransAmerica will be one of our portfolio companies, headed by me. Your legacy won't be destroyed, and we'll teach Timothy Voss a lesson about playing by the rules. In the meantime, until it reaches that point, we'll be on standby."

Voss Industries, a company which got its start in Big Pharma, is a scumbag in the business world, notorious for using tactics falling within the gray zone of legality to achieve their goals. There have been SEC investigations into their practices because everyone suspects they use illegal methods in their arsenal such as blackmail or espionage, but no one has proved it. Timothy Voss is a disgusting man known for his terrible treatment of women and his shady business dealings.

They're a disruptor to the old school handshakes and greasing of elbows the business elites are used to, and no one is keen on them growing their influence in the commerce and financial industries, which TransAmerica is currently a big player in.

Father's demeanor changes before my eyes as he contemplates my words. He's always made it known he wishes I would take over the helm at TransAmerica, but being a publicly traded company, that'd involve board approval and votes, and now there's no time for that. Plus, there are still plenty of old geezers who believe someone only twenty-eight years of age cannot possibly manage a multi-national conglomerate despite my resume and successes at Pietra.

Father now sits up straighter, a small swath of color returning to his cheeks. It's as if the life slowly leaking out from his body has been stemmed.

I see hope in his eyes.

Perhaps this is the only way for me to fulfill his dreams. To take care of his legacy from afar. Maybe someday, he won't regret staying behind all those years ago. He won't think of my sisters and me as a burden.

He would believe he made the right choice.

"You think you can save TransAmerica?" He sounds buoyant for once, like a castaway finally seeing the silhouette of a ship on the horizon.

Determination whips through me. A want—no, a need—to show him his choice back then was not in vain.

"Yes. Yes, I can."

"Do it the right way, son. We don't sink down to their level."

He's honorable, even to the end. Well, honorable in all matters except for his family. The fucking irony.

My head throbs after we hang up. I wanted to hate TransAmerica and him because of that fateful night almost eighteen years ago. But despite multiple attempts, I just can't.

Why do I still fucking care so much?

I thought my emotions were long dead, but apparently, I still care about his approval.

It's fucking pathetic.

Clenching my fist, I briefly close my eyes, only to be interrupted by a chime from my phone.

Ryland

> Dipshit, are you still alive? I haven't seen you in at least three weeks. Drinks at The Orchid this week? Or at least send me a proof of life text.

My foul mood lightens a smidge at the message from my good friend, Ryland Anderson, who seems to be battling with some issues himself these days. Aside from the one night with Liesel, work has been my mistress for the last few weeks, with the days blurring into nights. I should send him a text later before he sends out a search team.

Knock. Knock.

"Mr. Kingsley, your team is ready for you in the conference room," Jane, my assistant, announces through the door.

"Coming."

My idiotic team. Remembering the purpose of the meeting, I grab the binder containing the world's most ridiculous analysis and stalk toward the conference room, all temporary relief from Ryland's text forgotten.

The office, which occupies ten floors in a modern skyscraper within walking distance to the Charging Bull sculpture on Wall Street, is bustling with activity, with morning sunlight streaming in from the floor-to-ceiling windows, illuminating most of the employees buried in their work within the confines of the glass cubicles separating the space.

Hushed voices and beeping of phones fill the air as bankers and traders make their first calls of the morning. Several flat screens hanging on the far walls showcase the market positions and the latest news of all the international markets, from the New York Stock Exchange to the Hong Kong Hang Seng Index.

The office thrums with energy and this normally gives me the greatest highs, except this morning, after my call with Father and the atrocity in the binder I'm clutching in my hand. A small group of unfamiliar faces linger by one cubicle—interns, maybe, since they start today. A few managers and vice presidents dip their heads in greeting as I pass by them.

As the youngest vice president of Pietra Capital, the reigning investment bank in revenues on Wall Street, I'm on the shortlist for a promotion to the newly vacated Chief Operating Officer position after Greg Marley keeled over last month from a heart attack on his seventy-foot yacht during his sojourn to the Mediterranean.

It was said he didn't even want to go on this trip in the first place, but his wife begged him for a vacation to relive their honeymoon, and he relented after much pestering from her.

Perhaps he would still be alive if he didn't have a wife, because he would've been in New York City, mere minutes away from the top hospitals in the world.

I see my colleagues' gazes filled with both begrudging admiration, doubt, and a slice of contempt. The crinkling in their brows indicates the idea of letting someone so young, twenty-eight to be exact, join their lofty ranks, is probably causing some uncomfortable acid reflux in the middle of the night.

But the numbers don't lie, and I couldn't care less about their so-called useless feelings.

I've increased our investment returns by three times since I was promoted to lead the investments department two years ago, an achievement my predecessors failed to accomplish. Not having entanglements or clouded emotions like everyone else allows me to see things with piercing clarity. To analyze every investment, situation, or person with a rational mind. I'm sure they've enjoyed the extra padding in their wallets since my ascension up the ranks.

My emotional brokenness makes me great at my job and that's the only thing still driving me to get out of bed each morning.

The never-ending need to succeed, to be better, to be more. After all, these are the things a Kingsley should want in life.

My fingers clutch the binder in a death grip. *These fuckers are messing with my path to success.* I grit my teeth and take in a ragged inhale to stop the anger from boiling over.

Smoothing my face into one of fabricated calmness when I want nothing more than to tear into my team for this piece of crap burning a hole in my hand, I stroll toward the conference room where my analysts and investment managers are waiting for me.

I push open the clear double doors and storm into the spacious room, finding my team of fifteen top performers sitting around the long central table, their excited chatter filling the air.

Heads swivel my way, and Bradley Chance, one of my investment managers, breaks into a big grin. "Mr. Kingsley, good morning! Did you see the analysis we put together for you?"

Letting out a controlled breath, I twist my lips into a serene smile. "This binder here?" I hold up the offending documents in my hand. "I did. Read it cover to cover. Did everyone review this and agree with the assessments?"

Bradley glances around the table, catching the eyes of most people in the room before swiveling back to me and nodding eagerly. "Of course. This is one of our biggest investments this calendar year. Everyone did their due diligence."

I hum noncommittally. "Based on these documents, perhaps we should wait a few months before upping our stake in Cameron Corp." The analysis actually suggested an immediate buy on the emerging home goods manufacturing company purported to rival some of the top brands in existence.

A questioning murmur breaks through the silence and Chuck Bright, who I nickname Chuck Dumbass in my mind, chimes in, "Exactly right, Mr. Kingsley. Brilliant assessment."

Bradley turns his frown into a smile and nods again, making me want to smack the grin off his face. "That's correct."

The rest of the room joins the approvals, nodding ridiculously, a bunch of lemmings leaping off the cliff after the leader.

I set the binder down and place my hands on the table, surveying each one of my team, supposedly the cream of the crop. My fingers dig against the glass surface, my muscles clenched tightly to fight the need to throw those documents across the room.

"I guess a different way of looking at the data may result in doubling our purchase of their shares," I murmur, my vision slowly turning red as I narrow my eyes.

Hayley Richardson, a redhead sitting in the corner seat, interjects, "I think that's a good assessment as well."

The lemmings now change their tune and chime in agreement.

Idiots. The whole lot. Fucking kiss-ass, brown-nosing idiots.

At this rate, I'll never be able to trust anyone with the growing problem at TransAmerica or the new investments management with Scott Enterprises.

The churning in my gut is corrosive, making its way up my throat. My jaw clenches before releasing, my lips contorting into a snarl, no longer able to keep up the fake façade. My hands slam down hard on the table in a loud *smack*.

The team practically jumps in their chairs.

"Did *anyone* fucking review this piece of shit before sending it over to me?" I push the offending black binder toward the middle of the table, the sheets fluttering chaotically from the sudden motion.

"If I tell you guys to jump out the window right now, are you guys going to do it? Is there *anyone* capable of thinking beyond the IQ of a six-year-old in this room today?" I stand up, my fists curling to my sides as the weight on my chest increases, nearly smothering my lungs.

"Can someone tell me what's wrong with the documents you sent over today?"

The silence is thick and loud in the room as my skin feels heated.

"Did *anyone* bring their brains to work today? Or are you all more concerned about kissing ass than doing your fucking jobs?" Slamming my hands on the table once more, I wait for a few seconds before straightening up and crossing my arms over my chest, not caring if I'm creasing the delicate, bespoke three-piece suit I'm wearing.

The room is eerily silent. Muted conversations from the outside filter in from the conference room doors. Someone clears their throat.

The idiots look at each other, equal in their flushed complexions and rapid breathing. I see sweat dripping down Chuck Dumbass's forehead. If it weren't for his father being one of our largest clients, I would've given him the boot ages ago.

Another person clears her throat. A few chairs squeak as several folks shift in their seats.

I swallow the ball in my throat, the heat in my chest mounting into a fire. I guess I have some emotions after all, like the rage coursing through me right now. Just as I'm about to tear into the silent group once again, someone in the back raises her hand.

"They have a huge cash flow problem," an unfamiliar voice, soft and melodious with a thread of nervousness, slices through the thick silence with the ease of a steak knife to butter.

I scan the room to locate this one brave soul, my eyes finally snagging on an unassuming brunette with a shaggy haircut, dressed in a black business suit several sizes too big. Everyone turns their attention to her, and I hold my breath, waiting for her to continue.

At my silence, the brunette slowly meets my stare, her startling eyes, a color I can't discern from this distance, brighten.

She straightens up, squares her shoulders, and continues, "The face of the financials...the balance sheet and income statements spin a beautiful story of exponential growth and income, but it's in the cash flow and the footnotes where the ugliness lies."

The burn in my throat briefly recedes, and I arch my eyebrow, daring her to continue. She bites her lip, her voice stronger than before.

"For a company with such large profits and not much reinvestment in their business, you'd expect their cash or external investment positions to increase rapidly as well. But that isn't the case. Their cash flow, while positive, is abysmal."

She swallows, a hint of nervousness still shining through her expression, and she tucks a lock of hair behind her ear. The brunette pauses and looks at me, as if waiting for my permission to continue.

"Come on, *intern,* you think we didn't consider that in our assessment?" Hayley interjects, her voice shrill and grating, her eyes glancing at me before shooting daggers into the intern's face.

The intern—she's a fucking intern, so this is her first day—shrinks at the admonition before her forehead crinkles. I bite my cheek to not reveal my thoughts, and cock my head, wanting to see what this little mouse will do in the presence of the hellcat that is Hayley Richardson.

After taking a breath, the intern sits up straighter and leans forward. She brushes the errant strands of hair which have fallen over her face and replies, "I'm just sharing my thoughts. I reviewed the documents this morning and am here to learn. If I'm incorrect, please explain it to me. I want to be an asset to the team."

Glancing down, I find my fingers no longer trying to dig a hole into the glass surface of the table, the knuckles no longer stark white. A slither of amusement snakes inside me at this rendition of David versus Goliath.

"I'll *educate* you later, Greta. This is not the time or place for it," Hayley seethes, her voice coming out in a hiss as she darts furtive glances at me. "You can come to my office—"

"It's Grace, not Greta."

I snort, unable to hide my amusement. Few would stand up against Hayley, the reigning mean girl on the floor. She's cutthroat and merciless and usually rakes in good numbers. Part of the reason she's on my team.

"Continue...Grace," I murmur, lifting my eyes to stare at the intern, my gaze cascading over her features, taking in the brilliant irises of mysterious hues, the smooth complexion without an ounce of makeup, a petite frame hidden in the black atrocity that looks like it was salvaged from the depths of her grandmother's closet. She looks young and fragile, small and breakable, but something about the way she carries herself tells me she is anything but.

She's a warrior masquerading as a weakling.

Grace swallows then wets her lips, my eyes involuntarily snagging on the movement and marveling at how her upper lip is perfectly symmetrical, shaped in a cupid's bow and other shit I don't usually notice. She clears her throat again.

"As I said earlier, their impressive performance is not translating over to hard cash, and that's usually a red flag. If we were to dig deeper into the financials and footnotes for the last few quarters, we'd see their inventory balances decreasing in line with the peaks in their cash flows, which may indicate sales of their inventory, normally a positive sign. But if you look at the subsequent periods, the inventory balances will then increase dramatically, and the cash flow would drastically decrease."

Grace's voice is assured, and she glances around the room, capturing the attention of everyone as she spins the story she's seeing in her analysis of the same documents I saw this morning. Bradley's brows furrow as he stares at her pensively, and Chuck taps his fountain pen on the table in a nervous rhythm. Grace's eyes find mine again and my lips tip up in the smallest of smiles, encouraging her to go on with her analysis.

Her eyes widen at my expression and a grin tugs at her lips, an impish glint flashing in her eyes. The thread of amusement winding inside me burrows deeper into my chest, and I give her a terse nod.

"This is all conjecture, but from my untrained eye, it seemed odd that they would have large cash flow with low inventory, followed by a drastic drop in cash flow with increased inventory, all the while showing immense profits on their income statement. It almost seems like there's some massive sale of their inventory at period end, followed by...large returns?"

Grace looks at me, her brows wrinkling, and my fingers twitch, wanting to smooth it off her otherwise unblemished face. *It's just my fucking borderline OCD at work.*

The conference room is silent as the lemmings slouch in their seats, no doubt wondering how they were all showed up by a fucking intern on her first day of work. The squeaking of chairs fills the room as folks twiddle their thumbs and turn their heads my way, probably gauging my reaction.

My lips curve into a genuine smile at the only person who dared to speak her mind today. Grace's lips part in an audible gasp, and I slowly bring my hands up and clap in acknowledgement. The room slowly joins in the applause. Grace's pale skin flushes pink and she gnaws on her bottom lip with a savagery it doesn't deserve.

Hayley opens her mouth to speak, and I hold up my hand for silence before turning to the rest of the room.

"I don't want this to repeat itself. Bring your brains to work and don't fucking kiss my ass. If you can't do that, don't bother coming in," I command, my voice deep and laced with threats. I stride toward the double doors but pause before I step out of the room.

Turning around, I give the intern one last glance and find her staring down at her lap, her face still pink, a curtain of hair falling over her face. Curious. Very fucking curious.

Pinning a glare at the three stooges, Hayley, Bradley, and Chuck, I growl, "Fix the damn analysis and have it on my desk within the hour."

CHAPTER 3

Grace

"HONEY, GETTING READY FOR work?" Mom walks up next to me in the pink pajamas I got her for her birthday as I brush my teeth at five in the morning, already clad in a boxy white blouse, a loose navy cable knit cardigan, and plain black slacks, completed with a pair of practical and no-nonsense leather flats.

I won't be winning any best dressed awards anytime soon, but the clothes are comfortable, cheap, and meet the professional dress code of the investment bank. I thrifted them for pennies two weeks ago as I was preparing for my internship at Pietra Capital. A thrill thrums inside me as I anticipate stepping into that bright office once again. I went through a rigorous interview process, beating over one hundred candidates for this position.

Change is in the air. I can smell it.

If I do well and get one of the three full-time positions, all our problems will be solved—getting us out of here before our impending eviction and paying off the loan Mom got saddled with when one of her asshole exes duped her into cosigning and then subsequently running off, just for starters. He borrowed from a loan shark and dragged us into the mess.

After spitting out the toothpaste, I grab the cup of water on the edge of the sink and take a big gulp, swishing the minty flavor in my mouth before expelling it down the drain and setting the glass down to the side. I squint at my appearance and straighten my back, determination racing through me.

I'm going to be the best intern they've ever hired. They won't even know what hit them.

My eyes dart to Mom's reflection, and I grin. "The early bird gets the worm. I'm going to show up earlier and work harder than the other interns there."

I grab a brush from the small metal ledge affixed to the cracked subway tiles below the mirror and work through the rat's nest.

"I'm sure you will. You're so smart and you'll do a great job," Mom murmurs as she takes the brush away from me and combs through the knotted strands in the back.

My heart warms at the gentleness in her hands, the way she smooths the strands with her fingertips, her fingernails lightly raking against the scalp, something she has done for me ever since I was a little kid. She used to say it helps with circulation and hair growth.

"You need to brush your hair more often. It'll—"

"Make it shine, I know, Mom." I smile, staring at our reflections in the mirror.

Even under the harsh florescent lighting of our tiny bathroom barely big enough to fit the two of us, the resemblance between my mom and me is unmistakable.

Mom is beautiful, stunning really, even now in her early fifties. Her thick brown hair is loosely braided to the side, with a few strands framing her face. Her porcelain skin has only a few telltale wrinkles showing her age, and her eyes, like mine, are a beautiful shade of violet, which in some lighting appear blue. I've since learned our eye color is a form of blue eyes and is a result of a rare genetic mutation and less than one percent of the population have them, but the color still surprises people.

She was a beauty queen in her heyday, fawned over by hundreds of men on the Broadway stage even though she was never the main character. Her talent, as she told me, was somewhat lacking, but her charm and energy more than made up for it. Now she works at a small burlesque club off Broadway helping take care of the dancers.

"Mom, things are on the up and up." I can see the finish line ahead and damn it, I'll reach it even if it takes my last breath.

"It's all my fault. I shouldn't have listened to him—"

"Mom, Carl is an asshole and an abuser. You believed him because you're kind. This is on him, not on you."

Mom purses her lips but doesn't say anything. I know she still blames herself for putting us in debt, even though technically it was Carl who put us there. There's nothing she can do at this point.

"And when I get the full-time offer, I'll be able to get us a new place in a better neighborhood and pay off our debt." Clearing my throat, I look away. "So, why are you up so early? Another breakfast date? Who is it this time? The new man from the theater? It better not be Carl, right?"

Mom flushes, her pale cheeks taking on a beautiful bloom and her eyes sparkle. My heart sinks at the lovestruck expression on her face, one I've become too familiar with over the years. All I hope is the man putting that smile on her face isn't her last boyfriend, Carl, a snake of a human being who was obnoxious and slimy, who also had a nasty streak of violence. Then there were the leering glances I'd see him sneak Taylor's and my way when he thought we weren't looking. My stomach churns when I think of him.

If this is what beauty gives you, then it's definitely a liability and not an asset.

"No, this is someone new. I really think he's the one, Grace. His name is Peter, and he's a doctor. He loves me. I'm sure of it." Her eyes take on a faraway look, something I'm also too familiar with. "He's tall and has the most beautiful eyes…"

Mom is addicted to love. Or to the pursuit of her one true love.

She's the type of woman who can't survive being single for too long, always needing the validation of a man to make her whole. The men would come in droves, drawn by her beauty and positivity, but then they'd show their true colors, and the relationships would end. With the exception of Uncle Bobby, her one ex-boyfriend who treated us well in the past, who gave me a taste of what having a father would be like, most of the men she dated were assholes dressed in the finest suits.

Despite all these years of men passing through our lives like we were a revolving door, her many excruciating heartbreaks, and the colorful scumbags she has dated in the past, she still wholeheartedly, desperately believes in love. She still thinks she's the main character of her fairytale and her happily-ever-after is waiting for her just around the corner. It's almost as if she was chasing something or someone she lost, and her heart wouldn't settle unless she found him again.

She used to say, *"A heart wants what it wants."* I'd fight the urge to roll my eyes. It felt like a cop-out.

Giving my reflection one last glance, I smooth a stubborn cowlick sticking out of my hair. The cursed strands refuse to stay in place. After half a minute of fiddling with it to no avail, I shrug, giving up.

It doesn't matter. I'm at Pietra to learn and to get that job offer, to be financially independent, so I don't need to depend on the support or love of any men, because the only person who'll never disappoint you is yourself.

"...Maybe we'll get married one day and you'll finally have a stepdad. Didn't you always say you wanted a father?"

Mom's question draws my attention back to her and I swallow a laugh bubbling in my throat. I *did* want a father growing up because I never had one. For as long as I can remember, it has only been the three of us—me, Taylor, and Mom. Taylor and I don't even know who our biological father is and Mom refuses to tell us despite our years of pestering her. I wonder if this man broke her heart and that is why she's so desperate to repair it, seeking comfort in the arms of asshole after asshole, hoping to recreate what she once experienced.

"Not anymore," I reply. "I only want to know who my birth father is."

She stays silent, and I wish I could say I'm surprised by her lack of response.

Every time I'd ask her about my birth father, a shadow would fall over her face. She'd turn away and tell us he's no one of importance and we should stop asking her. Then, she'd fake a laugh and change the subject, but the pain would linger in her eyes.

So, over time, we stopped asking but there's an aching hole in my gut and I feel like I'm missing part of my identity. Maybe someday she'd tell us. A familiar weight returns to my chest, and I inhale a deep breath, releasing it slowly when I feel the knot loosening.

I shake my head softly at the thoughts before turning away and walking into the living room to gather my purse and my reading tablet for my bus ride and the 4 train to get to Wall Street.

A loud yawn follows us into the living room and my lips quirk into a grin before I turn around, finding Taylor, my younger sister by less than a year—Irish twins they say—trudging out from the bedroom we share, her long hair piled up high into a messy bun as she rubs her eyes.

"Why are you up so early, Tay? I thought you had at least five more hours of sleep in you."

Her nose piercing—a tiny black skull this morning—glints in the soft light from the one lamp we turned on in the small living room, the size only marginally bigger than the copy room at Pietra. But this tiny two-bedroom apartment near Melrose in the Bronx is rent-controlled and isn't in the projects. It's considered quite a steal in the current economy, which is probably why the landlord is evicting us in a few months when he sells the building to a large developer. Gentrification of the city is alive and well and now we'll need to find a new place to live.

Despite the less than ideal surroundings and the small space, Mom did the best she could to liven up the apartment—hanging artwork we made when we were younger over the faded floral wallpaper, draping chenille blankets and thrifted pillows over our gray sofa to cover up the ruined fabric from a mishap I made when I was in fifth grade and decided to decorate it with glitter and permanent marker.

Wonderful memories are held within these walls, and I wouldn't trade them for the world. But as I stare at the overdue bills on the countertop and the red paper sticking out from the pile of mail—the eviction notice our family has been trying to ignore for the longest time—I know our time in this little slice of heaven is ending soon. *Unless you get the damn job, which you will, Grace.*

"Auditions are at fucking eight this morning at Petit Jeté, which means I should probably be there by seven at the latest. What motherfuckers have auditions so early? Crazy people," Taylor grumbles, her lips curling into a half snarl. She sticks her middle finger in the general direction of the door.

"Taylor Gianna Peyton! Your language!" Mom scolds, but her voice barely holds any venom. Tay has the potty mouth between the two of us, quite at odds with her elegant ballerina persona, but Mom still makes it a point to try to "correct" her coarse language.

Taylor smiles sheepishly and mumbles something sounding like an apology before yawning again. She stretches her hands overhead, her large sleep shirt riding up her thighs. "I don't even know why I bother. It's not like I'll get in and even if I do, it's not like we can ever afford it."

Taylor is the artistic genius of our family, and her art is in the form of dance—a combination of ballet and hip hop, her dancing a juxtaposition of styles, the elegant with the edgy, much like the rest of her. Her angelic face is always caked with dark eyeliner which makes her slate-colored eyes look more piercing, and she sports equally ominous nails and has multiple piercings on her body. She always says her body is an extension of her art and her ever-changing nose piercing reflects her mood for the day.

She is truly talented, and this gift secured her a full-ride scholarship to the New York Institution of Dance and Performing Arts, a decent performing arts school on the East Coast, but Taylor has her sights set on something better, something higher, the crème de la crème of all ballet and dance companies in the country, the American Ballet Theater Corporation. And this Petit Jeté dance group has close ties with the lauded institution.

So, despite her I couldn't care less attitude, I can tell she's as nervous as fuck.

Grinning, I sling my arm around her much higher shoulders, her willowy, tall frame different from mine. I'm once again filled with dismay over my petite stature.

"Break a leg, sis. Go kick their asses. And don't worry about money. We'll figure it out as we always do. I'm going to get the job, then no one can stop us." I hop on one leg and attempt to ruffle her hair. Even though I'm shorter than her and am only ten months older than her, I take every pleasure in treating her like the little sister she is.

"Ugh. Your early morning energy is super annoying. Are you even human?" Taylor mutters, pushing me away like I'm a nuisance, but I see the beginnings of a smile twitching on her lips.

"Do you know why they say, 'break a leg?'"

"Oh God, another piece of interesting trivia. It's not even six yet, Grace."

I ignore her and Mom shuffles past us, laughing softly as she enters the kitchen, no doubt to prepare our coffees and breakfast so we can eat them on the go.

"In the olden days of theater, there was this line where ensemble actors were supposed to stand in. It was called a 'leg line.' If actors didn't get to perform, they had to stay behind this line. So, people would say 'break a leg' to wish them good luck in getting out of the line and get paid to perform. Cool, huh? Maybe you can use that to impress some folks today." I waggle my brows at her.

"If only it were that easy." Taylor rolls her eyes and plops down on the wobbly wooden stool in front of the linoleum counter of our kitchenette. As I predicted, Mom slides a steaming hot cup of coffee in front of her along with a toasted bagel with peanut butter. Taylor takes a sip, letting out a deep sigh of contentment.

"You and your coffee." I poke her backside as I walk behind her and grab my to-go tumbler and the sandwich bag with my piping-hot multigrain bagel nestled inside.

I kiss Mom goodbye on the cheek and double back to get my reading tablet charging on the kitchen counter—got to have my books with me. I beeline for the door again and perform my special doorknob dance—aka shake the doorknob to the right, then tilt it up—to open the creaky old door.

A gust of stale, humid air with the remnants of motor oil and something smelling suspiciously like urine fills the air. Far away chugging sounds of the subway train passing by filter up the exhaust vents. Got to love a hot and humid New York summer day.

"You and your books!" Taylor yells back and sticks out her tongue, her eyes glinting in laughter.

"Don't you dare make fun of my book boyfriends, Tay. At least I know how to read!"

"Girls, it's not even six in the morning. Will you guys ever cease bickering?"

We laugh and I throw back a wave of my hand, then march eagerly onto the sidewalk, a bounce in my step as I head to the bus stop.

I may currently only be an intern at Pietra Capital, but this is my first step to independence, my first foray into the business world, my first taste of financial freedom, and one day, everything will be very different.

And I hope it's for the better.

CHAPTER 4

Grace

Millie

How's the internship going?

Belle

She's smashing it, I bet. Millie, you don't know this, but when we were in criminal psychology class during freshman year, she set the freakin' curve. I'd hate her if I didn't love her.

Taylor

You should've seen her this fucking morning. I hadn't seen anyone more bright-eyed and bushy-tailed before six.

Millie

I have no clue how you girls are sisters with your opposite sleeping habits. Grace, meet up at the end of the week to tell us all about your fancy job?

I GRIN AS I stare at the messages from the girls. I haven't been able to hang out with them for the last week or two because of studying and the new job, but this weekend looks promising. I type out a reply as I hear the *click clack* of stilettos hitting the floor at a brisk pace.

"He's coming. Look sharp," Hayley announces as she waltzes by the cubicles, a seductive breeze of floral and spice trailing after her. The afternoon sun cast a bright glow through the windows, illuminating the sleek hallways of chrome and glass of the ultra-modern office as folks amble in after lunch.

Traders and analysts flutter around in their seats, the men puff out their chests as they flick away from the sports websites on their monitors to their work programs, the women sneak out a mirror to adjust their hair and reapply their lipstick.

I don't know who's coming, but I'm having a hard time not rolling my eyes at this superficial production.

This is probably why I never had hordes of men chasing after me like Mom. What you see is what you get with me and I'm never good at this artificial preening and fake smiling. But it's better this way. I don't need the useless distractions the opposite sex provides. I don't need the attention of men who only want a beautiful woman in their arms and someone they can spend the night with every so often.

I certainly don't need the leering glances of the Brad Brunswicks of the world, who spent more time undressing me with his eyes than dancing with me when we went to Homecoming as seniors in high school. He was my one and only boyfriend and the experience was extremely underwhelming.

She pauses by my seat and taps her perfectly manicured hands on the glass partition. She clears her throat. "Intern."

Her voice is sharp and no-nonsense.

I blow out a deep breath, my pulse spiking from the tone in her voice. I knew I didn't endear myself to her when I spoke up in the conference room. But I learned long ago watching Mom let men walk all over her to never let that happen to me.

"Yes, Hayley?" I hold her gaze steadily, willing my nervousness not to show through.

Hayley, in her dark green couture dress which probably cost more than one month's rent and her brilliant red hair swept in a flawless updo, looks every inch the girl boss I hope to be someday, but of course, I'd be much nicer.

"I'll be watching you today. I want no outbursts from you. If you have anything you want to share, you run it by me beforehand, understand?" She pins me with a hard glare, her blue eyes a sharp blade.

I swallow and nod.

I may not be good at office politics since this is my first white-collar job, but I'm not stupid. After we left the conference room the other day, several seasoned financial analysts took pity on me and gathered around my cubicle, giving me the lay of the land and a rundown on who's who in the office, and how Hayley is the woman we all aspire to be.

She's fearless, gorgeous, rakes in more deals than half the men on the floor combined, and her annual bonus alone could purchase a spacious apartment in Tribeca, but unfortunately, she has the tongue of a viper. As the intern pool is shared by all the managers on the floor, it'll be in my best interest to avoid pissing her off in the future. Wall Street is cutthroat enough as is, so I don't need to make any enemies.

After holding my gaze for a few seconds, she nods before striding away, patting her perfectly arranged hair no doubt to ensure everything is still in place, before disappearing into her office, which is in the prime real estate next to the corner office Steven Kingsley occupies.

Steven Kingsley.

I've read articles about him in my advanced business management class last quarter at NYUC as I was preparing for my summer internship. *Forbes* and *Wall Street Journal* have featured him as the most powerful person in finance under the age of thirty.

He hails from an old-money family in Los Angeles. But the Kingsley family, while influential, was going into debt after generations of mismanagement of funds until his father married his mother, an heiress from Asia. Using his wife's money, his father rebuilt the Kingsley empire and along the way, Steven and his sisters were born.

Instead of philandering about or sowing his wild oats as most rich guys do, Steven is a workaholic, climbing the ranks at Pietra Capital at a record-breaking speed so unheard of it's as if he's smashing the proverbial sound barrier in the stuffy circles of the industry elite.

My skin heats when I remember the way he stormed into the conference room, a whirlwind of power and coiled energy, his presence sucking the oxygen out of the room; how his eyes flashed with molten anger, his lips curling into a sneer as he hurled the binder across the table as if it were his worst enemy, even the papers within tried to plan an escape.

There's something compelling about him. A thread of danger. A dash of darkness lurking behind the surface. An abundance of restrained energy tethered tightly in his grasp.

As if his sanity is held on by the thinnest thread and he's mere moments away from snapping.

And God help whoever is around him whenever that happens.

But then he listened to my ideas like they were worth something. He took me seriously. And his brief smile after I shared my analysis in the room. The jolt of electricity hit me in my chest and I could barely hold his gaze after the applause because my skin felt heated—no doubt I was flushed.

It was disorienting and I can't stop thinking about it.

Brisk footfalls on marble floors echo from the direction of the lobby, the pounding sounds mirroring the quickening pace of my pulse. The floor is abuzz with activity, with traders throwing out numbers to their clients, the nonstop ringing of the phones the soundtrack of a busy workday, analysts whispering furtively in their corners, mumbling questions about capital gains and leverage ratios, but I feel the sudden drop in temperature, the collective holding of breath from everyone as the footsteps tread closer to the bullpen.

"Get me London in an hour. They need to liquidate their positions before this fucking shit blows to hell," Stevens barks out, his voice laced with impatience. Jane, his assistant, practically trips over herself as she scurries away to do his bidding.

I hold my breath as I witness him striding down the hallway, a furrow creasing his brows as if he's deep in thought.

I didn't get a chance to see him up close before, but he was compelling enough from afar, a powerful hurricane blowing by in the vicinity, leaving nothing unscathed.

But now, up close, it's impossible not to be awed by his presence, his imposing figure poured into a three-piece deep gray suit, a crimson tie knotted to perfection, and a hint of the same-colored pocket square peeking out from his suit jacket. He's tall, at least six-foot-three from my estimate, and from the way he fills his clothes, I can tell he has a lean but powerful physique underneath the luxurious fabrics, which yields to his body during each controlled movement. His hair, pitch black, almost glints dark blue under the office lights, is arranged carefully, longer on the top and short on the sides. His jawline is clean-shaven, sharp enough to cut glass and make cover models weep with envy.

But it's his eyes that tell you everything you need to know about him. Eyes I couldn't see well from where I sat in the room, but still drew me in like a moth to a flame. They're burnt gold, rimmed with stark green, the colors shifting under the light like tiger stone, which I learned during one insomniac night of aimless scrolling on my phone, fittingly, symbolizes confidence and protection. There are shadows underneath those mesmerizing eyes, like he hasn't seen over four hours of sleep a night for a long time.

His long legs purposefully stride in my direction, which is along the path to his office. My lungs seize and an unknown thread of anticipation and exhilaration wraps tightly around my chest.

This is just nerves. After all, you need to impress him to secure a full-time offer.

I want to turn back toward the spreadsheets opened on my monitor, but my body refuses to obey, my eyes automatically tracking his movements.

Steven looks up from his phone, his eyes sweeping the room like a king inspecting his subjects before they pause on me.

My mouth dries, my heart threatening to escape my rib cage, and I freeze, ensnared by the molten gaze, which seems to see past my shoddy haircut and baggy clothing, unpeeling the layers to examine the deepest parts of me, parts even I don't want to face.

He slows his movements, his eyes slowly drifting to my parted lips then back to my gaze, his cool countenance an unemotional art critic perusing galleries for his next acquisition, but I see the faintest spark in the amber pools, which disappears as quickly as it appeared. A faint hum of electricity hangs in the air, and my muscles tense in anticipation.

I must be imagining things.

"Grace," he murmurs, his voice deep, my name from his lips sounding intimate somehow, like this is how my name would sound on the lips of my lover as we're tangled within bedsheets, and my traitorous heartbeat kicks up a notch, my skin feeling fevered.

He remembers my name.

Steven dips his head, a corner of his lips curving up slightly into a ghost of a smile, and he continues his way down the hallway before entering his office, disappearing from view.

The pounding in my chest fades into a dull thrum as the floor exhales a collective sigh of relief and conversations resume, punctuated by the occasional bursts of laughter. My computer pings incessantly as my inbox fills up.

I shake my head, my mind fuzzy from what could've only been a few quick seconds of interaction, and fevered, ridiculous thoughts. I blink and grab my mug, slowly lifting it to my mouth and flinch as the scalding tea I poured from the carafe in the break room moments ago singes my lips. My hands jerk and the tea sloshes onto the table with my cardigan taking the brunt of the impact. I groan at the mess I now have to clean up.

"Not your day today, huh?" a bright voice interrupts me as I dab my sweater with a tissue, helplessly watching the wet mark spread on the fabric. "Here. More napkins for you." A wad of paper towels land on my desk from the cubicle on my right.

Jamie Chang, my cubicle neighbor, a bubbly first-year analyst at the firm, smiles at me sympathetically, her head poking above the glass wall. "At least it's green tea. It shouldn't stain."

"I swear, I'm not normally this clumsy." If anything, I'm the careful one in my family. Giving up on my sweater, I carefully blot the keyboard and surrounding surfaces, thankful I don't have any papers or binders lying about. The last thing I need is Hayley being on my case again.

"Eh, it happens to the best of us. By the way, a bunch of us are going to Lunasia after work on Thursday for drinks and karaoke. Want to come?"

I pause my clean up and take in her warm brown eyes crinkling at the corners, a pen perched on her ear. She twirls a strand of black hair around her finger and grins at me. My chest warms, liking her instantly. Unlike some women I've met here who view others as threats or competition, Jamie seems nice and welcoming.

I wish I could go. I've heard so many good things about it. Lunasia is a hot new club slash karaoke bar a few streets over. It opened last month by the entertainment and hospitality empire, Fleur Entertainment, to cater to bankers and analysts needing to let out some steam after work, and their admission alone costs an arm and a leg. Plus, I don't have anything appropriate to wear.

If I eat salads for a week, maybe I could go?

I blow out a sigh. "I don't think I can, but maybe—"

The ringing of my desk phone interrupts me, and I practically jump in place, my arm close to knocking over the mug of tea again.

Damn it. What's wrong with me today?

"This is Grace," I answer without looking at the caller ID.

"Can you come into my office?" A deep, masculine voice greets me, the question posed as a command, the smooth timbre I've only heard twice before, with the last time being mere seconds ago.

Startled, I glance at the screen on the phone, noting the name Steven Kingsley, extension 3108, emblazoned in black and white.

"Yes, sir."

Click. The line disconnects.

I stare at the receiver in my hand, stupefied, my heart beginning a lap around the track after the brief respite.

"Everything okay?" Jamie asks, her voice tinged with concern.

"Mr. Kingsley wants to see me."

"Oooo, don't want to be you. The man terrifies me. Good luck. Break a leg."

I snort, thinking how I said the same thing to Taylor before. Standing up, I smooth my hands over my clothing, my fingers pausing at the large damp spot on my sweater. I curse myself for not being extra prepared and bringing a change of clothing just in case. But who the heck would think you'd need a change of clothes for a desk job at an investment bank?

I shrug out of the damp outer layer, goosebumps pebbling my arms from the chill of the AC, which apparently is always adjusted to a balmy sixty to sixty-five degrees for the men in their suits, another interesting tidbit I learned online. My shirt didn't escape unscathed from the tea, but at least it's not as wet like the sweater in question. This will have to do.

Tucking in the large blouse so it appears to fit more properly, I hurry toward the corner office, keenly aware of the pairs of eyes trailing me on my journey, no doubt wondering why an intern is meeting with the head of the investments department.

Straightening my back, I knock on the frosted door, and am met with a terse, "Come in."

I swallow the ball in my throat and step into his large office, which is bigger than our apartment at home. The faint scent of eucalyptus hits my nose. Steven sits behind a sturdy oak desk, his cell phone tucked by his ear as he finishes a conversation. He motions me in with one regal flick of his hand.

Nodding, my eyes sweep the room. The blinds are drawn up over the floor-to-ceiling windows, letting in warm rays of sunlight. At one hundred floors above ground level, there's an impressive view of Wall

Street and surrounding buildings; the city laid out like glittering crystals and sharp planes of glass.

A dark leather sofa and black marble table atop a navy-blue carpet are on one side of the room. A backlit wet bar completed with a stainless-steel refrigerator is tucked away in the corner. The office is decorated mainly in navy and black, the shelves immaculately organized, the books stacked by height, and various placards and photo frames shine under the warm overhead lights. It's masculine and tasteful and even without knowing him, I'd bet he picked every piece of furniture in this space.

I'd also bet there's not a speck of dust in the place and everything is arranged in its precise order.

The room is even colder than the bullpen and I shiver, my hands rubbing my arms as I take a seat in front of the enigmatic man who's now typing something on his computer, his eyebrows pinched in concentration.

"You won't regret it. I'll call you with good news. Golfing next weekend?" Steven chuckles, his voice raspy, almost like a soft caress, and I sneak another glance at him, my hands on top of my thighs, and notice him staring at me, all the while conversing with the person on the other line.

His hazel eyes glow in an ethereal shade of amber as a ray of light from the windows hits him at precisely the right angle, highlighting the sharp planes of his face, his strong nose and thick lashes that have no business being on a man, and while his lips are curved into a smile, his soft laughter reverberating around the room, the merriment doesn't reach those brilliant pools.

If I were to close my eyes and listen to this conversation, I wouldn't have known he was putting on an act. But now, sitting mere feet away from him, it's obvious.

My chest constricts at the coldness on his face, and I wet my parched lips. There's something about him that makes me want to stare at him some more and figure him out.

To find out why a man who looks to be on the top of the world with everything he could possibly want, appears so...unhappy and unsatisfied with life.

Someone who looks empty. Lonely.

It's almost heartbreaking.

I pinch my wrist, mentally slapping myself across the face at the strange, whimsical thoughts crossing my mind.

He's probably just like the other rich men you've met in the past—a different woman each week, shirking responsibilities just because he can.

Steven mutters some nonsense about golfing and sports. His brows furrow as he glares at the desk before him, as if the pens scattered on the tabletop annoyed him somehow. His nostrils flare as he picks up all the blue and black pens, leaving only one of each, aligned precisely next to his writing pad, and places the extras, sorted by color, into his pen holder. Then, he stacks the various binders on his desk, red ones on one side and black ones on the other.

I stare at his motions, my mouth slightly agape, as if watching some transcendental meditation in progress, the thudding of the papers and binders sounding like ASMR therapy. A few moments later, his desk is clean. Impeccable. Cleaner than my entire apartment has ever been, even before Mom brings her new boyfriends to visit for the first time.

Steven lets out an inaudible exhale, the lines between his brows relaxing. He hangs up and sits back in his chair, the fake smile he was doling out toward the end of the call promptly slipping off his face. His veneer is guarded as he twirls a fountain pen around his fingers and swivels his chair, leaning further back, and props his ankle on top of his knee.

We stare at each other for the next few seconds, and I hear the clock on the far wall ticking, separating the next few moments in a barrage of staccato fragments—me trying not to fidget under his intense gaze, my breath coming in quick pants, my skin feeling feverish. Him looking as cool and as beautiful as a statue in the Louvre, one arm on top of the handrest of his armchair, his fingers lightly tapping his jawline as if he's trying to solve a mystery.

The moment stretches on, a strange tension hums in the background, the air feeling thin in the room, and we engage in this silent, staring contest, my hand gripping my pants while I fight to remain still, to keep eye contact while maintaining a soft smile on my face. Whatever he is trying to prove here, I'll pass with flying colors.

His lips slowly curve into a smile, a real one this time, a glint of amusement appearing in those tiger stone eyes.

"So, Grace Felicity Peyton, twenty-three years old, grew up in the Bronx, going to graduate from NYUC at the end of the summer..."

I gnaw on my bottom lip and wait for him to continue.

"You nervous?" he murmurs, the infinitesimal smile still gracing his face.

My pulse is thready, and I want to open the doors to let in some fresh air, even though the AC is at least five degrees cooler in here than out in the bullpen.

For such a cold man, he sure needs a lot of air conditioning.

"No," I fib. My fingers twist around each other as I tilt my face up and sit up straighter.

Never let men see your fear.

Because once they do, they'll back you in the corner like Marvin, another one of Mom's exes, did at the burlesque club while we waited for Mom in the dressing room when I was sixteen. *"Come on, honey, you and I can have a little bit of fun while your mom is at work."* I remember his beady eyes glued to my chest and how his slimy voice made my skin crawl. It was then I learned how effective a swift kick to the balls is for incapacitating handsy men who thought their money could buy the world.

"I'm just waiting to see if there's a question attached to your statement." I cock my brow despite the beads of sweat gathering behind my neck.

Steven laughs, the sound loud and jarring, but mesmerizing all the same. Breathing in slowly, my lips tug into a grin, the early ache in my chest slowly dissipating. A hint of the ocean and leather, no doubt an expensive cologne, wafts to my face.

An addictive, seductive scent. One I could see myself falling under the spell of.

The cologne, not the man.

For a moment there, the harsh angles of his face soften as the smile lingers on his lips. His eyes are lighter and brighter. His shoulders loosen, which I doubt he even noticed how rigidly he was sitting moments ago.

His chuckles fade into the silence once more and he frowns, as if surprised at something, and the strange stillness befalls us again.

"You're one interesting woman, Grace. Fearless, even in the den of the wolves."

"I intend to rule the den one day. Fear won't help me on the journey."

Steven cocks his head, a flash of admiration in his eyes, and nods, as if agreeing with my assessment. "I like your honesty. Don't lose it as you move up the ranks."

He steeples his fingers and leans forward, the glint in his eyes sharpening. A different energy filters through him as he focuses his attention on me, like I'm interesting. I find myself wishing I could keep the spark burning in those tawny irises always.

He clears his throat. "I called you in here because I want to know how an intern could notice something the rest of them didn't see."

Relaxing into my chair, I smooth out the wrinkles I inflicted on my pants, my body still on edge from our mere minutes in the same room.

When in doubt, I always go with honesty. "I grew up in the seediest part of the Bronx, so we needed to pay attention to everything, to keep our eyes out to make sure we didn't end up as a target to be taken advantage of. And we needed to be on the lookout always, as three single women in one tiny apartment."

Steven's gaze is intent on mine, his intense eyes darkening at my brief description of the less savory parts of my childhood, probably reading between the lines on what I'm not saying. His hand taps a slow rhythm on the table before curling into a fist, but he doesn't comment.

"Most of us don't make it out of there without some battle scars. And even fewer of us end up graduating from college. So, I'm used to working hard, studying more than anyone else in class, and being meticulous in my work. I learned to read everything I could get my hands on, and to pay attention to details others may miss."

"And so, you read the footnotes," he murmurs, his eyes narrowing slightly, his gaze never trailing away from mine.

"Yes," I reply on an exhale. "I memorized the details."

"And familiarized yourself with every word but also understood everything that was unwritten." His voice almost comes out as a rasp, his eyes still pinned on mine, his hand gripping the pen tightly in his palm.

My rioting pulse is now an unsteady drum in my ears, all my senses attuned to the mysterious man before me, the thickness and intensity in his voice drawing me in like a lure. I release a shuddering exhale and whisper, "When some things appear too good to be true, they usually are."

The AC hums to life in the background, the burst of air sending a chill down my body. I shiver despite the strange heat gathering in my chest. My tongue dips out to wet my lips again, a nervous tic, but Steven misses nothing, his eyes flaring slightly, darting to the movement. His gaze drags down to my chest, pausing for a brief second, then flickers back to my eyes once more.

He stands up abruptly, strides to the coat rack by the bookshelves, retrieves the suit jacket I saw him wearing earlier, then hands it to me, his eyes darting down my torso before looking away.

I glance down, noticing my thin bra doing little to hide the pebbled nipples protruding against the damp fabric, and I gasp, quickly snatching the jacket from him and wrapping it around my body.

He clears his throat and sits down in his chair, the strange tension dissipating instantly, like everything was just figments of my overly creative imagination. His eyes are once again dispassionate, his bearing as cold as a statue, looking every inch the King of Wall Street as everyone calls him behind his back.

Only the faint pulsing of the vein on his forehead indicates the last few moments had impacted him somehow.

"I'd like you to join the two projects I'm kicking off next week. Have you heard of Scott Enterprises and TransAmerica?" His voice carries a tinge of hoarseness, and he takes a leisurely sip from a cup on his desk.

"Of course. The real estate empire is headed by the billionaire, Adrian Scott. I've also read online he's your brother-in-law, and TransAmerica, well, everyone knows them. Your father plays a big role in the company."

He nods, a faint smile on his lips like he's pleased I've done my research on him. "Adrian just signed an agreement for us to manage half of his investment holdings. As for TransAmerica, we're mainly research gathering right now, but things may change quickly. I only want the best and the brightest on my team, and not only because this relates to my family, but also because of the size and influence of these companies on the broader business community."

Steven cocks his head to the side before dipping into a curt nod. "I'm usually good at reading people. I'll send Hayley an email to let her know you'll be joining us. Kick off meeting is eight a.m. sharp. You may go back to your desk now."

My chest bursts with pride, bubbles of excitement flooding my insides, and I bite my cheek to keep from screaming or squealing. I climb to a standing position, my feet practically bouncing on the floor.

"Thank you, sir!" Steven's eyes lift to mine once more, the irises darkening a smidge, but I'm too excited to care. I rock on my heels, my lips splitting into a wide smile. "Thank you so much for the opportunity. You won't be disappointed."

Spinning around, I take a few steps toward the office door, only to find my fingers still clutching the lapels of his expensive suit jacket.

Turning back, I begin to shrug off the jacket—

"Keep it until your shirt dries. Just leave it on your desk before you leave. I'll pick it up before I go home," he instructs, his eyes pinned to the computer, his fingers flying over the keys in an incessant rhythm. He has put on a pair of thin, metal-rimmed rectangular glasses, the ensemble only making him more devastatingly handsome.

My heart skips a beat.

"Thank you, sir."

The clattering of keys stops briefly, then restarts, and he proceeds to ignore me as I walk the rest of the way out of his office, the elation thrumming through my veins better than any coffee or alcohol in the system.

I inhale deeply, the intoxicating scent of the ocean breeze with a hint of sandalwood, pear, leather, and spice sifting into my nose, and I burrow deeper into the jacket, which wraps around me like a warm hug. I try to convince myself even a blind woman would find Steven attractive and the clamoring in my chest and the butterflies flapping their wings in my stomach are just reactions to being excited about being part of his team.

That's all there is to it.

CHAPTER 5
Steven

THE DARKNESS SWALLOWS ME whole, tangling its thick tendrils around my wrists and ankles as I fight to escape. I teeter at the edge of consciousness, my arms and legs flexing and kicking to no avail as dense smoke glides over my body, the swirling midnight pulling me back down into its murky depths.

I jolt, my eyes blinking open, and I find myself standing in the dark hallway of my home. The wind whips against the windows, the glass rattling along with the haunted howls, and I shiver, even though I'm wearing my favorite blue sweater and the brand-new jeans Mother purchased last week when she was out shopping with her friends.

Nana visited a few days ago and sewed a superhero patch on the right pant leg. It's so cool. She told me I was now a superhero myself. It's what I wanted for Christmas, but Mother said I was too old to play with action figures anymore. But this is better than a toy because Nana said these pants are now magical.

"I'm only eleven, Nana. How can I be a superhero?" I gripped the jeans, my grubby fingers softly tracing the red cape. Mother was going to be so mad Nana ruined the pants.

But I love it.

"You only need to have a brave heart to be a hero, my darling Stevie."

I look up, finding the face before me fuzzy, a light glowing behind her head. *Nana? Why can't I see you?*

I miss Nana. She gives me the best hugs, outside of Emily, that is.

The floor moves beneath me, and I'm back in the scary hallway once more. A large wail travels in from the outside and lighting flashes through the dark room in a streak of white. My heart pounds in my chest just like the time Emily dared me to watch that scary movie about a ghost with her last Halloween.

She said the movie was for big kids and because she was thirteen, she wouldn't be scared, but she said I would cry. I was buried in the blankets for half the movie, but I stuck through it, because I wasn't going to lose the bet with Emily. And I didn't cry at all.

A low rumble ripples through the hall. Squeezing my eyes shut, I put my fingers in my ears, knowing what's about to come. A piece of paper I forgot I was holding flutters to the ground.

Don't be scared, Steven. You're eleven now. You aren't allowed to be scared. You're a Kingsley, and Kingsley men don't let emotions get the best of them.

I keep repeating what Father told me two nights ago in the library before another piercing roar of thunder shakes the windows. Whimpering, I curl myself into a ball on the floor and try not to cry, but tears fall down my cheeks, just like the rain outside. My lips wobble and I scrunch up my nose, swipe my face, my heart pounding so fast I could barely breathe.

Father will be so disappointed if he sees me crying.

Taking a deep breath, I swallow a shriek when another bright flash of light floods the hallway, followed by a clap of thunder.

I can do this. I'm a Kingsley. I'm a big kid now, not a baby.

Gritting my teeth, I curl my hands into fists and stand up tall even as the branches from the trees smash against the windows and the wind lets out a painful scream. I hurry to pick up the paper from the ground and pad down the carpeted floor, wishing Jess or even Emily were here, but they're both at a sleepover with their friends.

If Emily were here, she'd probably turn on all the lights in the house because she's afraid of the dark too. And she doesn't care if Mother or Father yells at her. She's brave that way. Or if Jess were here, she'd give me a big, warm hug.

Fumbling in the dark, I refuse to turn on the lights because I want to show Father and Mother I'm a big boy now, not a little kid. I'm not afraid.

I walk down the stairs, my hand touching the wall so I don't trip and fall down. Father should be in the office right now. He always works at night after he comes home from his company. He probably wouldn't want me interrupting him, but he'd be happy if he sees my test scores.

Maybe he'd tell me good job or give me a hug.

I really want a hug right now.

Clutching the paper tighter in my hand, I puff out my chest, thinking how Mrs. Davis told the class earlier today I had the best score on the math test. She gave me a gold star. Everyone in class clapped, even Derek the big, mean bully who smelled like sour pickles all the time. I can't wait until Father sees the test. Mrs. Davis even wrote "Excellent job" on top of the paper. He'd be so happy with me. Maybe then it'd be okay for me to ask him for a hug because I'm scared, or to stay with him in the office while the storm is outside. Maybe he'd play a game of dominoes with me or read me a story.

The office door is open and a warm light shines from within. I walk past the dark living room and poke my head through the doorway.

"Father?"

Frowning, I look around the bright room, seeing Father's tall wooden desk full of binders and papers, all neatly organized in straight stacks, and his big computer screen turned on. He always said being organized is the key to success and failure always comes to those who let their guard down.

His favorite mug, an old cup with a big letter R and a palm print on it, has steam coming out, but he isn't here. Mother hates the cup and says it's ugly and she wants to buy him a new one, but he always tells her it's his favorite mug and not to touch it.

"Please, don't do this."

Noises filter in from the outside—a screech of a monster. A blood-curdling scream. I inch toward the living room, a shriek tearing from my mouth as I find myself suddenly in the dark pools of the sea. I find her swimming toward me. A predator.

She's a monster, grotesque with red eyes and a shapeless form. She's ruling the ocean with her tentacles and venom. She's approaching and I'm frozen in place.

Swim, Steven. Swim away. Don't chase after it.

The monster opens her mouth, hundreds of razor-sharp teeth gleaming in front of my face, and I close my eyes and scream—

I jolt awake, my lungs drawing in oxygen like I just broke through the surface of the water right before my breath ran out. Sweat beads my forehead.

A dream, it's only a dream.

The winds wail outside the windows, sounding eerily like that night all those years ago. My heart races inside my chest as the sounds wrap themselves inside me, once again restricting my airway, and I'm drawn back into an old memory I wish were only a dream.

"Please, don't do this."

Noises filtered in from the outside—they sounded like a woman's cries.

A thumping echoed loudly in my ears and I gripped my test tighter to my chest as I quietly followed the sounds, which seemed to come from the direction of the living room. My feet stumbled and I caught myself on the side of the big couch and winced, my toe hurting when I stubbed it on the floor. My eyes burned, the tears making them blurry, and I wanted to pinch myself for almost crying again.

I thought I heard wailing and screaming as I climbed onto the big blue reading chair by the living room window so I could pull the thick curtain aside and peek outside to the front lawn.

"Just leave them, please. Come with us," a tall lady cried as she grabbed Father's arm. "Please, just come with us. You know you want to."

A little girl was hugging her waist. She was so small I almost didn't see her in the dark. The skies were pitch black tonight and the only light came from a small lamp by the front door.

The rain was pouring and water glided over the windows like I was underwater in a submarine. I pressed my face against the cool glass and held my breath, even though they probably couldn't hear me.

The lady was wet, like she took a shower with her clothes on, but she didn't seem to care. An umbrella laid on the ground, twisted and out of shape. Her dress was sticking to her skin, and I could only think how Mother wouldn't ever let that happen to her clothes. She said her dresses were too expensive and we needed to be careful when we hugged her to not make them dirty.

Father's head was bowed down, and his hands were on the lady's shoulders. He was shaking, like he was freezing, and I looked around the room, seeing if I could find another umbrella or his jacket. Father's dress shirt stuck to him too, like he had been standing out in the rain for a long time.

Father looked up, his hands traveling from the lady's arms to her face. His body was still trembling even as he shook his head. He glanced up toward the sky, even though there was nothing up there tonight. There were no stars, no moon, only rain and lightning.

A flash of bright light was followed by the loud clap of thunder, and I huddled closer to the window, even though I really wanted to duck and curl into a ball, but I didn't, because I wanted to know why Father was out there with this strange lady and little girl.

And why he looked so sad.

In the few seconds when the night sky lit up by the flash of lightning, I saw Father's face. He wasn't shivering because he was wet and cold.

He was crying. Crying so hard, I could barely tell his tears apart from the rain.

My eyes burned and a thick lump formed in my throat. I tried swallowing, but it wouldn't go away.

I'd never seen Father cry before. He was always so calm, so serious, and even when I cried, he'd tell me to wipe the tears away and be strong, because Kingsley men didn't have weaknesses. Because emotions were for weaklings. My lips wobbled as I saw Father choking back his tears, his sobs loud, like someone was tearing him up from the inside.

Swiping my arm on my wet cheeks, I curled my hands into fists, wanting to run out there to push the lady away from Father. Because she made him cry, and Father never cried before. I scampered off the chair, my hands wiping my eyes furiously because my tears wouldn't stop falling, and—

"I can't leave them. This is my life. I wish I could. You have no idea how much I wish I could."

Dad's deep voice, the same voice telling me to stand back up when I scraped my knees after falling off my bike before, stopped me in my tracks.

A loud rumble was in my ears and a voice inside me told me to run away, to not listen any further, because I'd regret it later.

But my body wasn't responding. Instead, my feet carried me to the corner behind the chair and in front of the windows. The wind was very loud, like it was crying along with Father, like somehow, the entire world was very sad, just like how I was feeling.

"Is the money really that important to you? You married her for money, but you aren't happy. I can see that. We can make you happy. Don't do this to us, please."

Father shook his head, stepping away from the crying lady, who was shivering, her arms curling around the little girl whose face was buried in her mommy's waist.

"It's over. If I weren't a Kingsley and I didn't need to keep the family name afloat, I would leave with you without a second thought. But I can't. We can't survive on love alone. I made my choice when I married her."

I hiccupped, my mouth opening in a gasp. *He'd leave us? Jess, Emily, and me? Didn't he love us? What about us?*

My heart twisted and suddenly I couldn't breathe. I wished I never came downstairs to look for Father. Was it because we weren't good enough or smart enough?

Father kneeled down and opened his arms and the little girl flung herself into him. He hugged her back tightly and peppered kisses into her hair. The girl was crying and for a moment she turned her head my way and stared at me through her teary eyes. I shrunk back into the shadows, not wanting to get caught, and yet, unable to look away. We were both sad but clearly for different reasons.

Father rubbed his hand on her back, and she buried her head in his shirt. A sharp pain hit my chest. He never hugged and kissed us like this.

She stole my hug.

I slammed my palm on the glass, a burning sensation inside my tummy, wanting to tear the little girl off him. *That's my father, not yours. Get away from him.* But they couldn't see me.

"Sweetheart, be good for your mommy. Take care of your sister for me. Don't cry. I love you so much." Father was sobbing again.

Headlights swiveled and cut through the darkness of the night. I heard a car door opening and a screech from Mother.

"How dare you, Robert? Bringing this woman here?" More screams and shuffling and another agonizing cry wrenched up from her. "You skank!"

I squeezed my eyes closed, tears dripping down my cheeks like a waterfall. There was no point in wiping them away anymore. My nose was runny, and I shook my head, my body finally obeying me, and I fled, running as fast as I could to my room upstairs.

I balled my test paper with my hands, and hurled it to the floor then stomped on it. Then, I climbed on top of my bed and hugged Fluffy, my special teddy bear, to my chest. The windows shook and rattled and lightning flooded the room with light, followed by the loud thunder.

Taking a deep breath, I forced myself to calm down. I wasn't afraid anymore. It was only scary sounds and bright lights. It didn't hurt, not like my heart was hurting right now.

"How dare you, Robert!" Mother's screams traveled through the closed door of my bedroom. "You promised me. You said you would

WHEN HEARTS IGNITE 53

stop. I gave you everything. How could you repay me like this? How could you love someone else when I love you?"

Mother then yelled a lot of words I didn't understand, something about TransAmerica, Father's company.

"Quiet down, Audrey. Steven is sleeping. And it's over for good."

Mother's cries echoed in the halls and I buried my head in my blankets, not wanting to hear anything else. I wanted to escape, to find Jess and Emily or Nana. I didn't want to be here.

"I-I love you, Robert. I gave you everything I could. Please don't do this. Don't break us up. What about our kids? They need you. We need you."

Maybe Father didn't give us hugs because his hugs belonged to that lady and the little girl.

Maybe we weren't good enough to deserve his hugs.

Maybe we weren't good enough to deserve his love.

I wished he'd love me.

The rumble of thunder crashed in the room again and the windows shook and shuddered.

But I wasn't scared anymore. I wished my sadness would go away.

Perhaps Father has been right all along. We shouldn't let our emotions get the best of us.

Liabilities. All of it.

Beep. Beep. Beep.

My eyes snap back open as I sit up, thankful for my phone to halt my trip down memory lane. My memories are spotty—I don't remember their faces—only the face of my father. How devastated he was. How the tears streamed down his cheeks, even though the sky was also crying that night.

Sweat drips down my back and I fling off the thick comforter from my body. My heart races, the rioting in my chest relentless, and I bury my face into my palms. My fingers rake over my hair, damp from my fevered dream.

A wave of dizziness hits me, and I breathe through the nausea churning in my gut.

It's in the past. Everything is fine.

A ringing reaches my ears and I turn off the market notifications on my phone—most likely information coming in from the Asian markets where it's still daytime. I must have forgotten to silence my phone before I went to bed last night. Wincing, I glance at the time.

Three-thirty a.m. Fuck. Only two hours of sleep tonight.

The room is dark. Stifling. The wailing of the wind cuts through the silence. The faint glow of twilight seeps through the gap between the thick blackout curtains. Muffled sounds of cars and trucks from the streets far below filter through the double-paned windows.

My breathing slows from the hurried pants to its usual rhythm.

I'm in New York, not LA.

It's all a dream.

A dream or fragments of memories I haven't thought about in a long time. The past only reoccurs when storms rage outside.

Another notification chimes through and I glare at the screen.

I roll out my tense shoulders and swing my legs off the bed. I trudge toward the floor-to-ceiling windows in my bedroom, turning the thermostat colder along the way. My chest is still damp from exertion and droplets of sweat drip down the valleys of my muscles like I just ran five miles on the treadmill.

The burst of cool air greets me in a chilly welcome, and goosebumps soon form on my skin, but I like the shock to the system, the extreme temperatures chasing away the remnants of unease inside me, temporarily allowing me to forget the extra weight on my chest.

I whip open the curtains, staring at the city below me. The buildings are lit up like stars in the skies, even though it's impossible to see the skies at this hour in the dead of twilight. From my windows, I can see trees swaying sharply to the wind—a storm is brewing on the horizon—but the city doesn't bend to its will, the electrifying energy couldn't be quashed, and the streaks of lights from cars hurrying to their next destinations, the illumination of tall buildings surrounding us, and even the glow of street lamps in the large expanse of Central Park below are all collective fuck yous to the bad weather.

Or bad memories.

This is why I love New York. It's the place where if you get back up after you fall down, you still have a shot of winning the race, of conquering your demons.

It's a place where only results matter, not the journey, and most definitely not emotions.

Letting out a ragged breath, I slide my hand over my face, my body exhausted, but my mind completely awake.

My mind floats to TransAmerica, to my father, who's probably still awake in his office in LA, trying to figure out how to best protect the company. Inside sources told me Voss has approached some of the smaller investors. Easier targets, I suppose.

I should've stepped in earlier. Maybe if I had, Father wouldn't be so worried right now.

Maybe if I had, he'd see me as worthy.

Gnashing my teeth together, my forehead drops against the cold window. It's not too late. I'm Steven Kingsley, and I will win this. I will protect his legacy. He'll understand then.

Another day, another race, another battle for me to win.

And hopefully, the famished beast inside me will be satiated, even if it's only for a little while.

CHAPTER 6
Steven

THE OFFICE IS A ghost town as I expected when I swipe my keycard over the sensor next to the double doors behind the lobby, which won't be unlocked by the receptionist for another few hours.

After fitting in a quick run on the treadmill and a shower, I spent half an hour reorganizing the contents of my closet, hanging the newly cleaned dress shirts by color. I made a note to yell at the housekeeper for forgetting the precise order, the darks on one side, the whites on the other with the colors organized by gradient in between. By the end of that exercise, the haunted darkness inside me quashed to a low simmer, and I felt like I could breathe again.

Then, I came to the one place I knew I'd feel at peace, the place where I understood my role as soon as I stepped through the entrance. I know a lot of men make much more money than they can spend on Wall Street, and they'd blow some of it on drugs or women, but I prefer to sequester my billions in investments and bank accounts.

It's not the money that drives me to work each day, but the satisfaction of each kill, each deal, the way the numbers always work in my favor after careful analysis and decisions on my part.

It gives me a thrill, a hit that jolts my system, livening up my senses.

Because only I can do it better than anyone else.

A heated rush churns inside me as I imagine the day ahead, the problems waiting for me to solve, to dismantle, and the last wisps of unease from my troublesome night finally disappear.

I stare at my phone, swiping through the unanswered messages I received last night.

Emily

> Adrian and Parker are on their way to NYC. Treat them well...or else.

I smirk, imagining my sister wagging her finger at me like I'm still the short kid in middle school who she can boss around.

Steven

> Consider it done. I'll take great care of your husband, Ems. Don't you worry about a thing.

Emily

> Don't you dare get him into something he shouldn't get into.

Steven

> You have so little faith in him?

Emily

> No, I have zero faith in you. But now that I think about it, what are you going to do to him, anyway? Gourmet fine dining him to death? Have an all-work all-nighter party? Seriously, bro, you need to stop working so much. Do you need me to introduce you to some women?

Chuckling under my breath, I shake my head. Everyone knows my penchant for fine dining, so that's no surprise. But come on, I have friends. I just don't see them as often as I should.

The sound of a chair squeaking catches my attention.

My steps slow and I look up, noticing a warm glow radiating from one of the cubicles in the bullpen. The rest of the floor is still dark, the faint blue light from the beginnings of dawn barely filtering through the windows.

Frowning, I slowly approach the cubicle in question—I wonder why maintenance didn't turn off all the lights before they went home after their daily cleaning. But instead of finding the space empty, I'm greeted with a sight so jarring and unexpected, I stop in my tracks and blink a few times to make sure it's not a product of my sleepless imagination.

The intern...Grace, is bobbing her head like she's at a psychedelic rave, her hands swinging wildly in front of her, a headset reminding me of the cheap free ones they give out on commercial flights perched on her ears. Her computer monitor is turned on, and she is now typing manically while looking at the spreadsheet in front of her.

After a few seconds, she glances at an open tablet next to the keyboard and swipes at it. She stares at the tablet for a few seconds, then emits something confusing like, "Aww...so swoony," and goes back to shaking her head like nobody's business, her attention returning to the spreadsheet on her computer.

An interesting sensation flitters inside me, like tingles traveling up my spine, and I bite my cheek to hold back a snort. I had bumped into her a time or two in the break room and she'd volunteer statistics or updates on her research with pride shining in her eyes. I'd swallow the urge to ask her more questions about herself, to prolong our fleeting interactions, because she is like a book written in an ancient script I can't read, and somehow, that makes me more desperate to understand.

Quietly, I creep toward her, wanting to observe this creature in her natural habitat, to see what she is doing at this ungodly hour. Standing silently behind her, I hear faint strains of music from her headphones and squint at the tablet, reading silently the text that had her so riveted a few moments ago.

Lord Bingley hauled her up on the table and shredded her clothes with the desperation of a dying man. His teeth nipped at her neck. She moaned, her nipples beaded in sharp points, and she cried, "Craig, it has always been you." Bingley groaned while his large hands palmed her breasts. He murmured, "I don't need anything in the world. I don't need success or money. I don't need my titles or estates. I only need you in my life."

Grace pauses her work on the spreadsheet again and turns her attention back to her reading tablet. Her head isn't moving anymore as she lets out a breathy gasp from those beautiful, cupid's bow lips of hers.

Heated blood rushes south at the little sound, which registers in my twisted brain as a half moan mixed with a soft sigh. Coupled with the erotic text and the faint fragrance of jasmine and something spicy lingering in the air, my cock stiffens inconveniently, and I find myself bending down, my nose seeking the source of the alluring scent.

My nose almost grazes her hair, tied in a simple ponytail at the nape, and I suddenly pull back a few inches, feeling every bit of a creep. *What the fuck?*

"Please, this Craig is just trying to get in her pants. 'I only need you in my life,'" I scoff, "how *ridiculous,*" I murmur, my voice sounding hoarse, even as my eyes wander back to the text, wondering what will happen to Craig and this mysterious woman.

Grace shrieks, her cry sharp in the silence of the office, and she leaps up from her chair, her head smacking me square on my nose.

"Fuck!" I grunt as I jolt back, and cover my smarting nose with my hand, my eyes burning from the piercing pain.

Grace whirls around, her hands covering her mouth, her eyes comically large. "Oh shit," she gasps. "Sir, I didn't see you there. I'm so, so sorry."

She flounders forward, her hands reaching out as if trying to check my face to make sure I'm okay, and I hold her off, blinking away the moisture in my eyes. The pain slowly dulls, and I scrunch my nose, wincing at the lingering soreness. Everything appears to be okay. I hope I don't have a bruise since I have a board meeting later today.

Apparently seeing I'm well, Grace narrows her eyes into slits. "Hold on, why are you looking over my shoulder? And reading my romance novel?"

"Is that what that drivel is?" I arch my brow, setting down my laptop bag on the floor and lean against the cubicle wall.

Grace frowns, her lips twisting in a cute little pout. "It's not drivel! It's beautiful writing, and I agree some of it may be unrealistic, but that's what fiction is all about, for us to escape from reality."

"Huh." I cock my head to the side. "At least you and I agree that shit you're reading isn't reality. I'd be disappointed if our most promising intern has her head in the clouds."

She breaks into a smile, as if pleased at my compliment, but her lips quickly flatten as she processes the rest of my sentence. "It's not shit. And my choice in reading material has nothing to do with my work abilities."

She tilts up her chin, her eyes defiant, which from up close I can finally make out the color, a brilliant shade of violet.

I cross my arms and level a chilly gaze at her just to see what she'd do.

She mirrors my pose and adds a cocked brow for measure.

We stare at each other for a few silent seconds, faint music humming from her headphones, which are now curled around her slender neck. My lips twitch in an effort not to grin.

The balls on this woman.

I clear my throat and motion to the computer monitor. "What are you doing here so early in the morning?"

She softens, her hands fiddling with the atrocity she has on today, some oversized purple knitted sweater with wide legged pants. She looks like she has been swallowed up by her clothes. "I usually come in early to get some work and reading done, but last night, I couldn't sleep because of the wind. So, I came in earlier than usual."

It seems like insomnia doesn't care if you're rich or working class.

"What are you working on?"

Her gaze flits up to me and she replies, "I'm compiling some statistics from the Voss Industries filings from the last five years. Just trying to see if I can identify a behavior pattern in their investments and performance. Maybe something in the past may indicate their strategy toward TransAmerica. I know your team already has most of the information gathered, but I like to do my own research as well, just in case—"

"Anything is missed," I murmur. *Just what I'd do if I were in her shoes.*

An unfamiliar warmth builds in my chest, and in the stillness of the office, I finally allow myself a few seconds to take her in. My eyes sweep down her face, noticing how translucent her skin is, how her delicate throat flutters when she swallows, to the elegant fingers dipped in a light shade of pink polish, seemingly out-of-place given the rest of her attire and her lack of makeup and adornment on her body.

She takes in a deep breath, the movement drawing my attention to the gentle swells hidden under the bulky sweater and for a second, a morbid curiosity enters my mind, and I wonder what she's hiding beneath those thick layers of clothing, like it's her armor against the world. Then I remember the way my groin reared to life the other day when she showed up in my office with a wet shirt, her dark nipples saluting me under the damp fabric, looking very much like a wet dream come to life.

Fuck. This shouldn't be happening. These impulses and thoughts. Insanity.

"Send me your analysis when you're done. I'm curious." My voice is hoarse, and I level my eyes at her beautiful ones, and am momentarily stunned by the vivid shade of purple. A breath lodges itself in my throat.

She grins, and the impish glint I saw the other day in the conference room reappears in her eyes, and I almost flinch as the full impact hits me in my chest. Fucking bad memories and the damn dream have me out of sorts today. "You want to see it? I'm only an intern though. It's probably not at the level of detail you're used to."

"Your level doesn't matter to me. It's your work that counts. Don't let titles hold you back. And somehow, I have a feeling you'll surprise me...in a good way."

Grace bites back a smile and nods. "Will do. I should have something for you within the next hour."

"Good."

"Yep," she murmurs, her eyes now dipping toward the floor.

I clear my throat and swallow, my mouth suddenly feeling dry. I should leave now and go back to my office where work is waiting for me. But having someone to talk to at this early hour when I'm usually surrounded by silence and paperwork is quite...acceptable, or appealing if I'm completely honest with myself. Suddenly, the work that was exciting to me moments ago is no longer drawing my interest.

Glancing at Grace, I find her still staring at the ground, her feet kicking some invisible object on the dark carpet. A few strands of silky brown hair hang over her face, and I wish I could ask her to look at me so I can see what she's thinking.

The silence stretches on, and I find myself wanting to ask her more questions, to find out why she wears ill-fitting clothes, why she seems so energetic and positive most of the time, even though based on her resume and what she told me in my office a few days ago, she's barely scraping by. What drives her to get up each day? Is it the same gnawing hunger and emptiness as me?

Somehow, I doubt that would be the case with her.

I tear my eyes away from her, not liking the direction of my hypothetical questions and my burgeoning curiosity toward this woman. Picking up my laptop bag from the floor, I turn around toward the hallway and—

"So, why are you here so early this morning?" Grace asks, and I look up, finding those startling violet eyes staring at me and I wish I could stand closer and look at the hues underneath a brighter lamp, to see if they are indeed purple and not a trick of the light.

Fuck. I'm not the type of man to wish for things. I take and ask for forgiveness later. But a nagging voice inside me tells me following my impulse wouldn't be a good idea in this situation.

Her question fully registers a second later, and a sudden heaviness blankets me, shocking me into silence. In the last few moments, I had almost forgotten the weight in my chest and the dark dreams haunting me at night.

Swallowing, I reply, my voice thick, "Couldn't sleep. The wind."

Wisps of my memories float to the forefront as an invisible rope coils around my lungs, slowly restricting my airflow. That dream is like an old nemesis, haunting me for over fifteen years, and like every time in the past, when it resurfaces, the memories would wrap itself around my chest in a vise, and a phantom ache would appear in the spot where my heart is.

It was one of the last times I felt bone curling sadness. Nana passing away a few years later finished what's left of my heart.

She stares at me, her lips softening into a sympathetic smile, her big eyes never leaving mine, and I have a distinct feeling she's somehow trying to see through me and read my thoughts. I want to shift my stance. A part of me wants to walk away and another part of me wants to stay rooted in place, to find out what she sees when she looks at me.

"Fun fact," she begins, breaking the moment of tension, and she gives me a quick waggle of her brows. "Do you know why the wind is measured in knots?"

My heart thuds loudly in my chest and I feel the lump loosening in my throat from the same tingling sensations I noticed when I saw her dancing at her desk.

"What?" I ask incredulously.

"Do you know why the wind is measured in knots?" she repeats, her smile smug.

I shake my head in bewilderment at this sudden change in topic. "No. Why?"

"A long time ago, sailors didn't have a way to measure wind speed, so some of them started tying knots to a rope and tossing the rope behind the ship, letting the rope uncoil and run its course for some time. Then, they'd count how many knots were submerged during that time period, and that was used to determine the speed of the ship under the wind. One knot equals one nautical mile."

"And how is this relevant to what we were talking about?"

She rocks her heels in place, her eyes sparkling with unshed laughter. "The best way to get yourself out of a funk is distraction. Whenever I feel troubled or sad, I'd search online for interesting facts. Then, I'd come out of that experience a little wiser and also get a reminder of how fascinating the world and its history are. And how little our problems are in the grander scheme of things."

The thudding in my chest speeds up, a sweeping warmth flowing to my fingers, which was chilly a few moments ago. Somehow, this unassuming woman, so unlike all the women of my past—who'd be decked out in their finest clothes, throwing teasing grins or coy smiles my way—can see through me even though she barely knows me.

My heart spasms and I let out a rough chuckle. "Thank you. I'll keep that in mind." My fingers twitch with an impulse to do something, but I don't know what.

"What do you do for fun, sir?" Her voice is sweet, a refreshing morning breeze against my skin.

My cock twitches at the word "sir" coming from her lips. Looking up, I find her once again smiling. "Why do you ask?"

"I have a hypothesis..."

"I'm beside myself with anticipation," I reply, twisting my lips to the side as a spark of amusement makes its way back inside me.

Grace squints, her full lips pursed as if deep in thought. "You're young, but you're in the office before anyone else, and I always see the light in your office on when I pack up for the evening. You don't seem to have any crazy gossip about you in the news. My guess is, you don't have any hobbies, really enjoy work, and are a complete bore, or..."

She pauses for dramatic effect, and I feel my eyebrow lifting. "You're using work as an escape from something. And since the wind keeps you up, and you have dark circles under your eyes, my bet would be the latter. But I wonder, what would keep someone like you up at night? And don't you have friends to hang out with?"

Her words are metal bolts to the chest, the arrows hitting much closer to the bullseye than I'd expect, and I still my body, fighting all impulse to move, to flinch, to give anything away.

Chuckling halfheartedly, I murmur, "Are you sure that's how you want to talk to your boss? You know you have to *please me* and make me happy in order to get a full-time offer."

Her eyes widen and I realize how my phrasing sounds.

A bolt of heat rushes south at the thought of her pleasing me, her knees on the floor, those big eyes staring at me as she calls me "sir" before choking on my cock, and I nearly groan out loud at the lurid direction of my thoughts. Something tells me she's not going to be obedient.

A pretty flush travels up her slender neck to her face and once again, I find myself wishing the lights were turned on so I could see the exact shade of pink and whether it extends all the way to her ears.

This shouldn't happen. I already had my session with Liesel. I should be able to hold these useless impulses in for another few months. I gnash my teeth as frustration claws inside me. Fucking biology.

"I mean," I mutter and clear my throat, "well, you know what I mean."

She wets her plush lips and gnaws at her tempting bottom lip again. I want to tug it from her teeth with my fingers and soothe the bite marks. My nose flares and my breathing ratchets up.

Grace lets out a nervous chuckle as her chest seems to lift and fall in rapid succession. "Well, it's not eight yet. So, you aren't my boss." She swallows and swipes her lip with her tongue again.

My eyes are glued to the motion, the way her lips glint under the soft light, looking so lush, so pink, so inviting. Dragging my eyes back to hers, I find her pupils dark. "You're right about that."

I shift my stance on the floor, thankful the space is dark so she can't see the inappropriate bulge in my pants. I'm going to regret this, but my mouth can't seem to stop the words from tumbling out. "How about this? Outside of work, you can call me Steven, and I'll give you a pass on all the crazy ideas from your mouth."

Her lips tip up into a bright smile and she nods before stepping forward, the sweet floral fragrance drifting to my nose again. I resist the urge to close my eyes and inhale deeply.

Grace extends her hand toward mine and says, "You got yourself a deal. And I'll do you one better. Since you look like you're a loner and don't have any friends, I'll even be your friend. I'll be team Steven."

She smiles at me and my heart spasms. "Hi, I'm Grace Peyton, future financial rock star on Wall Street." She throws me a wink, the beguiling gesture causing my heart to skip another beat, and I can't stop the smile from appearing on my face.

"I'm Steven Kingsley, the King of motherfucking Wall Street," I reply, and clasp her hand tightly in mind.

The simple touch sends a sharp jolt to my system, much more alarming than the boiling hot water in my shower or the chilly breeze of my colder than normal air conditioning. But I ignore the warning bells in my mind as I stare at this alluring woman in front of me, watching her smile widening, the whites of her teeth blinding.

"Team Steven, huh?" I whisper, looking down at our hands.

I revel in how small her hand is compared to mine and now, standing a few feet from her, I realize she's much shorter than me, completely at odds with her colorful personality, and my nostrils flare as I'm hit with another whiff of her intoxicating scent.

"Yep. We're a team. You're stuck with me now."

I drop her hand and clench mine into a tight fist, wanting to keep the lingering warmth in my chilly palm.

"So, what now, *friend?*" I ask, unable to stop the smile from seeping into my voice.

She gnaws on that plush lip of hers again, but this time, it doesn't seem to be from nervousness. Her eyes take on a mischievous glimmer and she replies, "It's my personal mission to make sure you get a life outside of work, friend."

I arch my brow. "And how are you going to do that?"

She taps a finger on her chin as if she's contemplating a flurry of ideas before responding, "Are you brave enough to enter a bet? A dare?" She matches my quirk of brow with a sardonic lift of hers, as if taunting me to say no.

My blood pumps loudly in my ears and my nerve endings sizzle with energy. A challenge. A Kingsley never backs down from a challenge.

"Don't come crying when you lose," I toss back at her. "What are we betting and what are the stakes?"

"Jamie and the gang are going to Lunasia after work on Thursday, so this is technically a work event. Word is out they're going to try out the karaoke lounge next to the club. I dare you to come and stand up in front of the room and sing us all a song." She grins gleefully at me, her feet bouncing on the floor. She looks smug, and that smile on anyone but her would look condescending. She waggles her brows again, as if saying, *gotcha*.

What the fuck. Me singing a stupid song in front of an audience?

No fucking way.

The blood slowly drains from my face.

Grace pauses, and adds, "Oh, and in order for this bet to be witnessed, I need to be there, so you also need to front me one hundred dollars."

"For what?" I can't keep the incredulity from leaking out of my voice.

She scrunches up her shoulders and sighs. "The cover is expensive, and I need to run to the store to pick up a top. They won't let me in if I'm wearing this sweater or anything else I have at home." She fiddles with the hem of the offending article of clothing again.

I narrow my eyes at her. Either she's good at the hustle and I'm completely being played here or she really can't afford to splurge on a top and the admission.

She adds, "Regretting it? It's okay if you don't want to bet. We can talk directly about the stakes. If I win, or if you forfeit, you need to listen to me for one day."

"And what if I win?"

She smirks and straightens her shoulders. "I'll do the same."

"What about the one hundred dollars?"

"That's the price of entering the bet. Take it or leave it," she deadpans, and crosses her arms over her chest.

Tapping my fingers on the glass partition behind me, I stare at her in silence, my eyes sweeping over this she-wolf clad in a husky's disguise, the petite Amazonian carrying a personality bigger and more unique than most people in this building. Images of myself serenading my staff flash to the forefront, and I inwardly cringe.

But the lure of the challenge is too intoxicating and fuck it, I never back down from a bet. Keeping my eyes pinned on her, I curl my lips up and murmur, "Deal."

CHAPTER 7
Grace

"WHO ARE YOU LOOKING around for?" Jamie hands me another margarita from the bar as she slides into the spacious booth the six of us are currently sitting at.

She claims this is her way of welcoming me into the Pietra family. The music thumps loudly from the speakers, a strobe light sweeping over the room rhythmically, and I can't help but tap my feet on the floor and lose myself to the atmosphere.

For tonight, I can forget about our impending eviction, the loan—recently, the loan shark made it his goal to scare us with newsletter clippings of unsolved murders in the Tri-State taped to hand scrawled messages with payoff date underlined twice—Taylor and I tried our best to keep this away from Mom so she wouldn't worry but it has definitely caused some sleepless nights for me.

But right now, with a drink in my hand, enjoying a rare night out at a pricey venue, I can temporarily stop thinking about scrimping and saving every dollar and cent, the murkiness of my future, and how everything rides on this internship going well.

I take a sip of the alcohol, reveling in the warmth flowing through my veins. This may be my second...or third drink for tonight. Remembering Jamie's question, I reply, "Uh...nobody. Just admiring the décor here."

Getting to go to somewhere as fancy as Lunasia is definitely a treat, and I can see why people are raving about this place, which isn't a surprise given Fleur Entertainment's domination in the nightclub and hospitality space. They know how to make every venue feel unique and exclusive.

This particular lounge feels like we're sitting in the middle of a galaxy, with the floors made from a glossy black surface that has specks of color-changing mini lights embedded throughout, such that in the dim environment, it looks like we are floating midair and partying among the stars.

There are private karaoke rooms besides the large central space we're in, and folks who want to perform for an audience can stride up to the stage, illuminated by a spotlight which also changes colors to the beat of the music. A large L-shaped bar sits to the side of the room, also built from the same unique material as the floors except for a clear subway tile backsplash which is lit up in rotating colors. Accent lighting highlights the extensive variety of alcohol on the shelves behind the bartenders who are hard at work, creating colorful concoctions supposedly to have won awards.

A piercing squeal filters from the speakers as someone sings an awful rendition of a popular ballad, which has us all collectively cringing. I take another sip of my drink, sneaking a glance at Jamie, who is bopping her head next to me, oblivious to the butchering of the popular song.

There's no way I'm telling her there's a kernel of hope inside me wishing a certain broody, dark-haired, sexy man will come by to serenade us and prove me wrong.

My heart thuds when I think back to the strange conversation Steven and I had in the office two days ago at the crack of dawn. Goosebumps prickle my skin when I recall the way his deep, raspy voice sounded as he whispered in my ear, reading off a few lines from my latest romance novel. Besides my heart leaping in my throat at the unexpected intrusion, I remember the sharp burst of heat traveling to my core.

Then, there was the way he stared at me when I asked him why he was in the office so early, his smoldering eyes dark under the dim light, the silent anguish that seemed to shine back at me. The way he held himself still, his jaw clenched, his eyes shuttered. I'd bet anything it was something upsetting that kept him up at night.

Most of the time, he hides behind his façade of beautiful bespoke suits, sharp intelligence, and a biting tongue, but in rare moments, it'd be a look I see on his face as he passes by my cubicle on the way to his office or like yesterday, in the silence before dawn, the haunted loneliness radiating from him, which somehow calls out to me. He has an aura about him, an air of mystery, a tension seeping out from his compelling presence so visceral, I couldn't help but be drawn to. I want to peel back the layers and see what lies underneath. I want to know what would make his eyes light up with joy.

Because, deep down inside, there are moments when I feel the same way. When putting on a brave face seems too exhausting, too soul draining. When there's nothing I'd rather do than bury myself under the safety of my blankets and pretend my problems don't exist—the loan, the threats from the loan shark, the eviction, the void left by my father. And that's why I collect random factoids about the world when I can't sleep at night. My attempt to turn something negative into something positive.

Perhaps, it's this shaky invisible connection between us—like kindred souls recognizing each other despite the distance—most likely one-sided from my end, that had me blurting out my idea of being friends and throwing out a dare before I could think better of it.

I just couldn't believe he agreed.

Now, I wonder if he's going to show up, or if he's like all the other men I've known in my life, all talk and no action. Disappointments.

It doesn't matter, Grace, he's your boss, remember that. That's all there is to it.

"So, Grace, how did you end up with an internship right before you're about to graduate? Most folks come in during their junior year," Jamie asks, just as our coworker Theo belts out an off-key verse of a romantic song, which will most likely chase the ladies away instead of his original intention. We collectively wince, sorry for our eardrums and everyone nearby.

"Thank God he's a good banker and doesn't have to rely on his voice for a living," Amber grumbles next to us before tossing back her glass of bourbon.

She stands up and hollers, "Dude, can it, Theo. I'm going deaf over here."

She makes a slicing motion to her throat. "Give me that mic. You're embarrassing the rest of us. Let me show you how it's done." She's a second-year analyst at the bank who has what she fondly refers to as a "resting bitch face" because she says it takes too much of an effort to smile most days.

"Burn! That's fucking awesome!" Bradley sniggers and elbows Chuck, who looks like he already had way too much to drink, his face flushed and his eyes taking on a glint which raises my hackles—the same way I've seen other men look when their inhibitions are lowered and they think they can bend the world to their will simply because they are loaded.

Chuck laughs and glances in our direction, his eyes trailing over my face and lingering on my chest, which is covered by a flowy white blouse I bought from a discount department store yesterday during my lunch break. The familiar sensations of ants crawling up my skin have me shuddering and turning away from his perusal.

"Grace?" Jamie pokes my arm, drawing my attention back to her.

"Oh, sorry, spaced out for a second there. Anyway, I missed the deadline for internship applications last year, but thankfully, I had good enough grades and recommendations from my professors and one of them told me I should apply as a senior. He secured a few invites to corporate mixers for me and the rest worked itself out."

Of course, I didn't tell her the reason I missed the deadline was because Carl beat Mom up when she broke up with him and landed her in the hospital. Luckily, she only had a few broken ribs and bruises on her face, but there was no way I could focus on interviews and applications when I was dealing with the police, explaining how Mom didn't provoke him, getting a restraining order filed, and was busy looking over our shoulders whenever we were out and about.

All the while trying to keep my temper in check because I wanted to find the asshole and bash his head in with a baseball bat.

I can't seem to get through to Mom, to make her understand things are good in our lives without a man mucking it all up.

As much as I don't agree with Mom on her beliefs about men, I love her with all my heart. Growing up, we didn't have designer digs or the newest toys, and sometimes we didn't even have enough to eat other than freshly sliced bread with a generous helping of peanut butter, but life with Mom never felt lacking.

When our classmates had birthday parties and we couldn't go because we didn't have money to buy presents, she'd stage pillow fights at home. When it was our turn to celebrate our birthdays, even though we couldn't have the large, rectangular cakes with swirling white frosting and sprinkles, she'd always have freshly baked chocolate chip cookies and snickerdoodles waiting for us when we got home from school.

She'd teach us to dance, to sing, to read storybooks we'd borrow from the library on the weekends. Our lives were never boring and always fun. She gave us all her love, more than enough to make up for the lack of a father in our lives.

We're happy. Just the three of us. We don't need anyone else.

Or at least that's what I tell myself, even though my heart aches when Father's Day comes around each year.

Jamie clears her throat, drawing my attention back to her.

"Well, I'm glad you're here. We need more women in this place. The bullpen is teeming with testosterone and aside from Amber and Hayley, who are as approachable as sharks, there aren't too many women to talk to. There are a few ladies on other teams, but they're bitchy. It's like we never left high school, if you know what I mean." She nudges me gently and flashes a bright smile.

I can't help but smile back. I definitely know what she's talking about. Just the other day, one of those mean girls, Andrea, I think, shoved my shoulder as she passed by me in the restroom. Then, instead of saying sorry, she sneered and muttered something like, "Can't believe we're letting anyone work here nowadays. At least put some effort into your attire."

Clinking my glass with hers, I wink. "Well, I'm glad you're my cubicle buddy. Let's hope I survive the internship and get the job offer."

Jamie nods vigorously, her black hair swishing like a shampoo commercial. "You'll do fine. Mr. Kingsley is impressed with you. In the last few team meetings, he's asked for your opinions. I think if you keep this up, one of the three open positions will be yours for sure."

My skin feels heated at the mention of Steven, or in this case, Mr. Kingsley, since we're technically at a work event, and I cringe, wanting to mentally slap myself for reacting this way about him. Any warm-blooded woman with eyes would think he's hot.

This is just biology.

Memories of Carl and her other exes wash over me, and suddenly, my body feels soiled from the leering glances and unwanted brushes of their bodies against mine in a variety of "accidents." The margarita curdles in my stomach and my appetite sours. As much as Mom broke off these relationships as soon as something fishy happened, each experience seemed to solidify my views on the opposite sex. I'd never voluntarily put myself in such a vulnerable position.

There's no way I'd ever make the same mistake Mom made over the years.

Falling for a man.

Any of them.

But then, there's something about Steven, the way he seems to listen to me and see me. The way he took me up on my dare like he really meant it and wasn't just giving me lip service.

Stop this train of thought and snap out of it, Grace. He'll probably not show up any—

A few gasps and collective murmuring pierce the air, shaking me from my trip down memory lane. I glance at Jamie, finding her mouth dropped open as she reaches blindly toward me and grabs my arm.

"What?" I frown, scanning the room, searching for what has her so stupefied.

Suddenly, I see it. Or more accurately, I see *him*. The person who has the room shrouded in silence, with people scrambling to take out their phones and turn on the camera function.

Steven Kingsley strolls through the entrance like he owns the club, his bearing tall and face fierce, as if he's riding into battle. He's dressed in an impeccably tailored gray suit today, much like many of the men in the room, but he somehow elevates the clothing he wears with his classical features and the scowl on his face.

Several equally tall and attractive men trail behind him, but I barely pay them any attention, my eyes transfixed on my boss and my new "friend," and how he seems to own the room so effortlessly, drawing everyone's attention to him, even without saying a word. My heart clamors into a chaotic rhythm, and I can barely hear the music blaring from the speakers.

Slowly, he unbuttons his suit jacket, his eyes sweeping the floor in concentration, his lips pressed in a thin line.

"Oh my God," I whisper, my hand covering my lips when his eyes meet mine, a full twenty feet separating us, but I can feel the raw masculine energy emanating from him as if he's standing right in front of me.

One corner of his lips twists up in a half grin as he lifts one brow in the classic sardonic manner of his. His eyes are dark from a distance, but I can feel the heat from his stare, the intensity stifling, all-consuming. My body feels achy, my skin hot to the touch. I can feel him peeling back every layer on me with the strength of his gaze, as if he wants to burrow deep into my soul. I gnaw on my lip, my hands clutching my bouncing knees in a death grip as he pauses in the middle of the room and stares at us.

"Shit. If I'd bat for the other team, I'd be pregnant right about now," Amber murmurs, having taken a seat next to me a few minutes ago after her awesome rendition of Billy Idol. Her phone is turned on and pointed toward the men, a video recording in progress.

I nod wordlessly, a knot forming in my throat, and Steven strides over, his brows furrowed with determination. He ignores the hollers and laughter from the men he's here with—I guess he has friends after all—and the greetings from the people seated at the other tables, who all apparently know him. I guess it should come as no surprise in the lounge mere minutes away from Wall Street, everyone would know the king himself.

"Team." His voice is deep, piercing through the chaos as he stares at us in acknowledgement. A muscle in his jaw twitches.

He whips off his suit jacket with a flourish and tosses it to me in one decisive move. My hand automatically reaches out and catches the soft material. The movement brings a fresh whiff of ocean breeze and leather to the air and my pulse careens out of control. Erratic like my heart. Scrambled like my mind.

"What on earth?" Jamie breathes, sounding as astonished as I am. I nod, my gaze transfixed on his retreating figure.

My mouth waters, my heart pounding so rapidly it may give up on me at any second. I grip his jacket on my lap and stare at his sharp figure as he makes his way up the dimly lit stage, unable to tear my eyes away from the way his muscles flex with each movement, his powerful body finely showcased in his crisp, sky-blue dress shirt and dark gray vest.

Steven unbuttons his cufflinks and slowly rolls up the sleeves, exposing the corded muscles of his forearms, and for a moment, I wish I were up close so I could trace the sexy veins that are no doubt there. Even though we're in the presence of at least a hundred people in the room, the way he adjusts his clothing feels so sensual, so intimate, like something I would see if I were his girlfriend in the confines of his apartment.

His face is still as hard as granite, looking very much like he'd much rather be anywhere else but here and with one harsh tug, he loosens the navy tie on his neck, then rakes his other hand through his meticulously arranged hair, rendering it into a sexy, disheveled mess.

He turns to the deejay and murmurs something before striding to the microphone propped on the stand in the middle of the stage. Exhaling slowly, the corded muscles of his throat rippling, he grips the stand with both hands and closes his eyes.

The room falls into a collective hush as we wait with bated breath for what he'll do next. The beginnings of a recent top fifty romantic ballad, "You're My Stars," plays from the speakers, the bass and beats reverberating, the evocative melody haunting, much like the shadows I saw in his eyes before. Flutters gather inside me and my spine sizzles with anticipation and trepidation at the same time.

He's actually doing it. The bet.

My mind is in chaos, and I can't seem to process any rational thoughts. My heart kicks out of control, trying to make its way out of my rib cage. My eyes are glued to the handsome man dripping with charisma and sexual appeal standing on the stage, the dark blue spotlight lovingly caressing every plane, reflecting the coiled tension in his body.

The opening chords fade and I can hear his ragged inhale under the silence of the room as everyone sits transfixed to the man on stage.

"When I look at you," he begins, his voice deep and raspy, making love to the microphone he's gripping on the stand. His eyes are still closed, but his face is leaning over the mic like he's pouring his soul into it. "I see my future in your eyes..."

"Holy fuck, he can *sing*, sing." That might be Amber. I can't tell anymore.

"Someone record this!" some guy commands, but everything ceases to matter as their chatters fade away into the background and I can only hear one soulful voice piercing my defenses.

Steven's.

My chest feels tight, like my lungs are bound with thick cords of rope. A spark inside me flickers alive, and nothing I do can stop the simmering burn from spreading like wildfire.

I clutch his jacket closer to my chest, needing support somehow, even though this is just a simple song—a performance—but it feels like so much more. It feels as though he's shedding a thick layer of armor after a deadly battle and I'm the one person he lets inside to see the bruises and cuts on his soul.

His intoxicating scent and lethal voice, full of emotions, dipping and swelling with the lyrics and melody about unrequited love and heartbreak, hold me captive. The man on the stage looks nothing like the coldhearted king in an expensive suit. He looks like a man of flesh and blood, with trapped anguish and aching want coursing through his veins and this song, these few precious minutes, is the only outlet he has.

His only escape.

My mind, long relegated to the backseat of my consciousness, calls me foolish and hollers warnings and red flags through its gagged mouth, but perhaps there's a thread of whimsical in me, perhaps the books I read have somehow left an indelible imprint of hope deep inside me.

All I know is, I can't look away, and I don't want to.

This sight is emblazoned in my mind forever, a scene I'll no doubt revisit again and again in the stillness of the night, as I lie awake in bed when the storm rages outside my windows.

Steven glances up, his brows furrowing as if in pain, then leans over the microphone even more, shifting his stance and bending his body down, his torso swaying to the music. His hands flex and grip the mic tightly, the muscles in his forearm rippling, and he takes in a heavy inhale. His molten eyes, blazing like the brightest fire, look in our direction and pause when his gaze lands on mine.

Pinning me with his intoxicating stare, he belts out the crescendo, his deep voice heavy with agony, threaded with pain, "You're the stars in my skies, the reason I breathe at night, how will I live now that you're not by my side?"

His words barrel through my defenses like a battering ram and wrap around my heart in a crushing embrace. His voice echoes and vibrates inside me and suddenly, I understand why women faint at concerts, and why people can fall in love with a tender voice on the radio.

Because the voice, the language of our soul, reveals the truth in every husky rasp, every ragged edge, and every smooth vibration. Under the guise of a heart-wrenching melody and devastating lyrics, the voice inevitably reveals part of your hidden soul, breathing life and meaning into the musical piece.

And it is in *his* voice, I hear the strains of emptiness and longing inside him.

I find myself leaning forward, an unfamiliar ache forming in my chest as I hear the sorrow and the heartbreak in the lyrics, and see the stark loneliness in his gaze, which he tries to hide from everyone, but something I can see as clear as day.

My eyes burn, my insides turning into a heated mush, and I can't do anything other than curl my arms tightly around the jacket which smells like him, wishing I could somehow rush up the stage to wrap him in a hug because I know this man hasn't had someone to hold him, to silently be with him, to whisper in his ears, "Everything will be okay," in a long, long time.

"Baby, don't leave me in my personal version of hell, take me with you, even if it's not in this world but beyond..." His eyes never leave my face as he croons the lyrics which had teenage girls weeping when the song was first released, and I blink, feeling a wetness misting my vision.

It's as if the tables between us have disappeared, the crowds have disintegrated, and only the two of us remain in this space, shields down, armor stripped and on the floor in scattered pieces.

It's as if I could feel the thread between us glimmering so bright it's almost visible and tangible.

I swallow the lump in my throat as I sit there, captivated by my friend, someone I've only recently met, and yet, something inside me recognized him from the start as someone I've known for a long time.

"Take me with you to the beyond...because you're the stars in my skies," he finishes, his voice hoarse, his body slowly straightening back up and releasing the microphone, but his eyes never leave mine.

He pants, his chest heaving with exertion, like he ran several miles to be here, to stand before us, to serenade us, and he swallows, his corded throat rippling from the motion as the music slowly fades into silence.

The room is still. Quiet. An eerie calm cloaking the tables.

I hear someone clearing their throat. The crisp rattling of ice cubes in a glass.

The room is held captive, just like me, and we don't want to wake up from the spell.

Steven huffs out a deep breath and bends toward the microphone again. "Well, don't everyone clap at once. And you guys," he points to us, "don't have too much fun. I still expect you at work tomorrow at eight a.m. sharp." He flashes a sardonic smirk, the spark not quite reaching his eyes, and I see a faint flush crawling up his neck.

The room erupts into cheers and laughter, and Theo stands and hollers, "Go, Bossman!" I follow suit, my mind still dazed, my body still reeling like it's suspended in an alternate dimension where I'm over-loaded with sensations and everything feels too much—too hot, too heavy, too intense.

My hands clap automatically, but I can't seem to bring myself to say or do anything when I watch him saunter over to our table, the usual chill befalling his features once more.

His hair is disheveled, his tie enticingly loosened, and at the closer distance, I can see a five o'clock shadow peppering his strong jawline. He looks like someone who has dressed in haste after a rough tumble between the sheets. My eyes sweep to his muscular neck, to the way he languidly moves his body toward us, his presence teeming with re-strained power, and my core involuntarily clenches.

Biological reactions, that's all.

Swallowing, I stare at him as he approaches us and leans over the table toward me, his arm outstretched, palm open.

I freeze, my brain still not functioning.

A glint reappears in those hazel eyes, and he unleashes a devastating half grin as if he knows what I'm thinking.

"My jacket, Grace," he murmurs.

Still rendered speechless, I hand over the jacket that has quite a few new wrinkles in it from my death grip.

The music resumes from the speakers and conversations and awful singing carry on like the world hasn't been transformed in the last few minutes like mine has.

He pauses, his head dipped slightly toward mine, even though there is at least half a foot separating us, and whispers, "Checkmate. And you're mine."

I gasp, my nipples pebbling at the rough timbre of his voice, the imagined edge of possessiveness in his words. He pulls away, his lips twisted in an infinitesimal smile, his searing gaze capturing mine once more before he turns away, walks toward his friends, and exits the building.

My day is his. That's what he said. I must have misheard.

My core throbs and my panties are damp. My skin is hot, and I feel oddly out of breath.

"Shit, that was intense. What was that about? What did he say to you when you gave him back the jacket, Grace?" Bradley asks from the corner of the booth.

Glancing up, I find everyone staring at me and I take a seat and let out a shaky chuckle, hoping I sound halfway convincing. *Thank God it's dark in here and they can't see my face.*

"He t-told me this doesn't count as overtime, to make sure I don't bill those hours."

Bradley and Chuck snort, shaking their heads in unison. "The boss is a jackass, no doubt."

Amber types rapidly in her phone, a mad grin on her face, resembling a deranged hyena. "I'm sending this video to the others. I think it's one of those things where no one will believe me unless they see it themselves."

I laugh half-heartedly, sink back into my seat, and release a deep exhale. Turning to Jamie, I find her squinting at me, her brows furrowed, her head cocked to the side.

Quickly, I look away, like I was caught with my hand in the cookie jar, even though nothing happened in the last few minutes.

Absolutely nothing.

It's the alcohol and the music. The environment and my subconscious acting up.

It's *nothing*.

The binds around my chest tighten and I swallow the lump in my throat.

CHAPTER 8

Steven

I SWIRL THE CONTENTS of my tumbler in my hand, my mind still racing from half an hour ago. When I took a leave of sanity, strolled right into Lunasia, and belted out a song in front of colleagues, competitors, and God knows who else was in that lounge.

It's not like I noticed anyone except her.

Grace Peyton. The intern. My new "friend."

The woman who is wise beyond her years and seems to surprise me at every turn. The one person I've met who doesn't carry any artifice, doesn't speak with hidden riddles or secret meanings. The only person who doesn't want anything untoward from me—not my money, not my companionship or dates, not publicity, and not even a leg up at work.

In fact, the only thing she seems to want other than my acknowledgement of her work performance is to be my friend, because she noticed the dark circles under my eyes and somehow noticed the darkness I typically find myself mired in.

I remember the way her plump lips parted in surprise when I walked over to her and tossed her my suit jacket. How she couldn't tear her eyes off me when I sang on the stage. The way she trembled in her seat, seemingly oblivious to everyone around her.

I was tempted not to show up today, but the nagging in my chest was relentless, a phantom itch prickling my skin, and I couldn't ignore it any more than I could force myself not to breathe. My thoughts kept drifting back to her and those violet eyes, large and guileless despite the experiences she shared with me growing up in the tougher neighborhoods of the South Bronx.

There's a saying in the Chinese language, my mother's heritage, *chu yu yuni er bu ran*, simply translated as "to be borne from the mud and be unsullied," a phrase typically attributed to the lotus flower, which blooms beautifully amidst the brown muck of the pond.

Somehow, the idiom reminds me of Grace and her personality. Even with her shields up, her desperation to prove herself to the world, her horrible taste in clothing, she still has an air of sweetness. She shines brighter than me, someone who was born with a silver spoon in his mouth and yet, somehow still defective and hollow, someone who swallows the light instead of spreading it to my surroundings.

And so I knew I couldn't disappoint her. I couldn't be another blip in what must have been a tough upbringing.

Plus, a Kingsley never shirks on a bet.

But when I got on the stage, with the heat of the spotlight on my face and my colleagues and acquaintances in the dim room staring at me, knowing she was sitting in the audience, her attention solely on me, something switched on.

A sudden shift. Intense yet fleeting.

A brief gale carried the heady fragrance of change and anticipation in the air. It was unsettling. An invisible harbinger to a different future I couldn't make sense of, a world where my usual calculations and logic were foreign languages.

The crowds faded into nothing when I closed my eyes and listened to the chords of the music, the sorrowful sweeps of the violin, the darkness in the silence between the notes, and the heavy strumming of the guitar.

It's a popular song, one I'd heard Emily and Jess gush about to each other the last few times we spoke on the phone. It was supposed to be a bet, singing a melody everyone would recognize, but somehow, out of my mouth poured a song with more emotions than I ever thought I had. Somehow, with her in the audience, feeling her eyes on mine, deep and penetrating, everything seemed different.

I could feel a burning rush in my chest, seeping through my voice, a voice which hadn't performed for a crowd since the violin and vocal lessons Mother put me through in middle school and high school. Extracurricular activities for the resume, or so she said.

For a moment there, I almost felt normal. Like the dark void in my chest was filled.

Filled with a burgeoning flame which slowly warmed up my insides.

At that moment, it was like I knew what the painful stabs of heartbreak would feel like, or the crushing agony and desperate longing of wanting to follow your soulmate to the great beyond because one life with them wasn't enough.

It felt as if an invisible gate deep inside my soul unlocked, and tethered thoughts I couldn't name or tame came flooding out, a tsunami crushing normalcy as I knew it, bringing in havoc and destruction.

It was almost as if I was singing for one person in the audience, the one soul who would understand what I'm saying or how I'm feeling without words.

"You're mine."

I remember these words tumbling out of their own accord. The rush of satisfaction. The piercing need. The way I gripped my jacket to stop myself from hauling her from her seat and dragging her out of the lounge with me. So I could dip my nose in the crook of her neck, inhale that sweet scent, and claim her with my lips.

Fuck. What a load of bullshit.

My hand trembles, sloshing the whiskey in the glass.

"What the fuck was that all about? Are you going to tell us?" Ryland asks as he hangs his jacket on the coat rack by the door of the private room in the gentlemen's club within The Orchid. He strides over to the immaculately decorated lounge area, which is a statement of old-world luxury, akin to the gentlemen's clubs from Regency England.

The spacious room is separated into two parts, a long glass table for work or dining and a lounge area with two large, black leather sofas, imported from Italy, several navy tufted armchairs, a fireplace, which, during wintertime, would roar with a well-tended fire. The furniture centers around a coffee table crafted from glass and dark oak, completed with a Persian rug from the nineteenth century on the floor.

Normally, these rooms are reserved at least a week in advance, but Ryland, being the second eldest child and the public face of the influential Anderson family, which controls the behemoth Fleur Entertainment Holdings, where he acts as Chief Operating Officer, pretty much has a room reserved all year round for his family's use. Clearing his throat, he levels his slate-colored eyes at me, a startling contrast to his dark hair.

I take a sip of my drink, relishing the smooth burn of the alcohol down my throat, and murmur, "Nothing. It was nothing."

"I can't wait to tell Emily about this." Adrian Scott, billionaire real estate mogul slash brother-in-law, leans back in his armchair like he owns the place. He rakes his hand over his dark hair, his icy blue eyes shining with mirth before he brings his glass of whiskey to his lips for a sip. "There's no 'nothing' about this."

"Already on it before you did. Check the group chat." Parker Wellington, architect extraordinaire and brother-in-law once removed, since he's married to Liz Chapman, whose brother, James, is married to my oldest sister, Jess, flashes his phone screen to Adrian. Both of them snort at what they're seeing there. He throws a shit-eating grin my way, his annoying dimples showing on his face.

I groan inwardly, not wanting to see what awaits me in the group texts.

My sisters are probably conspiring to plan my wedding at any moment.

"There's nothing to tell. It was a bet, and a Kingsley never backs down on a bet." *Sure, keep telling yourself that.*

Charles Vaughn, a business colleague and close friend, also the CEO of the Bank of Columbia, rolls his eyes and mutters, "Keep telling yourself that, Kingsley. Maybe I'm the only person in this room who doesn't have a woman, but your abnormal behavior today has all the signs of the beginning of the fall of Rome to me. So, what's her name and what's your relationship with her?"

"I'm single too," Ryland interjects, staring at the glass in his hand with a pensive frown, his forehead furrowing. He glances briefly at Adrian and Parker before he looks away, his jaw tensing.

"You wouldn't be if you weren't doing two jobs at the same time. Why *are you* doing the professor thing again? Isn't being a COO of Fleur busy enough for you?" Charles asks, but Ryland stays silent, his eyes unfocused, his attention elsewhere if his anguished expression is any indication.

The man has secrets, and my gut tells me it's a woman. But he's been silent about it.

Charles sighs and turns his focus on me. He crosses his arms, his striking blue eyes narrowing, and along with his blond hair and tall frame, he looks every inch a stock photo model for Scandinavian royalty, a joke coined by my sisters and their friends, which garners a roll of his eyes every time we bring it up. He raises an eyebrow at me, and I let out an exasperated groan.

"There's no woman. Work is my wife. I don't do relationships. They're messy, distracting, and completely unnecessary." I look at the men in the room, pining them down with my glare, only to be met with bemused expressions on their faces.

"That's because you haven't met the right woman," Adrian responds, the normal coldness on his features softening as he is clearly thinking about my sister and their rags-to-riches, star-crossed lovers epic romance, which had its fair share of drama and turmoil, another cautionary tale of the perils of emotional entanglements, in my opinion.

Parker nods. "With the right woman, your life could very well change for the better. Liz saved me."

"There's nothing wrong with my life!" I slam the glass on the table and stand up, the sudden outburst shocking everyone in the room, including myself.

I could feel my face heat, a burning sensation spreading from the center of my chest to my extremities, and I grit my teeth, wanting to hurl something at someone, anything to dispel the perturbing sensations coursing through me. My stomach churns and protests, and I feel as if my dinner will make a reappearance at any second. Turning to face the windows, I drag in a deep breath, trying to calm myself and chase away this insanity plaguing me.

"Hey, man. Are you okay? We make fun of you and all, but we're just worried about you. You don't look so good these days. Is it TransAmerica?" Charles furrows his brows.

I let out a sigh. "That's part of it. Things are going to shit soon, I can tell. Voss is circling like a fucking vulture. We're on standby, ready to go to battle if they drop the first bomb. I don't know what Father would do if something happened to the company."

"I thought you weren't going to get involved."

Shaking my head, I sit back down and stare at the drink on the table in front of me. "I guess I'm not coldhearted enough for that. If he loses TransAmerica...if I don't save it for him, he'd be heartbroken." Or at least, whatever's left of his heart.

"You know, you don't need to prove yourself to him." Ryland's piercing gaze settles on me.

I attempt to swallow the lump stuck in my throat, but it doesn't dislodge.

Ryland sighs. "Anything we can do to help? You honestly look like you haven't been sleeping. And don't think I haven't noticed how you've scrubbed the face of your watch at least five times since you got here."

Looking down, I find my fingers hovering over the glass face, and I wrench them away. I force my lips into a half smile. "Don't worry. I have it all handled for now. If things get worse, I'll let you guys know."

Knock. Knock.

The crisp knocks on the door interrupt my chaotic thoughts and seconds later, three more Andersons waltz into the room. Rolling my eyes heavenward, I groan, burying my face in my hands. Leave it to me to pick the day I have an irrational meltdown, or whatever we want to call this, to be the day I finally meet up with friends, all powerful players on both coasts who can see right through any bullshit I spiel.

"What's with the face, Steven? What did I miss?" Rex, the party animal of the five Anderson siblings—four brothers and one sister—the classic troublemaker middle child, prances in, unbuttoning his suit jacket with one hand. His eyes, the same color as his elder brother, are already sparkling with interest at the idea of gossip. He ruffles his already disheveled brown hair and smirks. The man sniffs out gossip like a shark detects blood in the waters.

"Steven here, the Mr. Workaholic who doesn't sleep or have time for us, decided to make a detour at a karaoke lounge and sing a sappy, romantic song in front of an audience, after a strange interaction with a mysterious woman from his office," Charles unhelpfully supplies.

"*Oh.* Tell me more." Rex happily plops down on one of the open armchairs across from me and leans forward, his elbows on his thighs, the face of rapt interest. I wouldn't be surprised if he had secretly turned on his phone and were recording this for leverage later on.

"It was a bet. How many times do I have to tell you guys this? Are you all a bunch of pussies with your panties in a twist?" My teeth gnash against each other and my jaw aches.

Maxwell, the eldest and broodiest of the Anderson brothers, Ryland's fraternal twin, a recluse who's usually holed up inside the family mansion, his office, or The Orchid, and is rarely seen in public, quirks a brow, his face devoid of other tells or emotions. He saunters toward the wet bar with a quiet confidence befitting his role as the current CEO of Fleur Entertainment and pours himself a drink. "Ignore him, Steven. Don't engage. You'll only encourage him."

"Well, Your Majesty, not everyone here has the weight of the world on their shoulders to contend with," Rex throws back, a smirk on his face. "Some of us commoners need gossip in order to get through our day."

"Like you can be considered a commoner," Ethan, number four in the Anderson sibling pecking order, mutters. "You're our Chief Marketing Officer, for fuck's sake, your net worth is more than most people in New York."

"Obviously it was a hyperbole, Ethan."

"But seriously, Steven, are you leaving the bachelorhood? I thought you'd be the last person to get together with a woman...for good." Ethan leans against the stone wall of the fireplace, looking bemused at this entire spectacle.

"No. They're blowing it completely out of proportion. This was a bet with a friend. She said I didn't have a life outside of work and if I did this, I'd prove her wrong. That's all that was."

"And this is not a 'friend' from our Rose floors?" I think that was Rex again.

"I already ended it with Liesel."

"Since when are you friends with women, anyway?" Ryland murmurs, his lips tilting up in a smile as if he read every thought in my mind the last few minutes.

I stand back up and toss my hands into the air. "And *this* is why I don't meet with you guys more often. I *do* have friendships with women. Your younger sister, Lana, remember? Where is she, anyway? She'd be on my side."

"I think I saw her as I was coming in. She mentioned something about using one of the spas on the upper floors with her friends from college and leaving us to our brawls," Charles pipes up and crosses his arms behind his head. "She's smart. I should do the same."

He grins and turns to my two brothers-in-law. "Adrian and Parker, I think we can go to the steakhouse and I'll wine and dine you guys while the ABCDEs of the Andersons, namely him, Mr. C over there," he points to Rex, "gets down to business and ferrets all the details from Steven here."

"What's with the alphabet?" Parker quirks up an amused brow.

Rex rolls his eyes. "It's a nickname. Apparently, there are too many of us and our family alphabetized our middle names by age as a joke. Maxwell, His Majesty, has a boring name, Angus, like the fucking beef, and Lana, our little sister, is Elise. We are your classic stuffy, boring rich-ass people with five names on our birth certificates. It comes with the territory when your ancestors are part of the aristocracy in England and our family still holds a dukedom and a marquessate."

"So, what's yours?" Also, Parker, the nosy prick.

Rex winks. "It's a state secret."

Adrian and Parker look at each other and dissolve into chuckles.

"Well, back to Steven's little problem, I'm ready to start a bet if anyone wants in." Parker takes out his phone and the rest of the room hollers obscene amounts of money at the idea of me being off the market within one year.

Pathetic. Ridiculous. Absolutely insane.

I look above the fray at Adrian, who is barely stifling a grin. "Aren't you going to talk some sense into them?"

"I would if I think they're wrong. But in this case, I think they're onto something. And why have we never seen you with a woman or a girlfriend? Emily worries about you."

Shaking my head, I mutter, "Not everyone needs a woman to complete their lives. Emotions are messy, complicated. Just look at what happened to you and Emily. It took you eleven years to get together after some crazy heartbreak. You built your adulthood around her. It's too much power to give to one person."

"But it's worth it, Steven. I'm saying this as your friend and brother-in-law. Emily makes me a better person. She gives my life color. Don't close yourself off because of fear."

"I'm not afraid of anything," I snap, the unease from earlier making a reappearance.

He holds my gaze, his pale blue eyes sharp and penetrating, and I look away, afraid of what he's going to find when he stares long enough.

"Whoever this is, Steven, if she is someone who could be more, give her a chance. Not everyone has one," Maxwell murmurs after placing his bid, a shadow crossing his face, but he turns toward the door before I see more.

Suddenly, he retrieves his phone from his pocket and holds it up. "Sorry, incoming call from Tokyo. I'll be back." He steps out of the room and Ryland and Rex trade frowns and a cryptic stare before looking at the back of their oldest brother.

"You guys are done ribbing me, right?" I pull my tie loose and let it hang around my neck.

Normally, this is something I'd do only in the comforts of my apartments or before my quarterly bouts in one of the Rose suites, but as annoying as this group of men are, they are the best of friends, all of them from old money and equally accomplished in their careers, and I feel comfortable enough in front of them to let down my guard.

Except for Parker and Adrian, who worked their way up the ladder from more modest means, everyone else understands the complications and pressures of old money families—the machinations, the rules, the way others get close to you with ulterior motives, the enemies lurking in the background waiting for a moment to strike and tear you down from the top of the food chain.

When they say life is lonely at the top, the statement is very much true. Everyone wants to climb Everest despite the risks and dangers. Many frequently lose their lives during the treacherous ascent. But upon getting to the top, many realize the air is too thin, the rough winds are too brutal, the view is marred by clouds and blizzards, and an avalanche may just be around the corner.

It's often not that glamorous.

"Adrian and Parker are visiting from LA for business, which concerns Fleur as well." I lean back in my seat now that the chuckles and jokes are behind us, and everyone is settling into place. "Parker is here to meet with his business partner, Dylan, who you all know, to discuss the remodel you're planning for The Orchid. Adrian is handing over half of his investments to Pietra, and we're thinking of putting some funds into Fleur. But he wanted to discuss in person."

Ryland leans forward and clasps his hands on his knees. "What information do you need from us? I'm sure between Ethan, our CFO, and I, we can provide you with detailed financials or operational plans, if that's what you're seeking."

Adrian nods. "That's a start. I'd like to see your five-year investment plan, growth strategy, and any forecasts you have regarding..."

The conversation flows freely between them, and I release the stale breath trapped inside my lungs.

My thoughts trail to Grace and her bright eyes and teasing smile, my friends' discussion fading into the background. It's almost as if my heart, the organ which has only served to sustain life in my almost thirty years, is awakening, the telltale sparks of an engine sputtering to life.

The sudden thumping is disorienting, the thrumming in my veins unsettling, and I can't help but think about what Adrian and Parker told me earlier about how meeting the right person could change my life. Then Maxwell's sullen utterance, the lowest of murmurs about giving someone a chance because not every has one, echoes in my mind.

The thumping intensifies, as if the muscle is warming up, readying itself for a sprint or a long-distance run, and I suddenly find myself bereft, wondering if they're all correct, if perhaps something precious and valuable is missing in that hole in my chest and if perhaps, there is someone out there who can fill the void.

And maybe one day, I'll sleep soundly through the harsh winds and thunderstorms again.

CHAPTER 9
Grace

"CHEERS! CONGRATULATIONS, TAY, ON getting into Petit Jeté." I curl my arm around Taylor while the girls and I give her a well-deserved toast for a job well done.

As I predicted, she passed her audition with flying colors and the director of the dance company personally gave her a call this morning with the good news.

Taylor smiles, her eyes turning suspiciously red as Millie and Belle pull her into a group hug. Millie Callahan, Taylor's best friend who goes to NYUC, rubs reassuring circles on Taylor's back, shushing her and murmuring words I can't hear, but are no doubt kind.

Annabelle Law-McKenzie, or Belle, as she'd like to be known to her friends, doles out a sympathetic glance my way. We met at NYUC when she sat next to me in criminal psychology, and promptly listed all the reasons women shouldn't be walking alone after dark because serial killers were afoot. After telling me why she was in the class despite being a fashion design major—morbid curiosity—she threw me an easy grin, tossed back her thick black hair, and announced we'd be the best of friends.

Since then, the four of us have stuck together and Millie and Belle even decided to be roommates. We are an odd quartet from outside appearances, with Taylor in her grunge makeup and thick braids, oversized T-shirt, and torn leggings, me with my thrifted professional attire, Millie with her girl-next-door tank top, jean shorts, and luxurious brown hair, and Belle with her couture linen dress and pearl necklace. Yet, these are the girls I can't live without.

We celebrate our highs at food stalls and restaurants inside Chelsea Market or drown our sorrows in tubs of handmade ice cream at Millie's and Belle's swanky apartment in SoHo while watching reruns of *Sex and the City*.

Belle's father hails from the royalty of American haute couture fashion, with the McKenzie brand going toe to toe with the classic Italian and Parisian labels; her mother is a supermodel from Asia, but she's the most down-to-earth person I've ever met, never showing off her wealth and always respecting our boundaries by limiting dining out or extravagant activities.

True to form, we're crammed at a bar table, elbow to elbow with other patrons who are celebrating the end of another work week in Corazón, a Mexican and Japanese fusion eatery nestled within the industrial stalls of Chelsea Market, where it makes sense to have jalapeños on sashimi and listen to a lively Mariachi band play while drinking hot sake.

"So, are you going to sign on the dotted line?" Millie pops a grilled whole jalapeno in her mouth and winces. I cringe, my tongue almost on fire on her behalf.

Taylor shrugs and takes a sip of her sake. "Not sure, to be honest. There are a lot of fees involved in their pre-professional program. The tuition costs a pretty penny, and I have it good at my current school with the full ride, so I haven't decided."

"You must though! It's your dream to go there and then onward to ABTC, right? This is once in a lifetime. You have to make it work. Do you need a loan? I can lend you some money, and even charge you interest, since I know your stubborn ass won't take the money otherwise." Belle spears a piece of California roll with her chopsticks and waits for a response.

"I can help as well! I have funds set aside," Millie blurts out, her hand covering her mouth, which is stuffed with food. "Actually, I have a good amount stashed away."

We glance at her in surprise. Millie has been private about her background since we met her. From what we have gathered, she lost her mother at a young age and has an older brother and a father. That's about all we know. We figure there are things she isn't comfortable sharing until she's ready.

Taylor sneaks a glance at me, her eyes narrowing pensively as she purses her lips. I smile, pat her hand, and give it a soft squeeze. "You have to do it, Tay. We'll make it work. Remember, I'm going to get that job offer and everything will be fine."

It must be. I won't lie and say the additional costs associated with this good news don't stress me out, but I can't have Taylor giving up her dream because of something so superficial, yet essential as money.

My shoulders ache as heaviness settles on my chest. There's so much riding on this internship and I hope—

Fuck that. I'm going to rock this. There's no alternative.

I'm going to work even harder, so the job is in the bag.

Turning to Belle, I clink her glass with mine. "And you, sister from *another mother and father*, we'll put a rain check on your offer. If I get the full-time position at Pietra, then we won't need to take you up on it. But you're the best."

Taylor's lips split into a wide grin and she tosses a wink at Belle. "Now that I think about it, I don't mind having you as a sugar mama, though."

Belle snorts and I roll my eyes. Taylor pours more sake into Belle's cup. "But in all seriousness, the best thing that happened to Grace at NYUC was meeting you. I hope we don't have to take you up on it."

She flushes and looks away—Taylor is the tough cookie in our family and always shies away from what she calls the mushy stuff. Her nose ring, a heart today, glints in the light.

"Aww shucks, you girls are going to make me cry. It's what anyone would do. I don't have anything to spend my trust fund on anyway, and this is a worthwhile cause. Tay, when you become a prima ballerina or dancer or whatever you call it, I want reserved box seats and first dibs on all merchandise. And you must wear the McKenzie brand at all times."

"Ever the businesswoman." I chuckle and she flips me off.

Taylor turns to Millie and curls an arm around her neck, hugging her close. "And you...you're the best thing that's happened to me since sliced bread. Fuck, where did that saying come from? It doesn't make any sense."

I volunteer, "Actually, there's an interesting story behind that one. Supposedly, it's a slogan—"

"Not now, Grace," the girls grumble in union.

Millie chokes on her food and tries to shove Taylor away, but Taylor just sniggers and slaps her loudly on her back.

"Those damn jalapenos are so spicy, but I keep going back for them. I don't know why I do that...going back for things that are bad for me," Millie murmurs, finally disentangling from Taylor.

Her eyes are watery and she lets out a soft sigh, a pained expression flashing across her face. She has been uncharacteristically sullen ever since she came back from Los Angeles, where she spent a year for a special business program.

"What's going on Millie?" I poke her with my finger.

She glances up and forces a tight smile. "Nothing. Enough about me. How are you, Grace? How's the internship going? We barely get to see you since you started."

I look at the small porcelain cup in front of me and trace my finger on the Japanese character, which I recognize as love. Except for the memorable evening at Lunasia last week, where in a few short minutes, I felt like a main character in the books I read, someone who believes in destiny and soulmates, life has been as normal as can be.

"You're mine." His words, and the raspy tone in his voice echo in my mind. It felt like a brand. A caress.

It's nonsense. Figments of my imagination. Everything is normal. Unchanged.

Yet, in the deepest parts of me something feels different. Something I can't name.

So, this past week, I spent my days quietly in the office, diligently working on the Scott Enterprises project and the TransAmerica research, trying to push these ridiculous thoughts from my mind.

But it was a hopeless cause.

My heart floated and careened out of control when I heard his baritone voice greeting me in the early morning hours when the office was cloaked in darkness. I pretended to be surprised every time he approached my cubicle as if each morning was a chance encounter. My pulse rioted inside me, his occasional smiles fanning the flames of the spark in my chest.

Each day he lingered, his eyes as intense and penetrating as ever, but we only talked about the weather, about my plans for the weekend, or the lack of plans on his end. Some days, he shared with me snippets of his life in the city, and I gathered how lonely he was from the smallest details he revealed. He laughed at my random factoids and we'd discuss the merits of fiction where he still insisted love stories were a waste of time.

I memorized the way a vein pulsed on his right temple, beckoning me like a temptation, and I wondered if my touch could soothe the throbbing. My fingers twitched with a need to release his pinched brows when we talked about our families. From what I gather, he has a close relationship with his sisters, and that's about it. A shadow crossed his face when he mentioned his parents, and he changed the subject.

Then, that vein on his temple would once again pound against his smooth skin, ticking like a time bomb.

As soon as the clock struck eight, we acted as strangers once more. Boss and employee. Mentor and intern. Not friends in the dark.

But the urge to smooth my fingers on his face remains.

During business hours, I'd only seen Steven once in a group meeting to discuss the performance of the investments we were managing for Adrian Scott.

In the large conference room, where I sat in my usual intern spot at the back corner, and he stood in front of the room, dressed impeccably in a dark pinstripe three-piece suit looking every inch the boss he was, an exact replica of my first day at Pietra, I couldn't help but compare how the feelings pulsing inside me felt different.

How, instead of simple excitement at being in the room with the A-team of Wall Street, my eager heart wanting to learn and contribute, I found myself silently observing, my eyes skating over the imposing man at the head of the table, cataloging the way his hair is immaculately styled, not a strand out of place, but the dark circles under his eyes more prominent under the stark lighting.

I couldn't help noticing the way his muscles seemed tense, how there was an overall weariness in his frame, and I wondered if he wasn't sleeping at night again. He wouldn't tell me when I'd asked him in the morning. But I suspected that was the case.

And when his eyes caught mine, I'd imagined the piercing intensity reflected in the cool hazel tones were for me, his friend, because he would sense my concern for him. His beautiful lips would slightly tip up on one side and I would find myself doing the same. My pulse fluttered, and I sat up taller. Then he looked away, addressing the rest of the room.

These barely visible, split-second moments feel like the beginnings of an ancient script on a well-worn tapestry, writing I don't understand, yet has been there since the dawn of time. Perhaps we are all just players in a story written long ago in the stars.

After that group meeting and another small smile of acknowledgement as we passed by each other in the hallway the same day, nothing has changed. No more mention of friendship or having a life outside of work.

Neither of us has addressed the bet or the evening at Lunasia.

If it weren't for the quiet encounters every morning, where he'd share my breakfast under the lone lamplight from my desk, it almost felt as if nothing happened. As if everything were figments of my imagination.

Then, he went on a business trip, leaving me in the office haunted by strange thoughts and a pit in my stomach which seemed to grow over time.

"Grace? Hello? You okay? You mentioned you found a lead on your father the other day?"

Millie's soft voice draws my attention back to the girls, finding them staring at me quizzically. Taylor's hand is frozen midair, as if she was about to grab her drink but got sidetracked by what she's seeing on my face.

"Sorry, I'm thinking of some things." I smile, fiddling with the cup in my hands. "I found some old love letters tucked behind the bookshelf."

Taylor sits up straighter. I haven't gotten a chance to show them to her yet. But during my careful dismantling of our furniture in my poor girl's search for our birth father, I found a stack of yellow envelopes, with the postage stamps still intact, bound in twine and wedged behind a few dusty volumes of books I've never seen Mom read.

"I wish Mom would just tell us so we don't have to play detective. We're grown women, we can handle the truth, whatever it is." Taylor sighs. "Anyway, what's in the letters?"

"I haven't gone through all of them, but the man didn't sign his name and there wasn't an address for the sender on the envelope. But the penmanship is beautiful, and from what I've read so far, it seems like he comes from money."

Taylor snorts and rolls her eyes. "Of course he is rich. Rich men are pigs."

I nod, the same belief carved into my heart by the currents of time and disappointments.

But not all rich men are bad. What about Steven?

I flinch, a pounding kicking off inside my chest. Bringing the cup to my face, I inhale the smoothness of the alcohol and toss back my drink in one gulp, relishing the scorching burn, which brings tears to my eyes.

I clear my throat, forcing my thoughts to drift to something else. "Anyway, more to come on that. Eventually, I'll make enough money to hire an investigator and we'll get our answers once and for all. For now, my internship at an investment bank is hard as expected. Long hours, cutthroat environment, but I'm learning a lot. My cubicle neighbor,

Jamie, is pretty awesome, and mostly everyone treats me well. I'm learning a lot. Definitely a lot."

"You've said that three times now. Sis, everything good with you? I see you with the same strange, vacant expression at home too. Something doesn't feel right. I don't think this is just from finding those letters alone. I mean, you've been searching for answers ever since you could read. Something else is going on." Taylor narrows her eyes and points her black polish tipped finger toward me.

"Come on, guys. I'm good. You're all overthinking."

"And you're working for the King of Wall Street, right? How's that?" Millie asks, her eyes sympathetic, as if she can sense the confusion swirling in my mind.

"It's fine." *That's all you guys are going to get from me.*

Millie gulps down her sake and lets out a sigh. "There's something I've never told you guys, but I think it's time for me to share."

We look up and find her biting her lip, nervously twirling a strand of hair around her finger.

She grimaces and takes a deep breath. "Your boss in my brother-in-law."

"What? Steven Kingsley is your brother-in-law?"

Millie nods. "You guys have heard of Adrian Scott, right?"

We all blink. "Of course. I've actually been working on some investments for him at the firm," I reply.

The lip biting is back again and Millie swallows. "Adrian's my brother."

"What? You're *loaded?*" Taylor shrieks next to me. "So why do I have to buy you freakin' gummy bears every time we're out and about? You should buy *me* gummy bears. And none of the no brand shitty ones. I want Haribo, the classic ones made in Germany from now on." She grins and throws out a teasing wink.

Belle waves her away. "Tay, missing the point here. Why didn't you tell us? And don't you guys have different last names?"

Millie looks down sheepishly. "It's a long story, but my brother changed his last name in college for a very complicated reason I won't go into. And well, I just don't want people to meet me and think...heiress or rich girl, and I try to stay out of those circles. I've always wanted to tell you girls, but the opportunity never came up and I didn't want you to look at me differently."

"What? I'm thrilled. Now I can have *two* sugar mamas." Taylor grins and I swallow a laugh, still trying to process how I've had this tenuous connection to Steven all along.

"How is that possible?" I whisper under my breath.

It almost seems like the fates have been conspiring behind my back, and at some point, one way or another I'd meet him.

And I'd end up here.

Which is nowhere, Grace. You had a moment of alcohol-induced connection, which is a physical reaction to listening to a beautiful man with an equally sexy voice singing a song about undying love. Anyone would feel unsettled.

Nothing happened. Men are still unreliable. Mind over body.

I'll never become my mom.

Nevertheless, if she's my boss's sister-in-law, maybe she can give me more information about him. Shed the mystery. Scuff up the shine. A magician's trick always dulls when the behind-the-scenes come to light.

"Is he always so intense?" I stare at the empty plate in front of me, willing my face not to twitch.

"Steven?" Millie thinks for a few moments. "He's always been the quiet, broody type. A workaholic through and through. I think he and my brother have an unhealthy fascination with work. But Adrian is better now that he's with Emily. He actually takes time to enjoy life. Steven, on the other hand, I don't think I've ever seen him not work. Even at family events, he'd take out his phone and type emails or get on conference calls."

The thought of him working himself to the bones makes me sad. I swallow the lump growing in my throat.

"So...he never has fun or...dates?" I gnaw on my bottom lip. *Why did you ask that? It doesn't matter to you.*

"He's fun when he wants to be, and I guess we have a good time hanging out at family gatherings. Hold on a second." Millie clears her throat and I glance up, finding her eyes narrowed at me. "Why are you asking me if he dates?"

"Just curious about the boss." I pour myself another drink and take a sip from the cup, hoping my face isn't flushed.

"Hmm..." she muses, trading glances with Belle and Taylor. "Not buying it. But to answer your question, I've never seen him with a girlfriend. Not that I blame him. Any woman he brings home will probably be crucified by his mom. Mrs. Kingsley gave Adrian so much grief when he fell in love with Emily and, from what I heard, that also happened to their oldest sister, Jess, as well. I don't blame him for trying to stay single to avoid his mom's wrath."

Somehow, I don't think his mom is the driving factor of his bachelor status. I don't know how I know that, but it's a gut feeling. A sixth sense. There's a sadness radiating from him, like he's hiding his scars behind fancy suits and dollar signs. My heart clenches at the thought.

A waiter brings the bill to the table and Millie snatches it, waving her wallet in my face before slapping a card on the tray. "This is an apology from me for keeping the secret from you guys and also to celebrate Taylor's admission!"

"Are you sure you don't want to come out with us? We're just heading over to Millie's classmate's party near our apartment." Belle arches an elegant brow in my direction while she gathers her things and Millie scribbles her signature on the receipt.

I shake my head. "Nah. I'm good. You girls have fun. I'm just going to walk on the High Line and enjoy the night before I head home. Tay, stay at their place if it gets too late. Don't want you walking around our neighborhood in the middle of the night."

Taylor salutes me. "Yes, ma'am."

I'm hoping some evening air strolling along the famous manicured pathways will somehow get me out of my strange funk and back to reality once more.

CHAPTER 10
Grace

INHALING DEEPLY, I BREATHE in the cool evening breeze, which has a hint of humidity after the brief showers yesterday. The sunset is fading in the sky, a deep swath of navy chasing out the remaining streaks of pink and oranges. It's an impressionist's dream. A flock of pigeons lands on the side of the pathway, eagerly pecking at leftover breadcrumbs or food scraps from earlier in the day.

The skies are clear tonight, the city having been cleansed from the rain, and I can even make out some stars vying for attention away from the artificial lights of the skyscrapers. The atmosphere is chill. Relaxing. A brief respite from the chaos and hectic lifestyle of the Big Apple.

Strolling on the High Line, a public park built on an old, elevated rail line, after grabbing a bite at the bustling Chelsea Market, is one of my favorite things to do whenever I have time to make it out here. The city is teeming with nightlife, cars and buses whizzing underneath us on the ground level. Tourists and other like-minded New Yorkers gather on the sidewalks or in clusters around the large art displays and sculptures peppered throughout the park or listen to live jazz in a clearing ahead.

It's the epitome of why I love this city, the way the cultures blend like paints on a canvas, and mix into something new, how there's something interesting for everyone, whether it be art, music, sports, or food. Anyone can have an adventure when walking on the streets and people watching, taking in hurried businessmen checking their watches or flagging down a cab, tourists with their cameras out, taking photos of everything under the sun, and local kids biking down the sidewalks.

I listen to other people chatting in groups beside me or on the phone as I amble on the structured pathways toward The Shed and Hudson Yards, marveling at the greenery and trees planted on the path, as if suspended in midair when looking from the ground level, an oasis in the middle of the city that never sleeps.

Foreign languages reach my ears, too many for me to attempt naming, and I can't help but wish one day I might travel out of the country and see the world myself.

My heart feels light as I push my worries out of my mind and think about the possibilities ahead of me. As long as I ace the internship, my future is secured. And someday, I'd be able to travel and take Taylor and Mom with me. We'd pay off the loan, move to a better neighborhood, and Taylor would have her career in dance. Mom wouldn't need to work anymore and hopefully, she'd realize she doesn't need a man to complete her life.

I'd finally find the answers to the secrets Mom keeps under lock and key in her heart. And perhaps that gaping hole in mine would finally be filled, and I'd be at peace.

Inhaling another deep breath, my body thrums with excitement, my nose practically smelling the sweet breeze of change in my near future, and before I know it, I've reached the futuristic Bloomberg Building of The Shed, a structure made mostly of glass planes with a large moveable shell of an exterior, which looks like translucent clouds tethered to a metal frame in a quilt-like pattern. It's apparently made of some sort of Teflon-based polymer, which makes it much lighter than glass so the entire shell can move, transforming the building into various arrangements for indoor/outdoor use, concerts, exhibits, and other events.

It's one of my favorite buildings near the High Line because if something so large, so immovable, can still transform and surprise everyone, then who says a girl from the South Bronx can't do the same?

My mouth parts in wonder as I marvel at the structure, lit up brightly by spotlights, with glittering fireballs of light taking over the nighttime sky and the full moon gracing us with her presence as the backdrop.

There's magic in the air tonight.

Perhaps it's the honeyed scent of gardenias wafting in the wind from an extravagant display of white blossoms by the doors in front of the building. There must be an event there tonight.

Perhaps it's the faint strains of a string quartet playing a lively tune reaching my ears, such that when I close my eyes, I can almost imagine myself as the main character in a movie, the plucky girl standing in the middle of a bustling city, refusing to let life get the best of her, twirling circles in the night, executing a pirouette here, a chassé there, muscle memory from Mom's lessons a long time ago, and feeling the night breeze on her face.

It almost makes me believe anything is possible and someday—

"Grace? What are you doing out here? Spinning around in the middle of Hudson Yards?" A deep and husky voice interrupts my daydream and apparently...twirling.

A voice I'd recognize from anywhere.

My feet grind to an abrupt halt and the world swirls around me. I pitch forward, my arms outstretched as the center-of-gravity shifts from below me and a pair of muscular arms clad in the softest black fabric wrap around my waist, stopping my would-be embarrassing face-plant to the ground.

I blink, my eyelids fluttering open, and I see the unmistakable face of Steven Kingsley looking down at me with the full moon shining brightly behind him.

For a moment, I think I'm hallucinating and perhaps I had too much to drink earlier tonight. My breath lodges in my throat, my pulse thundering in my ears, and I can only stare at the man holding me in a position resembling a low dip in ballroom dancing like a scene from an old Hollywood movie.

The smirk on his face slowly fades as his eyes darken, the pupils overtaking his irises. His gaze trails down my features, landing on my lips, and I see him swallow. Our breaths mingle and I can smell a hint of mint mixing with his expensive cologne. His face dips toward mine, the movement so slight it's almost imperceptible, but I can feel with every cell in my body. My eyes begin to close, my skin on fire.

Then he flinches.

A muscle twitches in his jaw before he slowly guides me back into a standing position.

My lungs heave in a big breath as my hands reluctantly slide off his powerful arms, which I'm not even aware I was grabbing before. Taking a few steps back, I put a respectable distance between us, because my mind can't compute logic and reason when my body is standing a mere few inches away from him, my nose inhaling the scent of leather and the crisp waves washing up the sand.

"Steven?" My lips part, my eyes finally taking in the rest of him, and I belatedly realize putting a few steps between us hasn't helped with my cause of clearing my mind.

"Grace," Steven murmurs, his hands tucked behind his back.

He stands before me like he has stepped out of a carriage in the regency romance I finished reading earlier—the one he rudely interrupted me in the office weeks ago.

He's clad in the finest evening wear, a sleek black tuxedo molded over his body like second skin, the silky fabric reflecting a subtle sheen of the moonlight. A matching vest and pants, along with a simple black bow tie complete his look. His hair is artfully swept up and his face appears clean-shaven, which only draws attention to those soulful eyes of his, which I realize, under the glow of the streetlight nearby, have flecks of gold dotted amongst the amber and green hues.

Realizing I've been staring at him for the past few seconds, I clear my throat and curve my lips into a forced smile. "What are you doing here?"

He motions to The Shed in the background. "A charity event tonight for lymphoma research. Adrian couldn't attend and he asked me to stand in for him, given this cause is near and dear to him."

I nod, my eyes finally registering the event banners, which were next to the gardenias all this time.

"And you?"

I glance back at him, finding him staring quizzically at me.

"Obviously not here for the event." I motion to my flowy black blouse and wide-legged dress pants. "I was having dinner with my sister and friends at Chelsea Market and took a walk afterward to clear my mind. Speaking of which, one of my good friends, Millie, turns out to be Adrian's sister. Such a small world."

"She never told you before?"

"Nope. She's a pretty private person, but she told us tonight."

He hums in acknowledgment and begins walking toward the High Line once more. Staring at his back, I frown, confused by his actions, when he suddenly pauses and turns back, his hand outstretched, waving me toward him.

"Coming? I'm in the mood for a walk myself after a stuffy dinner and forced socializing." A small grin transforms his face, softening the harsh lines and rough edges, letting through a rare display of boyish charm.

"Come on, *friend,* I won't ravish you in the dark if that's what you're worried about," he adds for good measure, the grin transforming into a smirk. A devious twinkle appears in his eyes.

My heart pitter patters, an unusual swooshing sensation sweeps through me, like I've slowly reached the top of a roller coaster ride, my car chugging to an agonizing stop before it abruptly plummets to the depths of exhilaration and freedom. *Maybe ravishment coming from him might not be so—hold your horses, Grace.*

I bite back a grin and stride up to his side and we walk in the direction I came from. The crowds have thinned out now. The pathway is quiet, with the occasional murmuring and chuckles of couples taking a romantic stroll under the moonlight. Tall trees and dark green foliage are lit up by small spotlights along the carefully manicured landscape.

Steven and I saunter down the winding paths, the occasional sound of cars passing below interrupting us. Even though we aren't speaking or touching, I can feel every inch of his presence next to me, and my heart pounds in response, clamoring to get out, to get closer to the warmth radiating from his body.

I look at the ground and see our shoes side by side on the pavement, his dress shoes shiny and probably an expensive handcrafted work of art, and my worn-down leather flats, scuffed at the edges. Our outsides don't appear to match, just like dancing and the pouring rain, the colors black and white, the patterns polka dots and stripes. But when I glance farther down the road and see our shadows cast on the pavement—mere man and woman strolling side by side, our hands swaying and almost touching—everything just seems...right.

Then I remember how fun it was when Mom threw on our raincoats and dragged Taylor and me to the sidewalk to twirl and dance in the first rain of spring. Our hair would be plastered to our faces, our dresses soaking wet, but there was something wild and freeing about giving the middle finger to common sense and going with instinct, flirting with the whimsical.

And black and white are often paired together, as are different overlapping patterns in fashion, the contrast elevating each element into something better.

So maybe...just maybe, a friendship between a king with an empty heart and a poor girl with more heart to spare makes sense.

Even if it only makes sense to the two of us.

Our breaths mingle, and our steps are in sync, with Steven slowing his long strides to match my short ones, the simple gesture warming my chest and making me smile.

I peek into the windows of the multi-million-dollar apartments on both sides of the pathway, noting how some folks have their homes proudly displayed, with the curtains wide open, like a work of heart to be admired by the masses. A startling contrast to the closed blinds in our humble abode, completed with metal safety bars.

"What are you looking at?" Steven asks, his voice hushed, as if talking loudly will disrupt this quiet tranquility surrounding us.

I stride to the right and lean over the railing separating us and the luxury apartments.

"It's like a work of art. These homes. I'm just admiring the way they have proudly displayed their interiors to the world. Look at this one." I motion to the floor-to-ceiling windows in front of me, which showcase a large living room with empty white walls except for a long abstract painting of brilliant reds and blacks splashed over the canvas, and clean lines, what looks to be Scandinavian-inspired furniture artfully arranged around the room. A strategic spotlight shines on the wall art and the unique glass coffee table in the center, where instead of regular wooden or metal legs, the base is a metal sculpture of a man lifting the tabletop.

"Would you want that for yourself?"

"A spacious apartment in a safe neighborhood in the middle of Manhattan? Sure." I sneak a glance at him, finding him staring at the living room with an inscrutable expression. "But I don't think I would open the blinds and invite the public into my private home."

He chuckles, the raspy sound seeming forced. "Do you know why they opened those windows? Want to take a guess?"

I don't reply, sensing his question is rhetorical.

At my silence, he continues, "What's beauty if you don't have anyone to share it with? What's a family if you don't have people who love each other? The rich and powerful have more money than they know what to do with, but oftentimes, they don't have anyone worthwhile to share their trials and tribulations with."

He lets out a deep exhale. "When you're at the top, plenty of people will pretend to celebrate with you while secretly plotting your demise. People will go to great lengths to preserve their wealth and quickly, you'll find you don't have anyone who has your best interests at heart. And so..." he motions to the window in front of him, "these people stay behind their locked doors and around-the-clock security team and safely invite others to admire their success, their wealth, the ultimate 'look what I've got' because if the public is envious of them, then perhaps all the loneliness and machinations are worth it."

His shoulders are tense, stretching the tuxedo to its limit as he leans forward on the railing, his eyes still staring into the dim living room. A lock of hair dislodges from his hairstyle and falls over his face. My fingers grip the railing and I take a breath.

My heart suddenly twitches and aches, a fissure forming in its seams, and I bite my lip, my body angling toward him but still not touching, but my heart desperately wants to wrap itself around his lonely silhouette, because somehow, I know he's speaking from personal experience.

"But that's not true happiness...is it?" I whisper.

My face is turned toward his now, my eyes greedily absorbing every detail up close, noticing a faint shadow on his jawline where his beard is coming in, a small bump marring his otherwise perfect nose and yet adds character, the luscious black hair that looks so soft, my fingers ache for a touch to test the texture.

"No. It isn't."

Three simple words. Followed by a ragged exhale.

Enough for the seams of my heart to split wide open.

"Well, I hope being here with me, friend, makes you happy." I breathe out, watching his eyes darken, his frame so still, almost blending into the surroundings.

His eyes remain on mine, unwavering. "Yes, friend. You make me happy." Those amber pools sharpen and his nostrils flare as his lips part.

It's almost as if he's surprised he's experiencing a moment of happiness.

My heart clenches and my fingers dig into the cold metal of the railing, so I don't draw him into my arms.

At that moment, a streak of light appears across the sky, so fleeting and fast. I gasp, my hand reaching out to grab Steven's arm before pointing toward the heavens. "Quick! A wishing star, make a wish."

"It's probably a plane or an asteroid," he grunts. "There are no such things as wishing stars."

I shove him hard at the side, reveling in the soft *oomph* uttered under his breath. "Be quiet. Make a wish. *Listen to me.*"

"Bossy." I can hear the smile in his voice.

Before I close my eyes, I squint at him, finding his eyes fluttering shut and my heart twitches and tumbles, the bleeding from minutes ago stemmed. I bring my hands to my lips and close my eyes and make a wish, my heart clamoring inside my throat, my pulse rolling with each beat inside my chest.

A righteous rhythm, one which tells me the wish I'm making is the right one.

Fated.

A minute passes by and I slowly open my eyes, my feet bouncing on the ground, and I look to my right, finding Steven staring at me, his lips parted, an arresting expression on his face.

My smile freezes and the moment is gone as quickly as the shooting star. Steven straightens up and steps away, putting some distance between us, even though we still haven't touched except for when I grabbed his arm to draw his attention to the skies.

I clear my throat. "Do you know how wishing upon a shooting star came about?"

His lips quirk into a lopsided smile, making him look a few years younger. "No, but I guess you'll tell me."

I nod. "That's right. Rumor has it, around the second century AD, the Greek astronomer, Ptolemy, said shooting stars traverse the gap between cosmic spheres where the gods would peek through the crack to spy on us mortals down on earth. Supposedly, the gods are very amenable to wishes made during these brief periods. So, here we are."

"That's one hell of a rumor."

I grin, enjoying his unflappable expression and his no-nonsense responses. But I catch a faint glint of amusement in those ever-changing tiger stone eyes. "Oh, I'm sure it is. It's like playing a game of telephone lasting over two thousand years, I'm sure his original intent was probably something much more scientific and boring, like 'shooting stars are shards falling off from the moon,' but where's the fun in that?"

He laughs, the smile lighting up his entire face and my chest seizes, marveling at the rich, melodious sound, the way his eyes crinkle at the corners, and that stray lock of hair grazes his forehead as his body quakes under his debonair attire.

Warmth spreads from inside me all the way to my hands and feet, a heady rush resembling pride because I made the cold king smile once more. I couldn't help but grin at him—two vastly different people in opposite walks of life, united in the expressions on our faces.

"You do know whatever you said about moon shards isn't scientific, right?" His laughter slowly fades into silence, and he tugs his bottom lip between his teeth, as if to bite back another smile.

I wish he'd smile more often.

Perhaps his soul wouldn't be radiating loneliness then.

And it's in this moment I realize I could never be friends with this man. Despite my best intentions, he evokes all sorts of irrational ideas and emotions within me. He makes me daydream about whimsical thoughts of soulmates and happily-ever-afters, ideas which have no place in my life.

He makes me want to forget how unreliable men can be. Especially rich men. How they may charm you in the beginning until you give your heart away and then turn around and beat you to a pulp while stealing from you in more ways than one.

I should stay away. It's the logical thing to do.

But somehow, I can't.

I want to be the one to put the smiles on his face.

Expelling a heavy breath, I turn toward the pathway again, heading back into the light. Steven follows suit. Checking my phone for the time, I glance back at him and say, "It's getting late and I don't want to be wandering the streets of my neighborhood in the middle of the night."

I motion toward the direction of the subway station, my hand lifting in a half wave. "Hope you don't work too hard this weekend, Steven. I was mistaken in thinking you didn't have any friends, but you obviously do. Have some fun. Relax. I'll see you in the office on Monday."

I turn away before he can respond, my heart still twisted in knots, a quiet sadness seeping through my skin as I realize the farce this friendship ever was, something I'll never be able to hold up my end of the bargain because the only person who'll end up getting hurt will be me.

Because it's always the woman.

Perhaps Mom felt the same way with Dad.

"Wait." Pounding footsteps sound behind me before I feel the warm clasp of his hand on my shoulders and he turns me to face him. "Let me give you a ride home."

"You don't need to. I'm pretty sure it's out of your way."

"It's fine. The gentleman in me doesn't feel comfortable letting you go home by yourself at this late hour. It's no trouble." He drops his hand from my shoulder and steps back, once again putting space between us. His hand balls into a fist before relaxing by his side once more. "Do it...for me, then. So I can sleep knowing my friend got home safely."

My nostrils flare and I wet my lips. The wings flutter inside me and while my mind wants to say no, my heart won't let me do so. "Fine. Just so you can get a good night's sleep and get rid of those panda eyes."

Steven huffs out a satisfied hum and leads me back to The Shed and after a few minutes, a valet pulls up a sleek, dark luxury sedan I've seen only in the movies. Steven opens the door and I slide into the passenger seat, my fingers trailing over the buttery soft leather, my nose inhaling the crisp new car smell mixed with a hint of eucalyptus coming out of a small oil diffuser on the dashboard. It is night and day compared to the gust of warm, humid air on the subway platform, tinged with the stench of sweat and urine, while one waits for the train to arrive.

I shuffle my feet on the carpeted floor, my fingers twisting nervously in my lap as Steven goes around the car and slides into the driver's seat. I feel out of place in this vehicle, but as soon as he sits next to me, the air stills, and the gnawing uneasiness recedes into the background.

Relaxing into my seat, I give him my address and he quickly sweeps us away into the night, and expertly maneuvers the car on to various side streets and shortcuts, heading toward a neighborhood he's probably never stepped foot in before.

I glance out the window, admiring the way the bright colorful lights of the city blend into streaks of rainbow, the world moving at a lively pace outside, but at this moment, I'm cocooned in this sphere of silence and peacefulness with the only man who hasn't disappointed me yet, and someone I'm inconveniently drawn to.

We pause at a stoplight, and I stare at a billboard in the distance, which advertises, "See the world at your fingertips. Your dreams and story begin now."

Turning to Steven, I ask, "Is there any place in the world you want to visit but haven't yet?"

He cocks a brow at me and purses his lips, his fingers tapping on the steering wheel. "I haven't given it much thought before, to be honest. The traveling part is not the challenge. It's the taking time off from work that's more difficult." He shrugs and asks, "What about you? Anywhere in particular you want to go that you haven't been before?"

I snort. In the span of this confusing night, Steven would inadvertently highlight how different we are, then somehow tow me back in by showing me how none of it matters. "I actually haven't traveled internationally before. I've only flown on a plane twice...one of which was a long time ago when my mom's ex-boyfriend flew us all to Hawaii for vacation. I was a little kid then and remember little of it other than how excited I was when I saw the clouds outside the airplane window and how awesome it was to swim with the dolphins and fishes."

Smiling, I lean back, thinking of the fuzzy memories of Uncle Bobby dancing with Mom on the beach while Taylor and I splashed our feet in the waves. Life felt wonderful then. Perfect even.

The other time I flew on a plane is an unpleasant memory, and I shove it away. The old ache resurfaces in my chest...the wistful longing I've tried to bury over the years.

"That was a good trip." I smack my lips and release a stale breath. "But if I get to go anywhere now...perhaps after I get my full-time offer at Pietra, *ahem*..." I clear my throat sarcastically, only to be met with deep chuckles which cause goosebumps to prickle in the back of my neck, "the first place I want to go to would be Paris."

"Hm." He turns on the blinkers as we approach the rundown neighborhood of my apartment, and I brace myself for the look of shock and disgust to appear on his face. "It's a beautiful place. Definitely worth a visit," he says as he takes another turn, the car slowing as my apartment lies ahead.

We pass by a group of teenagers smoking weed on the doorsteps, neighborhood kids I've watched growing up over the years. I feel the curious stares and whispers as the car stops. Steven tenses, his bearings alert as he walks around to open my door, every inch the well-mannered gentleman in which he was raised.

"I'll stay here until you go inside." He stands by the car as I walk up the steps of my apartment, wedging myself between Tony and Jimmy, who let out a loud whistle after I pass by them.

"Landed yourself a rich one, Gracie? Just like your mama?"

I roll my eyes and take out my keys. "Oh shove it, Jimmy, or the next time I bake cookies, you won't get any. And that's my boss, you dumbass."

Sliding my key in the lock, I turn around, finding Steven still standing there like a dark knight, his arms crossed over his chest, his eyes sharp and watching every movement from us, as if he's ready at any second to come to my rescue if anything goes awry. My heart skips another beat and I smile before waving at him.

"Go home, boss. I'm good here."

He gives me a terse nod and motions me in with his hand, apparently not satisfied until I'm physically inside those double doors.

My chest warms at his protectiveness, and I step inside the building, my eyes adjusting to the bright fluorescent lights of the stairwell, which flickers intermittently. I turn around, seeing him frowning before slowly getting back into his car and driving away.

Later that night, after I washed up and changed into my sleep shirt, I walk to my bedroom window to close the blinds before I go to sleep.

Looking up at the brilliant dark skies, the stars still glimmering brightly as they did hours before during my walk on the High Line with a mysterious man who doesn't speak a lot, but holds so much inside him, I'm comforted I get to shoulder his burdens for a moment...albeit only by walking alongside him under the darkness of the night.

A star streaks across the sky once more, and the pounding renews in my chest. I make the same wish I did standing next to him then.

I wish he would find true happiness and let his soul fly.

CHAPTER 11
Steven

"YOU'RE IN EARLY TODAY."

I bite my cheek to suppress a smile wanting to form on my face when I see her hunched over her tablet, the lone lamp illuminating the bullpen as dawn is on the verge of breaking through the inky darkness of the night. I wonder what romance novel she's reading this morning. My heart is scrimmaging, my hand finding comfort in the hot drink I'm clutching in my grip.

Grace swivels her chair and faces me, her eyes widening in over-the-top shock and her cheeks twitching in suppressed humor as well. "Mr. Kingsley! Fancy seeing you in so early."

We have done this strange dance every morning the last few weeks without fail, me coming in at six-thirty on the dot, her acting like she hasn't seen me in the office so early before. Suddenly, waking up in the middle of the night to a dark room doesn't bother me as much anymore. The stillness doesn't seem as suffocating, the heaviness in my chest seems more bearable, like I have the strength to push it away and focus on something else.

Or someone else.

When I saw her on the High Line twirling about with a smile on her face, her beautiful hair fluttering around her, my breath caught in my throat and my heart seized. She looked ethereal, something out of the fairytales I read to little Violet whenever I'd visit Jess and James. The moonlight bathed her in a soft glow, imbuing her with...magic.

It's fucking stupid. Completely unrealistic.

Yet, I find myself ensnared by her aura. When I stepped out of The Shed, I wanted to reply to a few emails regarding TransAmerica that came through during yet another boring speech by some donor of the year. But as soon as I saw her dancing to her own melody with the stars as her company, all my thoughts of work flew out the door. A heady rush of warmth coated my insides and the only thing in my mind was the *need* to talk to her, to see what had her so mesmerized.

So, for the second time in my life, after the karaoke incident, I shed my heavy cloak of responsibilities, my mind barely registering the buzzing of my phone from more emails and text messages, my brain forgetting the American Lymphoma Research Society gala wasn't finished yet, and I was supposed to make a speech on Adrian's behalf. When it finally occurred to me late last night on the drive home, I hastily dictated apology notes to the organizer of the event and to Adrian, who'd no doubt barrage me with questions later.

A sharp pinch of guilt pierced my gut when I realized everything I dropped because of this insane impulse to spend time with her. Father's warnings in the past echoed in my mind. *Kingsley men don't let emotions get the best out of them.* I shoved the thoughts into a black box deep inside me.

I was selfish for once, and I felt alive.

Strolling with her in the darkened pathways, surrounded by carefully manicured gardens and cloaked in silence, I'd never felt more at peace. When she stared at me with those dazzling violet eyes and we talked about the loneliness of being at the top, I didn't find myself flinching or wanting to run away from her penetrating gaze.

She saw me.

She saw through my words and everything I didn't say. It wasn't my wealth or fancy title she noticed, but the deep murky hole inside me, yearning for something to fill it. When she gripped my arm and demanded I make a wish upon a shooting star, the abyss in my chest flooded with bright light, and in that moment, that brief second, I'd remember always, my world shifted on its axis.

I wanted to kiss her.

It wasn't a fleeting impulse or desire.

It was a desperate need, a sharp craving.

I don't kiss women. I don't want the intimacy with any of them. But with her, I found myself hungry for it, the sudden urge flooring me. Even if she'd later curl her lips at the ugliness in my soul, I still wanted to lie bare at her feet.

I wanted desperately to taste those luscious, plump lips, to embed a part of her inside me and to leave a part of me inside her.

It took everything in me to stand still, to not act on this insane desire.

"Steven?"

Glancing up, I catch those inquisitive eyes on me once more. I smile and pull a chair up from the side of the cubicle. Yet another unofficial routine neither of us would admit to. Instead of retreating to my office to begin my workday, I sit with her in her little glass cubicle, surrounded by the peacefulness of the early morning hours, with only the warm glow of her desk lamp illuminating the space.

Wordlessly, like the other days, she takes out her toasted bagel slathered with peanut butter from a Ziploc bag and gives me half. I place the hot coffee I "happened" to have, the drink with brown sugar and oat milk, what she once told me she enjoys on another early morning, and we'd sit down and have breakfast together.

It feels intimate. Better than any dates I've been on in the past.

Energy sizzles between us, every cell in my body feeling alive, and I tether down the impulse to touch her, to smell her jasmine scent at the source.

Every day without fail. With both of us acting like each morning was an act of serendipity.

Steven and Grace, two "friends" sharing a meal in the dark.

But friends don't dream about the taste of the other person's lips.

Friends don't jerk off in the morning shower, imagining her in there trembling as I drill my cock inside her. Friends don't come while growling her name under his breath.

Emotions are liabilities, Steven.

The warnings are faded signs on a chain linked fence, yellowed with age and missing a corner. Trespassers couldn't care less.

"Any plans for the weekend?" Her eyes glint with laughter as she asks me the same question each day. Like she's completely invested in whether I have a life outside of work. Like she senses I'm dry drowning in front of everyone.

I swallow a bite of the bagel, which has grown soggy in her commute from home. One day, I'll have fresh gourmet bagels delivered to her.

"No plans," I tell her the same answer every morning. "Work and more work."

My thoughts trail to TransAmerica once more. I want to start a defensive strategy now, but I need board approval. My gut tells me Voss will take their plans up a notch soon. My mind flits to Father, who sounded more exhausted when I spoke with him last night, and the ache resurfaces in my chest.

I should've stepped in sooner.

I wish I was the little boy again and I never went downstairs to search for him that night. Perhaps I'd be none the wiser, and his terse nods and deep grunts of approval would be enough.

Perhaps I wouldn't feel so resentful and yearning for something I'd never receive.

"What are you thinking?" she whispers.

"A little boy who got his hug stolen by a thief."

The answer is nonsensical, and yet, an understanding dawns in her eyes. Seconds pass by, us staring at each other in relative silence, and I watch those beautiful eyes darken, a pulse fluttering at her throat.

"Maybe the thief needed that hug more than the little boy. Maybe what the little boy wanted wasn't hugs, but something far more valuable," she murmurs, her gaze never leaving mine.

A thickness forms in my throat and I'm rendered mute, wondering how she seems to know everything, even though I haven't told her anything.

She understands.

She tucks a curl of hair behind her ear. "Maybe the little boy already had what his heart desired, but he just never saw it, because he was too focused on the missing hug. Tunnel vision happens to all of us."

Her smile is a jolt of electricity to my heart, sending it off in another flurry of erratic beating. "This little boy is loved, I'm sure of it. I can't imagine a world that wouldn't love this innocent boy with a huge heart, a heart he keeps hidden from view."

Her throat ripples as a flush spreads on her skin like wildfire. I see the swath of pink swimming from the creamy skin peeking out from the collar of her blouse to her slender neck, then to her smooth face. A swarm of tingles spreads throughout my body, obliterating all common sense, and all I can do is stare at her, memorizing the way her thick lashes fan across her face, the darkness of her pupils encroaching on the vivid purple, the small beauty mark at the edge of her lips, drawing me in.

The tip of her tongue darts out, the motion capturing my attention.

A few crumbs and a smear of peanut butter are stuck on her plush bottom lip.

I reach out before I can think otherwise, my finger lightly grazing the lips tormenting me the last few weeks, slowly wiping off the peanut butter. Her eyes flare and she intakes a sharp breath. Her legs squirm in her chair and her thighs clench.

Holding my breath, I continue tracing her lips far longer than necessary, reveling the softness and the texture. My finger sizzles from the contact. A sharp need throbs in my chest, heated blood circulating in my veins, and my groin flickers to life. Her lips part in a small moan, the sound hardening my cock in milliseconds.

Letting out a ragged breath, I dip the tip of my index finger into her mouth, my eyes flaring when I feel a hesitant but quick swipe of her tongue on my flesh, the sensations shooting straight to my cock, which roars to full mast. Lurid images of her dropping to her knees and wrapping those plush lips around my throbbing dick have me gripping my free hand on my chair, my body shaking with restraint.

I want to haul her against me, grind that little body on my cock. Make her scream in pleasure as I wring out orgasm after orgasm from her, knowing anyone could step in at any moment. And then I want to do it again.

"Steven," she whispers, her eyes glazed over.

"You're right," I rasp, my voice hoarse as I lean in, slowly caging her in her chair. Her head falls back against the headrest. I bring my finger up between us, the tip still shining from that tortuous lick.

A taste of her.

Her lips part, her eyes darkening and she whispers, "I'm always right."

Slowly, I slide my finger into my mouth and suck on the tip, my tongue swirling around the digit, tasting the sweetness of her mixed with the lingering taste of peanut butter.

Grace moans and lets out a shuddering exhale. I can see her beaded nipples saluting me in this position, with her head on her chair, her chest arching up.

I can smell the need from her, and fuck, do I want to respond.

"You're right," I repeat, my rock-hard dick threatening to break free from my pants, "perhaps the little boy didn't need hugs...maybe he just needed a *friend* who understood him."

I continue to lean down, my face hovering mere inches above hers, far too close for friends, but fuck who am I kidding here. My eyes drift to her lips again.

Plump. Shiny. Inviting.

So fucking tempting.

"A friend." Her voice is a whisper, her eyes fluttering shut.

Our chests touch, her nipples grazing me through our clothing, and I groan, the deep rumble sounding foreign to my ears.

I dip closer, my mouth watering for another taste, a more thorough taste.

Clang. The harsh sound of the door opening, hitting on something, is piercing in this heated silence.

We pull apart with a jolt and Grace snaps up in her seat, her chest lifting and falling rapidly. My breathing is labored, like I ran up thirty flights of steps even though nothing actually happened. My pulse pounds in my ears.

"Mr. Kingsley," Hayley greets me, her eyes taking on a shrewd glint as she notices a flustered Grace sitting as stiff as a statue, her face beet red. "Grace."

I clear my throat and straighten to my full height. Keeping my torso away from her line of sight, because there's no way I can hide the flagpole sticking out in my pants right now, I reply, "Hayley. You're in early today."

"Wanted to prepare for our meeting to discuss the Scott investments and the TransAmerica takeover in two hours. Going to review the documents the team prepared for me just to be thorough." She keeps her gaze on me, but I can see the wheels turning in her head as she's no doubt wondering why her boss is sitting with the intern in her cube so early in the morning.

"Thank you. Keep up the good work."

Hayley nods and with one last lingering glance at both of us, she disappears into her office.

Grace trails her fingers over her hair, as though her ponytail was dislodged in the last few moments of...nothing, and yet, everything. "Mr. Kingsley," she addresses me, even though the flush still lingers on her face.

Keeping my stare on her, I palm my aching erection, giving it one hard tug, my teeth biting back a growl. *Look at what you do to me.* Then I slowly adjust my raging hard on, watching her eyes widen and flare as the pink on her face deepens. She lets out another soft whimper and I swallow my groan.

Fuck me.

"Grace." My voice is husky and thick. "See you at the meeting."

After retrieving my laptop bag, I step out of her cube and walk toward my office, feeling the heat of her stare on my back. Every step is torture, my body wanting to turn around and stride back to the woman behind me.

But the growing distance is a cool breeze to my fevered thoughts and rash impulses, and eventually, the haze of lust and a heady emotion I don't want to name slowly clear my mind.

Friends, Steven.

Emotions are liabilities. Don't forget.

This time, the warnings stick, the adhesive barely clinging on, and I clench my fists and step inside the room.

CHAPTER 12
Steven

MY EYES JOLT OPEN from the sound of a chime from my phone.

For a moment, I'm disoriented and the world swirls around me, a kaleidoscope of confusing bright lights and colors. My lungs heave in breaths of air as the cobwebs slowly clear from my mind.

The smell of eucalyptus hits my nose.

The blue light from the computer monitors in front of me.

Faint sounds of telephones ringing. Muted conversations. Cabinets opening and closing.

I'm in my office.

I must've fallen asleep—the late nights and early mornings are getting to me, my body protesting at the consistent three hours of sleep. But my mind lingers back to yesterday morning, when Grace licked my finger, giving me an experience more intense than any blow job I'd ever received, and a renewed heat travels through my veins and I groan.

This morning, when I showed up at her desk with her coffee in hand, she looked so flustered, her cheeks pinkened. She repeatedly gnawed on her lip, and I kept trying to make her squirm with low murmurs and raspy comments.

A perverse need to elicit a reaction from her.

God, I've regressed to being a teenager. Fuck.

Every nerve in my body is primed and zeroed in on her, this petite woman so resplendent, I wonder how the world doesn't see it. Despite my best intentions to stay friends, those restraints fall away under the cloak of the darkness, and I just want her at my mercy.

Every graze of my hand on hers when I give her the drink, my fingers brushing a stray lock of hair fallen loose from her ponytail, my muscles clenching when I temper my need to wind those luscious strands around my hand before I plunder her lips.

It's reciprocated. I can tell by her dilated pupils, her quickened breaths, the way her tongue keeps swiping at her lips. Despite my mind telling me to stop, my body disobeys and continues to perform this intimate dance with her.

Knock. Knock.

Straightening up in my chair, I holler, "Come in."

My boss, Pietra Capital's CEO, Sean Andrew Henry, III—if there's a contest for the most pretentious name, he'd win it—strides in and takes a seat in front of me to have an impromptu meeting.

"Steven, this should be quick. Thought I'd get it out of the way before I forget."

Cocking my brow, I clasp my hands in front of me. The way he's shifting in the seat, his finger fiddling with his blue suit jacket which barely covers his waistline, is making me uneasy as my bullshit radar turns on. "What's going on?"

"How do you feel about our crop of interns this year?"

My mind snags on Grace, the shining star out of the group. Her insights are sharp, and she frequently identifies issues or trends others don't notice. It hasn't escaped me how some analysts would huddle around her cubicle, asking her questions when they thought no one was looking.

"They're decent, but one of them is stellar."

Sean nods absentmindedly. "Good, good. Who's the stellar one?"

"Grace Peyton, a senior from NYUC."

He frowns and shrugs. "I don't recognize her name. If she's good, keep her contact information for next year."

A cold front whips through me, sharpening my senses. I lean forward on my desk. "What do you mean? She's getting one of the offers this year. I know two of them are already spoken for because they're recommendations from our largest clients, but this last one is hers. She's the best of the group."

Sean waves me away, a shiny lock of blond hair falling over his face. "No can do this year. I just found out Greg Marley's niece is one of our interns. His widow called and asked if we could offer her a position. The family has been devastated with his passing and this would mean a lot to them."

Fuck this shit.

Grace never told me, but I sense she needs this job more than anyone else in the group.

"What about the other two openings then, can't we give one of them to her? She deserves it, Sean. She'd be an asset to the firm."

Shit. Why am I arguing with Sean? What he's saying makes sense. You know that, Steven.

Sean leans back, his lips flattening in apparent displeasure. "What's the matter with you, Steven? This is unlike you. You're a man of logic and common sense. The other two offers as favors to keep our largest clients happy are no-brainers. This intern, whatever her name is—"

"Grace. Her name is Grace." I grit my teeth together as I fight to keep my facial expression neutral.

"Grace is a nobody. The other three are somebodies. And we can give Grace an offer next year and double the signing bonus. She'd be a fool to say no then." He stands up, straightens his jacket and stalks toward the door.

Pausing before he turns the handle, he looks back at me, his steely gaze cold. "Steven, you're after the COO promotion. You want to run the TransAmerica deal, do what you do best, and use your fucking common sense. I'm not having this conversation with you again. Give the three interns their offers on Friday."

He lets out a laborious sigh, as if this entire conversation is tiring him. "I support you, Steven. You're the man for the job. Just do the right thing."

Sean walks out the door and disappears around the corner, leaving me reeling with the implications. My chest clenches, a burning anger crawling up my spine. I release a breath and rake in another. And another.

The right thing.

It's funny how that has changed in the last few weeks.

Logic and common sense, Steven. Grace can always get another job. I'll give her a recommendation. It'll be okay. She'll understand.

She'll hate you.

My thoughts are scrambled, my compass not knowing which way is north anymore.

Emotions are liabilities, all of it. My mind taunts me with Father's warnings.

Fuck, fuck, fuck.

My phone rings, the ringtone of a video call. I frown, picking up the device and staring at the caller ID.

Jess and Emily.

My chest twists as my shoulders tighten. I hope everything is all right. They rarely video me together. My first thought goes to Father, worried something happened to him because of the war zone no doubt at TransAmerica.

His life's work. The Kingsley family's redemption—instead of an empty old-money name, we are now synonymous with power. All because of Father.

His sacrifice by staying behind.

The thing he loves above everything else, everyone else. Now I have a chance to save it. I *need* to save it.

My sisters' faces flash on the phone screen. I don't think they'd stop calling unless I pick up.

Emily's impish face fills the screen. Her warm brown eyes, which she got from Mother, narrow at me, her lips twisting in a scowl. "Why did it take you so long to pick up?"

Sitting back in my chair, I lift a brow at her. We've bickered all throughout our childhood and that doesn't stop at adulthood, apparently. "I'm busy at work, unlike someone."

"Hey! I'm a busy career woman too!" She's a top PR consultant at a global firm, so she has a point there.

"Ems, focus," Jess chides gently as her hazel eyes shine warmly at us.

"Mama, I want to talk to Uncle Steven!" I see a small tuft of brown curls at the edge of the screen and a warmth fills my senses.

Jess hoists her toddler up on her lap and Violet flashes me a cheeky grin, her lips messy with chocolate sauce smeared all over them.

"You're not at work today, Jess? And how are you doing, little Violet? Are you a good sister to your little brother?"

"I'm not little! And I'm the best sister. Lucas would tell you, but he doesn't know his words." She pauses as she squints her eyes at me. "Why do you look tired, Uncle Steven? Are you staying up past your bedtime?"

"See? What did I tell you? You need to stop working so much. You're going to end up with a heart attack before you're thirty," Emily chimes in, her arms crossed over her chest.

Jess rolls her eyes at her sister and ruffles Violet's hair before handing her a tissue. "I took today off from work. Spending a little bit of time with this rascal before she heads back to school in a few weeks."

Jess is an audit partner at a major public accounting firm and she's usually mired in work, but summer is her slower season, which she takes advantage of now that she has little kiddos afoot.

"So, what's with the call today?"

Emily perks up, her scowl replaced with a blinding smile. "Happy birthday, Steven! Enjoy your last year before you hit the big three zero."

Frowning, I glance at the calendar on my computer monitor.

Shit. It is my birthday today.

"You forgot. So, I'm guessing you have no plans other than work?" Emily's lips flatten into a thin line. "Don't make me fly over there. And you know I can. Adrian can get the jet ready within the hour."

I hold up my hand. The last thing I need is Emily trailing after me, nagging my head off about having a life outside of work. She doesn't understand this is the one place I feel at home, the one place I can keep the dark thoughts out of my mind.

Except now, there's someone who can calm the rough waters. Someone who can—

No.

"Don't fly out there, Ems. I'm sure Steven has plans already, don't you, Steven?" Jess's soft voice interjects, but there's a sharpness in her gaze. Nothing escapes her notice.

I clear my throat. "Yes, I have plans. But thank you for calling."

"We won't take up too much of your time. We just wanted to say happy birthday to you, little brother, and we love you. Can't wait until you visit at Thanksgiving."

My nose prickles at the warmth in Jess's voice. Growing up in the empty halls of our mansion, where my life consisted of tutors and studying, the endless pursuit of being at the top in class, the best in everything, all duties of Kingsley offsprings, Jess had been the one to sneak me my favorite sour cream and onion potato chips on special occasions, even though Mother forbade junk food in the house. Jess had been the one to give me a hug when I got anything less than an A on my tests. She was the one who told me she was proud of me when I brought home awards and lacrosse trophies.

These accolades would only garner a terse nod from Father and a passing ruffle of my hair, if I were lucky. Mother would flatten her lips in approval, noting this was all to be expected, as we should never settle for second best.

Knock. Knock.

"I have to go. Someone is at the door. Thank you for the birthday wishes." I smile at my sisters and my little niece, who is stuffing a chocolate chip cookie she procured out of nowhere into her mouth while garbling something which sounds like happy birthday. Chocolate is smeared all over those cute little lips again, and Jess lets out an exasperated sigh.

Emily points her index and middle fingers toward her eyes and then toward the screen, the universal hand signal suggesting she'd be watching my every move.

Chuckling, I wave goodbye and set down the phone.

Knock. Knock.

The rapping at the door is more incessant. My muscles tense as I prepare myself for whoever is at the door. I hope it's not Sean again.

"Come in," I holler, trying to focus my attention on the texts I missed when I dozed off. There are at least a dozen from the idiots I call my friends.

Charles

> Don't make me come over there and haul you out of your office.

Ryland

> Welcome to almost being thirty. Enjoy your last year before you become old like the rest of us.

Parker

> Considering I'm the oldest out of everyone, that is a bit offensive.

Maxwell

> Ryland is a coldhearted bastard. Ignore him.

Rex

> Burn. The man who never speaks always tells the truth.

Lana

> My brothers are idiots, and I'm still in the twenties club. Happy birthday, Steven. Dinner soon?

Charles

I'm not getting in the middle of the Anderson squabble. As your good friend, I'm obligated to make sure you aren't burying yourself in work today. I have spies at your firm. If they report you're at the office past five today, don't blame me for taking more extreme measures.

I smirk at the text messages; the vines circling my lungs loosen slightly, and I turn on the silent function on my phone. At this rate, in a matter of minutes, there'll be at least fifty messages from the group chat, which they changed the name from "The Orchid Shenanigans" to "Save Steven from Himself."

Soft footsteps approach me. A hint of jasmine wafts through the air and I inhale the sweet scent, my heart beginning to kick up in rhythm because I already know who'll be standing in front of me when I look up.

Someone who makes me want to spill the heaviness in my soul, letting her shoulder part of the burden, so I can rest my head against her warmth for a brief respite.

Someone whose quiet conversations in the morning sustain me for the rest of the day. It's as if the world has stopped and we're the only two people left standing. And everything is still fine. More than fine.

Someone who drives me crazy. Insane. Mad with emotions I never thought I had, gifting me with the liabilities plaguing my father his entire life.

Someone I'll have to deliver a devastating blow to on Friday.

Grace.

My hands slowly curl into fists, and I swallow the sudden lump forming in my throat. I feel as if my carefully crafted world is spinning out of control, and I don't know what to do.

She'll understand.

She's considerate and kind and can see through me. She knows me better than most people. She's also logical and reasonable. She'll understand this is a business decision and has no bearing on us—whatever we are.

My reassurances are weak, even in my mind. Looking up, I find her standing in front of me, her hair tied up in a simple ponytail, her face devoid of makeup as usual. She's wearing another variation of her grandmother's closet, but I don't seem to notice the details anymore.

All I see are her large eyes, almost sapphire in the mid-morning light, with a hint of gray at the edges, her pert nose, those perfectly symmetrical lips. Her tongue dips out, the movement reminding me of yesterday morning, and my groin clenches in response.

"Mr. Kingsley," she says, her sweet voice slightly breathless, as if she could read all the nonsensical thoughts flittering through my mind.

"Grace." I have an irrational impulse to whisper her name against her soft skin, to feel goosebumps pebble her flesh as she shakes beneath me.

Fuck. *Something is terribly, horribly wrong. The insomnia is getting to you, Steven.*

We stare at each other, the soft blue light from the windows highlighting the way her pupils widen as the silence stretches on. The way her breath seems to catch in her throat. The way her delicate throat ripples as she swallows.

She blinks, her long lashes fan against her cheeks, and subtly shakes her head. She shoves a stack of binders on my desk. The *thump* reverberates in the quiet room.

"Hayley asked me to give these to you. We just prepared a fresh set of analysis on the Scott portfolio," Grace whispers, her fingers twisting in front of her before clutching the sweater in a death grip. She gnaws on her plump bottom lip again.

My eyes dip to the motion before trailing back up to her gaze. Lifting a corner of my mouth, I rasp, "Nervous?"

Her eyes flare and spark before her lips quirk up into a big grin, no doubt thinking about a similar conversation we had the first time she stepped foot into my office.

"No." She crosses her arms and stands taller. Definitely an Amazonian disguised as a weakling. "I'm just waiting to see if you have a question for me."

I smile at her near verbatim response from that first morning when she sat in front of me, determination laced in her voice as she fought to stay composed, to not cower in front of the King of Wall Street.

The organ in my chest thumps harder, pumping the warmth to the rest of my body. A tingle appears at the base of my spine and my breathing comes out in soft pants. I slowly stand, watching her lips part as she looks up at me, towering over her by almost a foot. My fingers trace circles on the binders she placed on the desk just now, fighting an impulse to reach out and haul her toward me.

And what? This is getting ridiculous. Common sense and logic, Steven.

The guilt wars with the desire as I try to shove these unfamiliar sensations back into Pandora's box. I need to pull away, to put distance between us. It's the right thing to do.

She'll understand.

I flinch at the thought, clutching to it like a life vest in the middle of a sinking ship.

She'll understand.

My fingers clench on to the binders. A muscle pulses in my jaw.

Grace swallows, her enticing mouth still parted, looking too inviting. Too tempting. She lets out a shuddering breath, letting me know I'm not alone in this strange insanity we find ourselves trapped in. She takes an imperceptible step back.

Creating distance. Letting the shutters fall.

It's smart. It's logical. It's rational. It's what I *should* do.

But damn if I don't want to stride around the desk and pull her flush against me so she can't escape. Then I'll bury my nose in the crook of her neck and inhale the sweet scent of jasmine and spice, giving my lungs a breath of life. Then I'd beg for forgiveness and tell her to give me one year so I can get the promotion, save Father's company, and give her a better job offer.

I'm going crazy. The abyss in my chest finally swallowing me whole.

"I-I couldn't help overhearing just now, before I knocked... Is it your birthday today?"

I nod. My voice is on a hiatus, every nerve ending in my body sizzling, the circuit on the verge of overloading from the barrage of sensations and...emotions scrambling inside me. I can't even begin to comb through and make sense of them all.

A spark of excitement appears in those gorgeous eyes, and she smiles, showing the whites of her teeth.

My heart skips several beats.

"I want to make a deal."

The tingles in my spine burgeon into a sharp current and I can't help myself but lean forward, transfixed by the energy she emanates.

"A deal," I murmur, watching the pulse fluttering in her neck as she holds herself still as if fighting an impulse to step back.

She nods vigorously. "I'm guessing you don't have any plans today. It seems like I can't leave you to your own devices."

"And what are you going to do about it?"

"I know you won the bet and one of my days is yours. But I'd like a rain check on that. Instead, I'd like to have one of your days."

My blood heats as I'm reminded of the night I didn't want to think about, and the strange emotions that coursed through me when I was standing on the stage singing...for her.

My life is about order. Papers stacked neatly in corners. Turning the faucet specifically three times to achieve the optimal level of heat. Making sure I only have one pen of each color on my desk before I start my day. Going to the gym at precisely four a.m. on the dot. Burying myself in my work, my only passion in life.

And she comes barreling in like a wrecking ball, toppling over my carefully constructed routines, teasing out the thoughts nestled in the deepest recesses of my mind, unlocking emotions I thought I didn't have.

My friend is dangerous. An atomic bomb packaged in an unassuming box. I can feel my fingers hovering above the number pad, slowly entering the nuclear codes which will obliterate the world as I know it.

She occupies my waking thoughts, disrupting the logic I've known as my companion all these years. The conversation from Sean flits through my mind.

I *should* stay away.

"And what do I get in return?" I murmur, the predator instincts in me roaring to life, telling me to strike, but not knowing if I'm going to lurch forward to tear her into pieces or to dive into her to savor every morsel.

She falters, the fluttering on her neck becoming more pronounced, and an enticing pink flush slowly spreads over her pale skin like watercolor. I want to be the one holding the damn paintbrush to tease out those beautiful streaks. To create art with my blunt strokes and her vibrant hues.

"Another one of my days." The answer comes out in a breathy whisper, one I can easily imagine funneling out of her lips when she writhes on the bed, her body draped in nothing but silk sheets as I feast between her legs.

Suddenly, all thoughts of guilt and job offers fly out the window. Dust in the wind. Sharp lust shoots straight into my groin, my dick stiffening in a matter of seconds. My body is malfunctioning, the urge to fuck overpowering, completely off track from my orderly schedule of one tryst per quarter.

These sensations are *not* friendly, the opposite of platonic.

The rational man inside me should heed to the advice Father gave me inadvertently that night when I caught him with the woman. I should remember the way Mother would secretly cry whenever Father disappeared on a "business trip," the way our fucking COO died of a heart attack because he listened to his wife, the woman he loved, such that he ditched his responsibilities and traveled to the middle of the sea where he couldn't get any medical help.

I should say no.

I should tell her to get back to work instead of tempting me.

I should disabuse myself of the notion this was ever a friendship.

Fucking shoulds. The most useless word in the dictionary.

My eyes flit to the calendar on my computer monitor. The meetings and calls I have lined up for the rest of the day, with precisely fifteen-minute breaks between each event to allow myself time to decompress.

"Fine. Deal."

The words are out of my mouth before I can stop them. It's almost as if my mind and my body are not communicating to each other, one turning against the other, and this warmth in my chest is taking the driver's seat, giving the middle finger to all the rules and thoughts governing my almost thirty years on earth.

Grace claps her hands in excitement and rocks on her heels. The current in my spine crackles, and I swear I could see sparks coming out of me. Her mouth splits into a big smile, warming up the entire room, which felt colder than usual this morning.

"Great. I'm cashing it in today. Meet me out front at four p.m."

She whirls around and takes her energy with her, leaving behind her intoxicating scent of jasmine, and a lingering heat in my heart.

I look at the haphazard piles of binders on my desk, the blacks scattered amongst the reds, papers sticking out, and a bittersweetness rises to the forefront.

She'll understand.

CHAPTER 13
Grace

I'VE LOST MY MIND.

Because nothing logical can explain why I'm doing this to myself. Why I took one look at his face, seeing the weariness he's trying to hide, and decided to take matters into my own hands.

When I heard outside his door it's his birthday today, I just knew he would spend it alone, surrounding himself with his work like armor, like it would save him from truly living and enjoying life.

Friendship or no friendship, I couldn't bear to see him spend this special day by himself.

Like it's somehow the greatest sin to live for himself. To be kind to himself.

And so, I've given one more of my days to him, my mind trying its best not to think about what he'd do when he ultimately cashes in.

Fevered eyes. His pupils dilated, ensnared on my lips as I swiveled my tongue around his finger. The way his nostrils flared when Hayley interrupted us when we were moments away from kissing. How his large hand palmed the sizeable tent in his trousers, his gaze never leaving mine.

My core clenches at the heady memory. My heart stirs into a rapid rhythm, much like this morning when I laid in bed, my sheets twisted around my waist, my panties wet, after a blurry dream featuring a beautiful man with soulful, sad eyes, and a banked fire inside him.

It has to be the heat of the moment.

I can't fall for him, the rich, powerful man with an equally important last name. He's everything I swore to myself I'd avoid because I'd rather commit myself to a nunnery before following in my mom's footsteps.

My heart kicks harder against my rib cage in protest as anticipation zaps through me like electricity from a live wire.

Now, I'm standing at the front door of our office building at three fifty-five in the afternoon, watching tourists strolling by, toting colorful gift bags inscribed with "I love NY" on them.

The air is sticky today. Humid. The golden sun beats down on the ground, and the swirling heat traps the scents of street dogs emanating from food trucks or exhaust from cars speeding down the streets. I regret not wearing a short-sleeve shirt today and I roll up my sleeves to the best of my abilities, the sweat plastering to my back and my foot thuds a nervous rhythm on the ground.

The automatic glass doors slide open, a burst of air conditioning blowing from behind me, the sudden chill eliciting a shiver down my back. My favorite scent of the ocean and worn leather travels to my nose.

My heart twirls in my chest.

"You got me where you want me." His deep, husky voice rakes down my body like a caress and the hairs on the back of my neck stand at attention. "Even though it's work hours, I'd consider this to be decidedly *not* work, so what plans do you have for me, *friend?*"

His tone is mocking in self-derision at the word "friend" and a sharp ache slices through my chest. He is correct. Whatever we have...it's not really a true friendship. It is something different all together, a purgatory in between heaven and hell, our feet dancing on a tightrope where the smallest slip would have us plummeting to our deaths. It's something infinitely more. Something I don't want to identify or recognize.

And yet, my heart can't take anything less. My mind seeks these passing interactions with him, these fleeting moments when he lets down his guard and shows me a version of him the world doesn't see often.

My mom is addicted to love, and I wonder if I'm heading down the same path, but instead of love, I'm addicted to him. The way his smiles make my heart seize, and I want to keep doing whatever I have to do to keep that expression on his face. The way his words only make me crave more time with him to understand the inner workings of his mind. The way my body hungers for his nearness, his touch, even the smallest graze creates the greatest highs for me. The way he makes me feel—safe, respected, admired.

"Well, unlike you, I'm not a billionaire, so don't expect to be wined and dined by me. But I'm a firm believer I can't have my friend working to death on his birthday. He only turns..." I glance at him, waiting for his response, realizing I still don't know a lot about him even though there are moments when I feel like I'm the only person who has seen the true him behind his masks, when I feel like I'm the only person who truly knows him.

"Twenty-nine." His eyes are covered in dark sunglasses, but his lips curl up in a sexy grin. The freaking man looks like a model for luxury menswear and doesn't seem at all impacted by the heat. Butterflies flutter in my stomach.

"Yes...twenty-nine once. So, I propose enjoying the city on a poor girl's...aka myself," I point to my chest, "budget."

"You know, I could just take us somewhere—"

I frown. "No. The birthday boy isn't spending a dime. And I don't need anyone spending money on me. I can very well have a fun day with my budget. Trust me."

"I can't wait," he drawls, his head dipping down to stare at me. Damn it, I wish he would remove his shades so I could see his eyes. "Can I at least drive?"

"No. Your day is mine."

"Who knew you were so bossy?" He scowls, but I hear the laughter in his voice.

"What, uncomfortable with relinquishing control?" I taunt back.

He steps closer, his alluring scent raising the stakes. "You have no idea. And I like my women bossy. All the more satisfying when they bend to my will later on." His voice is hoarse, barely above a whisper, but I can feel every word between my legs.

I fight an urge to clench my thighs. My blood heats and I rake in a breath, watching his corded throat ripple. His cologne surrounds me, and I can feel his bodily warmth seeping through the layers of the clothes, as if the distance between us is nonexistent.

"No one is your 'woman,'" I mutter, turning away to face the street, hoping to hide the flush no doubt spreading like wildfire.

"No," he murmurs softly. "You're my friend."

Friend. Yes, that's what we are. If even that.

"Which is much more important than my woman," he adds, his voice barely above a whisper, but my heart heard him loud and clear.

He's staring away, refusing to look at me, but his words cloak me in a soothing warmth, which feels nothing like the sticky heat of the summer. I glance at him, noticing his tense jaw, his still as a statue bearing, his hands fisted by his sides. He's struggling with something. I only wish he'd tell me.

I'd understand.

Taking pity on him, I pretend not to hear him, even though my heart is tunneling its way out of my chest.

"Come on, we're going to grab an early dinner in Central Park and then watch a movie." I beckon him to follow as I speed toward the nearest subway station, navigating the throngs of crowds no doubt headed toward the iconic bull statue a block over, drawing some much-needed distance away from him, hoping the physical exertion will dull the heated sensations flowing through my body.

"What are we going to eat?" His footsteps thump behind me, reassuring like my heartbeat.

"You'll see."

<hr />

"You've got to be kidding me."

"Nope. Take a bite. Be a team player—we're a team, remember? Come on, it won't kill you." I quirk my brow at him as we sit on a bench, facing an endless expanse of green grass and towering trees, blocking most of the surrounding skyscrapers.

It never ceases to amaze me how in a large city filled with millions of people, where every square foot of land costs an exorbitant amount of money, there'd be this huge park, filled with nothing except carefully manicured Mother Nature, located smack in the middle of Manhattan, where all the action is.

Steven grumbled the entire half-hour ride on the 2 train to the park. The man has never taken public transportation before. Not when he was younger in LA, which made sense, since I heard there were more cars than people over there, and definitely not when he moved here after college because he either drove or had a chauffeur at his beck and call.

These little vignettes he shares continue to make me wonder what we are doing. And yet, like two magnets driven by invisible poles, we're drawn to each other. For the first time in my life, I want to throw caution to the wind, to spend these moments with him as my "friend," ignoring what my mind is telling me, the hypocrite living in delusion.

I want to collect all these memories because I've been in the ugly, dirty trenches of life, and I know happiness is hard-earned and fleeting, and some day, this friendship or whatever we have will fizzle out, like the men in Mom's past who've ultimately deserted us, leaving us to tend to our wounds in the confines of our small apartment.

I want to be irresponsible, to be selfish, and to ignore all the red flags my mind is waving in front of my face—the erratic heartbeats in his presence, how my body becomes heated, no doubt a flush spreading on my skin, the way my nerves spark with electricity even when we aren't touching.

I laughed at how he dusted off his pants after taking a seat on the train, his fingers flicking off invisible lint or dirt. He looked so uncomfortable and out of his element as his eyes darted around the surroundings, like he was cataloging every scratch or blemish on the well-used seats. I saw how his hands swept over his slate gray tie, like he wanted to yank it loose from his neck to take a calming breath.

Now that we are settled on the park bench, watching the world go by, his tensed shoulders slowly relax. He has long given up on wearing his entire three-piece-suit. His jacket, a deep royal blue, is draped over his lap as he stares at the staple of the city in his hand like it offends him.

A hot dog.

His sunglasses are stowed away in the pocket of his vest, his shirtsleeves are rolled up, showcasing his muscular arms I was desperate to peek at that night when he stood on the stage at Lunasia and the sexy veins traversing over his muscles, which flex as he brings the hot dog in front of his lips.

"I could be having foie gras and filet mignon cooked by a Michelin chef right now," he grumbles before he swallows, as if he's trying to dislodge a lump in his throat. His lips flatten in displeasure.

"Ew. Do you know how they make foie gras? They fatten up a duck or a goose just so they can harvest the liver. It's barbaric! That's why they banned it in the city for a few years."

He arches a sardonic brow. "You and your bleeding heart. Why don't you become vegan then? They do the same things to chickens."

I throw my hands into the air. "That's different. Just eat the damn hot dog. How do you even call yourself a New Yorker without having a street dog?"

"Technically, I'm an Angeleno," he retorts, a smirk on his face.

Swallowing a laugh threatening to break free from my throat, I watch him wince as he takes a big bite of the hot dog ladened with ketchup and mustard. We bought it from a random street vendor who was parked in front of the entrance. Steven looked squeamish as I paid for his birthday meal, muttering about how unsanitary everything probably was and how he could have his chef fix us gourmet hot dogs if that's what I was craving.

Steven chokes, his face turning a tad green. "This is *revolting*. The meat is so overcooked...if you can even call this meat. God knows what's inside it. The bread is soggy, and don't even get me started on this wannabe ketchup."

He grabs the bottle of water next to him and chugs half of it down in a matter of seconds. "Fuck. This is nasty."

"Really?" I take a bite out of my own hot dog and cringe. Of course, the day I take the King to eat street fare, I'd buy from the wrong vendor. This hot dog tastes stale, even I have to admit it's pretty disgusting.

I slap him on the back as he chokes down the rest of his dinner because I lectured him beforehand about the perils of wasting food. "Think of it this way. This is a birthday you'll always remember. Instead of spending it surrounded by glass windows and piles of work..."

"And air conditioning," he mutters, sweat dripping down his forehead.

I snicker, watching him take out a tissue from his pocket and blotting his face.

"And gourmet food," he continues, his brow lifting higher, almost touching those luscious black strands of hair. "God, how will I ever survive the tragedy?"

"Sarcasm doesn't become you." I grin, even though I feel a pinch of guilt, since I dragged the king out of his comfortable castle to experience the call of Mother Nature with us serfs. "But look around you...see those tourists walking around. Even though sweat is dripping down their faces, they are wearing smiles because they get to enjoy the sun in the middle of the day. And look at that woman walking her cute little dog...or those kids sunbathing on the lawn. You don't need money to enjoy yourself."

Turning to him, I ask, "When was the last time you took a few hours off work and sat in a park to just...be? Enjoy the stillness? Savor the warmth of the sun hitting your skin and the way the breeze carries a hint of freshly mowed grass?"

He stares at me like I grew two heads.

"Well, my present to you this year is the gift of a new experience. And a reminder there's more to life than money and work."

"But isn't that why you want to work at Pietra? To make money...just like the rest of us?" Steven's eyes are piercing, glinting almost gold in the bright sunlight and I look away as the flutters, which have subsided for the last twenty minutes, begin anew in my gut.

Staring at a little girl with pigtails and her dad playing frisbee on the grass, her giggles filling the air, my heart clenches, the old ache resurfacing. "The difference is, I make money because I want to move into a better neighborhood and to go to Paris."

And pay off the loan, Taylor's tuition, find the identity of my father, and ask him why he left us.

But I don't tell him that because even to me, it sounds so sad, so pitiful, and I don't want sympathy from him.

I add, "Because I want to enjoy life, not slave away for the sake of making money."

Steven is silent as a soft cool breeze flitters by, much welcomed in the sweltering heat. The smooth notes of jazz music carry through the air, and I turn, seeing a street musician playing his saxophone by a stone bridge, the sultry sounds echoing in the short tunnel, lending an air of romance to the park.

The high notes mingle with the low chords, the music ebbing and flowing in a sensual rhythm, reminding New Yorkers to slow down and take a breath, that amidst the chaos and commotion in the city, we should all take a few moments to relax and enjoy these little moments in a beautiful park and celebrate the joys of being alive.

I see four people slowly rising to their feet—one elderly couple, a thin old man wearing red suspenders, clutching his wife or lady friend to his chest, the other a younger couple looking to be around my age, twin smiles on their faces. They twirl on the pavement, moving their bodies to the smooth notes of the music. Worries seem to elude them, and their life is not about the past or the future, but only about the present and these magical moments spent in your lover's arms.

I smile, a sudden wistfulness creeping inside me, a different ache forming in my chest. Romance, when it works out, is beautiful. It's the reason I keep flipping the pages of my books in pursuit of the elusive happily-ever-after.

Too bad reality is often uglier.

Clearing my throat, I look away, finding Steven's eyes on me, his brows crinkling at whatever he sees on my face. His gaze trails over to the dancing couples and I see his throat rippling as he swallows. He balls the hot dog wrapper in his fist, a muscle twitching in his jaw.

"What?" I whisper. The whimsical wings of unrealistic dreams beat harder inside my chest as a sudden heat spreads to my cheeks.

"You don't ask for much."

A statement, not a question. His words are a quiet murmur, a heaviness lacing through his voice. His beautiful hazel eyes ensnare mine, holding me captive as the magic of the jazz music swirls around us, threading the sweet, scented air with a dash of enchantment. For a moment, I want to ask him to dance, to let our bodies guide us into a world without troubles, without storms and winds, without sleepless nights.

Instead, I give him a shaky smile as my heart clenches, a slither of pain snaking its way through me.

If I don't ask for much, I never get disappointed. And life, often-times, is one giant ball of disappointments.

Steven

I can't look away.

Instead of staring at the giant screen in front of us, watching the classic *The Sound of Music,* while we lounge on my suit jacket, which no doubt will be ruined after tonight, I'm watching her instead.

She huddles close to me, our bodies not touching, as we sit next to hundreds of strangers at Pier I of Riverside Park South. I remember how her lips curled into a smug smile when she told me she'd bet I didn't know you could watch movies for free in the city, before whisking me here to take part in my first Summer Nights on the Hudson: Movies at Pier I.

After my birthday dinner of the atrocious hot dog, we took a stroll around Central Park, walking past Belvedere Castle, the granite tower and parapet walls sticking out like a sore thumb in the middle of the metropolis yet somehow blending in seamlessly all the same—one of the city's magical abilities. We stopped by Turtle Pond, watching the little suckers swim in the dark waters or sunbathe on rocks.

For once in my life, I didn't feel the itch to return to work, to bury myself within the world of dollars and cents, where winning was everything that mattered. My mind wasn't occupied by thoughts of TransAmerica and my father.

As the day bleeds into the night, the sunset washing the skies in a brilliant array of colors, I find myself raking in the sweet scent of jasmine with each breath, my lungs expanding with air with each inhale.

I can finally breathe.

And the irony of it is, it hasn't cost a thing.

The last few hours spent with Grace, wandering the city like tourists, I wonder if the emptiness inside me has something to do with my relentless pursuit of success, to climb higher on Mount Everest, to be the first person to ascend to the top.

And for what? So I could wake up in the dark, staring at the ceiling in the middle of the night?

Grace lets out a sigh, drawing my attention away from my thoughts, and I glance at the screen, watching Captain von Trapp dancing with Maria in the dark gardens, where anyone can tell love is brewing in the air, that the normally stoic man is falling for the charms of his sweet governess.

My chest clenches, and a heat unfurls in my gut, spreading to my loins. My skin feels warm as I sneak a glance at the beguiling woman next to me, who, without an ounce of artifice, without beautiful clothes or fancy hairstyles, shines brighter than any woman I've ever met.

Grace's eyes take on a dreamy gleam, her body swaying softly to the music as if she's dancing alongside the couple. I remember seeing the wistfulness in her expression when she saw the couples dancing on the lawn at Central Park earlier. My fingers twitch, an irrational impulse burning through my veins. I want to tug her in my arms and swing her in circles to the sound of the music.

I want to see how the violet of her eyes sparkles under the moonlight.

I want to see how she looks when she melts in my arms.

I want to taste her lips at the source.

I want to bury myself deep inside her body and never resurface.

My body jolts as my mind finally catches up to my thoughts. My father's crying face as he stood out in the rain in front of his other family floats to the surface.

Years later, when I was in high school, having my first and probably only heartbreak when the girl I liked said no when I asked her to the Valentine's Day dance at our fancy prep school, Father sat me down and told me it was best not to allow our hearts to become attached. Because once a woman slipped in and captured the tender organ, she'd never let it go, even if she were no longer in your life. And for the rest of your life, you'd lose part of yourself, knowing you'd never be able to reclaim it.

I knew he was talking about the mysterious woman, the one who broke his heart. I could see the sadness radiating from his hazel eyes, the way he'd cradle his favorite mug with the handprint, tracing the imperfections on the ceramic.

At the time, I was glad my heart wasn't ensnared yet, and was still in one piece. It was one of the few occasions Father truly spent time with me outside of academic events. We looked at the bright stars from our backyard deck, sipping on hot cider. His warning to me came from his broken heart.

Kingsley men don't let emotions get the best out of them.

A cool breeze sweeps through the pier, and the couples around us shift closer, with the women burrowing themselves in their partners' chests. Grace shivers, the tremor so slight I'd miss it if I wasn't staring at her. A thickness forms in my throat and my heart kicks into a rapid rhythm, pounding so loudly I'm afraid she'd hear it.

I slowly shift behind her before drawing her into my arms. She freezes, her muscles tense, and I can feel her eyes staring at me before I shift into position. Wordlessly, I cradle her, my fingers trailing over her arm, drawing out a sigh from those beautiful lips. Closing my eyes, I breathe in the sweet scent of jasmine, an aroma I want to bottle up and carry with me always, because it'll forever remind me of her, the only woman who has tempted me, dismantling my barriers as if they were made from paper.

Grace's body softens against mine, her head lolling to the side, baring her smooth, slender neck. Unable to resist, I lean down and press my lips against her fluttering pulse, where her scent is the strongest. She lets out a soft moan, the sound shooting straight to my groin, and I increase the suction, letting myself be selfish one more time. If I can't taste her lips yet, and I shouldn't until she knows about the job offers, at least I can taste her skin and feel her tremble against me.

"Steven." Her breathy voice is light as the breeze and her hand clutches my thigh.

My tongue dips out, swirling around the pulse, which is dancing with my lips, tasting the sweetness, the saltiness, the delicious flavor of her. Her fingernails dig into my muscles and I hiss in the pleasurable pain.

My skin is on fire and I want to touch her without all the clothes between us. I want to see her writhe in pleasure. My teeth scrape across that tender spot on her neck and her chest arches, her breathing quickening into deep pants. Her hips gyrate on my jacket on the ground and I know she's wet. I can satisfy her, make her come with no one knowing.

A desperate need claws inside me, but I know I can't touch her. Not until Friday, if she'll still have me. It's dishonest, not that I'm a paragon of integrity. I'm afraid I won't be able to stop, and I'll pull her into the abyss with me, snuffing out the flame shining brightly within her. I'm damaged, irreparable, and my broken pieces will slice and stab her until there's nothing left.

My nerves spark alive in those small areas where our bodies graze each other, and all my senses are alert. Reluctantly, I pull back, a surge of satisfaction rushing through me at the pink mark on her slender neck.

Mine.

Grace stills and turns toward me. She doles out a shaky smile, her eyes shining with unsaid emotions, emotions I'm afraid to read or recognize, because I won't be able to give her what she's looking for.

My nostrils flare and I hold her gaze for a few more seconds before I tear my attention away from her to focus on the screen once more.

My heart threatens to escape my rib cage, my pulse hammering in my ears.

For the first time in my life, I finally feel the agonizing want of needing another person more than I need my next breath.

And I want more. I want to leap into the flames and put my heart in her hands.

CHAPTER 14

Grace

"SOMEONE'S IN A GOOD mood today. Where did you disappear to on Wednesday, anyway? I came back from a meeting, and you were gone." Jamie leans against my cubicle wall as the office bustles with excitement.

Unofficial word is out that there should be an announcement on the full-time offers later today and gossip always livens the floor.

My gaze flickers to Jamie, finding her eyes narrowing to slits. The girl is much more perceptive than people give credit for.

Curving my lips into a grin, I fib, "I had a doctor's appointment and had to leave a bit early. Why, something happened?"

I will my heart to stop racing and hope my face isn't flushed pink. Burying my lips against the cup, I take another sip, watching Jamie as she purses her lips in contemplation before her eyes turn animated.

"You completely missed it, but Mr. Kingsley left the office before five. Everyone was talking about it. Bradley said he's been here for five years and has never seen Mr. Kingsley leave before him. There are so many conspiracy theories floating about."

I turn my face back toward my computer and make a show of staring at the spreadsheets, even though the numbers are not registering in my mind. I feel my face heating as my mind floats back to that night for the thousandth time today.

Sitting with him shoulder to shoulder at the pier, watching one of my favorite movies, was one of the best experiences I had in recent years. I can still feel the way he'd sneak glances at me throughout the film, the way he curled his arms around me under the guise of keeping me warm from the chilly breeze. I've never felt as safe as I had in that moment.

The way he kissed my neck, and how each suction and swipe of his tongue made me want to tear off his clothes and return the favor. My clit throbbed the entire night, my body ready to combust, and no amount of leg clenching offered any relief.

When he dropped me home that night, because once again, he wouldn't let me take the subway afterward, he walked me up the steps of my apartment, ignoring the hoots and hollers from the punks on my street. We stood on the top step, with the pale moonlight shining down upon us and my hands fumbling in my purse for my keys. When I found them, I looked up, finding his face dipped down slightly, blocking the moon in the inky darkness of the night skies.

But I didn't need the moon to illuminate my surroundings when he was there, standing mere inches away from me, the warmth from his body wrapping around me like a security blanket. He shone from within, his soul calling to mine, and it was impossible not to notice.

For those few blessed seconds, we stared at each other, oblivious to the cackling of the delinquents in the neighborhood, the backfiring of an old car starting up down the street, the blast of punk rock music from the speakers of a passing car.

Steven stared at me, his eyes turning more heated with each passing second, and my lips parted of their own accord. My nerves sparked and sizzled, the hairs on the back of my neck stood at attention, and I watched his chest lift and fall rapidly. His brows furrowed, like he was grappling with something inside him, and I remembered the way my heartbeat careened out of control, ready to dive off the deep end.

"Happy birthday, Steven," I whispered, our breaths mingling in the small distance between us, cloaking us in our small slice of heaven. Somehow, it felt like I was telling him a lot more than simple birthday wishes.

A muscle in his jaw twitched, and he swallowed. The tawny irises weren't visible then, long eclipsed by his swirling black pupils. His eyes

darted to my lips again, and I felt myself leaning in, almost imperceptibly, and him following suit, but then he stiffened and backed up a
smidge.

Enough to tell me the spell was broken.

"Thank you, Grace, for the best birthday I've ever had. You're right,
I didn't need to spend a lot to be happy."

His voice, threaded with tension and regret, echoes in my mind as
I stare at the spreadsheet in front of me, my heart still pounding that
staccato rhythm, a pleasure laced pain sifting through my chest.

It's almost as if I'm grieving a loss for something I've never had in the
first place.

I remember how my lips trembled when I whispered in his ear,
"Steven, you'll come to learn, I'm always right."

Riiing.

The blaring of the office phone pulls me out of my brief bout of
melancholia, and I mouth my apologies to Jamie, who nods before
walking back to her cubicle.

Glancing at the caller ID, I smile.

"Stev—Mr. Kingsley?"

A heavy exhale filters through the phone and a chill seeps through me.

"Grace, can you come in for a few minutes?"

"Y-Yes, sir."

Minutes later, I sit in his beautiful office, the warm sunlight draping
over him in what should've been a beautiful moment. But he looks
haggard as he rubs his palm over his jaw, his lips pressed in a firm line.
His forehead pinches, and he takes another deep breath before bringing
his cup up to his lips.

Like he's bracing himself for something bad to happen.

The AC churns on and I shiver as I take in those beautiful hazel eyes,
which seem sad and full of regret today.

"Mr. Kingsley? Is everything okay?" I sit up straighter, my fingers
twiddling with my shirt, and a heavy sense of foreboding sinks into my
chest.

He leans forward and clasps his hands together. "Grace. You're the best intern on my team this year. Your intelligence and hard work haven't gone unnoticed. If this were only up to me, we wouldn't be having this conversation." He pauses as if to gauge my response.

My chest feels like a freight train has slammed into it. I can't breathe as my mind processes his words. *Oh no. This can't be. I need this job offer.* My stomach churns, and I grip the hem of my shirt tightly in my fist.

My skin heats as I stare at my clenched hands, white-knuckled, and an avalanche of emotions buries me alive, turning an otherwise beautiful sunny day into the darkest nightmare. Anger, indignation, disbelief, grief, and a myriad of burning sensations rob me of my breath and all I can do is to keep breathing, to not fall apart in front of him.

I've worked my ass off for this offer and it's evident.

I deserve it more than anyone else in the internship group.

How could he do this to me?

How dare he?

My mind latches onto the scalding anger, and my nostrils flare.

Steven swallows and continues, "This is out of my hands, but I just found out the three offers were to be given to others. This was a decision made by people above me."

"But I need the job, Steven. I need…" *The large signing bonus.* My voice trails off, leaving the last sentiment unsaid as a burning sensation appears behind my eyes. *Never show men your fear.* Nothing will change. And I don't want him to feel sorry for me. But the betrayal hits deep.

Heaving in a shaky breath, I look up and whisper, "How *could* you?"

He flinches at whatever he sees on my face. I grit my teeth and look away.

"I'm going to give you the best recommendation possible. I can call up a few folks to see if there's an entry level position somewhere for you."

His words pick up in volume. He sounds desperate, frantic even. "Next year, one of our fall offers will be to you, and I'll make sure you get an extra bump on the signing bonus. Grace, everything will work out, and I—"

I hold my hand up, my eyes blinking rapidly as the implications of this slowly sink in. The loan shark payment. The eviction. Taylor's dream. Everything that was supposed to be solved by the offer. Now all my plans are burned to a crisp and suddenly I don't know what to do anymore. My lungs are squeezed in a vise and I choke in a deep breath, then another.

It's okay, Grace. We Peytons will find a way to get out of this. We don't need to rely on another man's charity. There are still a few months left before the loan is due. Maybe Steven can come through with recommendations, maybe things aren't so dire.

My mind swirls with chaos as my breathing quickens into pants.

"Grace?" Steven's voice sounds worried, but I can't bring myself to look at him.

He stands up and walks around the desk, leaning down and wrenching my hands away from abusing my shirt. His expensive cologne of the ocean and leather wafts to my face. His palms feel warm and safe.

Illusions. All of it.

Looking at him through my blurry vision, I want to lash out, to scream, and to tell him I desperately need this job. My chest spasms in pain, and while my mind tells me it's not his fault if the regret radiating from his being is any indication, my heart feels otherwise.

Utter and complete betrayal.

It feels like it has been stabbed a thousand times and the perpetrator is trying to stitch it up, but I'm the one bleeding at his feet.

It's always the woman.

Letting out a ragged sigh, I swallow the pins and needles in my throat and return his gaze. His eyes are dim with concern, his jaw tense, his hand still clasping mine, his thumb tracing soothing circles on it.

"I-I can't say I'm not disappointed, because that would be a lie. But I know it's not your fault...and I..." I release a deep exhale. "I understand. Thank you for telling me the news in person."

Steven heaves out a heavy breath, as if he were afraid I was going to say something else. He looks down at his hand on mine, his thumb still grazing my skin in a reassuring pattern.

He swallows, his throat rippling. "Grace, I swear, I'll make this up to you, I'll—"

"Mr. Kingsley, do you mind if I return to my desk?"

Even though my rational mind knows it's not his fault, my battered heart doesn't want to hear anything else from him. Because deep down, an insidious voice is asking, *couldn't he have done something? He's a vice president.*

I need to get away, to breathe and process everything without him being next to me.

I don't want him to see me cry.

Steven lets go of my hands and his hands curl into fists as he slowly steps away. "Very well. I'm sorry, Grace."

I scramble off the chair and walk toward the door.

"Grace." His voice stops me as I pause by the doorway. I still can't bring myself to look at him. "You still mean a lot to me, friend. I hope this doesn't change anything between us."

The word "friend" feels like a slap in the face.

I nod, unable to answer, and leave the room.

The day passed by in a blur and after management released the offers to the three lucky candidates, the rest of us got to go home early. Next week will be the last week of the internship. Steven was trapped in his office the entire day, and I didn't get to see him when I left.

My chest is heavy and my shoulders ache from tension as I step into the apartment, my fingers pulling off yet another red eviction notice taped to the door.

Taylor is curled up on the sofa, her eyes red with tears streaming down her face.

My heart plummets to the ground.

Dropping everything to the floor, I hurry toward her. My throat narrows, restricting my airflow, and my heart thumps rapidly in my chest.

My rebellious sister, who defies modern conventions, never cries. The only time I remember her in tears was when Mom and I picked her up from her sleepover and I told her Uncle Bobby wasn't going to be with us anymore. He was family to us at that point. We wrapped our little arms around each other while she sobbed into my chest. Since then, like me, she never grew attached to anyone or anything that would warrant tears.

"Tay? What happened? Please tell me you're okay." I wrap my arms around her shuddering frame.

"I'm fine, b-but the loan shark came by. He moved up the date of the payment to next Tuesday. He said something about his boss having cash flow issues."

Her words ring in my ears and I feel lightheaded.

"What! He said we have another three months."

"I don't know. He mentioned the deadline got moved up and if we don't pay, he'll hurt Mom. I'm scared, Grace." She gazes up at me, her eyes bloodshot. "These people are dangerous."

"Tay," I whisper, my voice choking up, "I didn't get the job. I'm so, so sorry. I know we were depending on the signing bonus, but something happened, and—"

Taylor shushes me, her face crumbling at the news. Her eyes take on a determined glint. "I'm going to drop out of the program and find a job, but that'll take time and it won't be enough—"

"No! You can't. You have talent, Tay. Let me think. Give me some time to think." I get off the couch and pace on the floor.

Even if she gets a job, it'll hardly make a dent in the amount of money we need right now. Steven's recommendations and connections will probably get me something mediocre in a few weeks, as all the excellent offers have most likely been made by large firms by now. Furthermore, we don't have weeks. I need something fast and lucrative.

"I'm going to take care of it, Taylor. Don't tell Mom about any of this. She'll only worry and there's nothing she can do, anyway. I'm going to call Belle and see if she knows anyone. She might have some connections. Focus on your classes. Everything is going to be fine."

CHAPTER 15

Grace

My lunch threatens to make a reappearance as I listen to the quiet pings of the elevator indicating the passage of each floor. The air smells faintly of lavender and I glance around the dark oak paneling and shiny silver railing, everything immaculately clean with no dust or smudges.

I guess I shouldn't expect anything less at the retreat for the rich and the famous here at The Orchid.

Belle came through when I called her earlier.

"Are you sure you don't want me to lend you money?" she offered. "I'd need to let my parents know with that large of a sum, but it's no trouble."

I shook my head, even though she couldn't see me. Money has destroyed friendships and relationships and I couldn't risk that with her. She means too much to me. I also don't want her to see us at our lowest. This is a mess we need to get ourselves out of, not something others should help us with.

"Thanks, Belle. But I need to do this on my own. You said she's expecting my call?"

Belle let out a sigh. "I knew you would be this stubborn. And yes, Sofia Kent is expecting your call. I don't frequent The Orchid a lot, but Sofia manages the Rose floors, and some of their dancers and companions come to us for custom designs and fittings. When I called her earlier, she said she had a position open which needed to be filled immediately and she could front a loan. I don't know what that position is, but you can call and find out."

Sofia has asked me to meet her on the lowest level of the Rose floors, which is situated toward the top of the fifty-plus story building.

An interview. To be a dancer. One that'll require me to shed my clothes.

I swallow, the nausea churning in my gut, and I can feel the sweat beading on the back of my neck. A weight sits atop my chest as I realize this is a pivotal moment in my life, because I'm about to embark on something I thought I'd never do. To use my face and body to make a living instead of my intelligence.

My thoughts flit to Mom and her years as a dancer on Broadway. In the good years, she'd have supporting roles. In the bad years, I'd see her dancing in burlesque clubs, where men would leer at her curves.

Her eyes would dim then.

I let out a shaky breath. *Snap out of it, Grace. Whatever happens, this is only temporary. You can go back to working in finance later.*

But still, the anvil on top of my chest presses down, making it hard for me to breathe.

The elevator doors slide open and I walk up to the receptionist, a beautiful redhead in a tasteful, black body-con dress, who smiles in a welcoming way when she sees me.

"I have an appointment with Sofia Kent."

Awareness dawns in her eyes and she asks me to take a seat in one of the tufted armchairs in the room.

The lobby is beautiful. Classy. Ivory marble floors with intricately designed medallions of black and gold coloring. The walls are white panels with delicately carved gold vines traveling up to the ceiling before swirling into a geometric design, which is the backdrop for a massive crystal chandelier.

The place is dripping in luxury. I'm sure even the lamps in this place cost more than one month's rent. I guess later today, I can tell Taylor I've finally made it inside The Orchid.

I remember passing by the modern building on 5th Avenue with Taylor when we were teenagers. We'd gape at the lofty exteriors, a structure seemingly constructed entirely of glass, which, aside from the front doors, was coated with a substance preventing bystanders from seeing the inside. Doormen dressed in the finest livery stood in front of the doors, their bearing tall, shoulders back, like they were proud to work there.

Rumors abound as to what's inside the building, the haven for the super-rich and superelite from all over the globe. Supposedly, if you want injections and cosmetic services from the best plastic surgeons in the world, all you need to do is make an appointment with their on-site spa clinic and you'd walk out looking ten years younger with the public being none the wiser.

I'd heard about the scrumptious cuisine found within the Michelin-starred restaurants inside. In fact, it's the only place in the world where a single building houses five Michelin-starred restaurants, all serving different international flavors in the heart of Manhattan.

Taylor and I would try to peek in from the outside, only to be dragged away by the doormen and given a terse warning. We wanted to see if the rumors were true. If we could spot celebrities lingering in the lobby. If people were pampered and their worries disappeared once they stepped through those doors.

I'd tell her as we walked amongst the throngs of tourists headed toward Central Park, someday I'd make it and I'd be able to enter this exclusive establishment and would tell her all about it. We'd sample fancy cocktails from their various wine and spirit bars and do whatever rich people do when they had free time. And I'd be able to do it because I'd have gotten there by myself, without depending on anyone.

I let out a heavy sigh as I see a tall, graceful woman with brown hair wearing a tailored gray sheath dress striding toward me with a sharpness in her green eyes.

"Hello Grace, I'm Sofia. Nice to meet you. Come, follow me."

After a brief, confident handshake, I follow her as she walks back in the direction where she came from.

A few corridors and turns later, we settle in her office, where she clasps her hands and looks at me expectantly.

"So, tell me why you're here."

I fiddle with my hands on my lap. "I need a job and my friend, Annabelle Law-McKenzie, mentioned you have an opening on the Rose floors. I'd like to be considered."

She quirks a brow. "I know we didn't go into details on the phone, but this job is a dancer at Trésor, which is our burlesque club."

I swallow and remain silent. My heart sinks at hearing the official confirmation of what this job entails.

"What's your background, Grace? Do you have any experience dancing?"

"I'm a finance major at NYUC. My mom was a performer on the Broadway stage when she was younger and she was also a burlesque dancer. While I didn't have official training, she taught my sister and me rudimentary ballet and jazz when we were kids. I'm not a professional, but I'd like to think I can dance fairly well."

She cocks her head to the side and stares at me for a few seconds, as if she's trying to read my facial expressions. I fight to remain still, poised, and neutral. Anything to prevent her from seeing the myriad of emotions inside me—the sadness, nervousness...disappointment at life's events.

"I'm good at reading people. You don't seem to fit the profile of our usual candidates for the job. You look like you belong on Wall Street. Why are you here?"

I heave out an exhale and lean forward. "To tell you the truth, my family is in a dire situation and I'm in need of a good amount of money in a very short timeframe. My job offer at Pietra Capital fell through at the last minute and I'm in a bind. When I called Belle, she mentioned your name. At this point, I'm willing to do anything. I'm a hard worker and I'm a professional. You won't regret hiring me."

Sofia hums under her breath. "How much do you need?"

I give her the sum, and she doesn't bat an eyelash at it.

"That can be arranged via a loan but will require you to be employed with us for at least two years. But before we get there, I need to see you dance. It's an interview or audition after all."

She opens her drawer and takes out a skimpy bikini, the black triangles barely big enough to cover any private areas. She sets it in front of me. "Change into this in the back and come back out."

My body freezes as I eye those tiny scraps of clothing, something I would never, *ever* wear normally.

"You don't have to do this, you know. The actual costumes are much skimpier," she says gently.

Her words jolt me into movement and I grit my teeth. *I can do this. If Mom could do it, so can I.* Without a word, I grab the bikini and head toward the restroom in the back, shed my clothes, and slip it on.

I glance at myself in the mirror, and a sudden urge to cry nearly overcomes me. My breasts are on full display, the tiny triangles cover my nipples and the bottom half of my swells. The bottoms are slim, barely concealing my slit.

Cold sweat breaks out on my skin as the burning sensation in my eyes doesn't appear to abate. My mind drifts back to all the men in the past who leered at my curves and made disgusting comments, and I know life is about to get much, much worse.

Blinking rapidly, I breathe in long inhales, followed by longer exhales. *I can do this. This is just a costume. This is not who you are, Grace. This is an act. Just pretend you're an actress.* I keep repeating the affirmations in my mind as I focus on my breathing, and I see a faint flush returning to my otherwise pale face.

Squaring my shoulders, I stride out, faking the confidence I don't really have.

If I'm going to do this, I'll be the best dancer they'll ever have.

Sofia's eyes widen, no doubt from my change in demeanor, and a small smile appears on her lips. "Good. Very good. I thought perhaps you changed your mind."

She plays a soft jazz piece and instructs, "Pretend you're on a stage in front of our clientele and dance."

The beats are slow. Sultry. My heart races inside me as I attempt to turn off all the noise in my head. *This is a task. A job. Focus on that.*

Closing my eyes, I gyrate my hips to the music, letting my hands skim the sides of my breasts as I roll my body in a series of moves I've seen Mom do from the backstage when I was younger. Dipping my body low, I flip back up, making sure to stick out my bottom and arch my back, my hands trailing back up my body. My eyes flutter open and I stare at a spot above Sofia and execute a pirouette, letting my body become one with the music.

"Good. That's enough." The music stops and my heavy breathing fills the air as I stand still, waiting for the verdict.

Sofia steps away from her desk and stands in front of me.

"The moves were rudimentary but well done, and we have teachers and choreographers here who will work with you." She smiles warmly at me. "You know, I have a feeling you'll do very well here. And your eyes...that beautiful shade of violet, they'll draw them in."

Them as in men.

The nausea, which disappeared for a few moments when I slipped on the dancer role, resurges and I fight to remain still.

She extends her hand again. "Welcome to The Orchid, Grace."

⸻

Later that night, after Taylor is fast asleep on her twin bed and Mom retired to her bedroom after work, none the wiser to the events that transpired a few hours ago, I sit at my desk facing the windows. The moonlight casts a faint glow through the half-opened blinds.

After my audition, Sofia took out a checkbook and wrote me a hefty sum, big enough to pay off the loan with leftover to move us into employee housing closer to The Orchid.

When I returned home with the check in my hand, my heart felt like it was razed by a bulldozer, and my eyes were on the verge of tears again.

Taylor pulled me aside, and I told her about the offer and that I'd be dancing. I didn't tell her about the stripping. I knew she wouldn't let me if she knew.

Mom fussed over us at dinner, her forehead crinkling when she asked us why both of our eyes were red and swollen. We made up some excuse about allergies and I tried my best to fake a smile even though my soul felt battered. Splintered into tiny pieces.

But now, in the stillness of the late hours, with the wispy moonlight as my companion, the sorrow I've been holding inside me threatens to unleash, the final quake of the earth breaking the dam wide open. My nose burns and tears gather in my eyes as I stare at the starry skies, my mind mourning the future I thought I had, but was cruelly wrenched away from me at the last second.

I'm young. I could start over.

It's only dancing. After two years, we'd be free.

It's not a big deal.

My mind whispers lies to my heart, trying to soothe its shudders and calm its cries.

Growing up, watching Mom depend on men, one after the other, using her beauty, her charms, but failing to keep any of them, I vowed to myself I'd never be in her shoes. I'd never resort to using my body or my face to eke out a living. I'd use my intelligence and my brain to carve a path for myself and my family.

But life is ironic, and Lady Luck is not on our side yet again. Now, I'm relegated to using the same features I never thought I'd use, to learn to stomach men gawking at me with lust in their eyes. I'm going to have to get used to my body not truly being my own.

Somehow, amid all this aching sadness, I think of him. The man from a different walk of life, his shiny dress shoes to my scuffed leather ones, his luxury car to my subway rides, his penthouse apartment to my hole in the wall with barred windows. Now, the distance between us will be even wider, even more insurmountable. I don't want him to see me as a dancer in skimpy clothing. I want him to remember me as the brilliant intern who could make him laugh.

Perhaps it's for the best. Men will always disappoint you and Steven has never made any promises to me. I know what happened with the job offer wasn't his fault—it was clear as day from the conversation in his office. But still, he wasn't able to protect me this time.

But you didn't tell him why you needed the job, Grace.

Does it matter? The results would still be the same and I don't want a job out of pity.

I stare at the moon, shining so brightly in the inky skies, even though the light within me has snuffed out.

He's only a friend, if even that. The way my heart beats around him, the way my skin sizzles from his touch? Biological reactions between a man and a woman. Nothing more.

Before anything could happen, not that anything would, our story would have to end. He'd live in his castle with air conditioning and fine dining, and I'd disappear from his life.

And perhaps, on the dreadful nights when the storm surges outside, the winds rioting against the windows, maybe he'd remember there once was a girl who felt the same way on those lonely nights. Maybe as he laid awake on his bed, waiting for the chaos to subside, he'd think about our afternoon at the park or the evening at the movies, or perhaps he might read a curious fact about the world and think of me.

The lump in my throat grows, and I retrieve a piece of paper from the drawer. I uncap the pen and scrawl out my farewell to him. Wetness slips down my cheeks as I realize he'd never know my feelings for him, that in these final words to him, written on a scrap and to be stuffed into an envelope and mailed later, he'd never know all the words I want to say but can't write.

How I wish I could stay by his side, to bring the spark dwelling inside him to the surface, to tell him to stop punishing himself by not living.

Even as our path diverges, I hope he can find peace in the night.

She disappeared.

Like everything was a figment of my imagination, my mind creating a soulmate because the hollow in my heart required it.

My heart, an organ I thought wasn't working anymore, spasms in pain.

Because of her, and the hole she left in it.

My mind flits back to us standing on her doorstep when I dropped her home after the movie at the pier, when she stood in front of me, mere inches separating us. I could smell the jasmine wrapping around me like a hug. I saw the way her bright eyes widened, how the moonlight added a sparkle to her glittering irises. I remembered her plump lips parting, the perfect, beautiful lips drawing my attention, begging me to taste them.

Begging me to taste her and feel her and surround myself with her.

It took all my willpower to step away because I thought I had more time. I thought if she forgave me, then maybe, just maybe, I'd let myself be selfish once again.

But after that night, she disappeared from my life without a trace. She didn't return my calls or texts. Worried she took the news of the job offers too hard, I lasted two days trying to distract myself in the office until I couldn't stand it and went to her apartment and knocked on her door because unease wound around my throat like a snake, crushing my windpipe.

Something was wrong. It was a gut feeling. And my gut was never wrong.

She didn't answer, and I tried again the next day. And the next. Until one day, one punk I'd seen lingering on the doorsteps before told me she and her family moved without a forwarding address.

I remembered how my three hours of sleep each night dwindled into one, if I was lucky, how she occupied every waking hour, and how for the first time in my life, I was worried about something, or someone, other than work.

Worried sick. The gnawing pain in my stomach grew with each passing day.

Until the following Monday, HR notified me she tendered her notice, and a small, unassuming letter arrived on my desk. Her farewell letter to me, asking me not to find her.

Perhaps it's for the best, because if I take her lips with mine, I'd fall into the path of my father, and one day, I'd sit with my son on the backyard deck, looking at the starry skies, thinking about the woman who captured my heart and ran away with it, because she couldn't stand how broken I was inside. I'd then tell my son not to get his heart entangled, because it'd only end up in regret.

But I realize the only regret I have right now is not kissing her and not knowing the sweetness of her lips.

9 MONTHS
LATER

CHAPTER 16
Steven

"PIECE OF SHIT!" I swipe the binders and pens off my desk to the floor, the crashing sounds echoing in my office.

The office soundtrack of muffled conversations and phones ringing comes to an abrupt halt like someone pressed pause on the music player. I don't even need to step outside my office to know everyone has stopped working and half the lemmings are no doubt straining to hear what's going on in here and the other half are probably scared shitless.

I haven't missed how Jane opts to call me on my phone instead of knocking on my door now, or how even Hayley, my bravest soldier, gives me a wide berth when she sees me storming down the halls. I don't know if it's the lack of sleep, the mounting pressures of the TransAmerica situation which has, as predicted, escalated rapidly in a hostile takeover situation, or if it's the one person I can't stop thinking about despite my best efforts. The person I've never forgotten.

I'm going crazy.

Staring at my monitor, tilted askew on my desk, I reread the email that landed me in a pit of boiling rage moments ago.

Steven,

Sorry, Voss made me an offer I couldn't refuse. Hope this doesn't change things between Pietra and us. My shares in TA are with them as of this morning.

Regards,

Pete McGinnis

P.S. I'd watch Hancock next. I know he said he wouldn't sell, but things have a strange way of changing around here.

Heaving in a deep breath, I wrack my brain at where things went wrong. In the last nine months, Voss has steadily increased their holdings in TransAmerica, and before this morning, they held ten percent of the shares or proxy votes, mostly acquired from smaller shareholders, but McGinnis is a board member, and he alone held fifteen percent of the company, which makes the loss of his shares devastating in our fight to save TransAmerica. Now, the score is Voss with twenty-five percent, Pietra Capital with twenty percent. Whoever gets over fifty percent first wins.

McGinnis and Hancock, another board member, were the most vocal about keeping TransAmerica away from Voss from what Father told me. His abrupt one-eighty this morning came from nowhere.

How did I miss this? Where did we go wrong?

I pace in front of my desk, the office still eerily quiet. A few muffled coughs travel through the door.

We missed something. Something obvious. There's no way McGinnis would sell to the scum of the earth, Timothy Voss, over keeping the shares or selling to us. What we offered was more than fair, we even tacked on a premium and discount on investment management fees.

Pressing a button on the phone, I listen to the ringtone of the call connecting.

"Yes, Mr. Kingsley?" Hayley answers promptly, even though I sense a thread of trepidation in her voice.

"Get me everything we have on Hancock."

"But he's a loyalist—"

"Things change, Hayley. We just lost McGinnis. We *missed* something," I growl, slamming my phone back on the receiver and burying my hands into my hair, tugging at the carefully arranged strands.

Imbeciles. All of them. I might as well do this job myself.

Blowing out a frustrated exhale, I collapse into my chair and close my eyes. An image materializes in my mind, one of many which rotates like a slideshow during random hours of the day. Violet eyes, which glow sapphire in dim lighting. Mischievous glint. Mind as sharp as a tack, noticing problems other miss. Lips spewing out random facts in the early hours of the morning.

Nine months, one week, and three days. That's how long she has been gone from my life.

My heart stutters before kicking into a frenzied rhythm as my mind drifts to Grace. Her memories have haunted me in the last nine months, keeping me up at night.

An anvil would sit on top of my chest when I walked into the office at the early hours in the morning, my heart clenching when I'd see her empty cubicle. My mind would relive the mornings I had with her, our quiet conversations in the dark, sharing a soggy bagel, which somehow tasted delicious in the faded thoughts of my recollection.

The hole in my chest has widened and deepened and I don't know how I'm still functioning each day. The yearning in my gut is a visceral jab from an ice pick, so intense I'd wake up in the middle of the night, my body drenched in sweat from fevered dreams with her laughter and smiles keeping me company.

Then the abyss would sweep in, cold and haunting, drowning me without water, and I'd wish I could fall back asleep and dream of her again. I'd give anything to experience the lightness in my chest, the warmth from her brightness, the peace I felt in her presence.

"I don't need anything in the world. I don't need success or money. I don't need my titles or estates. I only need you in my life." The insane line from the drivel of a romance novel I read over her shoulders that first morning in the office suddenly makes sense, and the realization knocks the wind from my chest, and I grip the desk before me for support.

Emotions are distractions.

Emotions are for the weak.

But why do I want to be carried away in the throes of it with her?

My chest clenches—a phantom ache, the constant companion to the murky hollowness in my rib cage.

Where is she? Why did she vanish? How is she doing? Is she safe? Is she taking care of herself?

More questions, but no answers.

Retrieving my wallet from my pants, I sink into my chair. My eyes feel heavy, another product of a restless night, and I pull out the worn sheet of paper, the size of an index card, which still faintly smells of jasmine.

Her farewell letter.

Unfolding the note from my wallet, I trace my fingers over the feminine, loopy swirls of her handwriting, the only sign she was ever real in my life.

Dear Steven,

I'm sorry I couldn't tell you this in person. Because of circumstances outside of my control, I had to move and end my time at Pietra early. The last two months have been a dream. I've learned so much from you and the team. I was excited to get out of bed each morning and eager for my future. But we don't always get what we want in life and sometimes, you have to face the sound of the music.

While the experience at the firm has been wonderful, I'm most grateful to have met you. I only wish we had more time, because I want to know why an aching loneliness haunts your eyes. I want to know why you can't sleep at night.

I hope someday you'll be able to quash the demons inside you, because you deserve so much more, Steven. You deserve to be happy.

Don't look for me. You won't find me. But know that wherever I'm at in the world, I'll be cheering for you, and when you see a star streaking across the nighttime sky, know that I will be thinking of you.

Your friend,

Grace

The phantom ache in my chest resurfaces, threatening to rob me of my breath as I reread the words I've long memorized. I can feel her pain and sadness in each stroke, each heavy press of the pen at the end of every sentence.

I can see the droplets of liquid, long dried, smearing the words at the corners.

Tears. I'd bet my life on it.

And the helplessness I felt nine months ago, the first time I realized I couldn't solve a problem, couldn't make it all go away, shakes me to this day.

What happened? It couldn't only be because she didn't get the job offer. It has to be something else.

I thought about hiring an investigator to look for her, but then what? She obviously didn't want me to find her, and she clearly distanced herself from me.

My mind swirls to my father and that one night when he sat next to me as we looked up at the stars in the skies.

Once a woman slipped in and captured the tender organ, she'd never let it go, even if she was no longer in your life. And for the rest of your life, you'd lose part of yourself, knowing you'd never be able to reclaim it.

Wise words from my father. I was too young to understand. And now, I wonder if it's too late. If perhaps my heart has been stolen from right under my nose and now I'm left bereft for the rest of my life.

Ping.

My cell chimes with a text message notification.

Emily

> Friendly reminder to be at The Orchid at five today. Jack's promotion celebration. I'm texting you the location of the secret courtyard. Don't be late.

Not a second later, another message comes through.

Emily

> I miss you, little bro. Can't wait to see your surly ass face. *Smiley face*

I chuckle under my breath at Emily's messages, which smooth the splintering edges of the ache in my chest. I don't know why I keep thinking about Grace, even after all this time has passed. *She was only a friend, Steven. That's all she ever was. Not everyone is meant to have a permanent place in your life.*

The words ring false. Complete lies.

My thoughts drift back to the last time I felt true heartwarming happiness spreading inside me, when my mind wasn't thinking about work or profitability, when I was actually present, with no worries in my mind, every cell in my body fully awake and aware of the person next to me.

The woman with nothing to her name yet is the richer person between the two of us.

The woman who made me feel alive, who made me feel the sultry heat of desire in my veins, who made me want to think about, to do impossible, ridiculous things. Things like hauling her against me, sealing myself with her, hearing her moans and whimpers as I find out what makes her scream in pleasure, drawing from her brightness, her positivity, and burying myself deep inside her and never letting go.

I just can't seem to forget her, even though her presence in my life was as brief as a passing hurricane, devastating all the same.

My thoughts drift back again to father's words...*bereft* is too little of a description for what I'm feeling every day. Time has not healed the wounds but widened them. Because now, I finally know what I'm missing.

I miss her. So goddamn much.

CHAPTER 17
Steven

JACK DRAWS SARAH CLOSE to him, and even from this distance, I can see the hunger in his eyes, the love seeping through this former playboy's soul. The two lovebirds are so wrapped up in themselves they don't even notice they have an audience.

The afternoon sunlight bathes them in a spotlight, making Sarah's orange tresses seem like a warm fire burning in the hearth, with Jack's inky black hair the coals keeping the fire alight. A soft breeze flutters by, disbursing the sweet scent of wildflowers within this hidden court-yard—one of many in this elaborate building—The Orchid. With the twining dark vines and vibrant hedges behind them, these two look like the definition of soulmates only needing love to sustain them.

"I love you so much, Sarah." Jack's murmurs travel across the intimate space.

My heart, the long dead muscle, spasms in an effort to come back alive, as if shocked by the defibrillator paddles of the emergency room. But the spark fizzles, leaving only a charred muscle and a flashing pain.

My eyes dart away and sweep over the rest of the long table where my siblings and their spouses sit, the couples very much in love with each other, smiling at the new lovebirds joining their ranks. A question I asked myself a long time ago resurfaces. *Don't you want what they have?*

For the longest time, my answer has been no, I couldn't care less.

But now, as I tell myself the same thing, a nagging itch forms behind my rib cage, my mind whispering, taunting with glee...*you liar.* I brush the voice away, not wanting to hear more nonsensical words, not wanting to know what or who caused the change.

My fingers fiddle with the paper chopstick sleeve and start folding it in half, and in half again. Unfold it and start over.

The damn corners won't line up.

Love is a liability and a game of Russian Roulette.

Yes, my siblings, and now Jack and Sarah, may have hit the jackpot, somehow all magically standing alive after their bout with the revolver. Perhaps their gun didn't have a bullet in the chamber. But not everyone is so lucky. The odds are grim and not on our side. Just look at my parents' marriage, two people who shouldn't be together, but are bound with no means of escape. One person forever pining for the love of the other, the love which has long been given away. A dreadful, hopeless torture until the end of days.

The one and only time I let a woman in my life, allowing her to peek under the first set of locks to my soul, she torched the chamber, then fled and disappeared, leaving me to deal with the ashes.

And it was only friendship, not even love.

It can't be love.

My chest spasms.

I'm a Kingsley, and Kingsley men don't let emotions get the best of them.

My hand curls into a fist, crushing the paper sleeve, as my chest hardens, a poor attempt at smothering the flames of pain with sand. I swallow the lump in my throat as I turn back to the new happy couple, who still seem to be oblivious to our presence.

"Jack..." Sarah whispers as Jack's head dips down, no doubt ready to demonstrate his love in more physical ways.

Even though love is not for me, I'm happy for them, having known both of them for years as Sarah Winstead and Jack Szeto are Emily's and Adrian's best friends from high school, respectively, who took the scenic route to get together, even though it was obvious to all of us, except for Sarah that Jack carried a torch for her for a very long time.

I clear my throat, not wanting to witness a make-out session from my two friends. "You know you guys have an audience, right?" I smirk at the shocked expressions on their faces when they whip their heads toward us.

Arching my brow at them, my eyes connect with Jack's. *You sappy piece of shit. How could you have missed us sitting out here all along?*

The happy couple blushes and Sarah tugs Jack toward the table.

My siblings all wear beaming smiles on their faces. Emily, her dark hair piled high on her head, is biting her bottom lip, her body bouncing with leashed excitement. Adrian has his arm around the back of her chair, his fingers tracing lazy circles on her shoulder. Jess smiles warmly and her husband, James, the sucker who spent his entire childhood and part of his adulthood in a sad unrequited love relationship with my sister, tilts his lips in a half grin.

Two servers, dressed in the crisp, blue uniforms of Kobayashi, one of the on-site award-winning restaurants at The Orchid, carry trays of an assortment of food, ranging from sashimi, hand and sushi rolls, *chirashi* bowls, the freshest fish I've tasted outside of the seafood markets in Tokyo. Platters of dishes decorate the table, an array of bright colors of pinks, oranges, and whites from the thinly sliced fish to the pops of green from cucumber, avocado, and side salads in sesame dressing.

"What's this?" Jack asks Sarah. She grins and they take a seat.

"A surprise celebration for your promotion. I know you didn't want to make a big fuss about it, but you deserve celebrating, Jack. Everyone, except Steven here, flew in yesterday. James and Jess even left the kiddos at home with her parents to come visit."

Jack is one of the key management members at The Orchid. He was the entertainment manager all guests sought after because he's infamous for solving problems creatively and seamlessly, which says something about his hustling skills since dealing with stuffy rich people who are used to getting everything their way can't be an easy job. Because he excels at his job, Ryland and the rest of the Andersons finally promoted him to a role he very much deserves.

"Director of Special Events at The Orchid," I comment, slapping him hard on his back. "Moving up in the world, my man." My lips curve into a smile. "Proud of you."

"All thanks to Adrian for giving me the opportunity in the first place. And..." Jack's voice turns raspy, as if overcome with emotions. He, like Adrian, grew up poor and had to fight his way up the food chain, so I'm sure this promotion means a lot to him. "Thank you all for coming all the way over here."

"It's all you. I only provided an introduction. Even though I wonder what they saw in you, jackass," Adrian mutters sardonically, but a glint of fondness shines brightly in those crystal blue eyes.

The meal goes without a hitch and all of us take turns making fun of Jack, who is completely besotted with the woman next to him. Now, with hearts in his eyes, he's saying some sappy shit to Sarah. "You're always right and I'm always wrong."

The men all groan at the table at his declaration. "Don't do this, Jack, you're setting a terrible example for the rest of us." James feigns puking, before Jess pokes him in the side, to which James curls an arm around her shoulder and presses a kiss to her hair.

"Completely pussy-whipped. *None* of this looks appealing," I grumble, feeling completely out of place with all this nauseating love in the air.

"What do you think about what Jack said, Adrian?" Emily bats her lashes at Adrian, who's staring at her like he worships the ground she walks on, a look I recognize when I first saw him twelve years ago when he was the poor boy who showed up to my sister's piano recital at school.

Adrian murmurs, "You're always right."

My heart pinches, a postmortem spasm, and I roll my eyes, before tossing my napkin to the table as everyone laughs at my expression.

Don't you want what they have? The annoying voice whispers in my head. I grip the napkin on the table and wet my lips, pasting a smile on my face.

Squeaaaak.

The door to the courtyard slams open, the sound echoing in the intimate space. The hairs on the back of my neck stand up and I can feel the prickling of goosebumps on my arm, which has nothing to do with the burst of cool air filtering out from the open doorway. My pulse picks up for no reason and the air thins and feels different.

I hear the faint sounds of someone sniffling as everyone looks behind me with apparent shock on their faces. Frowning, I begin to turn around to see what the commotion is all about.

"Excuse me, miss. Are you okay? Do you need help?" Jack's deep voice travels across the courtyard as I finally get a look at the interloper interrupting our meal.

Time, for all intents and purposes, ceases to matter.

My heart resurrects, the sight before me more effective than any electrical paddle in the hospital.

My pulse rushes in my ears with the force of a cyclone.

My lungs seize as I slowly rise to a standing position of my own accord.

Everything slows and every cell in my body hums to life after a long slumber.

A beautiful brunette stands mere feet before us.

My eyes cascade up her toned legs, which glimmer with whatever makeup or lotion is on them, to the luscious body with curves for days, clad in this dress—if you can call it a dress—made only of chains of pearls, no fabric to be seen, revealing an expanse of smooth, pale skin playing peekaboo between the chains, heavy teardrop breasts swaying with each breath she takes, small nude colored stickers covering the nipples, and a skin-tone scrap of underwear between her legs.

But it's not the obscene display of flesh designed to entice our amorous natures that gives me pause—beautiful women are a dime a dozen at The Orchid, it's the elfin face, slimmer than I remember, and the large, brilliant eyes, a deep purple in the sunlight, and the perfect cupid's bow lips, coated in a deep red lipstick.

The face that has been haunting my waking hours and lonely nights.

My lungs finally release the breath I'm holding, the sudden shift of the weight off my chest disorienting, and I rake in another deep inhale before I find my voice.

"Grace?"

My voice is rusty, my breathing coming out in pants.

I step forward, my mind and body not registering what I should do next.

I want to run to her and wrap her up in my jacket to block her from the eyes of everyone else in the courtyard. I want to grab her arms, pull her against me, and ask her what the hell is going on and why she disappeared without a trace. I want to know why the tears are trailing down her face. I want to know who hurt her so I can tear them apart piece by piece, delivering revenge tenfold. I want to fold her into my arms and whisper everything will be all right because I'll take care of her. Because we are never alone when we have each other.

I want to curl my hands around her face and finally fulfill the biggest regret I've had in my thirty years on this planet.

I want to kiss her. Fuck, do I want to kiss those pouty red lips.

Instead, I bite my cheek and do nothing. Other than asking, "Is that you?"

My heart is a tsunami behind my rib cage, every muscle in my body fighting the impulse to act on my desires.

The world is suddenly in technicolor again, the vibrant hues of spring after a barren winter.

The brunette gasps in surprise as she turns her attention away from Jack to me. Her eyes widen, her beautiful lips trembling for a split second before her expression shutters. She takes a deep breath and wipes the wetness on her cheeks with the back of her arm.

"Y-You're mistaken, sir." She stares at me like I'm a stranger. Her face is devoid of emotion. Cold. Numb. Indifferent.

But those eyes...I'd recognize those eyes anywhere.

She turns back to Jack and murmurs, "I'm fine. Just some bad news at home. Sorry for the interruption. Please enjoy your day."

As abruptly as she appears, she whirls around and darts back inside, her long, wavy hair flying behind her.

The door closes behind her with a resounding *bang*.

My heart threatens to escape from my chest to chase after the one person who resurrected it, and I fight the urge to rub the soreness that's spreading like wildfire.

It can't be. It has to be her.

My breathing comes out in erratic bursts, my mind a series of still framed images of the vixen from a moment ago as the hint of jasmine finally travels to my nose.

"Do you know her, Steven? From her outfit, I think she's one of the girls working on the Rose floors."

Jack's question is muffled, like I'm underwater, seconds away from reaching the surface, from relieving the burning in my lungs when I take my first breath of much needed oxygen.

The Rose floors? What?

I shake my head, not understanding anything that just transpired in the last few minutes, which could very well be a few hours for all I care, as the concept of time no longer registers, the reality of my world somehow shifted without me having a hand in it.

It can't be. It has to be her. I saw the brief flash of recognition in her eyes. Those violet eyes. Those beautiful, mesmerizing, penetrating eyes.

My hands feel around the air, latching onto the cool metal of my chair before I sit down. My mind finally notices the stilted silence, and I look up, finding Jack staring at me, his brows furrowed in concern. He just asked me a question.

"I must be mistaken. Sorry about that." I twist my lips into a smile and force out a few chuckles, which don't even sound convincing to my ears. "Yes, I must be wrong."

Clutching my chair in a death grip, I compel my muscles to relax and my lungs to expel the air I can't seem to empty as my body isn't functioning properly, the electrical wiring short-circuited from the cyclone that appeared out of nowhere.

Letting go of the chair, my hand grasps the cup on the table and raises it in a toast. I can feel the blood slowly returning to my face and I smirk, hoping it will put the others at ease. "Cheers to you, Jack, for your well-deserved promotion. I can't wait to see what's next in store for you and to have you be at my beck and call when I visit."

It seems to have worked, as everyone laughs, and Jack says something in return.

But my mind has already drifted back to the goddess with violet eyes, my missing flame on a moonless night.

As abruptly as she vanished nine months ago, she has reappeared in my life, as if a higher power has finally granted me another chance, another wish upon a shining star.

And this time, I'm not letting go.

CHAPTER 18
Grace

Millie

> Miss you, Grace. We really need to hang out again soon. You know, I asked my brother, and he has an open clerk position in the accounting department at his company if you want it. I know you won't take money from us, but it's a stable job even if the starting salary is not very high. If you don't want to dance anymore and want to pay off your loan with the Kents sooner, I can ask him to throw in a signing bonus.

Belle

> I've asked her the same too, Millie. Our Grace is stubborn and is determined to do this on her own. Whatever you decide, know that we love you and support you. You're wonderful, beautiful, and smart. But know that it's not a weakness to ask and receive help.

MY EYES PRICKLE AS I reread the text messages from my friends. I told them I was a dancer at a club within The Orchid but never told them I was at the burlesque club to be exact. I don't want them to know how I'm flaunting my body as my job now. A sticky shame slithers inside me, even though I *know* I shouldn't feel this way. I'm making an honest living and not crossing any moral boundaries I set for myself.

When I lay on my bed at night, reflecting on why I feel this way, I realize it's not about the job itself. The hardest part is getting over everything I lost and doing the one thing I swore to myself I'd never do—the future I had imagined since I was old enough to learn that education is my way out of living barely above the poverty line, the way I was going to work hard, graduate from college, secure a financially stable job and be set for the future. But instead, I'm following in my mom's footsteps. This is the cause of the heartburn in my chest.

It feels as if my dreams are gone like a poof of smoke because a shitty man duped Mom into signing a loan agreement with a loan shark. The only silver lining was I was able to graduate from college, and I now hold a diploma I won't be able to use until later.

I've had offers from the girls to work at their companies, to lend me money or gift it as bonuses, but I don't want to go from being indebted to one man, Elias Kent, to being indebted to other people, including Adrian Scott. I've seen how money changes relationships, and I couldn't bear it if what I have with the girls changes flavor.

It's not worth the risk.

Plus, the only person you can truly depend on is yourself. Life has taught me that lesson.

This is temporary, a blip in the broader scheme of things.

I stare at myself in the reflection, my fingers absentmindedly fiddling with the straps of my tasteful, yet sexy black bandage dress. My fingers graze the soft fabric, which crisscrosses over my chest and torso in a curve-hugging way, offering glimpses of the full swells of my cleavage, and the hem ending right above my knees.

Dark chocolate colored hair, with subtle streaks of mahogany and caramels and loose curls for days, expertly done by the on-site makeup artist, purported to be award-winning and best in her field. Lips coated in blood red, with a hint of gloss for plumpness. Large, doe-like eyes in the same shade of sapphire laced amethyst, are lined in a sultry cat-eye, and coated with at least three coats of mascara, making them pop on my otherwise pale face.

A breath lodges in my throat and I can see a wetness gathering in the eyes staring back at me in the mirror. Quickly blinking, I inhale the lavender scented air deep into my lungs, hoping to stem the impending tears. I can't ruin the makeup.

I look beautiful. Stunning. The spitting image of the starlet who took Broadway by storm all those years ago despite never being the main character.

I don't recognize myself.

And it's the loss of these dreams that haunts me the most.

My chest trembles as I exhale. Lately, it seems more and more difficult to breathe.

This beautiful, sexy woman is the one men flock to at Trésor. Cheers erupt when I finish a performance on the stage, each one leaving me in various stages of undress. The tips are endless and there are many requests for me to perform private dances, which I've always declined.

I'm a sensation. Unparalleled. A starlet within the Rose floors.

The lump in my throat grows and I roll my lips inward. Images of the bright-eyed girl in the frumpy clothes typing madly into the keyboard at the crack of dawn in a cold office shine behind my eyes. That girl was respected because of her intelligence, because of what she offered with her work ethic.

A handsome, dark-haired man with eyes the color of fall leaves swirls to the forefront. The quiet mornings in the office discussing everything under the sun. The way I still vividly remember his intoxicating scent of the ocean breeze and worn leather. How his eyes would spark and smolder when he stared at me when we were watching *The Sound of Music* at the pier. The way he reminded me not all men are sleazy disappointments.

But then, there was the look of regret when he told me he couldn't give me the job offer I very much deserved.

And yesterday, the searing shock on his face when he saw me in the courtyard. Tears streamed down my face because it was my first birthday after Mom's death. The most heartbreaking thing in the last nine months didn't end up being what happened at Pietra or the dancing at The Orchid.

It was the crippling loss of Mom.

The wonderful woman with a heart so full of love never ended up getting her happily-ever-after. Instead, she took her secrets away with her, taking the identity of my father to her grave when her vibrant soul was snuffed out by a driver who had too many drinks at a party and careened into her as she was crossing the street at the end of her shift at work.

A beautiful soul obliterated in a matter of seconds, leaving Taylor's and my hearts in tatters. It has always been the three Peyton women against the world.

Now, there are only the two of us left.

Despite how I look absolutely nothing like I did when he last saw me, Steven somehow recognized me in a split second.

I noticed the way his eyes skated over my attire, not lingering on my exposed flesh the way the other men would within the walls of Trésor, the way those amber pools darkened with concern as we stared at each other for the first time in nine months, the way he took those few steps toward me as if he wanted to see up close if I was all right.

But I don't want to face him. I want him to remember me as the intelligent woman he admired back then, the future rock star of Wall Street, and not a woman using her feminine wiles to eke out a living.

I've become the person I didn't want to be, and while I'd make the same choice all over again, I still haven't reconciled with this situation. If Mom could see me now, she'd be sad. Even though she used to say I should use my looks to my advantage, I somehow doubt she meant this.

My feelings are convoluted, a scrambled mess of knots in my chest. At least we were able to fool her into thinking I still worked on Wall Street until the end, since I'd leave our new apartment in my professional attire, only to change once I was at The Orchid.

"It's not too bad, is it, Genevieve? It should be an easy job tonight, just schmoozing with rich men at some event in the ballroom downstairs.

The tips will be enormous, and we don't need to dance," a raspy voice questions behind me.

We all had to take on French stage names when we started working at Trésor. All the more to sell the illusion, the mystique.

I turn around, finding Camille standing there with a grin on her pretty face. She also dances at Trésor, but the difference between her and me is, she loves her job. She loves wielding her body like a forbidden fruit, enticing men with her lingering gaze and the sultry sway of her hips.

She's proud and happy with herself, so much she opted not to hide behind a stage name, because she said Camille is already French. A confident badass. And I love her for it. It's wonderful she finds dancing here empowering, and the pay is indeed nothing to sneeze at. I can see where she's coming from, controlling the narrative, feeling confident with your body.

I wish I could feel the same way. But this is not the life I wanted for myself. And often, in the brief moments of silence within these walls, I find the sadness curling around my chest, its thorns prickling my bleeding heart.

Suck it up, buttercup. This is temporary, not forever. A temporary setback.

I muster my lips into a smile, watching as Camille strides toward me in a fetching red dress made of the finest silk. She throws her platinum blonde hair over her shoulders before pulling me into a hug.

"I know this is not fun for you. Have you thought about talking to Elias? He's not unreasonable. Maybe he'll let you out of the situation. He doesn't make girls work here against their will. And he likes you and trusts you." While Sofia was the one who wrote the check, the money actually came from her brother, Elias's pocketbook.

I shake my head. Part of me doesn't want to deal with my enigmatic boss. The fewer interactions I have with him, the greater the chance I can escape this without further complications.

Everyone in the city knows about Elias Kent. He is the mysterious criminal underboss who stays in the shadows but wields his dark influence ruthlessly, making his enemies disappear left and right. The local gangs in our neighborhood are terrified of him and these thugs are the very definition of dangerous animals.

After I joined The Orchid, I learned Sofia is his sister, and Elias provides The Orchid with the candidates and security for the men and women working on the Rose floors. The more I'm embroiled in his shady businesses, the less likely he'll let me go. And as is, I'm already doing some financial work for him on the side to speed up the debt repayment.

I've even hired a private investigator to find the identity of my father, the only parent I have left in this world if he's still alive. I cringe as a pinch of guilt makes an appearance. Mom would hate it if she knew I'm searching for him.

But don't I have a right to know?

There's only Taylor and me left in the world now, and if Mom's death has taught me anything, life is fleeting, and I wouldn't want to carry this regret with me when I leave this world.

"Ladies, ready?" A deep, rumbling voice speaks from behind us. I take a deep breath, steeling myself for the person I'll see when I turn around.

Elias.

He's leaning against the doorframe, dressed in all black, just like his soul, his fingers playing with an antique lighter I've seen him toy with whenever he makes the occasional appearance at The Orchid. The odd thing is the man doesn't even smoke.

His piercing green eyes meet mine, but unlike most men in this establishment, they don't stray from my face. "I don't need to remind you this event is important to the Andersons and myself. I'm running all the games tonight. So, you know what to do. Don't disappoint."

Elias steps into the light, drawing our gazes to the sharp scar slicing across his left cheek all the way to the temples. It's almost a shame how the cut adds rugged appeal to his otherwise handsome face.

"And Genevieve, thank you for the analysis of my investments. It's better than the ones my banker put together. I've said this before, and I'll say it again. If you don't want to dance, all you need to do is ask. There's a spot in my finance department with your name on it."

I swallow and dole out a terse nod. "I'm fine here."

Without changing his expression, he returns my nod with a brief dip of his head and stalks away.

I sense the weight of Camille's stare at the back of my neck. "Camille, he'd never let me go if I enter the belly of the beast and see whatever details are in the little black book of his."

Camille links arms with me as we walk toward the elevators. "Well then, you have one more year to go, and I'll be here with you every step of the way. I say let's go get buzzed with some top-shelf alcohol and duck or goose liver or whatever fancy crap they have downstairs."

My heart pinches.

"Ew. Do you know how they make foie gras? They fatten up a duck or a goose just so they can harvest the liver. It's barbaric! That's why they banned it in the city for a few years."

Steven arches a sardonic brow. "You and your bleeding heart. Why don't you become vegan then? They do the same things to chickens."

That day at Central Park was one of the best days of my life.

Steven, I miss you.

⸻

Lotus, one of the four ballrooms in the building, is buzzing with people when Camille and I make our appearance.

Most of the rooms in this building are named after flowers. Along with the name of the establishment, The Orchid, and its parent company, Fleur Entertainment, I guess the Andersons must really love flowers. In the past, I would be curious enough to pull up the search engine in my phone and immerse myself in research, not resting until I find out the reasons or history behind this.

But it's as if the innate curiosity I used to have has disappeared in the last nine months. And I don't find any reason to care anymore.

Still, it's impossible not to be awed by this palatial room, with its towering ceilings and stained-glass windows depicting the delicate lotus flower, with its white petals unblemished, floating in the waters. Lamplight from the outside filters through the windows, cascading the illusion of crystalline waters dotted with swaths of pink and white to the floors. Floor-to-ceiling gilded mirrors adorn the walls, much like what I'd imagine I'd see if I ever get to visit the palaces in France.

The mahogany floors, laid in a herringbone pattern, are clean, and shine under the spotlights dotting the ceilings. Tall, round tables are interspersed throughout the room, with towering glass vases filled with peonies of every color on the surface, its sweet scent lingering in the air.

Next to the floral arrangements are longer tables with the classic green velvet covering—blackjack, poker, roulette, and craps—the theme tonight, Monte Carlo in Spring suddenly makes sense.

Clusters of well-dressed people gather around the tables, men in pristine suits and women in beautiful gowns focus on the cards in front of them, small crowds cheering as a gorgeous woman in a champagne dress blows on a pair of dice before her partner, a man who's clearly already had too much to drink, tosses them onto the table.

The space hums with excitement, with energy, as the top one percent of the world mingles in throngs, eager to spend thousands of dollars like chump change.

I've heard this is a mixer for the elite in the financial industry, which means everyone who is anyone on the East Coast is probably in this room. My hands grow damp, and I sweep my eyes around the room, hoping I don't see the tall, handsome silhouette of the man I've never forgotten about.

Pasting a smile on my face, I waltz up to the roulette table and smile at the gentlemen gathered there. *I'm Lady Luck, and I'm here to put you at ease and learn your secrets.* Secrets I'll then relay back to Elias, whose rise to power, I suspect, has everything to do with the amount of sordid information he knows and barters for deals to be made. *Violence is so last century*, he would say, before he disappears into the shadows.

"Hello, beautiful. Which firm do you work at?" A middle-aged man whose waistline tells me he knows gourmet food intimately smiles at me before extending his hand. "I'm Harold Jenkins from Finch Capital."

"Genevieve, nice to meet you. I work here at The Orchid." I gingerly place my hand in his.

His fingers tighten as understanding dawns in his eyes, and the professionalism from a moment ago slips away like a snake shedding its skin. He steps closer, temporarily forgetting the game as his eyes drift down my body in a languid perusal.

Acid churns in my gut, but I force myself not to move and to maintain the smile on my face.

Finally, his eyes meet mine again and his lips curl into a sneer. "A Rose girl? Are you open for companionship?"

Looking down at my manicured hands, I feign demureness, when I want nothing more than to kick his balls and relish in his howl of pain. "I'm not a companion. I'm a dancer at Trésor."

"Ah. The burlesque club. I have not been there before, but..." he steps back and eyes me from head to toe, "I think I should visit."

Revulsion curls around my throat like a noose and I murmur, "We'd be delighted to have you. In the meantime, would you like me to place a bet for you?"

Harold grins and holds his hands open, giving me access to his chips. Smiling, I take a few chips and place them on the red number thirty. Glancing at the dealer in front of me, I touch my right ear, the universal signal for a round to be in our favor. With an infinitesimal nod, the dealer, a young man with reddish brown hair, rolls the ball into a wheel, which—I'm not sure how Elias engineers this—will no doubt land on my number of choice.

Stepping up to Harold, I watch his pupils dilate as my fingers graze his tie. "So, Harold, I hear Finch is working on a deal to offload TransAmerica with the hostile takeover. I have some stocks in TA myself," I bat my eyes at him, watching his oily face flush, "I'm worried about losing my savings. Would you know something about this?"

I bite on my lip softly, as not to ruin the lipstick, and the crowd beside us cheer and the dealer announces, "Red, thirty."

Clasping my hand to my mouth, I gasp in mock surprise. "Lucky me! Look, you doubled your investment, Harold!"

Harold laughs and slides his hand on top of mine, giving it a quick squeeze. "You're my lucky charm for tonight." He leans in and whispers, "And I'll have you know...Finch is selling the shares to Pietra. I'd look at liquidating what you have...things will get ugly soon, honey."

My pulse skyrockets at the name of the firm *he* works at. The place I used to dream I'd work at after graduation instead of here. My eyes dart around the room, searching for the unmistakable man, hoping the stars are on my side.

"Genevieve?" Harold's eyes are glued to my cleavage again.

I let out a soft laugh, hoping I'm convincing, and lean in to kiss him on the cheek. Mission accomplished with the first target.

Pietra is in active pursuit and Finch is one of the marks. I knew Steven had plans months ago. I guess they are in action now. Elias should be pleased with this tidbit. Hopefully, he'd considered this as part of the signing bonus repayment.

"It was lovely to meet you, Harold. If you're ever in need of entertainment, Trésor always welcomes you."

With one last smile, I spin away, walking as gracefully as I can toward the refreshment table, so I can grab a piece of tissue and wipe off any remaining trace of him from my lips.

One more year, Grace. You can do this. My thoughts race as I hasten my stride to the table ahead, bitterness swarming in my gut. Life is one big adventure. Even on the scenic route, there'd be rough paths and winding curves. A beautiful view lies ahead.

Affirmations, mantras, whatever you want to call it, the flimsiest thoughts keeping me sane.

At least Taylor is doing well at ABTC now. The sacrifice was worth it. Two months ago, ABTC poached Taylor from Petit Jeté, and with my generous wages here, I was able to support her dreams. Taylor called me two days ago after her first showcase there. The excitement seeping from her voice over the phone brought me to tears. My sister is happy, so happy, and living her best life.

What's one more year? If I could turn back time, I wouldn't have changed a thing, other than maybe killing Carl myself.

I'm so entrenched in my thoughts, I make a rookie mistake, momentarily forgetting the first lesson Mom taught us as young women growing up in the underbelly of the Bronx—pay attention to your surroundings.

A flash of black slams into me from the front with the force of a linebacker and before my lips can part in a cry, my feet, clad in five-inch heels, wobble from the impact, and I topple backward, my arms flailing.

Time slows as the ceiling lights swirl together and my muscles tense, my eyes clamping shut as I brace myself for the hard impact on the wooden floor.

But the floor never comes.

Instead, strong arms curl around my back, stopping what would've been a humiliating disaster in an already difficult night.

My nose registers the spicy cologne of the ocean and leather.

My body registers the familiar warmth and strength of the man holding me upright.

My heart gallops, my lungs drawing in deep inhales of the familiar, intoxicating scent.

Then my eyes finally flutter open.

Steven's beautiful face stares down at me and in a moment of weakness, a blip of disorientation, my fingers curl into the hard muscles of his forearms.

And I want to cry.

Relief. Security. Sadness. Elation.

My lips wobble as I watch his tiger stone eyes darken with intensity, his brows furrowed with concern. My fingers dig harder into his flesh, as if to verify he's really here, standing before me. My grip must hurt, but he doesn't even flinch.

In this split second where the world stops spinning around me, where my thoughts are waylaid by the rush of emotions inside me, everything ceases to matter, because I'm Grace, and he's Steven, and we're just friends, and he found me...even though I ran away from him, but fate brought us back together and everything will be okay.

The feeling of safety only he can give me cloaks me in its warmth, and if this is a dream, I never want to wake up.

"Grace?" His deep, raspy voice jolts me awake as effectively as a bucket of ice water over my head.

He pulls me to a standing position, and I drop his arms like they've burned me.

The wires in my brain finally connect and thoughts race in like a barrage of texts on your birthday, except this isn't joyous. It can't be. The sticky heat of anxiety coats my insides, and I shrink away. He can't know I work here. He can't know what I do here.

I want him to remember me as before.

"S-Sorry, sir. You're mistaken."

Without waiting for his response, I turn away, striding toward the game tables once more, desperate to reach the exits at the far corner of the room, my feet feeling like they're weighed down by lead, but I persist.

"Wait, Grace!"

I hear his calls behind me as I dart back into the crowds again, hoping he'd give up on chasing me. Pushing my way through throngs of expensive suits and fancy dresses, I walk faster, as fast as these heels can carry me, all the while trying to maintain a serene expression on my face, because nothing is unusual about a lady dressed to the nines, crossing the room with the desperation of criminals fleeing the scene of a crime.

Just as I am about to reach one of the double doors to the ballroom, a strong hand grips my wrist, halting my escape.

"Beautiful Genevieve, I never thought I'd say this, but you look almost as gorgeous in that dress as you do without your clothes on." The interloper tugs me to him and his hand slides over my stomach as rancid breath hits my nose.

I close my eyes and bite my tongue to keep from cringing. Focusing on the sharp pain in my mouth, I turn to the man behind me and tick my lips up into a demure smile.

"Mr. Voss, you are too kind." Gently, I pry his hands off me and step back. "And I've always worn costumes at the club."

Timothy Voss, the bane of everyone's existence, especially TransAmerica, is a frequenter to Trésor—every other Friday, to be exact. Unfortunately, he always "greeted me" there, his grubby hands always a millimeter away from my skin and oftentimes he'd have "accidents," where his fingers would skate over my breasts or he'd press up against me in the guise of having to move and inadvertently grind his disgusting bulge on my stomach. Then there were the many unwanted solicitations and lewd comments I tried my best to forget about.

Sofia has posted a bouncer next to me whenever Timothy steps through those rosewood doors and I know he's a few strikes away from being kicked out of the establishment. But as of now, he is still a patron.

Which means I need to grit my teeth and put on my big girl pants.

Timothy's thick hands circle my waist again, his fingers splayed over the tops of my ass. "Your little scraps of clothing aren't costumes. They are an invitation. We're not at Trésor, sweetheart. The no touch rule doesn't apply here. Why don't I book us a private suite upstairs and we can have some fun tonight?"

My fingers attempt to pry his hands off me, but this time, he holds on tight, a smarmy smile decorating his face. "I'm not interested, Mr. Voss. Unhand me, please."

Instead of letting me go, he spreads his legs and pulls me closer to him, so I'm now standing half an inch away from his suit-covered beer belly. "Come on, sweetheart, you've enjoyed our conversations, right? I've seen you shake your body at me on the stage. I tip *very* well."

His hand moves suddenly, and he paws my cleavage. "Your tits are so fuckable," he whispers in my ear.

My stomach roils in an uproar, and I swallow the revulsion creeping my throat. I grab his hand to wrench it off from my chest, my body feeling soiled, disgusting from his caress. My pulse riots and fear slams through me. His hand grips my arm instead, and he smiles at me, clearly enjoying my discomfort. "No, Mr. Voss—"

"Let go of her this instant," an unmistakable voice barks from our right, drawing the attention of many people in the vicinity.

Six simple words. Venom-laced anger.

As if his sanity is held on by the thinnest thread and he's mere moments away from snapping. And God help whoever is around him whenever that happens.

My thoughts when I first met Steven bubble up in this inopportune moment and I let out a hiccup. My mind is going mad.

Timothy glances at Steven, who has caught up to me with the stealth of a black panther prowling the forest at night. "Kingsley, I don't think we've met. I'm—"

"I don't give a flying fuck who you are. One last chance. Take your filthy paws off her or I'll rip them off and shove them down your throat and watch you choke to death. I swear, there'll be murder on these floors tonight," Steven growls as he curls one hand around Timothy's blood red tie and pulls, his knuckles flashing white.

Timothy chokes and gasps for air, his face turning red, his hands immediately falling away to grip his tie that is quickly becoming a noose under Steven's wrath.

Shrieks and gasps surround us as the sharks in the room are drawn to the display of bloodlust in front of them.

My heart pounds a mile a minute, threatening to break apart at its seams and my breathing comes out in rapid bursts as my attention is focused on the tall, threatening man in front of me, his molten eyes flashing with violence, his lips parted in a snarl, baring his blinding white teeth. A vein pulses in his forehead as he pulls harder on the bastard's tie and Timothy's choking sounds fill the air.

"Don't you fucking dare touch her. Don't you fucking dare even look in her direction, you disgusting pig. If you try anything again, I'll make sure that's the last thing you ever do."

Steven's face is twisted, flushed, his deep voice sharp and rough like a hacksaw. Everyone shrinks away, obviously fearful of the cold Kingsley losing it in the ballroom.

But my heart clenches, the tears which abated making a resurgence. I let out a ragged exhale, which somehow draws his attention away from Timothy. His head spins toward me, his eyes skating over my face and my body as if making sure I'm okay.

I nod, my cheeks wet, and I realize the tears I've been holding in for so long have finally broken past the dam inside me.

I'm not alone anymore.

It's as if my body knows everything will be okay because he's here.

And I can finally cry.

A flash of pain appears in Steven's eyes, and he locks his jaw before releasing a growl. Whipping his face toward Timothy, who is turning purple, he leans in, and murmurs, "How does it feel, being completely helpless? You fucking piece of shit—"

"Steven. Hey, Steven, let him go." Jack Szeto appears out of nowhere, bringing at least a dozen staff members who are busy dispersing the crowd surrounding us, and waiters float by with trays of alcohol, as if plying the bystanders with spirits will somehow make them forget the insanity happening now.

Jack whispers in Steven's ear as his hand slowly releases Steven's clenched fingers. Steven's broad frame shudders before his head dips in a curt nod. Blowing out a deep exhale, he releases Timothy, who bowls over and gasps for breath.

"K-Kingsley," he chokes out, "You'll be sorry. We'll s-sue you—"

"Mr. Voss, please kindly shut your trap and recuperate in the backroom," Jack commands, his voice strong and clear, leaving no room for arguments. "We don't condone sexual assault or harassment at The Orchid toward any of our patrons or our employees. Your membership is revoked immediately."

Timothy staggers to his feet, his face still flushed red with sweat dripping down his forehead. He points to Jack. "Y-You can't do that. You aren't an Anderson."

"He can, and just in case there's any confusion, I'll repeat what he said. Your membership is revoked, effective immediately, and I don't recommend bringing in the lawyers, or else you'll have to deal with my family and I'm sure we can out-lawyer you." Ryland Anderson steps up and signals a few security members to drag a screeching Timothy away.

"Nobody gets away with treating me like this, Kingsley. Fuck you, your family, and your whore!" Timothy roars as he disappears from the room.

Steven growls and darts toward the man, looking like he's ready to finish his threats.

Jack grips his arm and holds him back. He murmurs something to Steven, who slowly relaxes and is now straightening his suit jacket as best as he can, his face completely devoid of emotion, appearing very much the King of Wall Street I met nine months ago in the conference room.

Ryland's gaze skates over to me and I mouth, *thank you*. His lips tilt up in acknowledgment before he and Jack stride away, disappearing into the crowds, no doubt to perform some damage control, leaving Steven and me behind in the corner of the room.

"Don't you *dare* say I'm mistaken, Grace," Steven grits out, his gaze pinning me in place. "Don't you *fucking* dare."

The pounding beats in my chest are now a war chant and all the nerve endings on my skin come alive. My chest lifts and falls rapidly as my breathing grows erratic, and I watch him prowl toward me, each step slow and measured.

"Steven, I..."

"What happened to you, Grace? Why did you disappear?"

My feet back up toward the wall behind me.

"Why are you here?" he rasps, his eyes darkening, his pupils flaring.

Three steps away.

"Why are you dressed like this?"

Two steps away.

"Why did you *leave me?*"

His words break toward the end. The anguish in his voice is a sharp knife to my bleeding chest, ripping my breath away.

He's right in front of me and I peer up at him, watching those pupils overtake his irises like the nighttime sky swallowing the moon. His breaths mingle with mine, and his fingers drag up my arms, eliciting a tremble from me.

My lips part as my voice continues to elude me. I can only stare helplessly at him, watching him fill my vision, my body softening under his as he presses me against the wall, and I realize he has backed me into a small alcove out of sight from most patrons. His heat surrounds me, obliterating any rational thought.

Steven's head dips, his gaze darting to my lips before returning to my eyes. He rasps, "I should've done this that night on your doorsteps."

Before I can even process those words, his hands clutch my face, and he slams his lips to mine.

His kiss is savage. Possessive. All-consuming.

He breathes life into my lips as he steals pieces of my soul away with each swipe, each suction. Groaning, he bears down on my body, no distance separating us, and a desperate ache forms in my sex as the last vestiges of rational thought fall away.

Moaning, I bring my hands to his neck, my fingers digging into the thick, soft strands of his hair, gripping it, tugging it. He groans as he deepens the kiss and thrusts his tongue inside me, tasting me like I'm a wine he can't get enough of. His steel erection digs into my stomach and wetness seeps through the thong I have on. My hips gyrate of their own accord, my body rubbing against his hardness and he grunts in pleasure or pain.

"Fuck me, Grace. Your lips taste just like I thought they would. Sweet. Addictive. Unforgettable. Just like you. God, the things I want to do to you," he rasps as we part for air.

Before I can respond, he pulls me under the sea of pleasure again, his teeth tugging and biting my bottom lip, sending sharp currents of pleasure straight to my clit. He angles my face and traces kisses down my jaw, sucking at the sensitive pulse points in my neck, his hand skating up and grazing the hardened nipples thrusted out from my dress, needing his attention.

"Steven, oh my God," I whimper as he plucks one of the beaded points over the fabric.

"Yes, Grace. Fuck, you're so sweet. You fucking drive me *insane*. I've gone mad without you. I don't know why the fuck I ever thought we could be friends. Grace, do you want me the same way I want you? Tell me you do."

He releases my nipple and moves onto the other side, and I melt against him, my thighs clenching, unable to relieve the building pleasure between my legs.

I need him. I need these clothes off our bodies. I need his cock inside me. If we weren't in public, I'd—

The thought is akin to a foghorn roaring next to my ear.

We're in public and anyone can walk in and see us.

The noises of the casino games rush in like a howling hurricane and I push him away, my lungs desperate for air. He looks stunned, his eyes glazed over, pupils blown. His lips are swollen—I must've bitten him back in the throes of passion.

Steven makes a grab for me again, and I tear myself away from him, and make my escape from the room, keenly aware of dozens of eyes trailing after me.

"It's not over, Grace!" he hollers at my fleeing back.

And I have a feeling life as I know it will never be the same.

CHAPTER 19
Steven

"WHERE THE FUCK IS the updated analysis on TransAmerica, Chuck? It was fucking due an hour ago. We have a hostile takeover situation on our hands in case you've forgotten. I have a meeting and it's still not here on my desk," I bark into my phone as stammers come through the line. Heat travels up my spine and my nostril flares at his ineptitude.

Fucking Chuck Dumbass. Only cares about the glamour the lifestyle of an investment banker offers him. The money. The women. Doesn't care to put in the work and sacrifices.

"Hayley was supposed to send it to you. I asked her—"

"Did I give her the work or give you the work, Chuck? Stop fucking with me. You're wasting my time."

"Sorry, sir. I'll get—"

I slam the phone on the receiver, not wanting to listen to any more excuses from this idiot. Yet another task he failed, and I don't want to put up with it anymore.

My team is only reserved for the best of the best and I've given him too many chances in the last few years. My patience and tolerance have disintegrated to nothing in the past few months. I don't care who his father is—if we lose him as a client, I'll figure out some other way to make up the fucking twenty-five percent of our portfolio.

My eyes sweep over my desk as I grit my teeth. *Fucking mess. Why is my desk a fucking mess?* Attempting to inhale a few calming breaths, my lungs burn with rage.

My fingers twitch, and I rearrange the stacks of papers on my desk. The binders by color. Red on the left for urgent. Black on the right for medium priority. I adjust the pens in the penholder. *Who the fuck took out all the blue pens?* One blue, one red, one black. Everything in its precise place.

Yet, the scorching anger inside me doesn't abate, the flames threatening to swallow me whole.

"Fuck!" I swipe the binders off my desk, my mood treacherous, a fuse lit by the smallest spark. I pace in front of the desk and rub my temples.

Everything is slipping out of my control—Voss suddenly declaring war and acquiring shares at the speed of light. Me embarrassing him in front of everyone at The Orchid didn't help the situation and despite the pinch of guilt for worsening the situation, I couldn't help the rage slashing through me at how he manhandled Grace. And now, we're stuck with a rapidly escalating situation and we're trying to play catch up. My sleep is nonexistent and my mood swings all over the place.

Calm down, Steven. What's wrong with you?

I don't want to know. I don't want to think. I just want to be the calm, collected self I used to be. The person who didn't feel anything.

The person who had the fucking void in his chest.

Closing my eyes, I think about my Plan B now that Chuck Bright failed my test for him. I always have a backup plan, my own set of analysis I put together over the last two days at the crack of dawn, when I'd arrive at the dark office, and be the only soul holed up within these concrete and glass walls.

When I could hear the sounds of my breathing and would inevitably think about Grace.

But now, she has reappeared in my life, and while everything is still chaotic, a sharpness has entered my vision, a clawing need to find her again.

Because as soon as I saw her crying that day when she barreled into the courtyard, logic flew out the window. My mind became even more restless, my waking hours no longer driven by work and dollars and cents.

That's the thing with time. In some situations, time is water, washing away dirt and grime, cleansing you from within. In other situations, time is wind, fanning the embers into a blaze, until the inferno blazes through everything in its path.

It's the latter with Grace and seeing her for the first time after nine long months of drought is the spark setting off an explosion in the fuel-rich, dried grasslands ripe for a disastrous wildfire.

I asked Ryland to look for a Grace Peyton working at The Orchid after Jack's celebration in the courtyard and he said he'd ask some folks for me, but they hadn't gotten back to him yet. But now that I saw her again last night at the casino party, I know she fucking works there for sure. Now, I just need him to track down where she works within the fifty-story building. My hands resist the urge to grab my phone and check the text messages to see if he has an update.

I have no time for this. Too much is at stake. Father. The way he looked so crestfallen when I flew out last month to meet with the TransAmerica board of directors, spewing out confidence I no longer carry. Timothy Voss and his increasingly unpredictable and unhinged behavior, leaving red herrings one after the other, sending my team on a wild goose chase trying to identify the next shareholder on his hit list.

Maybe my thoughts of Grace have derailed my much-lauded focus, allowing Voss to sneak in like a venomous snake and latch himself onto his next victim.

I should be furious with myself. Angry at her for vanishing, then reappearing out of thin air, causing me to become distracted, my logic and clarity thrown to the wayside like yesterday's trash.

But then, when I saw her again last night amid the crowds gambling, dressed in a tight, curve-hugging black dress, all thoughts of anger and my last vestiges of control vaporized. She looked like a seductress, sweeping around the room to collect the hearts of unsuspecting men.

But it's her eyes, the beautiful violet eyes that made regular appearances in my dreams the last few months, that robbed me of my breath when I caught her before she could tumble to the ground. The spark may have dulled in them, but a glimmer of a fire still shined within. A sadness cloaked over those irises. Loss. Heartbreak. Shock. And many more emotions flitted across those purple hues before she pushed me away, sinking a dagger in my chest at yet another refusal to acknowledge me.

To acknowledge us.

And when I saw the fucker put his hands on her, touching what's mine, scathing, fiery blood coated my vision. I would've killed him if Jack didn't pull me away. If he didn't whisper in my ear, "Don't scare her off. She's rattled. She needs you."

Then there was the kiss. How I finally allowed myself to taste her, letting my lungs inhale a full breath for the first time since she disappeared. The way she melted in my arms, her soft little body rubbing against my hard muscles and steel cock, the little sounds she made as we dug into each other like we were feasting after walking in the desert with no food for weeks.

I can't bring myself to regret, to care about Father's warnings about the liabilities of emotions.

And perhaps the price to pay is TransAmerica.

Gritting my teeth, my eyes flutter open and I stare at the way the late afternoon sunlight reflects on the ceiling, the ripples dancing on the smooth surface like a lover's embrace, as if it's latching onto it, knowing as soon as the sun moves position, they'll be torn apart and have to wait for another day to be reunited.

Whimsical thoughts. Irrational dreams. All symptoms of a sickness only she can cure.

"Fuck," I mutter under my breath as I get up from my chair and drop to my haunches by the floor, picking up the binders and pens scattered on the carpet like blood splatter in a crime scene.

I heave in a breath, exhale, and repeat the motion. I sort the binders and pens by color and place them in their proper spots on the desk. Red on one side, black on the other. Three pens of each color are precisely aligned by the notepad.

But my heart wouldn't stop racing, the slideshow of Grace in my mind wouldn't stop playing. The peace and calmness wouldn't come. The longing, which abated briefly when I held her into my arms, when I almost fucked her in public, comes roaring back in full force.

Ping.

Grabbing my cell phone, I swipe to the incoming text message.

Ryland

> Grace Peyton works as a dancer at Trésor. She goes by Genevieve. Her shift begins in half an hour. Don't do anything rash, Steven.

Too late.

I'm already shrugging on my suit jacket, grabbing my keys and halfway out the door before the sentence fully sinks in.

I need to see her. I need answers.

And I want those motherfucking lips on mine again.

——— · ———

My fingers fiddle with my watch in a nervous rhythm. I'm probably getting smudges on the stainless silver straps and glass face, but I don't care anymore. I take it off, tracing the carving on the backside, *mind over matter*, wishing it were that simple, that somehow, my mind can stop this desperate craving I have for her.

All I know is, behind these elaborate double doors decorated with an intricate, glass crescent design, I'd find the woman who has become an obsession, her absence only stoking the flames of the fire which began all those months ago.

The Rose floors, which take up several floors of this building, house different clubs and rooms for various proclivities. There's something for everyone. Rumor is, there's even an indoor "forest" with sounds of the nature, faux moonlight, and star-lit skies for people who like to do the deed in the great outdoors but don't want to worry about a shutter happy paparazzi capturing photos that should never see the light of day.

I've never been to any of these specialty clubs or rooms because I've never felt the need to. One night with a companion every three months in a luxury suite equipped with adult toys and specialty furniture feels enough. Sufficient to slake an inconvenient urge.

An urge that vanished ever since she disappeared.

I can't believe she's been right under my nose all this time.

Taking a deep breath, I push open the doors and enter Trésor, the burlesque club I know many of my peers spend their evenings in, claiming the girls are sexy, the atmosphere is sinful without being gaudy, and the service is impeccable.

Sultry music plays from the speakers, the bass vibrating in my ears. The central space is large, almost three times the size of the bullpen at Pietra, with the walls lit up in dark violet, just like her eyes. Four lighted columns are at the corners of a rectangular stage, which is also backlit by the glass floor and punctuated by three silver poles, currently being occupied by three svelte women in glittering lingerie, contorting their bodies into impossible poses. Groups of men sit at circular tables surrounding the stage, apparently mesmerized by the dancers twirling around the poles.

My dick doesn't twitch at the half-dressed women, my blood doesn't heat from the spicy, smoky fragrance lingering in the air, my loins don't stir as I scan the surroundings, noting several private rooms on the right and a row of private, darkened stalls on the left where some men are groaning as they receive lap dances from the girls.

Sex and sin are in the air, but my mind is only focused on one thing—finding Grace, or Genevieve, and the desperate tugging renews in my gut. Suddenly, the music changes to another sexy, jazz piece, a singer decked out in a sequin dress rasping sultry lyrics into the microphone, something about sirens and possession. The three dancers disappear into the small crowds and giggles and hushed laughter fill the air.

My breath freezes in my lungs as a vixen appears on stage, her rich brown tresses curled into loose waves, falling over her chest and back. She's wearing a glittering, fitted jacket, which covers her entire torso, ending at the tops of her thighs, hiding everything, and yet showing swaths of skin and legs clad in fuck me, leather boots.

Grace.

She smiles coyly at the crowd, her hips swaying to the music, her fingers playing with the lone gold button keeping the blazer from falling open and revealing her charms. Her cleavage glimmers under the violet light, tempting anyone with a pair of functioning eyes. She bites her luscious, blood-red pout and dips her torso toward the floor, thrusting out her round ass, still mostly hidden by the jacket.

Blood rushes straight to my cock as the chattering in the room quiets into the background, the pulsing in my ears matching the sultry thumps of the song. My mind can't reconcile the innocent intern who was temptation embodied in those early hours in the office and this sexual seductress on the stage.

My legs move of their own accord, my mind mucked with lust and heat, and I find an empty table in front of the stage and sit down, my hands grabbing the cool, marble table in a last-ditch effort to keep my wits about me.

Grace unleashes another deadly smile as she gyrates her hips to the music, her motions fluid and languid, her fingers trailing over the jacket to cup her breasts, giving them a thorough squeeze. Her lips part as if she's moaning, and I almost come in my pants.

She flicks open the lone button on her jacket and the flimsy material pools on the floor, revealing her tight little body clad in a diamond-studded bra and thong, the lingerie barely concealing anything. Her tits sway and shake with the music as she closes her eyes, her hands trailing down the slender column of her neck, graze her luscious, creamy tits, smooth over her the pale expanse of her belly, and cover the little scrap of fabric over her pussy.

My mouth waters as I curl my fingers around the edge of the table, the marble digging into my palms, but I don't notice the pain.

She falls to the ground and humps the floor, her plump ass rising and falling in rapid succession, and a collective groan of torture reverberates in the room as everyone focuses on her sensual rhythm. It's almost like she's fucking an invisible person in full view of everyone.

My cock is rock hard, the boiling heat in my veins burning with a mixture of lust and anger. My hands curl into fists as I attempt to swallow the lump in my throat, every muscle in my body fighting the impulse to rush up on the stage and pull her off it, to hide her from the leering glances of the men in the room. I want to haul her to one of the private rooms, kiss the living daylights out of her as I tear the little scraps of clothing from her body, and pound into her tight pussy until she sees stars.

Her eyes flicker open as she scans the room, a teasing grin on her face, but the merriment doesn't reach those violet pools. Somehow, that dimness is a blade to my chest, the scything agony so piercing, it shatters the mist of lust and I break out into a sweat.

Her eyes widen when they fall on me, and her rhythm falters. She gnaws her lips—this time it's not a ploy to be seductive—her legs trembling for a second before she twists her mouth into a smile, much more forced than before. Her gaze flits away and a flush creeps up her pale skin and her body moves in a series of practiced moves, but now they seem more robotic.

The last chords of the music soon fade into silence with her last pose being her lying supine on the ground, her tits arched up in the air, her chest rising and falling rapidly. The room erupts into applause and hollers from the men. She flies off the stage in a hurry, like she's being chased by a monster.

I don't think so, little Grace.

I follow suit, my legs carrying me as fast as I can toward the innocent vixen who has my heart in a twist, my dick as hard as a rock, my mind in a craze.

I ignore the pointed stares and hushed whispers as I run toward her, my hand tugging my tie loose from my neck, my lungs needing more air, more oxygen to clear this murderous rage scorching inside me like a volcanic eruption. Reaching her in a few strides, I grab her arm and spin her around right before she darts into a door to the back rooms.

"Grace." Her name comes out in a hoarse pant, my voice barely recognizable.

Her eyes flash in something unrecognizable as she wenches her arm free. "It's Genevieve."

"I don't care. We're leaving."

My free hand flies over my torso, unbuttoning the double-breasted jacket—there are too many damn buttons—and I throw my jacket over her shoulders, wanting to hide her from the world. I grip her wrist and tug her toward the front doors, not caring I'm causing a scene as she struggles half-heartedly before stomping on my feet with her shoes.

Pain flashes through me and I let go of her, the lava in my veins corroding my insides in an agonizing burn. Another refusal. Another rejection.

"Why?" That's the only word I'm capable of at the moment. The ache shoots to my chest and I can't breathe once again.

She swallows and wobbles back a few steps. Her large eyes glisten with unshed tears in the dim light and she shakes her head. "I don't want you to see me like this."

Unable to comprehend, I close our distance and grab her hands again. Rational thought has pulverized into dust. I just need her to leave this place with me. Then we can figure everything else out.

I don't know what happened all those months ago. I don't know how she ended up here. I don't know why she seems so despondent.

I just know I want—no, need—to take care of her, to get her out of here, to solve all her problems. For the first time in my life, I want to risk it all—my heart, my emotions, all the dead pieces of me I've accumulated in the darkness over the years. I want to curl myself around her and surround myself with everything that's her. I know she'd take good care of all my broken shards, invisible scars, and ripping seams.

And I want to do the same for her.

And she wants me. I know she does. That scorching kiss. She has to want me back, right?

"We're leaving. You're miserable. You can't work here," I growl, renewed resolve lacing through me, pulling her beside me once more, the red haze from moments ago still clouding my senses.

"No!" She flings my hand away, her eyes flashing in anger. "You don't get to waltz back into my life after everything. You don't get to tell me what I can and cannot do. I'm doing fine. Leave me the hell alone."

She whirls away and darts into the back rooms, leaving me with a bleeding wound in my chest, my tattered heart lying at her feet.

CHAPTER 20
Grace

I CAN'T STOP THINKING about him.

Truthfully, I don't think I've ever stopped in all our months apart.

Even now, as I'm typing away in front of a computer, my thoughts drift to how he stormed the halls of Trésor looking for me. I knew he was going to find me again sooner than later, but nothing could've prepared me for how my skin would tingle when I felt his gaze boring into me as I danced on the stage. This fierce possessiveness in his eyes.

But then he had to come and act like a caveman, dragging me out like I had no free will, not even attempting to find out why I was there and why I didn't want to face him.

And that really pissed me off.

"You almost done here?" Sofia asks as she sweeps up her dark brown hair into a ponytail.

"Almost. Maybe five or ten more minutes."

Typing a few lines of Excel formulas in the spreadsheet on her computer, I run the latest assessments on companies that have peaked Elias's interests in the last few months. Sofia lets me use her office for my research on her brother's behalf.

"You know, my brother's company has a great research position. He'd be more than happy to forgive our loan to you. You're clearly happier amongst numbers than on the dance floor."

I shake my head. The curious thing is, if the Kents were not embroiled in the criminal underworld, I wouldn't have minded working under Elias. He's sharp and seems to respect my intelligence. He always comes back with thought-provoking questions on the investment run-downs I provide him, which, ironically, has sharpened my skill set in the financial analysis arena much better than textbooks and courses could do. He may be a walking dark cloud simmering with danger, but I don't typically see that side of him.

Part of me wonders why he's involved with the Andersons, and I asked him a few months ago when he left The Orchid the same time I did after my shift ended.

He let out a deep, raspy chuckle and said, "Perhaps you think I'm the bad guy, the criminal. But don't you think these large corpo-rations are criminals too? They're just more accepted. And it's the twenty-first century. The days of flinging around knives and hustling on street corners are over. It's all about connections, whether you're a legitimate business or a company with a more *colorful* background. And connections are the one thing I do have."

With that interesting tidbit, he strode away, disappearing into the night like a phantom in some gothic story.

"I want to do this on my own, pay off the debt once and for all, and start off with a clean slate." I give Sofia a smile and she nods in understanding.

As the most powerful woman on the Rose floors, Sofia's looks can be very deceiving. Her tall, graceful physique reminds me very much of Taylor, but when chaos happens on the floors, you'd see the transformation to a sharp, lethal predator before your eyes.

"Well, lock up when you're done here. If you need me at Trésor tonight, you know how to find me." She gives me a wave and disap-pears from the doorway.

The last thing I want to do is to depend on another person or be indebted to a man. Look what happened the last time I opened up my heart to trust a man? He took away the very opportunity that would've saved my family.

But he didn't know. You never told him, Grace.

I've had this argument in my head many, many times and while I don't directly blame Steven for what happened with the job offer at Pietra, I'm angry at the patriarchy, at the men sitting at top of the food chain, making all the decisions, holding onto all the power.

I should've gotten the job offer. My performance alone spoke volumes. But alas, one man decided I wasn't worthy, and therefore, took it away without even giving me a second thought. And Steven, well, he delivered the death blow with sympathy, but it was still a fatal hit, and he had absolutely no idea how much it devastated me.

He should've fought for me.

How do you know he didn't?

Logic doesn't come into play when you're hurt.

Regardless, it was a necessary reminder not to get my hopes up, and rich men always hold the power in relationships.

It's always the woman getting hurt in the end.

The power imbalance is too great, and if I were to tell him everything now and he came in riding on his white horse, rescuing me from my job here, I'd be indebted to him for good. It'd set my heart up for more heartbreak, for more disappointments.

The only person I should rely on is myself.

After I sent off the completed spreadsheets and answered Elias's probing questions in his email, I lock Sofia's office and head to Trésor for my shift for the night.

I change into my outfit for the evening, the pearl and chain minidress, the one that shocked Steven into stillness in the courtyard. It's one of my favorites really, if it only had more fabric affixed to it. I check my reflection in the mirror, noting my makeup, a sharp cat-eye with classic red lipstick I've come to love, and whirl toward the lounge.

My pulse races at who I may encounter there tonight. Will he show up now that he has found me? Or would he stay away?

"Genevieve! I'm so glad I caught you before you went out there," Camille screeches in excitement as she nearly smacks me in the face as I am about to step through the dressing room doors.

"What? Did something happen? Are you okay?"

"I'm completely fine. In fact, I have the night off...with pay, I might add." She grins at me, her face beaming like she won the lottery.

"And here I thought you like shaking your ass off in public."

"Hey! It's because I like *the power*, lady. You still don't get it. We hold *all* the power out there. When on earth can we literally, well almost literally, grab rich men by their balls and make them obey us?"

Rolling my eyes, I move to brush past her, but she stops me with her hand. "Aren't you going to ask me why I have the night off with pay?"

"I'm assuming some rich guy gave you a hefty tip?" Which happens often as Camille, with her sunny disposition and California bombshell looks, frequently has men throwing themselves at her feet.

"No! Some rich dude bought out the entire place for the evening. Paid for all the girls for the night. Said we can use it as vacation. But..." She bites her lip, and her large eyes appearing a tad guilty. "His only request is you have to stay. Sorry, Gen."

Fucking Steven Kingsley. I'd bet my life it's him.

My lips flatten as heat rushes up in my chest. My heart breaks into a sprint, making laps inside my rib cage. Whether it is from anger or in celebration, I can't tell. Part of me is furious at him forcing his way into my life again despite my rebuffs, but a tiny piece of me, tucked carefully away with the girl who once believed in wishing stars and interesting facts of the world, flickers alive, sending out shivers of anticipation through my veins.

He cares about me enough to try again.

Swallowing the sandpaper in my throat, I force out a smile. "Thanks for letting me know. I'll see what he wants from me. Enjoy your night."

"Rock his world and let loose! Remember, *you* hold all the power," Camille calls after me before dissolving into chuckles.

With my breath lodged firmly in my chest, I step into the darkened lounge, finding Steven Kingsley, in all his modelesque physique, looking far too good in a black, slim fit suit, sitting man-spread on one of the tufted sofas in the back, with the sole spotlight of violet hues shining on him, as if I'd miss him.

The King of Wall Street in full force.

I heard from Elias he got promoted to Chief Operating Officer at Pietra three months ago, the youngest man to head up the most prominent investment bank in the country.

But he looks tired. Haunted. Alone.

I don't miss how he seems to be more haggard than nine months ago, or the pain reflected in those piercing hazel eyes. I don't miss how there's a day's worth of scruff on his usually clean-shaven face or how his tie is not perfectly knotted and is slightly askew. His beautiful lips are flattened, like he's trying to leash in his emotions.

The same lips that took me in savagery at the casino event and made me forget about everything around me.

My heart seizes and clenches, much like the way it did when he said my name in the hallway as he passed by my cubicle to his office. Except now it's much worse. The butterflies, which I thought to have long disappeared, flap their wings wildly inside me as I walk toward this intimidating man who has stolen my heart without my permission.

I need to calm myself and put some mental distance between us until I can figure out what I want from him, if anything.

"Grace." His deep, rumbly voice, sexy and smooth like the finest whiskey, ghosts over my skin, sending shivers down my body.

Letting out a small exhale, I fight the urge to clench my legs and instead stand up straighter and sway my hips for good measure as I approach him, the pearls of my dress colliding together in a soft rhythm. His eyes darken as they drag down the length of my body, his nostrils flaring, and I can see the rippling in his corded throat as he swallows.

"Mr. Kingsley. I thought I told you not to come back." My voice is huskier than I'd like. It seems like my body disobeys me whenever I'm in his presence.

I stop two feet in front of him, watching his gaze trail up from my legs, pausing at my heavy breasts, then up to my face. Instead of feeling gross like I usually do when other men focus their attentions on me, my skin feels hot and my nerve endings spark with sensations as heat travels to my core.

His posture is deceptively relaxed, like a king lounging on his throne, assessing his empire before him. But a vein pulses on his forehead and I see the quickening of his breathing.

"I don't give up." His voice is a low rasp. "I need to know what happened, Grace. Why did you quit out of the blue and disappear? Why are you here now?"

I bite my cheek before responding, the wings flapping even more violently in my gut. My body wars with two impulses, to tell him to fuck off and to crawl onto his lap, bury my face in his chest, and breathe in greedy gulps of ocean breeze and leather.

I hold on to the first emotion arising from his question.

Pride.

"I don't want to tell you."

Steven sits up, his gaze sharpening as the predator wakes up inside him. "Did someone threaten you? Please, tell me. Let me help you. It can't be because of the job offer, right? I told you I was going to put out recommendations for you."

"I'm here voluntarily. That's all you need to know. I don't think we have anything in common anymore, Mr. Kingsley. I'm no longer working for you. I'm no longer your employee. I don't owe you anything."

My body spins away as I ball my hands into fists. *Distance, that's what I need, and the madness will dissipate. It's always the woman that gets hurt in the end.* I take one step toward the dressing room.

"Aren't you my *friend*?"

The words are soft, and yet they sound the loudest of them all. Heartbreak seeps into those simple four words, and I roll my lips inward to stem a sob choking me in my throat. My chest clenches, the pain of a thousand cuts threatening to cave me in, but I remain standing.

I won't fall for anyone, or any man.

I won't let myself be hurt again.

Clearing my throat, I reply, "We were never ever really friends, Mr. Kingsley. Can a bird ever be friends with a fish in the ocean?"

I hear his sharp intake of breath behind me, followed by a deep shuddering exhale.

My heart constricts, and I regret my words instantly, knowing I've inadvertently wounded him.

"We'll never end well," I whisper into the darkness in front of me, more for myself than for him.

A few seconds of silence is punctuated only by the sounds of our heavy breathing, as we're no doubt embroiled in our own emotional turmoil.

The swirling madness threatens to pull us back into its grasp.

"I won't rest until I find out what you're hiding." His voice is molten steel, the blade sharp and deadly.

It helps. His anger keeps me tethered to the deep waters, where I should be instead of daydreaming about soaring in the skies.

"Well, I can't help you there."

I take a few more steps toward the dressing room, my pulse pounding in my ears.

"I bought the place for the night, *Genevieve*," he spits out my stage name like it's a dirty word. "Is this how you treat your paying customers?"

The agony in my chest flares and throbs, his cruel tone slashing fresh wounds in my chest. *Yes. Be angry, Steven. It's better for us this way. It'll never end well.*

Pulling my shoulders back, I paste a fake smile on my face and turn around, finding Steven's intense gaze boring holes into me. A muscle tics in his jaw, his lips flattening in displeasure, very much like the day he ripped into his team in the conference room, his control barely held together by the thinnest string.

"Why, Mr. Kingsley, that was remiss of me. I forgot you were my *paying* customer. Please forgive me for my oversight." I stride toward the control panel in the corner, my fingers shaking as I hit play on the random shuffle mode for the music.

Walking back toward him, my feet falter as I hear the first chords of "You're My Stars" radiating from the surround-sound speakers, every sultry beat and aching melody wrapping around my heart in a firm grip.

My eyes flash to Steven, finding his gaze impenetrable, a bottomless pool of black. His own chest rises and falls rapidly. His hands are clenched tightly, fingers digging into the plush seating.

I remember how he stood up on the stage at Lunasia, slowly rolling up his sleeves, revealing his sexy, muscular arms. How I wanted to trace the veins there and to kiss the tension out of his frame. Resuming my walk, my heart kicking against my rib cage, I approach him and gently push his tense shoulders back so he's settled on the sofa.

Slowly, I crawl on top of him, my legs straddling his, and I take my first inhale of his intoxicating scent, which rushes in my veins like a shot of adrenaline, giving me an instant high.

The song plays in the background and I sway my hips over his lap, my hands finding purchase on his shoulders. His nostrils flare and the inky darkness of his pupils completely overtakes the amber hues. His lips part and our breathing mingle in the mere inches between us, cloaking us in a sensual haze.

An aching heat climbs up my body, my skin feeling fevered as I press closer to his hips, rotating my ass in a way I know men love, and a moan escapes my lips as my chest grazes his.

Everything is different with him. The heavy-lidded gaze, the harsh pants of his breath, from any other man would make me cringe with revulsion, but with him...it makes me feel alive in a way I've never had before. I inch my dress up and settle my bottom firmly on his lap, my core clenching as his hard erection hits my clit. He hisses, his hands finding my waist.

I throw my head back and thrust my breasts toward his face, my nipples pebbling under the crystal pasties I had on tonight. Everything feels so heavy, so sensitive.

Belatedly, I realize his hands are on my body, and I wrench them away and whisper, my voice a throaty moan, "You can't touch me. Those are the rules."

Gritting his teeth, his nostrils flaring, he gives me a terse nod and fists his hands to the sides of his lap. I slowly unclasp the fastening behind my neck. I've never done a private lap dance for anyone before. It wasn't something I was comfortable doing, but somehow, when I saw him sitting here, all his coiled energy and banked tension focused on me, I couldn't stop myself. I want to drive him crazy with need, like he has ever since I met him.

You have all the power.

Camille's words echo in my brain, and for the first time, I believe her.

What else could explain the fevered gaze in Steven's eyes, the way his lips are parted in a half snarl, the way his muscles are locked and tense, like he's using all his remaining restraint to stop himself from reaching for me?

The thought gives me another rush of euphoria and I slowly let the top of my dress fall to my waist as I lean back on his lap, my hips ghosting over his steel rod in a rhythm driving me wild. I can feel my breasts swaying, mere inches away from his face.

"Fuck me," he groans as I straighten back up, my hands skimming my stomach before curling around each breast, playing with the heaviness, pushing them together, squeezing them, molding them. Every sensation is a caress straight to my core, and I can feel myself leaking out of my thong, but I couldn't care less.

The song crests, the singer belting out, "You're my stars in the skies, my everlasting high...our souls intertwined..."

I let out a whimper. The music. His body heat. The way his hardness yields to my softness. The way everything feels too sensitive, too raw.

My eyes flutter open, finding his heavy, half-lidded gaze moving from my aching breasts mere inches away from his mouth to my parted lips as I let out another moan.

The sensations in my pussy heighten with every pass over the tent on his pants and the last vestiges of rational thought leave my mind as I bear down on him, grinding my clit along his length.

"Holy fuck," he growls as his hips arch up, thrusting into me.

His hands find the tops of my ass and his fingers dig in so tightly it almost hurts, but only adds to the maddening pleasure gathering between us. The thought he shouldn't be touching me barely registers because I need his hands on me more than I need my next breath of air.

I gyrate and move faster, my tits shaking and swaying to the song. His nose skims the tips of my breasts, his teeth making an appearance as he scrapes across the tender flesh. I mewl, my body bouncing on him harder, the burning heat gathering between my legs like a storm. His thrusts are stronger, every movement swiping precisely past my entrance to my clit, unleashing fresh torrents of wetness, no doubt leaving a mark on his slacks.

But I don't care. My mind is on hiatus, my body a slave to the sensations only this man can provide to me.

He brings his lips up to my neck, softly kissing and sucking the tender column as I fall back once more, bouncing on his hard cock, which I'm surprised hasn't dug a hole out of his pants yet.

He nips and grazes my pulse points and growls, "Yes, you greedy girl, make yourself come on the cock that has been hard only for you for the past nine months."

His words belatedly register in my mind as the sharp pleasure builds to an aching point and I bear down, rubbing his tip over my swollen nub and everything explodes in a flash of white light and glittering stars. I let out a throaty scream, and he smashes his lips on mine, his hips thrusting erratically, humping my wet, thong-clad pussy. His tongue dives in and he conquers my mouth in a blazing heat and a thousand sensations, prolonging my orgasm, as the walls of my pussy throb in aftershocks.

With a loud groan, he shakes against me, his mouth still tangling with mine, as if trying to swallow me whole. I feel a wet warmth seeping from his pants, and he drops his head onto my breasts, his mouth panting heavily, his breaths sending shivers over my damp, sweat coated tits.

Another song is playing from the speaker now as my body cools down from the most mind-blowing orgasm I've ever had, and we didn't even have sex.

The sounds of our breathing are harsh in the room and a renewed heat crawls up my face as I realize what we just did, how I performed my first lap dance for him and came all over his lap.

Belated horror crashes into the party, an unwelcome guest, and I scramble off his lap, my hands shaking while I adjust my dress and pull everything back in place.

My legs wobble and my eyes finally sweep back up toward his face and what I see sends another scorching heatwave through me.

Fevered eyes. Parted, swollen lips. My lipstick smudged on his face.

His hands are curled against his lap in tight fists once more as he sits there, stupefied, his nostrils flaring, like he wants to haul me back into his arms and finish what we started.

My core clenches, feeling empty, needy, achy for him, and I quickly back away a few more paces.

"Hope my performance was satisfactory, Mr. Kingsley. And you're banned from Trésor from now on. You can't disrupt my life like this." If I explain to Sofia about the situation, she'll back me up. I know she will.

He flinches.

And like a coward, I run away.

CHAPTER 21
Steven

JAB. SWISH. JAB.

I parry and dodge the foil aiming for my neck and torso from what seems to be multiple directions as Ryland and I move on the piste, the mat in the fencing club next to the boxing gym within The Orchid.

Sweat drips down my hair within my mask. My body, encased in the classic white fencing uniform, is burning with residual energy from last night at Trésor with Grace. She fucking ran away from me again after she came so sweetly on my lap, leaving me with a hard on to end all hard ons even after I came in my pants.

Why won't she let me help her? Grunting, I block an attack from Ryland, my mind in a convoluted mess.

Then there was the blistering phone call I received from Mother this morning.

"I couldn't believe it when Linda Winstead told me. You bought out a strip club for the entire night at The Orchid for a dancer? How could you? You're a Kingsley. This is appalling."

"It's none of your business, Mother. I'm not like Emily or Jess, and I won't listen to you."

She shrieks in my ear, her voice sounding more desperate, because she knows it's true. "Listen to me, Steven. You can't cavort with Grace Peyton. And yes, before you ask, I know all about her, about how she was an intern and now a dancer," she spits out the word like it's a curse, "and her background in the slums. You aren't allowed to be with her, Steven Kingsley, or I'll—"

I cut her off and hang up. No time for her bullshit when my life is literally in tatters.

Then, to add fuel to a roaring fire, my sources told me Hancock met with Voss early this morning and Hancock subsequently stormed out of the meeting in a fit of anger, his face purple as he sped away in his town car. I'm livid, pulling my hair out in trying to figure out what Voss is doing to get the board members of TransAmerica to dance to his tune.

I should be working, concocting my counterattack, getting on a plane to fly to LA to talk to Hancock and ask him what the hell he's thinking. But instead, I'm here, restless, unease swirling my insides, permeating every cell, every atom of my body. My mind is filled with fragments of her, twisting, resurfacing, coming together and falling apart again.

Everything is her.

Her smell. Her taste. Her touch.

The way she sauntered toward me, her tight body swaying in a sensual rhythm only innate to the opposite sex. The way those little pearls did the bare minimum to hide her smooth flesh from onlookers, each movement from her earning us a perverse peekaboo of those full tits and curvy hips.

How she felt against me, soft and silky, her scent of jasmine driving me crazy as my lungs clamored to draw in deeper inhales, to commit this sweet fragrance in memory, in case I didn't get to smell it at the source again.

The clang of our foils draws me back into the match as the heated blood circulates in my veins, carrying traces of her inside me, a high that has never waned with time or distance, an addiction that has only gotten worse with time.

My arm and wrist work in unison, my body lunging forward as I flick the sharp foil toward Ryland, my aim missing, and he easily parries away before counterattacking, a series of moves hitting me in the torso, the neck, the back. Each attack adds to the frenzied circus of my mind and my focus temporarily shatters into fragments as memories from last night force their way back into the forefront.

How my cock was as hard as a steel pipe when she unlatched the top of her dress, letting it pool around her hips and I got my first view of those heavy, tear-drop breasts, the outlines of her nipples beading into tight buds protruding from the sparkling stickers she had on.

The spicy smokiness of her arousal and the wet mess she made on my pants when she rubbed that hot little pussy on my dick like it was her favorite toy. How I nearly died on the chair from the need to pin her down and fuck her until we were both delirious from pleasure.

The way I came in my pants like an untried teenager after watching her eyes glazed over, her head tossed back in passion, her body spasming and melting against mine as she came with the sound of my name on her lips.

Then there was the glint of hurt and sadness in her eyes. The heartache in my chest when she said we were never friends.

And I recognize she's right.

How can we be friends when all I want to do is kiss her, taste her, sheath myself inside her until the end of time?

How could we be friends when I want to see her fall into pieces beneath me, coming apart at the seams from pleasure?

How could we be friends when my heart, this organ I thought was long charred and dead, reawakens in her presence, the thumping, fluttering, beating, rendering me into an incoherent mess, slicing the chain mail of my armor into pieces and scattering them onto the ground in her presence?

No. I want her. All of her. I want her to be *mine*.

Spotting an opening, Ryland lunges forward and jabs his foil in a series of moves, variations of high and low outsides, high and low insides, and before I knew it, the referee calls the match.

We perform a salute as a sign of respect before I rip off my mask and hoist it under my arm even though I want more than anything to fling it across the room, but that would be bad form in the sport.

"Fuck!" I mutter under my breath.

I should've taken up boxing like Adrian, Parker, or James. I used to make fun of them for how barbaric they were, wanting to use their fists to inflict bodily pain like savages, but now I see the wisdom, because this restrained sport with all the fucking rules and manners don't even make a dent in obliterating the swirling chaos inside me.

Ryland walks alongside me toward the locker room and showers. "What's going on with you? And don't tell me you're fine because whatever that performance was just now, that spoke volumes. Is it Genevieve?"

"Grace, her fucking name is Grace," I growl as I hurl a blistering stare at him.

He raises his hands and mimes backing off. "Fine, fine. Grace. That's the same girl from your company, right? The one you did the impromptu serenading for?"

At my silence, his brow arches. "Why is she working here, then? As a dancer? And why do you care?"

"I don't know why she's here. She didn't fucking get the offer from us because of some internal BS and then she disappeared without a trace. I bumped into her a few weeks ago at Jack's promotion celebration, and this whole fucking mystery has been haunting me ever since."

"And yet, you still deny having feelings for her."

Feelings don't even begin to describe the rabid obsession I have toward her, the craving to have her by my side again, as my woman, my partner at work, my...everything.

Shit. Shit. Shit.

I glare at him and head toward the locker, my mouth spewing curses as I miss the combination and have to try again. Even the fucking locker is conspiring against me today.

"Shit. You're in the deep end. I don't even hear a denial anymore," Ryland murmurs as he sheds his soiled uniform and drops it off in the hamper for housekeeping to clean. He wraps a towel around his waist and crosses his arms, his bare torso glistening with sweat, not giving me any personal space.

I wrap a towel around my waist and toss my hands into the air. "What the fuck do you want from me? To admit I'm a mess and I can't eat, sleep, think, or even focus on work? To tell you I'm feeling like a fucking failure because TransAmerica is getting stolen right under my nose and there's nothing I do can stop it? To tell you this maddening woman has driven me insane with need for most of this year and I fucking miss her so much my mind is filled with nothing but images of her, and now that I've found her, she won't tell me why she left me and why she's working for you instead of being with me?"

Ryland's mouth drops open, his slate eyes widening at my outburst. My pulse hammers like a drill in my ears and a sharp pain pierces my head. Headache. Just what I need at this moment.

He steps back and holds his hands up in surrender. "Technically, she works for Elias Kent since he provides us with the security and personnel for the Rose floors, but that's beside the point."

He swallows, his eyes dimming as he looks away. "Women are complicated. That's why you and I don't do relationships. But they have a way of sneaking past the gaps in our armor, attacking us when we least expect it."

He rakes his hand over his soot-colored hair and stares at a spot behind me, like he's in his own world, swimming in his own set of problems. "And you're helpless to stop them. But I know this. Sometimes they don't want us to be strong and to be assholes. They want us to be vulnerable and tell them our feelings. Just because I can't be that man doesn't mean you can't be."

His eyes sharpen as his gaze falls on mine again. "From what I can see, you're all in already. Why don't you try telling her how you feel? Maybe if you open up, she will as well."

With that parting thought, he disappears toward the showers, his head dipped low, his bearing rigid.

My lungs heave in a deep breath as I step into one of the private shower rooms and lock the door. I turn the faucet knob clockwise precisely five times, my body flinching at the icy rain washing over my sore muscles.

Father's warning from years past echoes inside me once again. A useless warning because he never told me how quickly it could happen to you. How, despite my so-called self-perceived brokenness, the moat and high walls of my castle, an unsuspecting storm from nowhere could come barreling in, toppling everything in seconds.

Emotions are liabilities, but it's too late for me. They escaped before I even noticed. She ensnared me without a single weapon.

Vulnerability.

It's something I've never done before because a Kingsley doesn't show weakness. A Kingsley doesn't flop belly up and hopes the other person pets you instead of stabbing you with a knife. Ryland's parting words filter in, digging their way into the quagmire of my mind, refusing to leave.

Would spilling my heart out make a difference?

Would telling her how I couldn't sleep the last nine months, not knowing where she was or how she was doing, how everything was tasteless on my tongue, how my world became dull and heavy again, make her come back to me?

Would telling her how the best time of my life was when we were sharing a bagel in the dark or when she curled against me as we watched a movie soften her stance?

As the frigid water cools my body temperature from the outside, a strange heat tingles at the base of my spine and travels to my newly beating organ.

My Grace is still in there...in that sexy vixen. The hurt in her eyes and the fierceness in her frame when we argued prove she still cares for me.

I've tried it my way—barging in and commanding, tackling the problem like any I've encountered at work, and it hasn't worked.

Of course it wouldn't work. She's not a project or a corporate target.

She's a fierce warrior with a soft heart, and there are no words in the world to describe everything that is Grace Peyton.

Could Ryland be right? What's the harm in trying?

Resolve permeates me as I scrub the sweat off my body, eager to find her and heal myself from this sickness once and for all.

I'm Steven Kingsley and I never lose.

Not now, not ever.

CHAPTER 22
Grace

THE RAIN IS COMING down in sheets, blurring the windows in a wall of water. I sit on the settee under the bay windows in the dressing room, having arrived earlier than necessary for my shift today due to the inclement weather. My hands trail the navy and white Chinoiserie fabric, no doubt imported from somewhere, like everything in The Orchid.

The skies are a swath of dreary gray, and the trees bordering Central Park sway against the fierce winds, the harried sounds muted through the double-paned glass. Storm clouds are low on the horizon, blanketing the city in an oppressive weight.

A relentless burning forms behind my nose. I know it's not because of the email I received earlier from Emerson Clarke, the investigator I hired in the search for my birth father. He mentioned while my birth certificate had no father listed on it; he was able to track down some leads through other records but would need more time to vet through them.

It's a disappointment, that's for sure. But it's not something completely unexpected. After all, the man never came to search for us. If he's so determined to stay hidden, he probably covered his tracks well.

I retrieve my purse from beside me, Mom's classic black leather flap bag she loved and protected her entire life. My guess is, it was a gift from my father, whoever he is. After unzipping it, I trace the inscription on the leather tag affixed to the inner lining.

The number of stars in the skies pales in comparison to my regard for you.

It's beautiful, if not bittersweet.

I could sense the love in the words, and yet, their story did not end well.

If only real life could imitate novels, where happily-ever-after is waiting for all of us at the end.

Maybe he isn't alive anymore, and Mom is finally reunited with him in the afterlife.

The pang in my chest deepens as my vision blurs. I failed the one thing I swore myself never to do, to give my heart away to a man who has no business being mine and followed in my mom's footsteps.

I can feel my resolve weakening, the temptation growing into a bottomless pit of hunger, famished for the exhilarating rush, the quickening of my breath, the fluttering in my gut only one person can give me.

Steven.

His impassionate words about helping me out of whatever predicament he thinks I've gotten myself into.

Would it be so bad to rely on someone else for once?

In times like this, when I'm staring into the dreary skies and the heavens pouring grief out from the clouds, I wonder how nice it would be to lean against a strong pair of shoulders, to close my eyes and relinquish all control, and to be loved and taken care of by someone else.

My throat tingles and thickens.

Riiing.

I look at the caller ID on my phone. My girls.

Forcing my face into a bright smile, I answer, seeing three concerned faces staring at me.

"What is this? An intervention?" I joke with a chuckle, which sounds fake even to my ears.

Taylor frowns, the black heart on her nose glinting from the lamplight in our apartment. "Grace, we're all worried about you. You haven't been yourself the last few weeks."

"What are you talking about?" I stand and pace around the room.

"You were staring into space when we watched the finale of *Sex and the City* last weekend. That's your favorite episode!" Belle frowns.

"I don't even know when the last time I heard a random factoid from you was," Millie adds and lets out a sigh. She looks like she's in her bedroom.

Taylor runs her hands through her inky strands and arranges them into a bun. "Don't bother denying it. You've been dull since you left your banking job and then everything went downhill when Mom passed."

Her eyes take on a wet sheen. She clears her throat, her voice thickening, before continuing, "I know it's been hard with Mom gone. I miss her a lot too, Grace. But I don't think that's it. You've been a shadow of yourself, especially the last few weeks, and we've all noticed it."

Plopping back down on the settee, my hand smooths the white silk wrap-dress, my fingers rearranging the fine fabric so the thigh high slit isn't as prominently displayed.

"Nothing is going on, girls. You guys are too sensitive. Can't a girl just have some off days?"

Millie raises her brow and exchanges a glance with Belle, who has joined Millie in the bedroom.

"Just ask," Belle hisses, nudging Millie in the ribs.

"Fine. Fine." Millie winces before turning her face toward the camera again. "You don't have to tell us if you don't want to, but is this sudden depression because of a man?"

"What man? You know I don't do relationships—"

"Adrian told me the other night during our weekly check-in call that Steven seems to be in a funk over you. I know you told us not to update you on him after you left the job, but he hasn't been eating, sleeping, or anything. I think he even missed some TransAmerica shareholder meetings, and that is unheard of. At least that's what Adrian said he heard from Rex Anderson, who I think heard from Ryland."

Belle rolls her eyes heavenward. "These men gossip more than we do, I swear—"

"What? Steven hasn't been taking care of himself?" My heart stutters to a stop at the image of Steven suffering.

His haunted eyes, gauntness in his handsome face, the skewed tie and otherwise unkempt appearance in his standards. The way he grabbed onto me last night that seemed much more desperate than sex and lust. It was almost like he was gripping a life raft and fighting to stay afloat.

My eyes burn and my lips tremble. I bite my cheek, hoping the sharp pinch of pain will keep me from crying.

Taylor and the girls exchange another glance, if that's even at all possible during a video call, and Millie straightens up. "Grace, we know you're hiding something, and we want you to know we love you and we'd never judge you for *anything* you're doing for whatever reason. We fully support you." Her eyes sharpen with knowledge, and I let out a shuddering exhale.

"W-What do you mean?" My pulse roars in my ears as dread snakes its way in.

Millie winces and blows out a deep breath before blurting, "We know you're dancing at a burlesque and strip club."

My face heats. "You girls *know*?"

She nods. "Adrian told me Steven made a scene at the casino night at The Orchid and also bought out Trésor for a night for you. And you told us you were dancing, so it wasn't too hard to put two and two together."

Millie leans closer to her screen. "Grace, we don't know what's going on with the two of you, but we know this goes way beyond a *friendship*. If you guys are both so miserable and pining for each other, why don't you give him a chance? From everything I know about Steven, none of this behavior from him is normal. It's decidedly abnormal."

My eyes flutter shut as I think about him, the only man my heart has clamored for, the only person ever to make it skip multiple beats, riot against my rib cage like it wants to break free and join its partner nestled in his chest. The only man who's made me feel safe, whose words felt sincere. The only man, despite all our talks of friendship and ridiculousness, is the person closest to making me feel romantic love and longing, such that every day without him feels like an agonizing chore, and everywhere I go, I see and experience fragments of life I want to share with him.

I blink my eyes and sniffle, moisture coating my vision, and my lips tremble.

I miss him. I miss him a lot.

Somewhere along the way, he'd stolen my heart and never gave it back. The bird and the fish, pining for each other in a story that'd never end well. And yet, the yearning won't abate, and I feel irrevocably changed, like I'm incomplete without him.

"Oh, sweetie," Millie whispers, her own eyes turning red. She's the hopeless romantic among the four of us.

I pour my heart out, telling them what happened with the loan shark, with the job offer, and Belle's face turns ashen when she hears her role in introducing Sofia Kent to me and what I do here at Trésor.

"I-I didn't know, Grace. I should've found out what work she was looking for before recommending you. There's nothing wrong with working at the burlesque club, and I'd wholeheartedly support you if it's something I know you'd be interested in, but knowing you, it was probably the *last* thing you wanted to do. God, why are you so stubborn, woman? You could've just taken my money and saved yourself a lot of misery." Belle's face is flushed now as stares at me.

"I just don't want to depend on anyone. I don't want money to affect our friendship!"

"You dummy! It's okay to lean on someone else when you need help. That doesn't mean you are weak. In fact, I'd say it takes strength to ask and receive help. That's what friends are for. At least the ones that are worth keeping. You'd do the same for me!" Belle shakes her fists at the camera, her voice impassioned.

I bite my bottom lip to stem the fresh onslaught of tears threatening to break free from my eyes.

"You don't judge me for it? Dancing in scanty clothing in front of rich men?" I whisper, my voice thick and shaky.

The girls shake their heads vehemently.

"I just wish you told me. When the girls told me earlier, I couldn't believe it. But then, of course...how did you get such a large sum of money in such a short time to solve all our problems without the job offer?" Taylor sniffles on screen, her dark eyeliner running at the edges.

Her brows furrow and her slate eyes are clouded with guilt. "I should've asked more questions. I know you did everything for me, for our family, and you never complained or said a word about it. And if anyone should dance, it should be me. Heck, I'm the dancer in our family. I wouldn't have let you—"

"And that's why I didn't say anything. And it's fine."

"But on a brighter note, the fashion mogul in me has been wanting to compliment you on your attire and makeup the last few months, because it's time you're embracing God's gift instead of hiding away in frumpy clothes, but that's beside the point." Belle gives me a teary wink, her nose red, and I snort, the weight in my chest lightening.

She continues, "And being a dancer is badass. I could only imagine how you're getting all the men to drool over you. They can look but not touch. It's the ultimate power move."

My lips tilt into a smile as I think about what Camille said last night.

Taylor murmurs, "You know. Beauty is not a fucking weakness or a sin. I know you've hidden yourself because of Mom and the men in her life. She wouldn't have wanted that for you."

The heaviness I've been carrying in my chest lightens a fraction and I realize life is all about perspectives. I was so afraid others would be disappointed in me or look down on me, but it turns out they don't care. Perhaps I have been wearing the biggest lens of prejudice, oblivious to how it's been affecting my life.

I did what I needed to do for my family and it's something I should be proud of.

I look at the girls, finding their eyes warm and kind, still the very girls I'd take a bullet for. Maybe I've been living life all wrong.

Taylor swallows and lets out a shaky sigh. "Not all men are the devil, either. I know it's hard for us to open our hearts to men and shit when everyone we've known is a disappointment, but from what Millie tells me, Steven seems to be one of the good ones out there. Why don't you give him a chance?"

My lips twitch from the emotional sentiments of my curse words-loving sister. She has a soft, beautiful soul underneath the black polish and grunge makeup.

Millie nods resolutely. "I'm not saying this because he's my brother-in-law. I know he may be a workaholic and a cold hard ass sometimes, but he has a warm heart inside those suits and he treats his sisters well, including me. I've never seen him get so worked up over anything or anyone before. I don't know what's going on with the two of you, but if you're miserable and he's miserable, don't you think it's worth giving each other a chance?"

Suddenly, the door to the dressing room flies open and Camille bursts in, a cloud of bright energy and sizzling excitement. She pants heavily, like she ran up a flight of steps in high heels. "Genevieve. You need to come."

"What's going on?" I stand up, my phone in my hand, the girls still on the screen.

"Your man showed up an hour ago, and Sofia turned him away just like you asked. Well, he didn't take the hint, and..." She heaves in another large inhale, a few strands of blond hair sticking to her sweat misted skin.

My breath lodges in my throat as I hold my phone in a death grip. "And what? Spit it out, Camille."

Silence permeates the room except for Camille's soft panting and the faint sounds of the wind howling and the rain splattering against the glass from the outside.

Camille's eyes widen and she says, "He's outside in the rain, yelling for you."

CHAPTER 23
Steven

I'M OFFICIALLY INSANE. CERTIFIABLE.

Because nothing else can explain why I'm standing in one of the private courtyards on one of the top floors at The Orchid, drenched in the pouring rain as the storm rages around me. Thoughts of routines and orders have long been cast to the wayside, the urge to see her overpowering everything else.

Violent winds lash against the trees in anger, the water from the skies its weapon. Dark branches swing wildly in the air, a desperate ploy to escape the onslaught. Young spring blooms of muted colors lay scattered on the ground, the swirling waters carrying away the petals.

Another stormy day. Befitting my mood.

I could blame my lapse of sanity on my prolonged lack of sleep or stresses at work, but that would be a lie.

And there's one thing Steven Kingsley isn't...a liar.

I'm starving for her in my love-sick soul, desperate for anything she could give me. Grace. My star in the skies. The moon illuminating the night or the sun shining during the day. The calm in my rough waters.

My mind isn't thinking clearly anymore as desperation swirls around me with each of our interactions, every rejection from her another deep carving into my newly beating heart.

And so, I'm standing, drenched head-to-toe in icy rain, rivulets streaming down my face, soaking every inch of my bespoke Italian suit as I'm standing under a window which opens to a backroom at Trésor, angling to get her attention because she refuses to see me. And if this is the only way I can get her attention, so be it.

This space, one of the many courtyards interspersed on the fifty floors of the building, is the best location I could find after she banned me from visiting her at Trésor again.

I know she's scared, and that's why she keeps sending me away. Something terrible must have forced her into this situation. And perhaps, when I delivered the news about the job offer, I became another man who has disappointed her in the past.

But never again.

I'll knock down those tattered walls and wrap my arms around her, building us a fortress, so she'll always feel safe. She'll know she can tell me anything and that won't ever change my feelings for her.

We're a team and we can solve this.

"Grace Peyton, I know you're in there! I'm going to stand out here until you come and talk to me!" I holler again, my voice raw and hoarse from yelling the past twenty minutes.

Curious heads have gathered at the window of Trésor and other onlookers are loitering at the balconies from other parts of The Orchid, a low murmuring joining the chaos from nature.

I barely notice them. My pulse pounds a loud rhythm in my ears, my heart taking on a frantic, desperate beat.

"Grace! Come out. I'm not going anywhere!" A heavier torrent of rain lashes across my face, and I swipe at the wetness to no avail, my eyes only glued to the lone open window, hoping to see the woman who has occupied my thoughts for all these months.

Footsteps travel to my ears from the courtyard's entrance. A dark umbrella slides over my head.

"Steven, come inside. We'll find another way to talk to her. You're drawing a crowd," Jack murmurs in my ear as he places his hand on my sodden sleeve.

I shake my head, barely sparing him a glance. "I'm staying put. Go back inside, Jack."

He sighs, probably knowing he won't get through to me since this is his third attempt. "God, you're such a stubborn ass. But who am I to argue with you? If I had a chance to win Sarah over earlier than waiting for twelve years and all it took was standing in the rain, I'd do the same thing."

Jack releases my arm and lets out a mirthless chuckle. "At least take the umbrella?"

"I'm soaking wet already. It doesn't make a difference anymore. Go back inside, Jack." My eyes remain pinned on the open window at Trésor.

He mutters something under his breath and shakes his head, walking back inside the glass door of the courtyard. I see him shooing away onlookers, no doubt plying them with alcohol or other means of distraction.

"Grace, whatever you're going through, let me help you!" I holler again, rawness scrapes against my throat.

A loud clap of thunder booms, followed by a flash of lightning, and I fight the urge to flinch as my mind drifts back to another stormy night where a little boy got his hug and innocence stolen from him.

It's almost déjà vu. The smell of the wet air, the howling of the winds, roaring of thunder, blinding light cleaving the skies in half.

Goosebumps pebble behind my neck, and my breathing becomes labored.

This time, I don't run away.

I stand and I fight.

My lungs heave out a deep exhale as the moments slow to a crawl. Another window at Trésor slams open, the frame hitting against the wall with a loud *clang*.

There she is.

Grace, with her beautiful brown hair cascading down her shoulders, her pale face somehow luminescent even in the dim light, her body clad in a white dress which makes her look very much like an angel descending among mankind from the heavens.

"Steven! What on earth are you doing out there? Get back inside."

I shake my head, my body no longer feeling cold as a fresh burst of heat rises inside me. "You locked me out. I had no other way of getting to you. I want to talk to you," I holler.

"There's nothing to say. We're not friends, we never were. Please go back inside. You'll get sick." She leans further out the window, and I can see the desperateness in her frame.

"No. I just need half an hour of your time, please. I'm not going to move until I can talk to you." My hand swipes at the water pelting my face. "You know I'm an asshole when I want to be. I'm not going anywhere."

She stares at me as emotions flit across her face, too quickly to name. She gnaws on that plump bottom lip of hers again. The seconds pass as we stare at each other, neither of us backing down. I fist my hands before slicking my wet hair away from my face.

She throws her hands in the air. "You stubborn man!" Grace whirls around and disappears from view.

Moments later, the courtyard door swings open, and she slowly walks toward me, her chest rising and falling rapidly. Rain continues to pour from the skies, quickly soaking her hair, running down her face, pelting against her dress.

She looks so beautiful.

So much my heart clenches and my lungs seize.

The heat from earlier resurges and spreads to my extremities as I watch her stride toward me, a long expanse of smooth thigh showing with each step.

Grace comes to a stop a foot in front of me and stares at me with those penetrating, soulful eyes. Her plush lips part and I can hear the faint sounds of her panting over the storm. She swallows, her elegant throat rippling. "I'm here now. What do you want to talk about?"

For a few seconds, I'm robbed of speech, the beating in my chest a frenzied rhythm, my nerves coming alive in anticipation of her being so close to me again. My fingers twitch with an urge to grip her arms and pull her to my chest so I can bury my head against her neck where the scent of jasmine is the strongest.

But we just stare at each other in silence, the *pitter pattering* of the rain as the backdrop. She's fully soaked through now, just like I am, and my nostrils flare at the sight of her dripping wet in front of me, like a goddess walking out of the water.

My gaze holds hers, my mouth unable to form words because there's too much I want to say and yet I suddenly can't find the language for them.

The air thickens with each passing second as another clap of thunder lashes from the skies. Everything feels momentous. Like I'm perched at the opening of an aircraft, about to freefall from the skies and hoping my parachute opens.

I feel achingly alive.

My heart skips another beat as a desperate need tears through me.

Only she can make my soul fly.

Vulnerability. Ryland's advice whispers in my mind and I swallow the thick lump in my throat and slowly step toward her, every step feeling fated.

After all, we're magnets that should've been pointing toward each other the entire time. It's useless trying to pull us apart.

"Grace," I rasp, coming to a stop a few inches from her. "Will you forgive me for whatever I did? Will you let me in? Please?"

My hand shakes as I slowly touch her face, my fingers trailing over her wet cheeks and jaw, wiping away at the water droplets as best as I can.

"I-I miss you, Grace. I was broken before, but with you, I feel whole... I feel alive. I know this can't be wrong. I don't care if I'm a bird or you're a fish. I'll become a swan so I can swim in the lakes. I'll be a falcon gliding above the waters, protecting you as you swim below me. I'll be a penguin who loves diving into the deep seas. *Please* don't lock me out."

Grace leans into my touch, her lips trembling. "I don't want to be my mom." Her response is a breathy whisper.

She chokes out a sob. "She spent her life pining over a man well above her station, who left her so heartbroken she spent the rest of her life trying to recreate him in others. Her heart had a hole that never recovered. She was addicted to him, and my sister and I resulted from the bittersweet union, and he never came back for her or for us. And she died heartbroken."

She squeezes her eyes shut. "I-I don't want to be like her."

My thumb swipes at her tears, even though it's useless with the rain. "I won't be like him. Your father. I won't ever abandon you."

"That's what they all say...but they leave at the end. They always do. And then I'm left with the pieces."

I shake my head, my other hand clasping the other side of her face. "*Never.* I promise you. Never. Grace, I didn't feel anything before you. My life was only work and even then, my chest was a bottomless pit, a dark abyss no light could penetrate."

My eyes mist as I lean down and tilt her face up, my voice hoarse and thick. "Then you showed up, with your sharp intelligence and brightness, and your ridiculous notion I need friends. You wormed your way inside me, toppling my walls, breathing light and life back into my heart."

I grab one of her hands and press it against my chest. "This has never beaten for anyone else before and it never will. Please don't push me away. Whatever you are going through, let me help you. Let us face it together. Please."

I swallow and heave out a heavy exhale. "Please, I beg you."

Her hand presses deeper into my chest, clutching the wet fabric of my dress shirt, as if to feel the drumming heartbeats. I can feel the warmth of her touch through the wet layers of clothes, like a defibrillator shocking my senses alive. I cover her hand with mine as my other hand cradles her face. Her eyes flare, the brilliant purple darkening to almost sapphire at what she sees in my gaze. Her lips part again, the plump, plush lips beckoning me to kiss, to bite, to taste.

"S-Steven," she whispers, her body trembling. "What if I tell you no?"

"Then I'll show up every day and convince you until you say yes." My voice is a low growl as I step in closer to her, so much our bodies are almost grazing each other.

She lets out a soft gasp, the sound inflaming my senses and sends heated blood straight to my groin.

"What if I'm scared?" A pulse flutters in her neck.

"Then I'll wrap you in my arms and shield you from the elements and anyone who dares stand in our way can go fuck off." I take another step closer and our bodies press together like they have always belonged to each other.

"What if I tell you I don't feel the same way?" Another breathy whisper.

A muscle twitches in my jaw as I clasp her face with both hands, tilting it up. "Then I'd call you a liar. Because no one, absolutely no one, can make you feel like this."

My head swoops in and I capture her parted lips in mine.

CHAPTER 24
Grace

His kiss is feral. Dominating. Passionate.

Unlike the kiss during the lap dance, fueled by lust and anger, this one contains his soul and his all-consuming love.

Everything I didn't know I wanted, but everything I absolutely needed.

His lips tangle with mine as he drags his fingers to the back of my head, curling them against my wet strands. Steven opens his mouth wider, like he's swallowing me whole, trying to get any piece of me inside him.

A moan escapes me as his tongue slips in, swiping and invading, obliterating all remaining rational thoughts, chasing away all remnants of fear. My skin feels fevered, hot to the touch despite the chilly rain bathing us in an onslaught, but we don't care. We find our furnace in each other, two flint stones striking against each other, sparking a roaring fire.

His teeth nip at me as he tastes me and I let out a whimper, my hands curling around his neck and gripping his hair. My fingernails score his scalp and he hisses before diving deeper into the kiss, conquering my mouth like it's the last armor to my heart.

"Liar," he rasps against my parted lips, "I've never had the urge to kiss anyone until you, and now all I can think of is the taste of your lips, the sweetness, the drug."

I let out a ragged breath. "S-Steven. I've missed you so much."

"Not as much as I missed you."

Steven dives in for another scorching kiss, sucking on my bottom lip like it's the most precious delicacy. "Fuck, you taste delicious. You taste like mine."

My breasts are swollen, my nipples beaded into sharp points, poking out from the white dress shirt plastered against my body and I rub them against him, the abrasiveness causing me to arch back in tortured pleasure.

"Yes," I moan, "I need you."

He growls as he slides his hands between us to cup my heavy tits, his fingers thumbing the erect buds. "All for me, huh? And you say you don't feel anything for me?"

Sharp pinpricks of pleasure shoot straight to my core, and I can feel wetness seeping out from my lace panties. Everything aches inside me, outside me. All my senses are heightened. The pulsing in my ears thunder with the rain pelting on the ground. This grip of his fingers moving to my butt feels like a brand. The scrape of his teeth over my neck sends bursts of pleasure to my clit.

He hauls me up like I weigh nothing, and I curl my legs around his waist, my wet shirt dress plastered to my thighs. His thick erection tunnels toward the waistline of his pants and, with each stride of his legs, it hits against my clit in a tortuous grind. I grip him tighter against me, my body moving on its own, bobbing on top of him, rubbing my sensitive, achy nipples against his suit and shirt, gyrating my clit over the hard outline of his cock.

Steven growls under his breath as he picks up his pace. I feel dozens of eyes staring at us, two dripping wet figures tangled in each other, halfway to having sex in public, but I couldn't care less. My mind barely registers how I'm supposed to be getting ready for my shift, and how due to the no fraternization policy of The Orchid I'll most likely lose my job after today.

Everything ceases to matter except for this man in front of me. The man who still makes me feel safe and adored, like I'm the center of his universe.

I nip at his neck, sucking the sensitive spot where his jawline meets his ears, and he hoists me higher against him, his arms lifting me up and down his body, continuing the tortuous onslaught of sensations building in my clit.

My cum leaks down my thighs and I can feel his dick getting harder, longer, if that's at all possible. Before I know it, he backs me into an open elevator and presses a button.

"You're so wet for me, darling. I can't wait to see you fall apart on my cock." He lets out a pained grunt as I gyrate my hips harder against him.

"Steven, I need you." Another whimper.

He growls. "You like it when I talk dirty to you, don't you?"

My core clenches and I can barely muster the strength for a nod.

"Fuck, you're so greedy. You need my dick in your tight little hole, don't you? You need me to fill you up and mark you up from the inside?"

His dirty words are like pouring gasoline into an inferno and the moan tearing out from my throat sounds like a soundtrack of an adult film.

"Answer me," he grunts, pausing his movements as I try to move shamelessly against him, but his body weight pinning me against the wall of the elevator renders me immobile.

My eyes flutter open, my vision blurry with pleasure, finding his fevered gaze, a madness shining at me, ensnared on mine. His lips are twisted in a half snarl, his panting breaths heavy on my face. Sweat or raindrops bead on his face, his hair slicked back like a model coming out of the pool in a cologne commercial. A muscle tics on his forehead.

God, he's so fucking breathtaking.

"Y-Yes," I whisper, "I need you to fill me up with your big, hard cock, stretch it out and flood me with your cum. I want to feel you leaking out of me when I move."

His eyes flare and darken impossibly more. The pools are pitch black and blazing with hunger. "Fuck yes, my dirty girl. God, you were made for me."

He slams his lips back onto mine as our bodies move again in an erratic rhythm, humping each other through our sodden clothes. I briefly register the *ding* of the elevator and the doors opening. Steven carries me toward a destination that could be heaven or hell; I don't care as long as he's there with me.

Another *beep* and he steps into a dark room. I bury my face into his neck and inhale greedy gulps of seaborne breeze and worn leather as his palms grip my ass cheeks beneath my dress, his fingers digging into my tender flesh as he spreads them, and the cold air rushes in like a shock to the system.

I'm delirious with pleasure, with lust, with want. I barely hear him murmuring something to another man, who disappears like a ghost.

Steven slips his index finger underneath my panties and swipes from my clit to the puckered hole in the back as he strides past the darkened hallways. "You're so wet and ready for me, darling. So fucking ready for me."

Seconds later he slides me onto the ground and my legs wobble, my feet finding purchase on a soft carpet. My vision clears enough to realize I'm standing in the middle of his bedroom in what must be his private suite at The Orchid. A small lamp is turned on, illuminating the room in a dim glow.

"You're fucking intoxicating. All of you."

I take in his dark eyes, finding his attentions lasered on my face, then to my chest and my pussy, and I realize my dress shirt is translucent, baring every dip and every curve to him, my nipples puckered and ready for his touch.

Slowly, holding my gaze to his, I unbutton my shirt, and slide off the fabric, which was abrasive to my skin, watching his eyes grow molten as he takes in my wet, heaving breasts, my hard nipples, my glistening body.

"Keep the panties on," he commands as he strides closer, shedding his clothes along the way.

My breath lodges in my throat as I take in the smooth expanse of golden skin, every muscle and ridge defined, the perfect carving of his Adonis belt, and a dark smattering of hair leading to—

Oh fuck.

Steven drops his pants and takes out his raging erection, which is curved toward his stomach. It's thick, with veins traveling up the sides and my mouth salivates, wanting to trace them with my tongue. The tip is dark red, almost purple, and wetness coats the mushroom head. It looks angry, furious even. His balls are heavy between his legs, and he grimaces as he gives his cock a nice hard tug.

More wetness seeps through my panties as I walk backward until my legs hit the bed. Our heavy breaths fill the air, an erotic soundtrack to what we're about to do. He prowls toward me like a predator.

Hungry. Intense. Desperate.

He pushes me onto the bed as he stands in front of me so I'm eye level with his raging cock.

"Suck it. It's upset with you for vanishing."

Steven grabs the back of my head and pushes my face toward the angry tip, and I let out a mewl before opening my lips and drawing his turgid length in.

Inch by inch.

He hisses. "Yes, darling, take your reward. This cock is yours. Oh, my fucking God."

His legs tremble as I dive onto his length, eagerly swallowing as much as I can handle, my tongue swirling around his salty flesh. It tastes masculine, delicious, just like the rest of him. My hands cup his heavy balls and tug gently, earning another tortured groan from those beautiful lips as my tongue swirls around the tip, tasting the pre-cum smeared all over the top.

Steven fists my hair and maneuvers my head in a rhythmic motion, guiding me into a quickening rhythm. My throat gags as his cock hits the back and I breathe through my nose and swallow, letting more inches tunnel down my throat.

"Shiiiiit." He pants as he moves me quicker against his groin, the sound of my sucking and gagging joining his heavy breathing.

With one free hand, I grab at my breast, pinching my swollen nipple as I quicken my pace and feel him harden some more. Then I slide my fingers under my panties and touch the hard, wet nub, feeling the juices gush out of me.

"You don't get to come until I say you can," he growls as he pulls me off him and tosses me back on the bed like I'm a rag doll to be used for his disposal.

His eyes are wild. Untamed.

The shackles I saw binding his body before completely shatter. Instead of the coiled, unaffected businessman who is as cold as ice, the man in front of me is a vanquisher, a predator about to tear into his prey.

My heart riots in my rib cage as I feel myself getting wetter, my breasts heavier, my breathing coming in quicker pants. My legs part of their own accord as I relinquish all sense of control, ready to take whatever he wants to give me, ready to submit to his hot intentions.

He climbs above me, gripping his long, thick dick in one hand and he gets between my spread legs. He takes off my underwear and tosses it behind him.

"Beautiful pink pussy, all spread wide and glistening for me, your cum already dripping down your thighs because you're so horny for me."

He rubs his hard tip over my slit, my back arching at the electrifying sensations. "Fuck me, Steven. Put me out of my misery."

"Fuck yes, darling. You'll never be miserable with me." His tip dips into my wet entrance, and we both hiss with pleasure.

I thrash my head on the pillow. "You're too big." He slides in a few more inches, the movement sending searing pleasure through me. More wetness seeps out of me. "Oh my God. It feels so good... I need everything."

He groans as he pushes in like the invader he is. "You're taking me so well, darling. Your pussy is so tight. It's gripping me like it's desperate for my cum."

I pant, my breath mingling with his as he plasters his hot body on top of mine.

My legs automatically curl over his tight butt and he struggles to push the rest of himself inside me. "I-It's because you're the second person I've done this with...the first and only time being prom night in high school."

He freezes, his face snapping up, his eyes widening at what I'm saying. "I never felt the urge to do it with anyone...until you."

With a growl, he slams his lips on mine again as he plunges in, his thick cock spearing me in half, the pain mixing in with a heady pleasure I can't begin to describe.

I arch my chest up as I let out a long moan.

"That fucking doesn't count." His voice is hoarse as he slides out and I let out a whimper. "Let me show you how a man fucks."

He laces our fingers together and moves his hips in a frenzied rhythm, and I shake and shudder below him, our bodies becoming one. The pain slowly fades as renewed heat gathers where we're joined.

"Oh God, Steven. It's so g-good," I stammer as the pleasure builds.

With each grind of his hips on mine, his cock hits a sensitive region inside me and sparks fly. My legs shake against his back, involuntary movements out of my control. I let out a keen wail and feel more wetness seep out where we're joined.

"You like that, huh? This pussy is mine. Only I can give it pleasure from now on." A rough possessive edge laces his voice as his darkened eyes pin onto me, his fingers gripping mine in a death grip.

His powerful thrusts quicken, the bed frame slamming into the wall in a harsh rhythm in tune with our slapping flesh. His balls hit my ass with each swivel as he ends each pistoning with a grind, his dick dragging against my clit on the way out.

My legs shake and tremble, flames spreading over my body like wild-fire, and my eyes flutter close from the onslaught of pleasure.

He hammers harder inside me and growls, "Open your eyes. I want you to look at me when you come, so you know who's going to be fucking you for the rest of your life." The rightness of his words causes my eyes to snap open as every cell in my body comes alive.

His eyes widen as if he's shocked at his own words and a determined glint appears in those black pools as his lips part in a snarl, his teeth baring and he slams harder inside me, like he's purging something from himself or stealing parts of me to take with him.

My body throbs and my lips wobble. Everything is too sensitive, the pleasure a fevered torture. I hear cries and moans reverberating around the room that I later realize were from my mouth. I careen headfirst into what I know will be a cataclysmic explosion, a first for me in sex.

The tension gathers, the sparks blistering where he fucks me. "Steven, oh fuck...I'm going to come, oh sh-hit."

"Come, darling. Flood me with your juices. Fall apart in my arms." He grunts in exertion as he doubles his efforts, pounding into me like it's the last thing he'll do, and the tension breaks as a wave of pleasure so intense spreads through my body and I come with a cry, my vision whitening.

The walls of my pussy throb against him as he grows impossibly harder and with a few more punishing thrusts, he lets out a guttural moan and shudders against me, streams of hot cum flooding my inside, prolonging my orgasm.

"Grace, Grace, Grace," he pants, his head dipping to my neck before he takes my lips in his again, his tongue swiping, licking, joining mine while his dick still throbs inside me in the aftermath. His thumbs rub circles over my hands, our fingers still intertwined.

"My home," he whispers, pressing softer kisses on my face and neck as we slowly come down from our high.

We're joined in more than one place, and my heart finally feels whole for the first time in as long as I can remember.

"Shit," I gasp as my body slowly calms down from this out-of-body experience, "we forgot the condom."

He freezes, his muscles tensing like he's surprised he forgot about protection.

"I'm on the pill and am clean," I whisper.

Steven leans down and kisses me. "I'm clean too. I've never been in anyone bare before."

A burst of pride funnels through my chest. *I, Grace Peyton, made him lose his mind.* The haze of melancholy in the last nine months finally clears away and a smile blooms from inside me, threatening to break free from my lips.

I didn't realize I was laughing until he asks, "What's so funny, darling Grace?"

"I'm still me, aren't I? Even after this."

He gives me a warm smile as his dark pools slowly fade into amber once more. "You're always you because you're strong. And nothing will ever change that. Only now, I'll be by your side and you won't ever have to fight your battles alone again, nor will I. We'll be stronger together. We're a team."

My eyes mist at his reference to my teasing before when I said we were a team in half-jest. But now, it feels true from the bottom of my heart.

This man, he's on my side. I don't know why I ever believed otherwise.

Steven leans toward me, tenderness in his eyes, his fingers swiping away a wet clump of hair sticking to my face. "Now, can you tell me what happened nine months ago?"

My pulse kicks into an erratic rhythm as my chest hiccups and the beginnings of unease gather at the base of my spine. I look at him, all traces of the hard billionaire vanished. I only find warmth, concern, and something deeper, much more intense, in those tiger stone eyes.

I don't want to rely on anyone, least of all a man. My impulse, developed from a lifetime of disappointments, is to don on the armor I've spent years crafting and perfecting, break into a smile and change the subject. But now, the tugging of my heart as I stare at the only man who has broken down my barriers, who is living with his own demons but still brave enough to be vulnerable in front of me, I find myself wanting to let go of the flimsy strings holding my problems and my fears together.

I want to lay everything at his feet, all the dull shards and shiny fragments, have him pick me up and carry me to the other side and let him take care of the mess I left behind.

My lungs constrict as my pulse ratches up. The words are perched on the tip of my tongue, but I can't find my voice. I swallow and inhale deeply, his scent of the ocean and leather giving me strength—

"Do you know..." he begins, his voice deep and husky, his fingers tracing circles on my forearms, sending shivers down my body. "Male falcons can be very possessive and aggressive and they protect their females with their lives?"

My breath lodges in my throat as the pounding pulse inside my ears eclipses the simmering of fear in my veins.

"And what does this have anything to do with our conversation?" I whisper, the butterflies swarming in my chest as I take in the soft, but mischievous glimmer in his eyes.

"A wise person once told me the best way to get out of a funk is to read interesting factoids about the world. Then we'd realize how miniscule our problems were. This person suddenly disappeared from my life and my soul felt bereft. So, when I laid awake at night, I'd search for interesting facts to keep me company. To remind me of her." His words are soft, but his eyes darken in intensity and he slowly leans toward me and presses a gentle kiss on my forehead.

My eyes prickle and burn as tears threaten to be unleashed. I roll my lips together in a desperate urge not to cry. I'm so tired and have been so exhausted trying to shoulder the burdens of my family for a long time, and seeing this strong man in front of me, treating me like I'm the most important person in his life, I just want to curl myself in his arms and never let go.

Steven's nostrils flare as he sees my expression, and as if he can read my mind, he tugs me close and pulls me against him, wrapping me in the warmth and safety of his embrace.

His voice is deep and melodic, and I feel the rumbling in his chest. "Peregrine falcons mate for life and ancient Egyptian deities had falcons as their sacred animals. Supposedly, their eyes symbolize the sun and the moon and they protect the world below with their mighty wings. They're special animals."

I tremble, the tears sliding down my cheeks and dripping onto his chest. The warmth flooding my chest ensnares me and terrifies me at the same time. I want to spill every ounce of worry from my soul, to sleep and rest in his arms, knowing he'll be there to handle everything coming our way.

I could get used to this warmth. I could get addicted. What will happen to me if I lose this later, like Mom did?

He shushes me and whispers against my hair, "Let it out, my darling. You don't need to do everything alone anymore. I'm here, Grace. We're a team. For the first time in my life, I care about someone more than myself. You've given me that gift. Please let me share your burdens."

Lifting my head, my vision blurry, I attempt to give him a wobbly smile. For now, I'd relish the feeling of his embrace.

I'd be brave.

"Nine months ago, when I lost the internship, I had to find another way of getting money to pay off a loan from a loan shark who threatened to hurt Mom," I begin, my voice sounding thick to my ears.

Steven's muscles tense, his brows pinched with regret as he listens to me tell him about my burdens all these years—the eviction, Taylor's tuition at Petit Jeté and ABTC, the loan payment, my choice to dance at Trésor for two years, my search for my birth father, Mom's tragic passing, and how no day goes by without me missing her.

The words pour out of me, like the dam has been broken, and I sob into his chest and tell him everything as he grips me tighter against him, wrapping his muscular arms around my back as if to protect me from my memories and worries.

My voice is hoarse as I tell him about the men who have rotated in and out of our lives and how I've been afraid of my feelings for him because experiences of abandonment by the men in my life.

"Perhaps, I'm a cliché, a little girl always missing her father. When I was younger, I used to dream he'd walk through the doors one day, kneel to the ground with his arms stretched wide, and we'd run excitedly to him for a hug. He'd smell like warmth and safety and tell us how he missed us and couldn't live without us."

And so, when we were kids, growing up in the questionable neighborhood of the South Bronx, I remember feeling the sharp edges of jealousy whenever I saw my classmates' dads picking them up from school. Even though we were all equally poor and wearing similar threadbare pants and scuffed shoes a size or two too big—since you'd get more wears out of them—my friends looked so happy sitting atop of their dads' shoulders.

It was the first time I learned how poisonous jealousy was. How it seeps inside the depths of your soul, sinking into every nook and cranny, coloring your vision of the world in a shade of ugly, despicable green, and not the vibrant hues of spring, but the vomit-inducing sludge of trodden weeds caked with mud after a rainy day.

"I'd be so jealous of my friends and classmates with doting dads. The only time this jealousy abated was the several years we had with Uncle Bobby when Taylor and I were little. He was Mom's only boyfriend who treated us well, like we were his own."

I smile at the memories. He'd pick us up from school and take us to Coney Island on the weekends so we could go on the big Ferris wheel and buy us hot dogs with all the toppings from the stands while we waited for Mom to get off from work at her dance club.

Whenever he visited, he'd bring us the watermelon gummies I loved and the cocoa crisps with real chocolate chips for Taylor. He'd read stories to us of princes and princesses, of faraway lands and magic. I still remembered his bodily warmth, his reassuring scent of leather and old books. For the longest time, I secretly hoped he was our father, and he would stay forever. But Mom would always shake her head when we asked.

But one day, he too disappeared, and I never wanted a father anymore. I just wanted answers.

It was easier not to get our hopes up than to get our hearts torn apart. Now, with the lens of childhood laid shattered at my feet, I'm too jaded to care.

I let out a shaky sigh as I doodle circles on his forearm with my finger. "Obviously, that relationship didn't last, and I swore to myself I wouldn't let my heart be ensnared by any man, because no one could be trusted outside of Mom and Taylor. And because I didn't want to depend on anyone because everyone outside my family had deserted us in the past, I didn't want to take money from friends. I'd much rather dance here for the two years and then start fresh later. So that's why I disappeared and why I ended up here."

Steven lets out a shuddering exhale, then he intakes another deep breath before repeating the motion again. I swallow the lump in my throat and while my voice is raspy from crying, my soul feels lighter than it has ever felt in recent memory. I glance up and find his impassioned gaze pinned on me, a vein throbbing on his forehead. His jaw is clenched. He opens his mouth as if to say something, but shuts it to swallow instead, like he doesn't even know where to begin.

Finally, after a few seconds of silence, our naked bodies intertwined under the covers, he rasps, "You sweet, strong girl. God, I'm so sorry for everything you've gone through. And yet, you still stand tall, smiling at the world. You still find it in your heart to befriend a lonely man who has everything he could possibly want in life and yet doesn't value his possessions when you had so little to live on. I don't deserve you."

His eyes cloud over with moisture as he raises his trembling hand to caress my face. I close my eyes and lean into his touch.

"And I'm the one who told you about the job offer, the person who set everything into motion." His breathing is harsher. The words take on a clipped edge, and I can feel the anger and self-loathing seeping through his words. "It's my fault—"

"Shhh..." I press my finger to his lips, halting his verbal lashing on himself. "It's easy to want to blame someone else for our problems. I know I wanted to all this time, and it was easy to blame it on you because the thing is...you are everything I'm afraid to have...my biggest temptation. It was easier to be angry at you than to show you all the imperfections in me. But I've always known it wasn't your fault. You didn't know everything I was dealing with. And even if you did, I wouldn't have let you help me. My pride and fear didn't allow it then."

"Will you let me help you now?" Steven holds his breath, his eyes intense, his brows slanted in concentration.

My pulse is a beating drum in my ears, and my heart threatens to give up inside my rib cage. My tongue dips out to wet my lips, but his gaze doesn't waver from mine. His muscles are tense, as if every atom in his body is waiting for my response.

I swallow and say, "Y-Yes. Please help me, Steven. I'd like to have your help."

I look at her slumbering form as the storm rages outside, oblivious to the way my life changed in the last few hours. The wailing of the winds sounds eerie, but I barely notice anymore.

Normally, in the thick of the midnight tempest, I'd be staring at the dark ceilings, an aching want drenching my skin in sweat. My mind would be restless, my body filled with unease.

But now, with Grace tucked in next to me, her alluring scent of jasmine cloaking the room in a soft scent I hope will never dissipate, my heart is at ease and finally at peace.

My mind reels from how our bodies came together tonight. Sex before was meaningless and bland, a means to an end so I can eliminate the biological urge and focus on more important matters. But with Grace, it's a communion, a transcendence.

I'll never forget how she melted in my arms, how delicious her mouth tasted, how every nerve ending in my body vibrated like a tuning fork when I thrusted into her hot, wet heat, how her channel clenched my cock in a vise as if she didn't want to let me go any more than I want to leave her body. I've never come as hard as I did tonight, our hands intertwined, much like our hearts.

It felt like...making love.

Unlike my past experiences, my body aches to do it again. And we did, when I carried her into the shower and fucked her against the tiles after I soaped up every inch of her delectable body and washed off the rain with warm water. Now, in the middle of the night, I want to rouse her from sleep and bury myself inside her again. I want to hear her screaming in my ears from pleasure as I lose my sanity with her. My cock throbs and my balls ache, but I swallow my impulse as I take in the sleeping princess once more.

She looks radiant even in her sleep, the murky glow of the night caressing her smooth face half-blurred in shadows. Her nose scrunches adorably and she buries her head closer to my chest, as if seeking my warmth.

I want to keep this expression on her face always. I'll do everything I can to help her so she doesn't have to shoulder her worries alone anymore.

She took down her walls tonight and decided to let me help her by paying off her loan from the Kents. I smile as I recollect her reaction.

"I still don't feel comfortable taking money from you."

"You won't. You'll come back and work with me at Pietra." My lips twist into a grin as I watch her eyes widen, like the idea is something that hasn't crossed her mind before.

"B-But there are no open positions available."

I shake my head. *"I don't care, I'll make one. This time, I'm not letting my boss turn me down. After all, I'm the COO now. I have the power to open a new position."*

A glimmer of hope and elation shines in those violet eyes. Her lips twitch into a wry smile. *"Oh, right, you got promoted."* Her fingers travel up my *chest, sending blood rushing to my stiffening cock.* "Big boss now. But the answer is no."

I frown. "Grace—"

"I want to be a consultant instead. That way, I get to be my own boss."

My lips quirk. "I can work with that. I'll hire you as my consultant, and you can help me on the TransAmerica takeover."

I sigh, my smile falling away. "Grace, I need help with it. It's my father's legacy, and no one in the company is up to snuff. They're all telling me what I want to hear, but not actually telling me what's wrong with our approach. I need someone to come in with a fresh set of eyes. Please come and help me. I need you."

She stares at me, her gaze sweeping over my face, the teasing glint softening into seriousness, and she nods. "I'll come help you. We'll save your father's business."

A thickness forms in my throat and I clasp her hands in mine. "Thank you. You're saving me, not the other way around, Grace. The loan repayment will be part of your compensation. It's more than fair for what TransAmerica means to me."

She gnaws on her beautiful lip. She blinks, her eyes glistening, and lays her head on my chest again.

My lips tilt in a smile as I curl her body against mine, wrapping my arm around her back. She grumbles something before letting out a soft sigh and buries herself against my heat, like she belonged there all along.

I'll make sure she stays happy by my side.

My problems haven't changed since yesterday. We're still losing the TransAmerica hostile takeover. I finally called Hancock the other day, and he told me Voss was leaning hard on him to sell his shares or to give him his votes. He was threatening him with an imminent takeover of his own company.

How do you win a card game when you're playing with a cheat? I want more than anything to give Timothy Voss a taste of his own medicine, but I know Father, with his strait-laced attitude, he wouldn't want to sink as low as the scum of the earth.

Despite this, I feel content, the dark void inside me disappearing with every moment I spend with Grace next to me. She's *my* grace, my breath of fresh air. She ignites my heart. The swirling warmth and sultry heat inside me wrap around my chest again. An emotion is on the tip of my tongue, but I don't dare voice it yet.

The rain pelts against the windows, this time sounding like a soothing melody, lulling me into safety, with the only woman I've ever cared for romantically sleeping soundly in my arms. My eyelids feel heavy, the unfamiliar warmth in my body blanketing me in comfort. A flash of lightning pierces the room, followed by a low rumble of thunder—all part of nature's soundtrack, a cleansing of souls—and for the first time, I fall into a deep, dreamless sleep.

CHAPTER 25
Grace

EXCITEMENT THRUMS INSIDE MY veins as I stare at myself in the full-length mirror of our one-bedroom apartment in Morningside Heights, a few blocks away from Columbia University. This was one of the best perks of working at The Orchid, to live in the furnished employee housing in Upper Manhattan and leave the sketchier area of the South Bronx we were in.

The one-bedroom apartment is small but bright. Scandinavian designs of sleek and clean lines and furniture made with natural materials make the space appear larger than it is. The large windows let in a lot of natural light, elevating the mood immediately.

"Looking good, Grace. You excited for work?" Taylor beams at me as she saunters in from her bedroom, which is an area we carved out from the living room with a beautiful Japanese shoji screen of Robin's egg blue, painted with delicate white blossoms. She insisted I enjoy the bedroom myself this time, since it was my job that got me this apartment.

"I am. I'm also glad we don't have to move."

Taylor grins. "So, things worked out between you and Steven?"

My face heats at the mention of him...the savage sex in what must have been his private suites at The Orchid, the vulnerability in his eyes as he laid his soul bare, and how it seems like every decision in my life, every breath I've taken, have culminated in those moments.

Despite my fears and worries, it feels right to be with him.

He insists I'm his woman now and the feminist in me normally would recoil at that description, but the female in me who loves romance novels is screaming in glee.

I find that I don't mind it...if it is with him.

"God, that look on your face. You don't need to answer me anymore." Taylor snickers.

I smile sheepishly at her. "Yes. We're together now."

"I'm so glad you didn't get in trouble at The Orchid since this is all so sudden."

I don't know what Steven did, but he must've called Ryland. All I know was, this morning, when I tendered my notice at Trésor, Sofia Kent gave me a soft smile, like she knew this was going to happen, which was no surprise given the very public manner in which Steven claimed me at The Orchid yesterday. I broke the cardinal rule—no fraternizing with patrons.

"Go get them, Grace. I have faith in you. You never belonged here in the first place," Sofia said with a knowing glint in her eyes. "And don't worry about the housing. Management said they would honor your apartment contract with them until the end of the year as long as you are on time with your rental payments. Go show Wall Street what you're made of. Elias speaks volumes about your intelligence. You'll go far, I'm sure of it."

It was uncomfortable to accept help from Steven or anyone else. But I knew it was necessary. My pride was a strong motivation in my life, but it would become my hindrance if I let it become the sole driver of my future. Then, there was the cathartic release I experienced when I bared my soul to Steven last night with him wrapping me safely in his arms.

I survived. The world didn't collapse because I accepted help.

Now, I'm looking at entering the profession I'm passionate about. This time, I'll start my journey as an independent consultant, something I thought I would do further down the line. This is my way of keeping my independence, so I'm not completely beholden to anyone for my career anymore. I can lose a client, but I won't ever lose my job. This way, I still get to work for Steven, but the power seems more balanced.

I gnaw on my lip as the beginnings of nervousness seep inside me at going back to Pietra, where everything began. My anticipation mirrors what I felt all those months ago when Mom was brushing my hair and massaging my scalp during the first week of my internship. This time, it carries a thread of bittersweetness as I think of the woman I miss so much, hoping she's looking down from above and feeling proud of how I've climbed back up after falling down, how I'm finally brave enough to take a leap, to believe in someone other than myself, to let another man hold my tender heart in his care.

I think she would be proud.

Wetness mists my vision as I stare at Taylor, and I find her eyes suspiciously red as well. Irish twin sense. "You're thinking of Mom, aren't you?" she whispers.

Nodding, I pull her into my arms, and she squeezes me back. Her braided hair tickles my nose. "Mom would be so fucking proud of you. And I'm so proud of you, Grace. You've achieved so much with so little, and now you have found someone who can take care of you the way you've taken care of us. No matter what happens, you're my badass sister, and I'll always be here for you."

She pushes me away, her cheeks pink as she gives me a once-over. "Belle would be proud too of what you're wearing. Thank God you aren't going back to your frumpy old granny workwear. You look like a girl boss."

Chuckling, I dab my wet eyes with a tissue, careful not to mess up my simple makeup of a nude eyeshadow and eyeliner, paired with a mauve lipstick. I smooth my hands down a sheath dress I dug out from Mom's old clothes. It's a classic black tweed dress with white trim, elegant and formfitting.

I'm not going to hide myself anymore. If there's anything I learned in my time at Trésor, I can be feminine and independent, embrace my physical attributes, and be powerful. I can have intelligence while taking care of my appearance. Things don't have to be mutually exclusive.

"Thanks, Tay. Do you need to go to ABTC today?"

"Nope. I get today off. I don't know what I'm going to do with myself. I might go bug Millie. She seems to be nervous about something but she won't tell me anything. But I have this." She grins as she holds up a bag of gummy bears, the classic Haribo version that is apparently the crème de la crème of all things gummies. "I'm going to fish it out of her."

I laugh, my voice feeling lighter than it has in ages. "Good luck with that."

Twisting the door handle, my heart pinches and warms at the memory of myself doing the special doorknob dance at the old apartment, with Mom and Taylor laughing as I left for work. A lump gathers in my throat again as I think of the beautiful woman who gave birth to me, who I take after, who I miss so desperately. The happiness is threaded with sadness, all part of the tapestry of life. Heaving out a sigh, I step out of the apartment, the sweet humid air of spring blossoms wafting to my nostrils.

"Break a leg, sis!" Taylor calls out behind me before the door shuts, and a smile appears on my face.

⎯⎯⎯ ◆ ⎯⎯⎯

Sighing in contentment, my soul brims with happiness and energy when I step onto the marble floors of Pietra Capital.

Back on Wall Street once again.

My lips twitch in an effort not to smile and look like an idiot as I take in the bustling bullpen. Traders pace in their cubicles, their hands waving in the air as they talk on their phones. Analysts type away at their computers, the staccato sounds soothing my frazzled nerves. My eyes widen when I see my cubicle empty and clean and I realize Steven has kept my old place for me.

But then, a chill befalls the room as I step toward the bullpen and colleagues glance up from their work. The furtive whispers begin, too low for me to hear. Hayley blazes by in a cream suit, her eyes giving me a once-over before she arches her brow, her lips flattening.

Then, I feel the leering glances of Chuck, who grunts something like, "Must be nice to be a woman these days." I frown, but he turns around to engage in a conversation with another person.

Unease prickles my chest, crawling inside and settling around my rib cage. *Why is everyone looking at me like this?* I can feel my face heating and I brush my hand through my hair before smoothing it over my outfit, looking for something amiss, anything that'll explain this cold reception I'm experiencing right now.

Gnawing my bottom lip, I approach my cubicle and see Jamie beaming at me, her smile blinding, the same pen perched on her ears, her black hair arranged in her usual bun.

"Welcome back!" she exclaims and gives me a friendly wink. "I've missed you so much around here!"

My chest warms and the earlier unease slowly melts away. First day jitters, that's all.

"I missed you a lot too. So happy to be back."

She blows me a kiss. "Lunch on me today, okay?" Her phone rings and she points to it apologetically.

I mouth, *go ahead,* and smile as she plops back on her chair and answers the call.

My fingers trail over my clean desk as elation flutters inside me and I roll my lips inward to keep from grinning like an idiot. Turning my computer on, I settle in place, eager to begin my workday and catch up on the latest happenings with TransAmerica.

The hours fly by and soon the late afternoon sun is shining its golden rays through the windows. I spent most of my morning perusing spreadsheet after spreadsheet, financial statements, and news articles. It'll take me some time to get through everything, but I know I can do it.

Then, Jamie took me to a nice sushi restaurant a block away and gave me the lowdown on everything that happened at Pietra in the last nine months and all the corporate drama I missed. I found myself laughing at her big expressions and truly enjoying myself over a meal—something I hadn't done in a long time.

I stretch my arms overhead and stifle a yawn before getting up and walking to the restroom. After I step into a stall, I lock the door and complete my business. I roll out my tight shoulders, no doubt a product of my intense typing from earlier.

Just as I'm about to stand up and flush the toilet, I hear the bathroom door opening.

"Mr. Kingsley hired her back as a consultant?" An unfamiliar voice whispers as a symphony of *clicking* and *clacking* heels step into the bathroom. I freeze and hold my breath. *They must be talking about me.*

"Did you hear she worked as a stripper at The Orchid? Chuck told me earlier. Apparently, his father is a member there and Mr. Kinglsey made a big scene over her at some casino night." This screechy voice I recognize—Andrea, the mean girl I ran into a few times before as an intern who always looked down on me whenever we passed by each other in the halls.

"No way! Our Mr. Kingsley is losing his cool over her? What does he see in her, anyway?"

"Who knows? Look at how she's dressed now. It's like she wants to be one of us when she used to be in those rags. Maybe she's a kept woman now. I mean, he's in such a good mood today after barking at us for months straight." Andrea snorts and I peek through the gap between the stalls and see her hunched over the mirror, no doubt reapplying her makeup.

The shock from the conversation wears off and ice forms in my veins as my pulse roars in my ears. I fist my hands as I realize the awful rumors swirling about my return.

"You guys shove it. Grace is super nice and smart. I'm sure those are just rumors blowing everything out of proportion. And whatever she did or didn't do isn't any of our business." A new voice joins them.

Jamie.

But now, listening to the girls gossip, telling sordid tales about what they heard I did or didn't do, with Jamie trying her best to smother the rumors on my behalf, a burning heat gathers in my chest and rises up my throat. Gnashing my teeth together, I clean up and flush the toilet, the noise shocking everyone into silence.

Pulling back my shoulders, I step outside my stall, my lips curled into a sneer as I arch my head up and stare at Andrea and the new girl with unconcealed contempt. I won't bow down to the mean girls. They don't get to talk shit about me and think I'll take it lying down.

Jamie lets out a shaky laugh and bites her lip. "G-Grace, the girls were joking, I'm sure."

Andrea snorts. "No, we aren't. You're a kept woman, making it look bad for the rest of us."

The new girl, a brunette with a haughty air, crosses her arms over her chest. "Slut."

Red mists my vision and I step toward them, ignoring Jamie's pleading. They glance at each other and step back until Andrea's backside hits the sink. I stare at her and the new girl, even though they're taller than me, but in this moment, height ceases to matter because of the fury burning in my chest.

I crowd in and bare my teeth. "If you guys spent half the time focused on your work instead of gossiping about things you know nothing about, Mr. Kingsley wouldn't need to hire me to help him with TransAmerica. I wouldn't need to come back to clean up *your* mess. So please, save me the holier-than-thou attitude and actually do your job. I couldn't care less about your so-called rumors or opinions of me. I'd have to respect you first before I care."

Stepping back, I wash my hands as the girls process my words, their frames shaking.

"Grace?" Jamie asks in a soft voice.

I ball up a paper towel and toss it in the trash. "Thanks, Jamie. I'm fine."

Turning back to the two mean girls, I growl, "I'm from the South Bronx. I came from nothing and am not afraid to get my hands dirty. You talk shit about me again, and you'll regret it."

I push open the door and stalk back to my cubicle, my heart still racing a mile a minute, and I close my eyes and take a few deep breaths, willing my emotions to settle.

Moments later, Jamie's voice sifts through the silence. "Don't listen to them, Grace. They're just jealous of you. You were always the smartest one out of all of us."

I turn and face her. "Aren't you curious if anything they say is true or not?"

"Of course I am. Curiosity is a natural thing, but it doesn't matter to me. You're kind and intelligent, and you deserve to be here more than anyone else in the room." Jamie unleashes a bright smile. "I'm really glad you're back, cubicle buddy."

Her words are a balm to my burning chest and I feel the tension slowly melting away. I thank her and turn back to my computer, finding an instant message waiting for me.

Steven Kingsley

> I thought I'd feel less distracted with you here, but it's only getting worse.

My chest tightens as I think about the comments from the women moments ago. I swallow. *It doesn't matter what they say. You and Steven know the truth and you'll show everyone your worth with the quality of your work.*

Blowing out a breath, I respond.

Grace Peyton

> How so, Mr. Kingsley?

Steven Kingsley

> I just want to call you in here and make you come all over my mouth. I didn't get a chance to taste you yet, and it's driving me insane.

Heat travels to my face as my core clenches at the image of him burying his head between my legs. I bite my lip to keep from smiling.

Grace Peyton

This is sexual harassment, Mr. Kingsley. We are on company software and I'm your consultant.

Steven Kingsley

I know people who'll wipe this clean. It'd be as if nothing ever happened. And your feistiness is getting me hard.

Grace Peyton

Sir, this is inappropriate.

Steven Kingsley

Fuck. I need to hear you call me sir while I make you swallow my cum.

My nipples pebble at his messages and I squeeze my thighs together, a poor attempt to relieve the ache gathering there. I bite my lips, a devious side wanting to show up and play.

Grace Peyton

Sir, get back to work. We are saving your father's company. And if you're lucky, maybe you get to have dessert later tonight.

Steven Kingsley

Damn. Your bossiness is so sexy. I can't wait to break it down and make you melt.

I glance at his closed door, part of me wanting to say screw it and walk inside and have him show me what he meant, but I refrain from my baser urges. There's still a war to be won and I'm here to earn my keep and show those gossipmongers I deserve to be here with everyone.

Steven Kingsley

Back to work, darling. Welcome back. I'm happy you're here. *Smiley face*

My heart melts at his words and the emoji that is so unlike him, I have a hard time thinking it's from the same icy-cold man I met all those months ago. But just as I suspected, underneath the bespoke suits and chilly outbursts lies a giving heart. I let out a sigh, the warmth from his words seeping inside me. I'd brave all the rumors and barbs to witness this side of him.

With a smile on my face, I focus on my work in front of me, an in-depth analysis on the North American subsidiaries of Voss Industries, which includes some grunt work of combing through several years' worth of financial statements and footnotes, tedious to many people but enjoyable for me. This is what I excel at, digging deep into the numbers, searching for anomalies, inconsistencies, red flags which might indicate nefarious activities.

Timothy Voss doesn't keep his hands clean, and no one is perfect. If there's dirt to be dug up, it has to be in the numbers. I grit my teeth as I think of the odious man, the bane of my existence when I was dancing at The Orchid. I'll relish being part of the team to take him down for his scummy ways when I felt so powerless against him before. He saw me as a body, but now, he'll remember me for my mind.

Determination whips through me and the hum of the office chatter fades into the background as I immerse myself in the world of numbers and fine print, highlighting areas worth looking into after my cursory review. Hours slip by and my breath catches as I pause on the footnotes of the financials on my screen. Frowning, I scroll back up and click to the statements on the other tabs opened in my browser.

My fingers tremble as my mouth parts in a gasp.

I think I found something. This has to be how Voss is getting to the other shareholders. I need to let Steven and the team know.

"Grace, Jamie, conference room one. Hancock just sold his shares of TA to Voss. We need to debrief now." Hayley comes out of her office, a burst of frantic energy piercing the room, and I quickly gather my notepad and laptop and follow her to the conference room, where Steven has gathered with Bradley and a few other individuals.

A hardness returns to his eyes, all traces of the flirtatious man from the instant messages disappearing.

A pulse thuds heavily on his forehead as he glares at the group in the room. "What does he have on Hancock that we don't? Why are we always one step behind Voss?"

Steven paces around the room, a thundercloud hanging over his head, and we scramble to take a seat. My eyes catch his and for a split-second, those tawny irises soften as I give him a subtle nod, a hug from afar.

He holds my gaze for a moment, his tensed shoulders softening as he exhales. "Does anyone have any updates? They are at forty-three percent to our thirty-five. The stock price is plummeting. This is impacting the entire market because the public thinks there'll be economic upheaval around the corner. Any thoughts?"

The room is silent other than the soft humming of the air conditioning in the background.

I glance around, taking in Bradley's pale face glistening with sweat, Hayley's normally perfectly coiffed hair falling out of her bun, and I slowly raise my hand.

Steven's eyes snag on mine, a flare of admiration reflecting in those amber pools. "Grace?"

"This is very preliminary because I only just got started. But I tracked down the financial statements of their most recent North American subsidiaries before they got acquired by Voss. There's an unusual spike of cash outflows earmarked as 'other' in the months leading up to their acquisitions. I don't see any corresponding purchases of equipment or headcount increases or anything that would make it seem like they need to use this cash. The notes are especially vague. This is a big hunch, but it smells like a cash payout of some sort."

His gaze sharpens, his expression darkening as his jaw clenches. "Fucking Voss. He's blackmailing them, isn't he? That's how he got to McGinnis and Hancock. Shit."

I purse my lips. "If that's the case, the next target would most likely be Senator Townsend. He holds ten percent of the company, and originally my focus wasn't on him, given how powerful Townsend is, but if Voss is resorting to illegal means, he's desperate for TransAmerica then. I think it would be prudent to find out why he is so interested in TransAmerica. That may be the leverage point."

Hayley volunteers, "I'll dig into any Voss and TransAmerica relationship." She arches her brow at me, her lips tilting up in something I recognize...respect.

"I'll take Townsend then. His son owes me a lunch, anyway," Bradley murmurs from his seat, some color finally returning to his complexion.

"Fine. Get to work, then. Grace, you stay behind." He doesn't look up as he rummages through a few binders on the table.

I glance at the others, noting the quirked brows and once-overs from Hayley and Bradley and my face heats. After overhearing what people are saying about me and Steven in the bathroom today, I have no doubt what they're thinking. Jamie smiles at me sympathetically as the group leaves the room, leaving Steven and me in the quiet space.

He finally stops fiddling with the pages, and looks up, the coldness in his gaze from moments earlier warming instantly, his eyes intense as he takes me in, like he didn't just see me hours ago when he dropped me off at my apartment after our night spent in each other's arms. He walks to the door and begins to close it.

"Please. Leave it open." My pulse quickens, but I don't want to be subjected to more murmurs and rumblings on my first day of work.

Steven's brows furrow as his eyes skate over my face, as if cataloging every infinitesimal twitch and meaning behind my placid expression.

I force a smile. *I'm fine.*

He shakes his head. *You're not.*

Slowly he approaches me, his steps light, and he pushes me toward the back of the room, out of sight of the bullpen and the windows. He steps up to me and tilts my head up.

"What's wrong, darling?"

"Nothing."

"Don't lie to me. We're doing this together, remember?" His hand comes up to my face and curls a lock of hair behind my ear.

I inhale his intoxicating scent, my body coming alive in his presence, and I sigh. "There are rumors about me in the office. I don't want to add fuel to a fire."

He stiffens, his eyes darting toward the open door again. "I'm not afraid. Are you? Your work speaks for itself."

He takes my hands in his, his long digits softly caressing mine, sending shivers through my body. "We're a team."

His soft words, uttered in that smooth, whiskey voice of his, send heat throughout my body, warming it up from my inside. He steps away, respecting my need for space in this environment, his warm gaze never straying from my face.

My eyes mist. A team. Someone I can depend on to shoulder my burdens. I'm no longer alone. Rolling my lips inward, I sniffle to stem the impending tears threatening to break free. He furrows his brows even more.

"Darling?"

I shake my head. Fuck this, I don't care about the idiots outside.

My hands travel to the back of his neck, and I pull his head down toward me and press my lips to his. He inhales sharply as I lick the seam of his smooth lips, slipping my tongue in and tasting him.

He takes control of the kiss, his hand traveling up my back and gripping the nape of my neck as he angles my head and deepens our connection. He groans and presses our bodies together, so that every hard plane of his chest and abs is pressed to my soft curves. I can feel the telltale bulge rubbing against my stomach and I whimper.

A faint sound of a phone ringing in the distance breaks through the swirling sensations and I reluctantly step away, but not before pressing another lingering kiss on his lips. With a smile, I walk out of the room, my head and shoulders held high, feeling his eyes tracking my every movement.

CHAPTER 26
Grace

Steven

> You sneaked off from work last night without telling me, you naughty girl.

I BITE MY BOTTOM lip as I stare at his text message while waiting by the printer in the copy room for a few analyses I'm putting together for a meeting tomorrow. My stomach grumbles and I check the time. Seven p.m. I'll swing by his office later to see what he wants to order for dinner.

Grace

> I was late for dinner with my sister! Why, you miss me?

Steven

> I more than miss you. I crave you. You've turned me into a monster.

My face heats at his message, and my fingers fly over the keys.

Grace

> You sound like a vampire from one of the romances I read.

Steven

> I'm beginning to understand the drivel you read. I just want to keep you tethered to me so I can kiss you and smell you and fuck you at my whim.

> You make me feel so many things. It's like I'm
> seeing the world for the first time with you.

My heart bolts to my throat at his words and what he's not saying. We haven't had time to be together since the weekend because every minute of our day has been devoted to work, whether it's late nights or early mornings.

He'd insist on driving me home each night. His eyes would rove over my neighborhood, a few blocks away from Columbia University, in approval. No more strange neighborhood kids smoking pot on the steps or graffiti on the walls. Considering we'd leave the office well after midnight each day except for last night, when I had a standing dinner date with Taylor, we were too exhausted to do anything else.

But he'd kiss me. Those bone-melting, heart racing kisses that made my panties wet. The ones that made us want to give the middle finger to catching a few hours of sleep to prepare for the next day, and instead tangle ourselves in each other's arms, finding the various ways we could make each other groan in pleasure.

"I've never had the urge to kiss anyone until you, and now all I can think of is the taste of your lips, the sweetness, the drug."

He told me that was his golden rule in the past and my heart can't help but skip several beats every time his lips touch mine. It's as if he can't get enough, like he has saved all his kisses for me. In the early morning hours, when we resumed our private breakfast dates, he'd bring the freshest bagels from Estrelle's, a popular bakery I had always wanted to try, but was too expensive for my tastes.

"Any plans for the weekend?" I'd asked, a teasing smile on my face. Just like the old times, but also very different.

"Spending it with the woman who has captured my heart," was his response, and I blushed, pretending not to know who he was talking about before he laughed in that sexy deep voice of his and he'd then kiss me softly on the lips. We spent half the time working side by side in his office, and the other half making out like horny teenagers.

The last few days have been like an extended foreplay.

He isn't like any other men I've encountered in the past. Not like my one ex-boyfriend, not like Mom's exes. He has made me feel treasured, loved, and safe. The only person who has ever made me feel a fraction of what he does was Uncle Bobby, who took that feeling of security with him when he left us.

The thumping in my chest, the way my breath catches when I see him striding down the hallways at the office, the way my nerves awaken and spark with energy when he grazes my fingers as he passes by, or when he pulls me into darkened corners for a brief kiss are all signs my body and heart are giving me that I'm in way over my head.

The feelings I have for him are burgeoning, growing at the speed of light, and I'm helpless to stop it. And if I were to be honest with myself, I don't want to stop it.

But deep down, there's an insidious thread of fear which reveals itself right before I fall asleep, a hollow voice from deep inside my soul warning me...this is the honeymoon phase, he's a rich man, and haven't you met enough rich assholes to last you for a lifetime? What if he's just like the rest of them? What if he ends up being a disappointment and leaves you after pulverizing the rest of your heart into powder?

A sharp ache slices through me at the thought, and I quickly brush it away as I type my response.

Grace

> You've given my world color too, Steven. You have a big heart that was hidden under layers of smoke and dust. If only you could see what I see.

He doesn't respond after that, and my heart can't stop the disappointment from creeping in. Was I too intimate? Sometimes, words can feel more intimate the sex and kisses.

"If it isn't our resident gold digger slacking off in the copy room," a nasally screechy voice draws my attention from my rioting thoughts. Andrea sneers at me as she and the other girl I bumped into that day at the bathroom stride in, acting like they own the company.

Rolling my eyes, I straighten up and cross my arms. "Cut it out already, will you? It's hard enough being a woman on Wall Street without us backstabbing each other. What's your deal?"

She snarls, steps forward, and raises her voice. "My problem is *you*. You've always gotten special attention from Mr. Kingsley. What does he see in you, anyway? Those wide, innocent eyes are as fake as shit."

I move to sidestep her, not wanting to draw a crowd, but she grabs my arm in a tight clasp.

"Let go of me."

"What if I don't want to? What are you going to do about it, you slut? You think you're better than us because you can crunch numbers and offer some insight? Well, I tell you, you're even more pathetic than us. You're from the slums, pretending you belong, and now you're just sleeping your way to the top. It's disgusting. God knows that's probably how you got the job in the first place—"

I twist her arm around and grab her wrist in return. We're officially drawing a crowd, and out of the corner of my eyes, I see the familiar silhouettes of Chuck and Bradley, along with some other colleagues hovering by the doorway, no one making a move to stop this banshee from attacking me.

Fucking lemmings.

Andrea shrieks.

"I got my job here on merit, just like everyone in this room. The reason Mr. Kingsley respects me is because I work hard. I come in before any of you show up, and I'm one of the last to leave. I offer insights that are useful for the team. And I want to remind you, since you conveniently forgot, I'm a consultant here, not an employee. Even if I'm with Mr. Kingsley, I'm not breaking any rules or violating any ethics. And frankly, it's none of your business. And it's because women like you exist, the rest of us have a bad reputation for being gossipmongers and overly emotional messes who can't be trusted to rise to the top. *You* set us back a few decades, not me."

I release her arm and grab my papers off the printer and move to turn around.

Then came the slap.

· ⸱ ◆ ⸱ ·

Steven

My eyes narrow at the email on my computer, my blood boiling at the contents.

Kingsley,

You made an enemy of me at The Orchid, and I never forget a slight. I heard the slut is working for you now. Before, I thought TransAmerica would be a great company to add to my portfolio, perhaps even to keep it intact. But now, I'm going to enjoy tearing it apart piece by piece, and watching your old man shrivel into nothing. You choked the breath out of me. Now it's time for me to return the favor.

And one day, you'll end up with nothing.

And stop tailing my team like a bunch of dogs. It's pathetic.

Voss

My upper lip twitches in fury as I clutch the mouse on my computer in a death grip. I sent him a very reluctant message last week, wanting to broker a deal to stop this madness. An olive branch, even though he's the last person to deserve one.

I should have known a pig like him would be scum all the way through. Calling him a pig is an insult to the animal itself. But what gets my vision red is seeing him call Grace a slut. It makes me want to find the man himself and finish the job I started on casino night. I won't experience an ounce of regret when I see his eyes rolling back in his head.

Huffing out a ragged breath, I take a sip of water from the cup on my desk, anything to keep me from throwing my computer on the floor.

Riiiing.

My cell phone blares loudly, and I swipe the screen to answer without additional thought.

"Steven, you need to stop frolicking with that woman."

Mother.

Rubbing my temples with my thumb and index fingers, I close my eyes and listen to more of her screaming. "That woman is Grace, and I'm not frolicking with her. She's my girlfriend."

My eyes flicker open as I realize girlfriend doesn't seem the right term to call someone who's so important to me, someone I need to keep myself afloat in swirling waters. She's the one person I'm sure of at the current moment with everything else going up in flames. My heart, something I thought was long missing from my body, pounds in confirmation, my lips curving into a smile as I think of our text messages from minutes ago, before Voss's email promptly soured my mood.

"Listen, Steven. You can't be with her. You just can't. Anyone but her. You'll damage the Kingsley name. It's just a fling, son. Break it off and we'll pretend nothing happened."

My hands clench the pen on my desk, the knuckles white as a burning sensation radiates from my chest.

I stand up and roar, "What the fuck are you talking about, Mother? I have no time for this bullshit. Grace is mine and there's nothing you can do or say to change my mind."

"I'm flying to New York tonight to talk some sense into you. Steven, don't you dare—"

I hang up the phone, the lava churning in my veins threatening to erupt from this screeching nonsense from Mother, coupled with Voss's unhinged tirade. Pacing in front of my desk, I rake my hand through my hair, breathing in a deep inhale of the eucalyptus scented air that used to bring me some semblance of calmness.

But it's not enough now. I want to go to Grace, to say fuck it to office optics, and pull her into my arms. I'll be able to find peace there. The pressure in my chest will lessen and settle. She'll chase away the demons and monsters in my mind as she always does.

My pulse is loud in my ears as I think about my angel with beautiful eyes and sparkling intelligence. The only person who truly understands me.

I need to find her. I'll apologize to her later, but I need to find her right now, and at least hold her in my arms for a minute so I can breathe.

With only the thoughts of her in my harried mind, I stride to the office door and wrench it open, only to come face to face with Hayley, who is furrowing her brows in what looks to be alarm and concern.

"Yes?" My voice is clipped and terse. I know I sound impatient, but I could barely bring myself to care as I stride toward Grace's spot in the bullpen. My forehead pinches as I notice the empty cubicles.

She's not there.

Hayley walks briskly next to me, her voice urgent. "Mr. Kingsley. There's a commotion in the copy room."

"What do you mean?" My eyes scan around the office, looking for my goddess with brown hair and violet eyes.

"Andrea has been jealous of Grace for a long time because of her *friendship*," she clears her throat, "with you. She's been spreading some nasty rumors about her. I've already pulled her aside and talked to her, but it didn't work. She has Grace cornered in the copy room right now."

Red haze coats my vision as the burning heat blazes into molten flames. Scorching fury fills my veins at the thought of Grace being attacked by an office bully. A low growl threatens to tear from my throat.

Nobody messes with what's mine.

My body jolts into action, my feet carrying me toward the copy room as fast as I can, my fists curled at my sides. Sweat beads my forehead as my strides quicken. My tie feels like it's choking me, but I couldn't care less. Logic and rational thoughts flee the scene, and I burn with a need to destroy whoever is making Grace upset.

She has to be upset. She has always wanted to be known for her intelligence and work ethic. She has pride and wants to be independent, to be respected because of her abilities, not because of her attractiveness. And she sure as hell doesn't want to succeed because of a man.

I, of all people, know how stubborn she can get.

I break into a run as I turn a corner and pass by the blurry faces of colleagues standing up from the cubicles on the side of the office. I hear whispers, see fingers pointing, but I don't care. My muscles ache from tension, from keeping my exterior in check and not fly off the handle in the middle of the trade floor.

A sizeable crowd has gathered in front of the doorway of the copy room. Men and women of all ages, some with hands covering their mouths clearly in shock, others calmly drinking fucking coffee as if they're watching a play.

Pathetic pieces of shit.

I can hear yelling and shrieking as I approach the copy room, with Hayley fast behind me.

"...Even if I'm with Mr. Kingsley, I'm not breaking any rules or violating any ethics. And frankly, it's none of your business. And it's because women like you exist, the rest of us have a bad reputation for being gossipmongers and overly emotional messes who can't be trusted to rise to the top. You set us back a few decades, not me." Grace raises her voice, her posture tall and elegant, as she peers up at an angry blonde who is flushed like a tomato.

Even from her backside, I can tell Grace is defiant, strong, and powerful.

Absolutely intoxicating.

A rush of admiration flows through me. A lioness snarling in the midst of hyenas. Then, my brain processes her words and my heart swoops and free falls.

She acknowledged us.

She pretty much admitted to the possibility of a relationship.

She isn't hiding anymore.

The warmth from her stance causes my chest to spasm, my heart to spiral in its tumble from the skies, a breathlessness returning to my chest. I want to pull her against me and plant a kiss on those pouty lips in front of everyone.

Then, before I could react, the blonde raises her hand high in the air and slaps Grace across the face.

Smack.

The sound echoes in the suddenly quiet room as the crowd gathering outside gasps in horror.

And I see red, and violence, and death.

A snarl tears from my throat, and I hurl forward, pushing apart the gossipmongers as I step into the room, my eyes only on Grace, who is holding the side of her face with one hand. Now that I'm closer, I can see her profile, and how tears pool in her eyes as she glares at the blonde.

The blonde smirks and raises her hand again and swings down.

Pushing the last interlopers out of the way, I reach out and block her hit.

My senses are fried, my pulse thundering, my vision only focused on the person in front of me who dared to lay a hand on *my woman*. My ears barely register the murmuring of the colleagues gathered at the door, my eyes barely seeing the blonde's friend trying to pull her away, her lips moving as if she was talking.

"No one," I growl. "No one hurts Grace and lives to tell the tale. I don't fucking care if you're important, if you have your reasons, I don't fucking care who you are. No. One. Hurts. Her." I step in between her and Grace. She scampers to her friend.

I raise my voice so everyone can hear me. I don't care if they talk about this later or tell everyone the King of Wall Street has gone mad for his consultant. My mind can't compute logic and rational thought anymore.

"Grace is a wonderful person. She is smart, capable, works harder than anyone else in this room, myself included. If anyone dares to hurt her or make her uncomfortable in this office, don't show up at work the next day and consider yourself blacklisted from every fucking financial firm in the country. You will be done. And if you aren't done, I'll make sure anyone who dares to hire you regrets their actions. And this goes for assaulting *anyone* in my office. There is *zero tolerance* for that kind of behavior here."

My eyes are glazed, unfocused, as I glance around the sea of blurry figures in the room and outside of the doorway. "Do I make myself clear?" I roar and I see some folks flinch and shrink back in terror.

A chorus of "yeses" echoes back.

"Back to work!"

The crowd scampers away like rodents and I whip my head toward the blonde and her friend, who are trying to sneak off inconspicuously.

"Don't move."

They freeze and the friend sneaks a glance at me before turning to the blonde, mouthing something that might be an apology before scurrying out of the room.

I step in front of the blonde's face, watching as her eyes widen, her complexion paling.

"You're fired. Pack your things and leave. I don't want to see your face on Wall Street ever again." My voice is low, lethal, as my fists tremble with the need to maim and destroy.

With a whimper, she nods and scrambles out of the room like the bully she is, torturing those she perceives to be weaker than her, but she is the true coward.

My lungs heave in large gulps of air as I struggle to calm the volcanic eruption inside me. A drop of sweat trickles down my forehead and my body shakes from tethered rage.

How dare they hurt Grace? How dare they hurt the woman I lov—

The thought sparks in my mind, a flame in the darkest night, and my heart slams to my throat, lodging it in place.

I love her.

Nothing could explain the way my world brightens with her by my side. The way my emotions spin out of control when it comes to matters involving her.

Just then, the sweet scent of jasmine wafts to my nose and I feel gentle arms encircling my waist and a warm, lithe body pressing on my back.

Grace.

I love her. My darling, Grace.

My heart slowly dislodges from my throat as my lungs draw in deep inhales of jasmine, the violence and anger surging inside me, slowly abating to a simmer, fading into a sultry, heady warmth.

A new burning sensation appears behind my eyes and I try to swallow the ball forming in my throat.

My chest rises and falls rapidly as I greedily take in more of her sweet, calming scent, my fingers gripping hers around my stomach.

"Grace," I rasp. My voice is hoarse and thick with emotions.

Slowly, I turn around, and what I see in her expression takes my breath away. Tears cling to her lashes as she doles out a watery smile. Her left cheek is pink from the slap and I want to find the blonde and tear into her once again.

Instead, my fingers tremble as I graze her smarting cheek and she bites her plump lip and swallows, her slender neck rippling.

My words are trapped in my mouth, my heart hurling itself against my rib cage as if it wants to leap into her arms. I can only stand before her, rendered mute by all the thoughts and sensations running wild inside me.

Chaos. Mayhem. Paradise.

She smiles again and whispers, "You make me feel safe. We're a team."

With those words, my soul free falls, and I link my hands with hers, our fingers twining, and I haul her out of the room toward the exit, not caring if dozens of eyes are trailing us as we leave the building.

CHAPTER 27
Grace

HE DRAGS ME OUT of the building without a word. His tall frame, clad in the same sexy double-breasted suit he had on when he first visited me at Trésor, is clenched in tension. I can feel the dark energy pouring off him in waves. But despite the thundercloud hanging above him, there's a softness in the way he holds my hand in his, like he's treating me with delicate care.

Like I'm precious.

He gives my hand a squeeze and walks faster.

My heels click on the cement floor of the parking structure in an erratic rhythm as I try my best to catch up to his long strides in my maroon pencil skirt, which restricts my movement.

"Steven?" I ask breathlessly as he swings open the passenger door of his sedan and pushes me inside.

He glances down at me, a vein in his forehead throbbing, his eyes darkening with intensity as they dart to my lips, and he swallows. His jaw clenches and he reaches over, gifting me with his comforting scent of leather and ocean, and buckles me in before slamming the door shut and striding to the driver's side without a single word spoken.

Steven starts the car, his gaze lasered to the path before him, and he speeds out of the structure and turns onto the streets. The streetlights blur in golden streaks through the windows, the car humming quietly as he takes me to an unknown destination.

The ride is silent; the air is filled with urgency. His jaw twitches and his hands are white-knuckled on the steering wheel. My pulse riots inside me as I sit next to him, knowing he's hanging on by the thinnest thread.

Twenty minutes later, most likely made faster because of all the shortcuts and what I'm sure is above the speed limit driving, Steven stops in front of a sleek high-rise made from cement and glass. He tosses the keys to an attendant and runs to my side to open the door.

"Come." His voice is deep and terse. A command.

He grabs my hand and hauls me out of the car before taking me to an elevator and pressing the button to the penthouse.

The elevator ride is also quiet, fraught with tension, the calm before the storm. I see his eyes flashing every time he glances at me before looking away. His large hands are fisted at his sides, and my heart races at the intensity I see on his face.

I move closer, wanting to touch him, to smooth my hand down the bunched muscles on his back, to tell him everything is okay, just like my impulse when he stood up on the stage at Lunasia, with his tall frame radiating loneliness. But this time, I can actually touch him, to feel him, to share his burdens.

He flinches as I caress his shoulders. He swallows before inhaling a deep breath and letting it out, the sound loud in the quiet elevator. My forehead furrows at the agony on his face, the way his brows are pinched, his amber eyes darkening to a deep brown. His nostrils flare when the elevator doors open and he links his fingers with mine and drags me toward the only door in the lobby.

Placing his hand on the sensor, he waits for a beep before opening the door and pushing me inside. Dim lights automatically flicker on.

My eyes widen at the tall ceilings, the white marble foyer leading to a spacious living room with floor-to-ceiling windows, pristine leather furniture, a modern glass coffee table, and tasteful art decorating the walls. This must be his actual apartment outside of The Orchid. My mouth parts at the skyline beyond the glass panes, the glittering skyscrapers rising above the darkened expanse of Central Park stretching far and wide.

I turn around, finding Steven staring at me. "Steven? Where—"

He curls his hands around my face and smashes his lips against mine, swallowing the rest of my sentence in a deep, drugging kiss. His lips and hands work in tandem as he hoists me up, his palms gripping my ass cheeks. At the resistance of the pencil skirt, he growls in disapproval before tearing it off my legs. I hear the seam ripping from his roughness.

"My skirt," I pant out between kisses.

"I'll buy you another one. I'll fill up your closet with everything you want so I can rip them off you piece by piece."

His palms return to my ass as he pins me against the door, my legs wrapping around his waist. His lips trail to my throat as his teeth scrape the tender column, sending sharp currents of pleasure straight to my nipples, beading them instantly. My core clenches as he unleashes his tongue. Licking, swiping down my pulse points, my clavicle, before burying his face in the cleavage revealed by my blouse.

"I can't get enough of you, Grace. When I heard what they said to you, how they made you cry, I went crazy. When she hit you, I've never wanted to commit a crime more than that moment," he rasps against my flesh.

His body weight keeps me pinned to the wall as he rips off the blouse with his hands, sending the buttons flying. "I'm mad for you and I want to burn the world for you. You unlock every emotion inside me and every moment we spend apart is torture."

He groans at the sight of my heaving breasts, clad in a black lace bra, a small present I gifted myself when I got my internship at Pietra. "Your tits are mine. Your pussy is mine."

He looks up, his fevered eyes flaring and snagging on me, rendering me breathless with anticipation. "You. Are. Mine."

The possessiveness in his voice is like a caress down my body, and my pussy floods with moisture. I curl my legs tighter around his waist and rub against the thick hardness saluting me from the confines of his pants.

"I don't care if anyone knows. Heck, I want the world to know that I, Steven Kingsley, am madly, insanely, over-the-top crazy about you." His lips ensnare mine in another passionate kiss, his tongue spearing inside my mouth like he owns it, like he owns every part of me.

I melt against him as he suddenly moves, carrying me past large spaces and rooms I have no interest in seeing right now. He walks up a flight of stairs and pushes open a door, his mouth never leaving mine, his teeth tugging my bottom lip, biting before smoothing the pain with a heated lick of tongue. He samples, tastes, and conquers, leaving me in a haze of delirious pleasure.

He drops me onto a soft carpet, my blouse lying tattered at my feet, my bra somehow unhooked and discarded, and he gets up, like an avenging god from Greek mythology. My eyes widen as I finally take in our surroundings.

We're in a solarium. The ceiling and walls are all made of glass. The stars glimmer brightly in the nighttime skies as the city sparkles around us. It's as if I'm floating in the middle of space, surrounded by glowing balls of fire and the mysteries of the universe.

My eyes shift back to his, finding his pupils blown, the inky darkness swallowing the irises like a high tide. He quickly sheds his clothes, revealing swaths of smooth skin and rippling muscles. His cock is long and thick, saluting me as soon as he crouches on top of me.

"I've always wanted to take you here. This is my favorite room in the apartment. This is the closest I can take you to the stars, the fissures of the cosmos, so the gods can see us and witness how I feel about you," he whispers as he cradles his face with my hands, his breath ghosting my lips.

He gives me a lingering kiss. "I don't know what you wished for that night at the High Line, but I can tell you this. You are my wish, and I don't need to wish for anything more. You saved me and healed me."

My eyes tear up as I recall my wish for him. I reply, "My wish for you was happiness, so your soul can take flight."

He stills, his lips parting. His nostrils flare, and he lets out a shuddering exhale. "G-Grace," he shakes his head as if he's in disbelief, "happiness doesn't even begin to describe how I feel when I'm with you."

He pants softly, our breaths mixing. "I love you."

With those three words, he slices the remaining bonds of doubt in my mind, and I bring his head to mine as we entangle ourselves in a searing kiss again.

This kiss is sweet and intense, all rolled into one. It's as if our souls are melding together, creating magic of its own. I whimper. He groans. Our sighs mingle. His hand slips to my breast as he gathers the sensitive mound, his thumb flicking at the hardened tip, and I let out a moan.

He grunts and moves down my body, pressing kisses on my heated flesh. His mouth captures one tender bud, and he sucks it, followed by quick lashes of his tongue, and I cry at the pleasure, my back arching, my fingers gripping his hair. My body is burning, coming apart underneath him.

He moves to the other side as his hands spread my legs. He tears my panties off and his fingers delve into the wet folds and he groans, "So fucking wet for me."

Trailing kisses down my stomach, he inserts a finger into my channel and I whimper at the pleasurable intrusion, my legs falling apart. His thumb circles my clit and I almost careen off the carpet.

"Steven, oh my God." I shudder underneath his onslaught.

"What do you need, darling?" A low, sexy drawl, sending more moisture between my legs.

"Taste me. Taste my cum. I need you." The words spill out of my lips with no forethought, and he growls with approval before he goes in for the kill.

He swipes his tongue up my slit from my puckered rosebud to my clit before he focuses his attention on my swollen nub. He sucks the clit inside his mouth, his tongue flicking and tapping, and he adds another finger inside my tight channel.

"Steven," I shriek as sparks gather rapidly in my pussy, spreading to the rest of my body.

I thrash on the carpeted floor, the fibers most likely giving me carpet burn, but I don't care as I'm delirious with pleasure, my hips arching off the floor as he doubles down on his efforts.

"You taste sweet here too. I'm addicted to this taste. To you," he whispers between licks.

He pauses and takes his fingers out, swiping it down my slit. "This beautiful pussy is dripping for me. Darling, you want to come?"

Then, without warning, he spears two fingers into my pussy and one in my puckered rosebud, the slickness of my essence acting as lubricant, and his mouth sucks on my clit like it's his lifeline.

"Steven!" I scream, my voice echoing in the room.

The sparks burgeon into electric shocks and override my system before exploding, sending shockwaves through my body as I come, my vision blacking out, a gush of liquid seeping from the onslaught of his tongue on my clit and the fullness in my pussy and ass.

"A squirter," he murmurs, his voice filling with awe, before he continues to lap between my legs, all the while pumping his fingers inside me. "Lucky me. I can't wait to make you scream again and again with my name on your lips."

My mind is blurry with haze, my skin and body on fire as I spasm on the carpet, the waves of pleasure never ending. He crawls above me again and widens my legs. He stares at me, his eyes dark and intense, and whispers, "I love you," and slams home.

I let out a keening moan as his cock spears me in half and he unleashes a punishing rhythm. My legs curl against his waist as I hang on for dear life and let him have his way with me.

"Steven, Steven, Steven," I chant his name between pants of breath. He's my prayer, my salvation, everything in one.

He captures my lips with his and intertwines our fingers together as his hips slap against mine, each thrust of his cock hitting me deep inside.

I feel myself blooming underneath him, my legs widening, ready to receive him.

This feels more than sex. This is a communion. A merging of souls.

My lips part on an exhale as my gaze remains tethered to his. My nipples scrape across his muscles with each of his punishing thrusts as fire builds between my legs once more.

"You're mine, Grace. No matter what anyone says. And I'm yours."

Thrust. Thrust. Thrust.

His pistoning grows erratic, the sweat dripping off his forehead, but I don't care. My heart is full to the brim, so full of emotions, of sensations, and I arch up, welcoming him inside me where he belongs.

"Come inside me, Steven. Give it to me," I murmur, watching his eyes growing wild, untethered as he jackhammers his hips inside me like he needs this as much as his next breath.

I can feel his dick hardening and throbbing, the telltale spasming telling me he's near. But something is holding him back, a last vestige of control, the very thing he's tethered to since he was younger, from what I've gathered in our early morning conversations. And I sense letting go is difficult for him and that one night at The Orchid was perhaps a blip, an explosion from a prolong period of aching want. This Steven before me—passionate, ardent, with muscles pulsing with control—is his usual form.

I want him to let go with me. To fly into the stars.

The words perched on my lips for the longest time finally break free.

"I love you, Steven. Let go. Give me all of your cum."

With a roar, he breaks into pieces in front of me, spurts of hot liquid coating my insides, sending me into a spiral of sensations as I fall off the cliff with him, my cries echoing in the spacious solarium. With the stars as our witness, my body and heart tangle with his, winding in a knot no one can ever untie. Tears slip from my eyes at the momentous thoughts, the love I never thought I'd feel for another person pouring out like a dam bursting.

Steven groans as he captures my lips with his once again, our kiss softening, yet intimate and searing. His hips gyrate, prolonging our orgasms, and my nerves are fried as sweat coats our bodies.

As our breathing evens out and my mind slowly clears, he lifts his head and stares at me, his eyes glittering like the stars above him.

"Is it true? You love me?" His voice is hoarse, dripping in disbelief.

Moisture mists his eyes and a sharp ache pierces through my chest. For a moment, he looks haunted, much like the lonely man I met all those months ago, the one I want to wrap in my arms and tell him everything will be fine.

How can I not love him?

It's an impossible task, and I realize I've tumbled headfirst into this emotion a long time ago. Ever since our eyes locked in the conference room, when he gave me a smile of approval and my heart skipped in my chest, I never stood a chance.

With a trembling smile, I nod. "Steven, I love you very, very much."

He chokes back a sob and unleashes a devastating smile, an errant tear slipping down his face. He leans his forehead against mine.

"We're a team. I'll never let anything happen to us."

And my heart, my traitorous heart, flutters in reply, the wings of hope soaring in the skies. A star streaks across the inky darkness above and I squeeze my eyes shut and make a wish.

I wish this man to be mine always and we'll never be apart.

CHAPTER 28
Grace

I HUM UNDER MY breath as I stride out of the bathroom at Carlisle's, one of the restaurants within The Orchid, lauded for their steak and fresh seafood, opened by two married award-winning chefs, each specializing in surf or turf. My chest warms at the thought of the enigmatic man who is my boyfriend. He said we were trapped at work for far too long and he wanted to take me to a nice dinner date at The Orchid.

I glance around the space, my eyes marveling at the tall ceilings and the décor of cream and tan. The windows are covered with heavy velvet drapes. Small tables dot the room but are spaced far apart, with long-stem candles burning brightly in silver candlestick holders. A harpist plays soft strains of music in the background. I feel like if I were to step into heaven, it would look something like this.

When I worked upstairs, I never took the time to explore the establishment, as we were not supposed to loiter outside of our work areas. But now, seeing bits and pieces of The Orchid as a guest of Steven's, I can see why the rich and famous like it here so much. You can find pretty much everything you want here without the disruptions of the public or the press. Why would you ever want to leave?

My lips quirk into a smile as I think about Taylor, a renewed flame burning in my gut. One day, I'll gain membership here and can finally bring her here, fulfilling that dream from long ago when we strolled past the building, attempting to peek in before being shooed away by doormen.

My phone buzzes in my purse, and I slow to a stop to take the call.

"Hi Emerson, sorry for the noise. I'm at a restaurant. Do you have something on my father?" My chest tightens as I wait for his response, wondering if I'll finally get some answers.

"Grace, I just want to let you know I have narrowed down your birth father to three candidates. I'm in the process of securing DNA samples and will run tests to make sure before I release the results. Don't want us to get ahead of ourselves."

A pulse kicks in my ear and I blow out a deep breath. I feel nauseated and elated at the same time. "Tell me, are those candidates alive?" *Please tell me they are. I already lost one parent, I don't want to lose another.*

"Yes, they are. But I want to be sure before I tell you their identities."

I release another exhale, the nausea abating to an uncomfortable churn in my gut. "Okay. Do you need a DNA sample from me?"

"Already have it."

I frown. "How?"

Deep chuckles filter through the line. "You don't need to know. Just as you don't need to know how I'm going to get the samples from the three men." We've never met in person before, but I can imagine the arrogant smirk on his face and I roll my eyes.

"Thank you. You have no idea how much this means to me."

"You'd be surprised." His voice turns solemn before he clears his throat. "And you don't need to thank me. You're paying me for this."

"Ugh. If you weren't so good at what you do, I don't know how I would put up with you."

More laughter sounds from the line before he disconnects.

My heart pounds in my chest, a vigorous rhythm, and my fingers tingle. I always believe in the sixth sense and something tells me my life is about to change again and I can't decide if I'm excited or scared.

There have been so many changes in the last year—the internship, the loan payment, dancing at Trésor, losing Mom. I look up, catching Steven staring at me from a distance, his elegant brow arched in question.

Him.

I smile and swallow the lump in my throat as heat spreads through me. Not all surprises are bad. Steven gives me a wink and bites his bottom lip. The teasing expression on his face makes my heart skip several beats. I wouldn't have thought this was possible when I first met him all those months ago, when he was the coldhearted King of Wall Street with pain and loneliness lingering in those brilliant hazel eyes.

He'll never be lonely again.

I'll be here to hold him in my arms when he wakes up in the middle of the night. I'll be here to wrap him in a hug when the darkness ensnares him in its vines again. I'll be here to tell him I love him, over and over again until he believes he is worthy of the love.

My eyes prickle as I saunter back to him, my heart so full, the rapid beats fluttering within threatening to spill outside of me. I've never felt this way before and I'm scared. Terrified of this feeling going away.

Perhaps this was what Mom felt with my father, and this was why she never truly recovered when he left.

"Everything okay?" His eyes darken as they rove my face. He seems to be able to read all of my moods.

I nod. "It was my PI. They're close to finding who my father is."

He nods. "That must mean a lot to you. Anything I can do to help?"

"No, Emerson has it all taken care of. But when I find out who he is, I might need some strength from you in order to meet him."

"I hope you find who you are looking for." The words are quiet and I sense a heaviness cloaking his frame. "Any man would be a fool not to want you for a daughter."

My heart clenches at the ache I hear in the deep timbre of his voice. From his lack of sleep, toiling away to save TransAmerica, his father's legacy, I can tell he has a tenuous relationship with his father. I reach out and take his hand in mine, delivering warmth and love to him with my touch.

He stares at our intertwined fingers, emotions working across his face like a slideshow—heartache, loneliness, sadness, love, loss. I don't know why he ever thought he wasn't capable of emotions before. I think he has too much of it and it became all too overwhelming and he erected a barrier to protect himself.

"I've tried to please my father all my life," he begins, his fingers now toying with mine, like he needs the contact in order to continue. "He's a brilliant man. Intelligent. Hardworking. Has a set of moral standards I can never emulate. He always insists on doing the right thing, winning the right way. No shortcuts, just hard work. Push and persevere. He isn't an affectionate man, but I knew he loved me, or so I thought."

He glances at me, his eyes taking a faraway look. "I still remembered when I was in second grade and he took me to watch the Lakers play for the first time. He taught me the game and the rules and when everyone screamed as we won, he'd sit back, silent, a smile on his face. Then, he gave me a pat on the knee and told me, 'This team began somewhere too. In fact, the team was formed from a disbanded team, which had one of the worst records in the National Basketball League back then. They worked hard and are now one of the best teams in basketball.'"

He smiles fondly at the memory. "He didn't hug me or ruffle my hair that day, but it was the happiest day I remembered in my childhood. He didn't work for the entire day and spent it all with me."

"Some people aren't good at expressing their feelings." My heart aches for the little boy who wanted physical affection but didn't seem to receive enough. How I want to wrap him in my arms.

He rolls his lips inward, a glimmer of hurt appearing in his gaze. "I thought that was the case for the longest time. He valued hard work and so I made sure I got top marks at school, won trophies, certificates, anything I could bring home to show him how I was worthy enough to be his son. I did everything I could do to earn a pat on the head or even a hug...but secretly, I really wanted another day at the games with him. But he was always too busy. But still, I'd see a smile grace his face whenever I brought home those report cards or test scores. And for the longest time, that smile was enough. I was content. The basketball game was like meeting a unicorn. It wasn't supposed to happen, but I still saw it, and it was magical."

Moisture mists my vision, and I clutch his fingers tightly in mine, feeling his hand tremble as his voice thickens. His eyes coat in a wet sheen as he continues to pour his heart out. The words I suspect were trapped inside him for years without an outlet.

His voice turns hoarse. "Until one day, I realized my father did have love to give. He did give out hugs and kisses. The problem was, the people he loved weren't me. Weren't my sisters or my mother. They were someone else."

I gasp, my chest flinching as realization slams into me. "He had an affair?"

He nods. "I wasn't supposed to see anything, but I caught a glimpse of his other family one stormy night and he gave all of his hugs and kisses to them. He cried for them. I had never seen him cry before. It was one of the worst nights of my life." Steven wets his lips as he exhales a heavy breath.

"Is that why you can't sleep when there's a storm outside?"

He nods, his face haunted with memories of the past. "I don't remember everything from the night now. The memories have faded. But somehow, my body seems to remember, and whenever there are howling winds and thunderstorms, the fragments of the past assault me, and I get to relive whatever pieces I remember over again."

The agony in my chest deepens and I want to travel back in time to when Steven was a little boy and punch his father in the face.

"What about your mom?"

Steven chuckles mirthlessly. "My mother is a tortured soul. She hides her hurt behind controlling behaviors and outward appearances because I think her heart got broken by my father and this was her way of keeping everyone together. If we were all perfect children—the right clothes, friends, schools, grades—Father wouldn't leave us. Maybe his heart was with someone else, but his body would be here."

I walk out of my seat, not caring I'm in public, and crawl on his lap and curl my arms around his neck. He dips down and clutches me to him, his body trembling. My chest spasms in pain at the little boy who got his world torn apart, who suddenly realized his father wasn't the person he thought he was.

The feeling of not being enough. Of not being loved.

Tears slide down my cheeks. I may not have met my father, but at least I had the love of my mom, who never let us feel anything less than.

"You are enough, Steven. You are so worthy of love, you incredible man," I whisper against his lapels.

Placing my hand over his heart, I can feel the reassuring thumping underneath his dress shirt. "This heart, even without money, successes, or fine things, is special, is one of a kind. Your parents are blind if they don't see that."

I lift my head up, my cheeks grazing his chest, and I find his teary gaze on mine. I whisper, "And I see *you*, Steven Kingsley. I'd love you even without your success, without your money, even if we were to live in the South Bronx in an apartment with gangs loitering outside and we have to eat stale hot dogs for the rest of our lives."

His lips twitch into a smile as I continue, "I'd love you even then. Because you are a good man and just you alone burn brighter than any wishing star in the sky."

His lips part, and I feel a shudder roll through his tense frame. "Grace," he rasps before he dips his head down and claims my lips in front of everyone.

I hear the furtive whispers, sense the pointed stares, but everything quickly fades away as the world becomes just the two of us, my mouth breathing life into his, his lips sending love to my veins, our body heat keeping each other safe and warm. My heart clenches and flies, my soul soaring into the night skies and I feel a rightness burrowing deep inside me.

This is perfection. Even if I don't find the identity of my father, even if what I learn will disappoint me, it doesn't matter anymore, as long as Steven is by my side.

For the first time in my life, I feel whole. There's no aching darkness in my chest. I don't need to hide or pretend. I can just be myself, and I know that'll be enough for this man in my arms.

And I can do the same for him.

A weariness snakes through me and when I look up, I see the same in his eyes. A cathartic release of emotions would do that to you, and God knows how long those wounds have festered inside him.

I only wish he'd heal one day, even if it means I have to kiss him and whisper I love you a thousand times every day, I'd do it, just to chase the darkness away from his eyes. Slowly, I disentangle from him, straighten my navy dress, and walk back to my side of the table.

A waiter appears from nowhere and pulls my chair out for me as I take a seat. Then seconds later, platters of food mysteriously appear on the table, everything served in a quiet, efficient manner by men in crisp tuxedos and perfectly slicked back hair.

My eyes widen, my mouth dropping open at the array of food in front of me. The earlier melancholia fades to the background as I'm hit with a barrage of fragrant aromas and artfully arranged dishes—food porn at its best.

There's lobster with grilled herbs and drawn butter, rib-eye steak which smells rich and fragrant, a pesto pasta sprinkled with what looks to be slices of truffles on top, and the artisan breadbasket, the perfectly cut, fluffy rolls, golden brown baguettes, slices of thick focaccia, strips of salt-flaked pretzel sticks. If I weren't in love with this man already, this meal would do it.

"The breadbasket," I gasp in awe.

Steven chuckles, the heaviness dissipating from his frame. "Of course, of all things you focus on, you'd focus on the least expensive item on the table."

He bites his bottom lip. "I want to put that expression on your face every day. You'll never want for anything anymore. You deserve to be pampered like the queen you are."

I smile as we dig into the food. Growing up, we never had opportunities for fine dining with our limited budget. A hot dog at Central Park was perfectly acceptable. I look at the man before me, who is carefully slicing the steak and lobster and putting them on a plate for me, so I could no doubt try everything on the table, and I feel my breath lodging in my throat.

How did I get so lucky?

He sneaks a glance at me, finding me staring at him, and the boyish grin appears on his face again. His eyes no longer look sunken, the dark circles have faded significantly, and he is sporting a five o'clock shadow, something I don't usually see on him. But he looks radiant. Happy.

"I want to put that expression on your face every day too," I whisper.

His hands freeze and his piercing hazel eyes meet mine. He swallows and rasps, "I feel like I can breathe when you are by my side."

We stare at each other in silence, with the soft melodies of the harp playing in the background and quiet chattering from other patrons in the restaurant as accompaniment. My lips part and I feel an intense tugging inside me, drawing me to him, like even the distance of this table between us is too far apart.

He has become my falcon, my protector, his presence above the waters letting me swim freely near him. Two people who shouldn't have gotten together yet somehow did. Two magnets made whole.

The prickle behind my eyes becomes a burn and I let out a wobbly smile. "We're a team."

A vein pulses on his forehead, his intense gaze boring into mine, telling me everything he's not saying.

A vow. A command. A wish all twisted together.

"We're a team," he murmurs, his voice thick as his nostrils flare.

Just then, a waiter comes by and pours water into our glasses, breaking the spell.

Steven hands me the plate he prepared and I take my first bite of the steak, which melts in my mouth in a swirling pool of savory flavors. I moan with pleasure. My mind flits back to his look of horror when he ate the first bite of his hot dog at Central Park and I giggle.

"What are you thinking about?" Another arch of his brow, his eyes twinkling with amusement.

"The hot dog."

He groans dramatically and I laugh. He shakes his head. "Now you understand why that hot dog was torture for me. This," he points to the dishes on our table, "this is what food should be."

I dig into the buttery lobster, which tastes so fresh it feels like it was just caught moments ago, and I nod my head. This food is unparalleled. The Michelin stars make sense.

After swallowing, I murmur, "Life is full of different flavors. You need to taste the bitter to enjoy the sweet, experience sadness to enjoy happiness." I quirk a brow. "Taste a stale hot dog to enjoy a scrumptious surf and turf."

He laughs softly. "One thing I love about you is your ability to see the bright side of everything. Even in the harshest situations."

Taking my hand in his, the touch sending a jolt of awareness through me, he whispers, "You're amazing, Grace, and I thank the stars for bringing you to my side."

My face heats as I dip my head down, bubbles prickling my spine and I feel like I can fly and be the fish that joins the swan in the beautiful blue skies.

With him looking at me with so much love in his eyes, I feel everything is possible.

Dinner is filled with laughter and seriousness as we trade stories of our childhoods and I tell him I nearly burned down the kitchen one time when I tried to cook dinner for Mom's birthday back when I was ten. I may shed a few tears when I tell him stories of Mom, how she was the most loving person I'd ever met, how her heart was always filled with kindness. How I wish she could've met him, how elated she would be now that I finally opened my heart up to love.

I tell him about the men in our past, how Carl beat mom to a pulp, how sleazeballs would leer at us and try to take advantage of us when they thought they could get away with it. I watch his eyes burn with anger, his jaw clenching, fists gripping the tablecloth like he wants to stand up and take on the world for me. Then, his stiff posture softens when I tell him how I ended some of these behaviors with a hard kick to the balls. I tell him how I ended up hiding my appearance, and dressed in baggy clothes to avoid more spotlight as I grew up.

"You're beautiful, Grace, no matter what you wear. You can't hide a soul. Back then, when you were in clothes I thought were from your grandmother's closet, I still couldn't resist looking at you whenever I passed by. It doesn't matter to me if you want to wear baggy shirts or curve-hugging dresses, not that I would ever complain. You're beautiful to me because of what's inside you and that brilliant mind of yours." Steven marvels as he lifts my hand up to his lips and presses a soft kiss there.

My lungs seize and I dole out a wobbly smile, a current of warmth unique to him swirling within me like a warm breeze on a summer night. And in this moment, I definitely feel like I can fly and soar in the skies.

"Steven, I—"

"Steven Kingsley!" a feminine voice hisses behind me as I watch Steven straighten up, his jaw clenching.

"Mother."

CHAPTER 29

Grace

STEVEN DIPS HIS HEAD into a curt nod and arches his brow. A chill sweeps in, hardening his eyes, and I fight the urge to tremble from the hard edge of his voice.

My fingers move to disentangle from his, but he only grips me harder, then ups the stakes by intertwining them and holding them up for all to see.

My heart can't help but burst at his show of possession. Yet another example that Steven is the person for me.

He isn't like the other men in my life. He's not like Mom's asshole exes. He's proud to have me by his side. I'm not a fling, a secret, but someone he deems worthy to stand next to him.

We're a team.

I exhale, my lungs finally drawing in air as I turn my head toward an elegant woman, dressed in a couture dress suit with her neck and ears adorned with pearls, her black hair swept up in a twist. Steven's mother is beautiful, her skin is smooth and pale—I can see where Steven got his inky hair and elegant brows from.

But her eyes are hard, her face ashen, a flitter of panic bursting in those dark brown irises as she looks at me for the first time. She swallows and sways, her fingers grip the table to keep herself upright.

I stand—it seems to be the right thing to do—and extend my free hand. "Hello Mrs. Kingsley, I'm Grace."

She levels a chilling glare at me, her eyes sweeping down to where Steven still has my hand in his tight grip.

Her nostrils flare and she murmurs, "I know about you, Grace. The woman who has my son behaving all out of sorts."

Her words are civil, but her tone is seething, venomous. I flinch as my skin heats. This woman doesn't like me. I'd bet my life on it. Of course, she'd think I'm below her son in every way she considers important. But then I'd think about what Steven told me just now, how his mother is a tortured soul, and my heart softens. Sometimes, a sad person can't help but be mad at the world.

Steven's mother straightens up and commands to me, "I'd like to speak to you, if you have a moment."

My brows furrow as my eyes widen in shock. I look at Steven, who has risen as well. "Mother, that's unnecessary. Anything you have to say to her can be said in front of me."

Mrs. Kingsley looks around the restaurant, a pink flush creeping up her neck at the attention we're receiving. She glances at me again, desperation reflecting in her tense frame.

I squeeze Steven's hand and turn to him. "Don't worry, it's just a chat. I'll be right back."

Turning back to Mrs. Kingsley, I wave toward the lobby. "After you."

She arches her head up, her nose high in the air as she spins away and heads toward the lobby outside of the restaurant and I follow suit, not before turning back and giving what I hope is a reassuring smile to Steven, whose face has darkened as if an enemy has swept in, threatening to topple his kingdom.

Retreating to a quiet corner outside the third-floor lobby, she turns to face me. I swallow and stand tall, my fingers tangling with each other in a fight to not show fear.

She stares at me silently for a few seconds, her eyes sweeping from my wavy hair to my emerald-green dress, a gem I found online at a discount but flatters my complexion.

I brace myself for what, no doubt, will be unkind words from her mouth.

"I want you to leave my son."

I flinch, my pulse rioting in my ears as her words sink in. I know we're from different classes and she doesn't approve of me, but I didn't expect the instant hatred she has for me.

"No. With all due respect, Mrs. Kingsley, your son and I are both grown adults and we don't need your permission to be together."

She purses her lips as if she expected my answer. "Very well."

She takes out a checkbook from her clutch. "How much would it take to change your mind? I've done my research on you. Raised by a single mom, living barely above the poverty line, fatherless. You must have a price."

My skin burns as scorching rage churns through my body with the swiftness of a tsunami. I fist my hands and stand up straighter. Taller. Never cower in front of your enemies. "Nothing would change my mind. Perhaps you think I'm not good enough for your son. Maybe you think I'm after his money. I don't care. I make a decent living on my own and I don't need to depend on him. I'm with him because I love him, so you can't buy me off, so don't even bother."

"You'll ruin him," she cries as she furtively looks around our surroundings, her frame vibrating with leashed emotions, something I've seen her son do time and time again. "He'll never recover. You need to leave him. You need to stop this."

Swallowing hard, I refuse to acknowledge the small slither of shame attempting to pierce through the armor I've carefully constructed all these years. I refuse to be belittled by anyone.

Holding my head up high, I reply, "I may not have a fancy last name, I may not be rich and have old money connections, but I have my abilities and my pride and I won't stand here to be shamed by anyone. Especially not for loving a man as wonderful as your son. Someone you and his father have overlooked all his life. I'll be civil with you because you are his mother. But I am done with this conversation. Good evening."

I spin around, my body shaking from anger as I stalk back into the restaurant, leaving the seething woman standing behind me, no doubt feeling stupefied at this turn of events.

My muscles soften as Steven strides toward me and wraps me in a hug in the middle of the restaurant by the open kitchen. I can feel the anger draining from my frame in his embrace, his scent calming me by the second, his touch chasing away any lingering sense of shame and anger. It doesn't matter if the world doesn't approve of us. All that matters is we are together.

I cock my head up and smile at him, watching his frown softening. "We're a team."

A corner of his lip curves up and he presses a kiss on my forehead. "A team. Now, tell me what happened."

He escorts me out of the restaurant toward the Menagerie, one of the small cocktail bars on the second floor, a space I heard is intimate and beautiful. Part of me wants to slink away and hide his mother's barbs from him. I don't want to cause a rift because I know, despite what he says about his parents, he still loves them. After all, why would he work himself to the bone trying to save his father's company? Another part of me wants to hide the shriveling heaviness in my chest—his mother finds me so unsuitable she wants to buy me off.

But then I think about our vows to each other, "we're a team," and how all our heartache in our time apart could have been prevented if I were more honest with him, if I let down my guard and let him in, and I realize, there's no more room for secrets between us.

I tell him what his mother told me and watch as his muscles clench, his tiger stone eyes hardening.

"Fucking bullshit. She pulled this on my sisters before they married their husbands. I won't put up with this, with her. I'll cut her off before she can say another bad word to you—"

Pulling him to a stop before the elevator bay, I reach up and caress his face.

"I don't care, Steven. I don't care what she says. You and I are all that matters."

He swallows, the flush in his face receding at my words, and he leans down and captures my lips with his.

He murmurs, "Fuck the world. We're living for ourselves."

I ignore the swirling in my stomach and bury myself in his embrace.

CHAPTER 30

Steven

THE OFFICE IS SILENT as I stare into Father's crestfallen face on the monitor. My chest is heavy, and I feel like the tie is a noose around my neck, preventing me from breathing.

"Voss got Townsend and a few other shareholders. Townsend called me this morning and told me he's not selling to us but will yield his shares to Voss tomorrow. It makes no sense." I watch my father's face crumble in front of me, and it's almost like I've been hit in the face by a two by four.

I failed.

I'm the King of fucking Wall Street, and I couldn't even protect my father's legacy.

He was right all along. I don't deserve his love and hugs.

I don't deserve to be a Kingsley.

Father shudders, and for the second time in my life, I see moisture welling in his eyes. He looks toward the ceiling, trying to stanch the emotions from bleeding through, a tough Kingsley until the very end and a javelin spears my chest.

I feel sick with regret and want to cast up the breakfast I had this morning in the office with Grace. I should've stepped in sooner. I shouldn't have waited until the last minute to help him.

I should've done so much more.

Perhaps if I took Voss off the board when he first started showing interest in TransAmerica or quit Pietra and gone back home to work for

Father and spend the time developing connections with the Board of Directors to promote me as CEO, things would've turned out differently.

Sweat beads the back of my neck, my hands shake on my lap. I'm a failure—

"It's over, isn't it? All these years. My entire life put into the company and he gets to come in and take it all away." Father seems to have aged years before my eyes. His normally tall, proud frame has shrunken into his seat, his eyes vacant and filled with loss and pain.

It reminds me of that night when he cried in the storm, when he gave the hug to the little girl and said goodbye to the woman he clearly loved with his entire heart such that there wasn't room for the rest of us.

"I need to go, son."

I have no words, no reassurances as he disconnects the call.

A quiet knock interrupts my thoughts, and the office door slowly opens. The scent of jasmine hits my nose and a burning sensation appears behind my eyes. Letting out a shuddering breath, I bury my face in my hands, my shoulders trembling, aching, a shameful heat filling my chest.

"I failed him, Grace. I'm unworthy. He was right all those years ago," I choke out, my breathing coming out in pants. I feel lightheaded, dizzy, sick with shame and sadness.

"Oh, Steven," Grace murmurs as she walks to my side and crawls onto my lap, lending me her warmth and her touch as reassurance. She twines her arms around my back, her hands smoothing down the bunched muscles as she presses kisses on my cheeks, which I belatedly realize have grown damp.

Her touch unmoors me. And those dreadful emotions come tumbling out of their own accord and I'm helpless to stop them.

I guess you can't only keep the good ones.

Life is full of different flavors. You need to taste the bitter to enjoy the sweet, experience sadness to enjoy happiness.

Grace's wise words curl around my tattered heart as she whispers endearments into my ear.

"You've tried your best. He knows that, Steven," she says gently.

I look up, my blurry vision finding her violet eyes glazed with moisture as well, as if she couldn't bear to see me in my current state.

Her thumbs gently swipe my cheek as she says, "You're enough, Steven. You're loved." She repeats these affirmations, and I tremble, my hands clutching her waist, needing her presence to keep my sanity, to keep the noose around my neck from choking me alive.

"I love you," she chants, her beautiful lips parting as she leans closer to me.

"I love you, Steven. You're loved," she repeats before pressing her soft lips to mine.

Her kiss is an elixir, an antidote to the venom spreading inside my veins. Her touch is a bandage, slowly wrapping my bloody wounds in loving care. Light slowly seeps into the void that was threatening to swallow me whole as Grace adjusts herself on my lap and presses her lips against me more ardently, her hands trailing to the back of my hair, her fingers scraping my scalp.

The heavy heat of shame slowly morphs into something else—a simmering flame as she swipes her tongue on the seam of my lips, begging me to let her in, in more ways than one. The atoms in my body vibrate with renewed tension, my soul eager to expel out the darkness inside me and replace them with the light within her.

My hands slowly travel up her back, a new heat gathering in my groin, and I tangle my fingers in her hair as I angle her head so I can taste her more deeply, so I can drink this magical elixir of hers and chase away the pain.

She lets out a soft moan as her lips part and my tongue sweeps in, sampling her, savoring her, my soul letting in more light with each passing second.

"I love you," she repeats as we part for air, and my eyes prickle for a different reason. Her words are a balm to the jagged edges of my soul, and I can't get enough.

I fist her hair and pull as I drag my tongue down her neck, tasting the saltiness of her skin, the sweetness of jasmine mixed with honey. I want to forget. I want to get myself drunk on her. I want the pain to go away and be replaced with anything else.

She whimpers, the sound turning my cock hard. I bury my face in her cleavage. If I'm going to die without oxygen, I'd rather be smothered by these smooth mounds. My teeth nip at the swollen globes peeking out from the V neck of her shirt and I can feel her hardened nipples saluting me from within.

Grace slowly crawls down from my lap, and she kneels on the carpeted floor under my desk as she slowly unbuckles my belt and eases my throbbing cock from my pants.

My heart still hurts, but her touch is giving me life.

I stare at her, my ragged breaths sounding loud in the quiet office, and she holds my gaze as she licks a long swipe from my heavy balls to the glistening tip, her hands cradling and moving along the shaft.

Her pupils are blown as she sucks me in like it's the best thing she's ever tasted. The darkness inside me is replaced with sharp lust and the heady warmth of so much love for this woman before me, a queen worshipping a commoner such as myself.

She bobs her head, moving faster, and the burning sensation crawls up from the base of my spine.

I grip her head and move her harder along my shaft, hissing at each glide, at each suction.

"Fuck, Grace. Your mouth." I toss my head back onto the chair and close my eyes, my balls constricting.

"I won't be able to hold it in long enough today," I groan.

Knock. Knock.

We freeze at the sound at my door and I straighten up as Grace hides under the sturdy desk.

"Yes?"

The door creaks open and Sean pops his head in. "Steven, I heard we're losing TransAmerica. You don't have any backup plans?"

My muscles tense, the earlier heaviness slowly creeping back in, invading my body once again. I let out a shuddering exhale as I try to keep my face passive in front of my boss. It's one thing to fail, but another thing to fail in front of vultures and sharks.

"Steven?"

My tongue is tied, twisted as the darkness wraps its tendrils around my throat and my world swirls again. Just as I feel myself sinking deeper and deeper into the void, Grace delivers a toe-curling lick on my cock from the base to the tip.

The sudden shock and sensation jolt me back to the present and I grip the handrest with one hand, my other hand fisting her hair, trying to stop her...or not stop her.

I clear my throat, my body flinching as Grace swirls her tongue around my tip. "I'm thinking of options." I feel breathless for a different reason now.

Sean mulls over my answer as Grace bobs her head on my cock once more, the rod springing back to life and hardening, lengthening at her ministrations. Sharp pinpricks of pleasure gather at my balls, traveling throughout my shaft, and I bite my cheek to swallow a groan. *Fuck me.* My legs tremble, sweat gathering on my forehead and the back of my neck as she moves harder against me.

"There has to be a way for us to stop them. Voss is unhinged and out of control. He's been poaching most of our largest clients and tossing money and enticements at them," Sean muses, his brows furrowing. "Something isn't right with the man. He's been crazy before, but this is on another level. We need to take him down."

I nod. My voice is rendered mute as Grace, fucking Grace, attempts to swallow my dick down her throat and my jaw clenches from the need to groan from the sharp pleasure. I hear a low whimper—my darling is getting turned on with this act—which I mask with a loud cough. The thought of her clenching her thighs down there and trying not to moan has me hardening even more and I feel her choke and gag on the length.

The pleasure swirls, and I can smell her arousal. My breathing is coming in quick pants and I can feel the flames gathering at the base, shooting up my shaft. My skin is heated, my cock feels ready to explode, and I grip her hair harder in my fingers, wanting to pull her off, but my hips arch up, not ready to let her go.

"You okay, Steven? You don't look too good." Sean narrows his gaze at me, his eyes cascading over my face, no doubt noting how I'm sitting rigidly, flushed and ready to blow.

My balls contract and my legs tremble as the pleasure sharpens to a boiling point. *Shit. Shit. Shit.* Her fucking tongue and throat are taking me to nirvana.

A muscle twitches in my jaw as my body shakes and I shift in my chair. I let out a ragged breath before murmuring, hoping my voice still sounds steady, "Indigestion this morning. And I'll handle this, Sean. Give me a little bit of time."

Sean straightens and stares at me for a moment and I fight to keep my face placid and cool when I'm about to combust in my chair. With a terse nod, he says, "Figure it out, Steven. We can't let him win."

He closes the door with a *click*.

A low roar rips from my throat as I push out of my chair and drag Grace up from her hiding spot. "You naughty, naughty girl," I rasp in her ear. She looks dazed, her lips swollen.

"You were so sad. I could feel it. I w-wanted to distract you."

"You distracted me all right. Ass up, underwear off, on my desk," I growl as I stalk toward the office door, my hand fisting my throbbing dick.

I engage the lock and turn around and I nearly come at the scene before me—Grace, her dress hiked up, panties on the floor, her breasts pressed up against my desk, her two, creamy ass cheeks high in the air, a glistening slit in between them.

"Fuck me. Look at that dripping wet pussy."

Not bothering to fully undress, I step behind her and line up the tip of my dick at her slick entrance. "You want to make me feel better, darling?"

"Yes, sir."

I freeze at the sound of the term on her lips and at my silence and stillness, she turns her head, her face flushed as she takes in my expression. Whatever she sees on my face has her lips curving into a sly smile.

Her tongue snakes out and swipes the cupid's bow of her upper lip before she moans, "Let me make you feel better, sir. Use me for your pleasure. Flood me with your cum."

My vision narrows and nearly blackens out, and with a low roar, I slam into the hilt. My mind is a swirl of chaos—the crippling loss and shame from this morning battle against the lust and love I have for this woman before me. There are too many emotions and sensations and I feel like I'm going crazy, delirious, and hanging on by the thinnest thread of sanity.

My hips piston inside her against the desk, her tight channel gripping me like she needs this as much as I do. She whimpers with each thrust and I curl her silky strands around my hand, pulling her head off the desk as I hover my body over hers, dominating her completely, never letting go.

"Steven," she moans.

Thrust.

"Yes, my dirty, dirty girl?"

Thrust.

"You are loved, oh God," she cries, her hand slapping over her mouth to muffle the sounds as I hit that tender spot deep inside her and I feel more wetness from where we're joined.

"Fuck yes. You love me."

Thrust.

"You're never leaving me." I bite her earlobe, earning myself a mewl.

Thrust.

"I'm goddamn crazy about you."

Thrust. Thrust. Thrust.

My cock throbs as her walls tremble and her cream gushes, our bodies coming together in an erotic symphony of skin against skin.

The darkness from the call earlier is in the background as every atom in my body is focused on the trembling woman beneath me and where we're joined. Her legs shake and she tries to arch off the desk but I pin her down and drive into her harder, faster and suddenly, I feel a gush of liquid dripping onto my thighs as her lips part into a cry, "Steven!"

I swallow my name on her lips as the dam bursts inside me and with a few shuddering thrusts, I groan into her mouth as my cock throbs in her tight heat, jets of hot cum flooding her insides.

She shakes beneath me from aftershocks and I feel lightheaded, my soul repleted but exhausted, and I curl my body over hers, relishing the way I cover her just so. If I'm failing as a son, at least I'm not failing as her lover and her man. I can protect her and give her everything I have left.

"I love you, Steven. Don't you forget that," she whispers, her skin damp with sweat.

I kiss her temple. The beautiful mind and soul of hers. She always knows just what to say.

"Thank you, Grace. Thank you for loving me."

She turns her head and flashes me a blinding smile and I look at her in awe. Even now, I still can't get over how this woman is mine. I press my lips to her, kissing her gently with reverence, tasting her sweetness at the source before pulling out of her and cleaning her with a tissue from my desk.

After adjusting our clothes, she grabs my hand and pulls me to the sofa. Her face is flushed, a beautiful glow on her skin that screams she has been freshly fucked, and I can't help but grin at her disheveled appearance.

"What?" The lip gnawing is back.

I tug it loose and press another soft kiss where her bite marks are.

"Nothing. You're just so beautiful...and not only on the outside, but especially on the inside."

The flush turns pinker, and she drops her head on my shoulders as we stare at the bookshelves lined up with accolades and placards from the sofa. All my achievements on paper, but none matters as much as the woman next to me.

Suddenly, she stills, and a tensed energy emanates from her being.

Frowning, I glance at her. "What's going on?"

"Steven, don't you think it's time for us to explore other options? We can't fight a cheat without using some tricks of our own."

Her brows are pinched as she stares at me. "I've been thinking about the TransAmerica situation and I think it's time to take it to the next level."

"He wanted to do things above-board. His way."

"But he'll lose the company. Isn't that what he wanted more than anything?"

I swallow, a phantom ache returning to my chest. Yes, that's what Father wants more than anything.

Grace turns toward me. "The times have changed, Steven. We can't go to a gunfight with our fists and expect to come out alive. We are not dueling amongst gentlemen of bygone eras now. Voss is a crook—and a crazy one at that. We need to think outside the normal boxes with him."

My fingers trail circles on her shoulders, enjoying the silkiness of her skin. "What do you have in mind?"

She sits up, her eyes holding mine, her teeth gnawing on that plush bottom lip of hers as if she's debating whether to say anything.

"Tell me, Grace."

She sighs. "When I was dancing at Trésor, I worked under Elias Kent."

My body stills at her mention of the infamous crime boss everyone in the city is terrified of.

She swallows and continues, "You may not know this, but he provides protection and candidates for the men and women working on the Rose floors. It's probably one of the more above-board things in his portfolio."

She crosses her legs. "He was a good boss, but part of my job there, when I was mingling in the crowds during mixers and such...like the casino night, was to obtain privileged information for him from the patrons. He collects secrets. I think that's part of why he's so powerful and feared."

My mind whirs with the new knowledge as a tiny spark of hope flickers inside me. "You want me to ask him for a favor. For a secret to topple Voss."

She nods. "If TransAmerica is your father's lifeblood, and his opponent isn't playing by the rules, why should we? I'm sure Elias has secrets on Voss. He knew about the takeover long before it was public."

Grace nestles her head on my shoulder again. "Think about it. He will probably ask us for a secret or a favor in return, but...having worked for him, I don't think it would be something we can't stomach. He's fair."

A roaring appears in my ears as I contemplate her words. I might not be able to decide yet, but I have to admit this may be our ticket out of this mess.

I squeeze her shoulder and press a kiss on her hair. "You're absolutely brilliant, Grace. I appreciate how you're thinking outside the box and treating this project as important as it is to me. Let me think about it. But thank you."

She emits a satisfied hum.

⸻ ◆ ⸻

That night, a new storm brews in the skies. I can smell the sticky humidity in the air, the charged tension in the atmosphere. The winds whine and wail and a flash of blazing light ricochets through the opened windows, followed by the quaking rumble of thunder.

My body awakes with a start, my breathing coming out in harsh pants, my mind filled with images of a sea monster swallowing me whole as I watched Father and his other family helplessly from afar. No one heard my screams as the monster bared her fangs.

My heart riots in my chest, a layer of sweat gathering on my upper lip and my pulse roars in my ears.

It's a dream. Distorted memories.

The ache from my muscles distracts me temporarily—I must've had them clenched as I tossed and turned in the blankets. I turn toward the open windows. The dark clouds are thick and angry, blanketing the city in tightly leashed anger, the beginnings of the morning light attempting but failing to break free from the suffocating thickness.

My heart races as my mind latches onto the sea monster, with her tendrils and razor-sharp teeth, cold sweat gathering anew on my chest and—

A low moan. A satisfied whimper.

The smell of sweet, calming jasmine.

A tiny package of warm heat and smooth softness burrows against my side, a shapely leg curling across my groin, followed by an arm on my chest.

I glance down, looking at my sleeping beauty and my pulse instantly calms, the ropes binding my lungs slice open, and I take in my first full breath. A deep warmth generates from within, spreading through my body to my hands and feet, and I gather her in my arms, arranging her so she's tucked inside my embrace as I spoon her on the soft bed of my apartment on the Upper West Side.

She lets out another soft sigh, a small smile tipping on her lips, like she's dreaming of wishing stars and butterflies and I find myself smiling, the earlier slithers of terror fading into the night.

Pressing a kiss on her head, I mull over her words from earlier, when she suggested contacting Elias Kent.

My father's haunted face rises to the forefront. Those sunken cheeks, thinning hair. The life leaching out of his eyes. It's as if he's given up on living. Father's heart is broken for the second time because I failed as a son.

If it weren't for his determination to win this above-board, playing the usual corporate tactics, I wouldn't have hesitated to use all means necessary to stop Voss in his tracks.

My father trusted me to solve this for him.

I saw the hope in his eyes all those months ago when he believed I would take care of the problem.

We've tried his way, and we failed.

It's time to do anything necessary to win this.

Sharp resolve races through my body, the spark burgeoning into a dark flame inside me. Heaving out a deep breath, I carefully roll to the side and grab Grace's cell phone from the nightstand. After swiping it open—we traded passcodes awhile back as we didn't want any secrets to be between us—I scroll to Elias Kent's contact information.

I grab my phone and type a message.

Steven

> Elias, this is Steven Kingsley. I'm sure you know who I am and who I am to Grace. I'd like to ask you for a favor to solve a problem.

A few minutes later, his reply comes through.

Elias

> I've been expecting your message. Let's talk.

After setting up a time to meet at The Orchid tomorrow morning, I set our phones back on the nightstand and curl my arms around Grace once more. For the first time in the last few months, I feel like I'm not fighting against the current anymore, that perhaps I have a chance to turn the tides around and win the war.

And if I don't, this woman will still be by my side, loving me with her heart, lighting up the darkness inside me.

Everything will be okay.

With that thought in mind, my eyes drift shut, the exhaustion of the day pulling me back under the cloak of sleep.

The storm rages on, the howling of the wind shrill through the windows, the quaking thunder and blinding lightning shaking the world outside—a swirling tempest looking to destroy everything in its path.

But a heaviness sits on top of my eyes, the sweet scent of her lulling me into safety, her warmth cloaking me in love, and slowly, I succumb to a deep, restful sleep, oblivious to the maelstrom.

CHAPTER 31
Steven

GRIPPING GRACE'S HAND TIGHTLY in mine, I stride down the quiet hallways of Voss Industries. The office, a sea of dark suits and dresses, very much like Pietra, is deadly silent, the employees' mouths agape, and they stare at us as we follow the receptionist to see their boss.

They can smell the blood in the air.

Grace gives my hand a firm squeeze, as if reminding me she's by my side, that I'm never alone, but I don't need her physical touch to know she's here. The air always shimmers and changes whenever she enters a room. The hairs on my arms would stand up as every cell in my body awakens.

My soul can sense her presence.

I glance at her, noting her brows furrowing, a determined glint shining in the purple gems. She's dressed in a dark red dress hugging her curves in just the right way, her shoulders hiked back, her stance tall.

A warrior heading into battle.

My lips twitch as pride slams through me like a tsunami. This woman never ceases to amaze me.

She's putting on a brave face to see the one person who caused her discomfort at Trésor. The person who harassed her time and time again, who made her feel like a piece of meat, who made her feel dirty.

She has never told me the details, but from the time I saw him pawing Grace at the casino night, I sensed it wasn't an isolated incident. The fucking asshole.

The thought makes my blood boil, along with what he's doing to TransAmerica—I should've strangled him that night at The Orchid, spectators be damned.

I told her she didn't need to come with me today, that I'd deliver his proverbial head on a platter for her later, but she shook her head. She squared her shoulders and told me, her eyes flashing, it was time to make the bastard pay for his sins, and she wanted to see the conclusion to the epic battle, to see him fall to his knees. She needed it for closure, to prove to herself that she was the one remaining standing. That despite everything he made her feel, he didn't win in the end.

I'll fucking slice him at the knees in front of her, so he'll kneel beneath her feet.

The secretary raps her knuckles in a furtive knock then opens the door, revealing the asshole sitting behind his large oak desk, his mouth splitting into an obnoxious grin, like he has already won the battle.

He locks his beefy hands behind his head and leans back in his chair. Victorious. Ridiculous. His eyes take on a heated, lascivious glint as his gaze rakes over Grace and a growl gathers in my throat as heated fury singes my insides.

Grace squeezes me. A reminder to calm down, and I let out a ragged exhale.

"I see you're with your whore. Are you going to trade her to me to save your father's company?" He sneers as my body stills, his words ringing in my ears.

"Timothy *fucking* Voss," I hiss, the rage which abated from Grace's touch seconds ago surges back with a vengeance. I hurl toward him, wanting to tear his limbs off for his insults, for the way he's making Grace flinch next to me, but she holds me back in a tight grip.

Voss laughs, his face flushed as he turns to Grace. "You should've chosen me, honey." His eyes harden and his voice takes on a clipped edge. "I never forget a slight."

Grace straightens and blows out a deep breath. "I'd never choose you. And we're not here to pander to you. You're vile and despicable. We want to see you in person as we deliver this news." She looks at me and clenches her jaw, reminding me of our purpose here.

To deliver the death blow. To watch the enemy fall onto his knees.

A new calmness enters me as I lead Grace to the chairs on the other side of his desk and we take a seat. My lips flatten before curving up into a smile.

"You've lost, Voss."

He freezes, confusion flittering in those beady eyes. "What are you talking about?"

"As of three hours ago, a mysterious package arrived at the FBI white-collar crimes division. In the package is a dossier of emails between you and your CFO regarding bribes and blackmail sent to McGinnis, Hancock, and Townsend regarding the hostile takeover of TransAmerica, and includes bank statements from Cayman Islands accounts and a voice recording of you discussing with your CFO the blackmail details and your illegal sabotage and corporate espionage of McGinnis's and Hancock's companies to acquire their shares in TransAmerica."

The color drains from his face. He leans over the desk, his hands thumping the surface and he snarls. "You have nothing on me. None of that evidence is admissible. You're bluffing."

My lips twist into a sneer, and I cock my brow. "Am I? Or am I just playing the game your way? Your CFO is now a star witness sitting at the FBI headquarters, pouring his heart out for leniency and he's providing his copies of those records to them—very much admissible, I'm afraid. And New York is a one-party consent state. Anyone in the conversation has a right to record...legally."

I stand up, and Grace follows suit. Leaning forward, I growl, "You're done, Voss. Your greed has finally caught up to you, and you'll end up with nothing and will be rotting in jail instead, where you should be. No one will lose any sleep over you. This is my final present for you after everything you've put *my woman*," I glance at Grace, "and my father through."

I slam a copy of his bank statement from the Cayman Islands in front of him, along with printouts of his emails between his CFO and him talking about blackmail and espionage. "I'm *not* bluffing."

Voss's eyes widen in shock as sweat beads on his forehead. He shakes his head in disbelief. His face grows mottled as his heavy frame shakes with anger.

He grabs the lapels of my suit and hauls me to him. "H-How did you get the evidence? John is loyal, he's my son-in-law. He'd never betray me. Tell me how you did it. Everything was done through the Caymans. They're traceless. I handled the interactions with McGinnis and Hancock myself so no one would have those records. It's impossible. I did everything right. He wouldn't have turned on me. It's impossible!"

He pulls me tighter against him. "How did you get this?"

Letting out a low chuckle, I grip his hands tightly and rip them off my body. "I have my ways."

I now owe Elias Kent a favor in the future. The man already had the dossier packaged in a fucking red bow when I met him this morning, all the while wearing a smirk on his face.

Looking at Grace, I heave out a breath. "You should've gotten a lot more for harassing her."

Stepping back, my hand takes Grace's again, and she glances at me, her breathing quickening and she blinks, apparently overcome with emotions in seeing the man who terrorized her cower at our feet.

"We're leaving, darling," I murmur and press a kiss to her hair.

We reach the door in a few strides and I wrench it open. Two men in loose gray suits, standard uniforms of government agents, it would seem, stand at the doorway and they walk in, holding out a warrant. A crowd of employees gathers in the background, shock registering on their faces.

"Timothy Voss, you're under arrest for corporate espionage and blackmail in relation to the acquisition of TransAmerica Corporation. You have the right to remain silent..."

"And in case there's any doubt about your guilt," Grace pulls down her neckline by a few inches, her eyes flashing in both anger and victory, revealing a microphone and a wire, "You just admitted it all on a recording."

"Y-You..." Voss points his meaty fingers at her, his face red with rage.

"You should've never underestimated me." Her voice is sharp. Cutting. A warrior slaying her enemies. A heat rushes through me. She's fierce and amazing.

And she's mine.

Giving the Feds a nod, Grace and I leave the room.

My pulse riots against my ears, my heart a swirling tempest in my chest. My eyes burn as my vision blurs. I hold my breath as I drag Grace behind me to the elevators, my hands shaking from the chaos—elation, thrill, anger, relief, too many emotions for me to name.

The elevators close and I haul her against me, needing to feel her warmth in my arms. She looks up, her violet eyes glistening with unshed tears, as if she knew how important this moment was for me, how she's proud of me, how relieved she feels now knowing Voss will be behind bars for good.

"You did it, Steven," she whispers, her trembling fingers caressing my face.

I nod, the lump in my throat thick, rendering me mute. Blinking, I attempt to clear the moisture from my eyes as my body shakes underneath her embrace.

She rises on her tiptoes and presses a soft kiss on my lips. "You saved your father's legacy. You took a bad man off the streets. You did it. You're worthy with or without this win. But I'm so, so proud of you."

I let out a shuddering exhale as a guttural sob escapes me. I collapse against her, my lungs raking in desperate gulps of jasmine scented air, and she holds me tightly in her arms, her hands softly rubbing my back.

"No, Grace. *We* did it. I couldn't have done it without you."

In this moment, a calmness enters my being.

And I realize, I'm fucking worthy.

Standing in front of the palatial mansion on the quiet hills of Palos Verdes Estates, my hometown, I breathe in the cool salty breeze carrying the scent of the Pacific. The air is drier here at my childhood home than in New York, but being a stone's throw distance from the ocean, a dampness from the marine layer permeates the air in the early morning hours.

The sun is hidden behind the clouds today, denying us its warmth and light, and a chill seeps through my suit and buries itself under my skin. A few seagulls squawk as they fly overhead, no doubt heading toward the beautiful beaches nearby.

Lush foliage decorates the massive front lawn in a sea of deep green. The California drought doesn't extend to the wealthy here, like everything else in the world. Every hedge is carefully trimmed, every tree well taken care of, including the large oak trees on the premise, the ones I would climb up as a kid and hide amongst the branches as I played hide and seek with my sisters. I remember Emily screeching as she ran around searching for me, and Jess...she always found me first but then pretended she didn't see me, even though I'd hear her pointing another direction to misdirect Emily whenever she got close to my hiding spot.

I smile at the fond memories of this front lawn. I played soccer with my friends here, stargazed into the heavens at night when I couldn't sleep inside the large house, which grew even quieter and lonelier when Emily and Jess both went away for college, leaving me behind. I'd look at the stars and wonder what was up there.

My mind flits to Grace when she grabbed my arm that night at the High Line and made me wish under a shooting star. I guess I found my answer years later. Perhaps during those nights when I was lying on a beach blanket, watching the stars twinkle in the clear night skies, a lonely girl on the opposite side of the country was doing the same, and we were all along tied by this thin string between us, which pulled us closer and closer until a year ago when she stepped into Pietra.

I smile as I remember her soft lips, the very ones I kissed late last night before I got in my jet to travel back here to deliver the news of Voss's downfall in person to my father.

I heave out a breath, my lungs taking in one more gulp of my childhood, and another memory cuts to the forefront as I'm standing on the manicured lawns, staring at the front door separating me and my parents.

This is the spot that ended my innocence almost nineteen years ago. When I found out Father wasn't a god, but a human, and he wasn't perfect. When I found out he had no heart to give us because he already gave it to a woman and a sad little girl under the pouring rain on a starless night. When I felt unwanted and unworthy because he said he would've left us if it weren't for his company and legacy.

When I wanted a hug I didn't receive.

When my heart broke into a thousand pieces and never truly healed.

The thought sobers me, clouding the good memories with a cloak of darkness and a heaviness creeps in and makes its home on my chest.

Fisting my hands, I straighten up and take a deep breath, attempting to dislodge the anvil sitting on top of my rib cage.

I'm here to rewrite the ending. To tell this man he made the right choice by staying behind all those years ago, that despite his heartbreak and the way the heavens cried alongside him that night, his sacrifice wasn't in vain.

Because I saved his legacy, the thing he cares most about in the entire world.

Because *I'm worthy.*

With that thought, I square my shoulders and unlock the front door, stepping inside the quiet foyer.

Mabel, the housekeeper, a portly woman with a kind face, comes to the door and greets me, but I shake my head. "I'll find my parents on my own. Thank you."

At this hour, Father should be sitting in the dining room, reading his newspapers—the old-school paper ones because he's a traditionalist—a frown on his face as he peruses the current events. Mother would be next to him, drinking tea and prattling about their social calendars or the gossip of the day, which would earn her an occasional grunt or response from Father.

I hear Mother's one-sided conversation as I approach the dining room. Some things never change.

And yet, many things have changed over the years.

Stepping inside the spacious room, lit up by the morning light streaming in from the large grid windows, my parents look up at me in surprise.

"Steven!" Mother gets up, her hair perfectly coiffed, her hands smoothing over the nonexistent wrinkles on her cream couture dress. "We weren't expecting you to visit."

She beams as she flutters around the room and hollers for the housekeeper to bring a set of silverware and some breakfast items.

Father sets down his newspaper and smiles at me, but the warmth doesn't reach his eyes. He looks skinner than when I saw him last. His gray-streaked hair is almost completely white. His complexion is sullen and pale. He looks like he has given up and is barely clinging to life.

I take a seat on the right side of him as Mabel sets down a steaming cup of coffee and a plate of toast, ham, and eggs. I thank her then stare at my parents, who have now given me their full attention, no doubt wondering about the purpose of my surprise visit.

After clearing my throat, I bring the coffee to my lips and take a sip. My fingers tremble. My pulse races. My palms grow sweaty.

Turning to Father, I say, "Father, as of last night, Timothy Voss was arrested for a multitude of corporate crimes. I imagine the news will break soon if it hasn't already."

Father straightens up, a tenseness radiating from his frail frame.

"I gathered some evidence of his wrongdoings and worked with the feds to take him down. The TransAmerica takeover will not happen. I know I didn't do it your way, but sometimes, we need to bend the rules to win the game. We can't bring our fists to a gunfight and expect to win." *Grace's wise words.* Staring at him, I swallow, watching his eyes widen as the implications sink in.

"TransAmerica is safe, Father. Your legacy is s-safe." My voice breaks toward the end and I watch a wet sheen appearing on Father's eyes. He trembles, his arms and hands shaking on the table, clearly from disbelief and shock.

Suddenly, it's as if a flame that was sniffed out has renewed, the fire growing as the seconds pass by.

"T-TransAmerica is s-safe?" His hands shake as he clutches his mug in a tight grip, his favorite mug with the R inscribed and the small handprint.

I swallow and nod. My heart beats a resounding rhythm. "Yes. We did it."

He heaves out a deep breath, his mouth opening as if he's trying to speak, but no words come out. He takes a few more gulps of air; the mug in his hand clattering against the table in an erratic rhythm, and the tea sloshes out, but he pays no notice.

"I-It's safe," he repeats, his eyes widening and taking on a faraway look, almost like he's trying to wake himself up from a dream.

Mother claps, her normally terse face warming instantly. She turns to Father. "Robert, what did I tell you? Steven would save the company. I knew he would do it, and you were so despondent over nothing. Your son is brilliant, just like you—"

My attention turns to Mother as our last interaction at the restaurant creeps to the forefront. My hands grip the table napkin in front of me as my heart thuds rapidly behind my rib cage in nervousness, excitement, and now...anger.

She wanted to buy Grace off.

She disrespected her and, by association, disrespected me in return.

The tsunami moves up my chest and I fist my hands.

Pushing my chair out, I stand up, watching Mother's brows furrow in confusion.

"Steven?"

"Mother, Father, I'm here to tell you we won and TransAmerica is safe. But I also want to let you both know I found the love of my life.

Her name is Grace Peyton, and she's *the* most important person to me. We will be together with or without your consent. She's it for me. The end game. My life is incomplete without her."

Glaring at Mother, I continue, "If you *dare* disrespect her like you did at The Orchid, I will never come home again. Our children will *not* know their grandparents. I won't let *anyone* hurt her again."

Then, my gaze returns to my father, who looks shell-shocked at the turn of events. "If it weren't for Grace, you'd have lost TransAmerica. She provided the contact to find the evidence against Voss. It's because of her you get to keep your legacy intact."

"G-Grace," Father whispers, his voice haunted, and he clasps his chest.

Mother stands up and tosses her napkin on the table, a rare display of outright anger from someone who always cares most about poise and outward appearances. "You can't do this, Steven. You just can't—"

I turn away and storm out of the dining room, my legs carrying me down the hallway, through the foyer, and I wrench open the front door and slam it closed behind me with a resounding *bang*.

I'm done with her. With them. No one can separate Grace and me. *No one.*

The door crashes open a minute later and Mother steps out behind me, her breathing frantic.

"Mother, I'm not going to listen to you—" I walk toward my car, desperate to get out of here and get back to New York where Grace is waiting for me. Where my home is.

"Steven!" She grabs my arm and pulls me to a stop, her heels dragging across the pavement.

"Steven, she's your *sister!*"

My heart flatlines in a matter of milliseconds, her words echoing in my ears. My lungs seize and my legs almost give out from underneath me. The void in my chest is so visceral, my hands clutch my shirt in a trembling grip. *Sister? What?*

It can't be.

"What?" I whirl around, finding Mother's face pale, her eyes frantic and wild.

My pulse rams harshly in my ears and every sound is too shrill, every sensation too sharp. Heat and cold sweat coalesce, like my body's barometer has shattered into pieces along with my sanity.

I shake my head. "Stop your lies, Mother. I've made my choice to be with her and it's pathetic you're resolving to this to stop me."

She shakes her head vigorously, her face flushed, her perfectly combed hair falling out of the pins, but she doesn't even appear to notice.

She hurls forward and grips my arm tighter, digging her fingers into my sleeve. "Steven, if she were a normal girl—even if she was poor and I didn't like her background—knowing how you felt about her, I wouldn't have stood in the way. Not after what I went through with Jess and Emily. I know how stubborn you kids are when it comes to love."

Her eyes well up and she continues, "Your father had an affair when you were younger. He had a lot of business in New York then and would fly out and stay over there for weeks at a time. Over time, I realized he spent more time there than at home and he grew distant, even more so than before. It was then I hired someone to tail him, and I..."

Her body shakes as she takes in a ragged breath. "I found out he had this entire family out there. A woman and two girls. I saw photos of how he took them to the park, to Coney Island, how he held the woman's hand as they walked down the streets and took the subway, like they were a happy, normal family. Then one day, the woman and one of their daughters showed up here unannounced, and I caught them. It was raining so hard and your father just stood there crying. He was going to leave us. I was sure of it."

I freeze and hold my breath as the world stops spinning around me and I listen to her side of the story of that horrible night. Mother's tears are streaming down her face now, her mascara running down her cheeks, but she doesn't seem to care.

I've never seen her cry before. I've never seen her look so *devastated*. Never in front of me.

"I confronted him and told him to make a choice. Us or them. I knew he married me for money, but I thought we were happy. He brought TransAmerica back to life with my family's help. We had three beautiful children together."

She swipes the tears from her face, the mascara streaking across her pale skin. "She was begging him to leave us..."

Her words fade into the surroundings as the breath I was holding swooshes out of my lungs like someone delivered a powerful liver punch to my gut. I'm rendered immobile, my mind in a haze, my heart fracturing, splintering, pulverizing by the weight of her words as she smashes my world in front of me, snuffing the bright stars in the skies, the warm sunlight behind the clouds.

I shake my head in disbelief. No, it can't be.

I can't breathe. The tie is choking me, winding itself around my windpipe with her words and my memories as assailants. A sharp pain stabs through my chest as her words echo repeatedly in my mind and I feel them so viscerally in my body, I flinch and fall to my knees. My fingers grip the wet grass, trying to find purchase on anything that'll keep me tethered to consciousness even as dots appear in my vision.

This is a nightmare, much worse than the sea monster swallowing me whole.

Mother's cries pierce the silence of the morning, which was once peaceful but now gruesome.

"I'm sorry, Steven. I'm so, so sorry," she sobs as she wraps her body around my back, and kneels next to me, not caring about the wet dirt ruining her dress.

Ironically, this is one of the few times Mother has fully wrapped me in an embrace.

One I thought I desperately wanted, but now hate.

My mind fills in the blanks of the spotty memory from that one stormy night a long time ago, when I stood behind the blue chair and peered out the windows and saw the tears pouring down from the skies as Father was overcome with grief. The beautiful woman, with sad eyes and dark hair plastered against her face and the little girl—oh God, the little girl who turned my way as she burrowed herself in her mother's side. Her beautiful, striking eyes. Her elfin face.

Grace's eyes. Grace's face.

The girl who stole my hug that night.

The girl who had my father's love all along.

His favorite mug. The little handprint.

My sister.

CHAPTER 32

Steven

"No," I HEAVE IN deep breaths, the world blurring around me.

I feel lightheaded, my heart spasming out of control. I feel like I'm standing at death's door, for nothing could feel as horrible as this. "No, no, no. You're lying. It's a mistake. It can't be."

I stand up slowly, my legs shaking as Mother grabs my jacket. "I wish I were, Steven."

Father. I need to talk to him. He'll tell me this is all a lie.

Wrenching myself free from her, I stagger toward the front door, then throw it open and storm back inside, not caring I'm tracking dirt into the house.

I need to talk to him.

My vision blurs at the corners and I can hear the harsh sounds of breathing in my ears.

My strides quicken, and I turn into the dining room.

"Father, is Grace the product of your affair?"

Father freezes, his complexion whitens. His hand clutches his chest as he wheezes, "Y-You found out? You know about her?"

Nausea makes its way up my throat and I stalk toward him. "I-It's true?"

It can't be. I refuse to believe it.

Father trembles, sweat gathers on his forehead, and he opens his mouth to say something but nothing comes out.

"Father, tell me this is all a lie! How could you do this to all of us? To me?"

My mind spins as I shake my head in disbelief. "I *finally* found the one woman I care about more than anything in the world, the one person who makes me feel happy and whole and y-you...you've taken her away, your actions have destroyed us, *destroyed me*. How *could* you?"

Father's face is as white as a sheet of paper, his breathing coming out in harsh pants and he gasps, "S-Steven, I-I'm sorry. I..."

His eyes roll backward and he collapses face forward on the dining table.

"Father!" I reach him and clasp his shoulders, pulling him back up. His head lolls to the side, his body lax and unresponsive.

"Robert!" Mother screeches behind me, and everything descends into chaos.

"He's sedated right now. I'd recommend letting him rest and not stressing him out further," the doctor instructs before exiting the private suite at the hospital.

I bury my face into my hands at his bedside as Mother cries next to me. Apparently, father experienced something called a vasovagal syncope, and the fainting was caused by a myriad of factors—his lack of sleep, overworking and overexertion, not eating or drinking water enough, and emotional upset most likely from TransAmerica and...

What I asked him this morning.

My mind is swirling and blurring and the world doesn't make sense to me anymore.

Grace, my sister.

Father all but admitted it before he passed out.

When he came to a few times in the ambulance and in the hospital, he started thrashing and uttering nonsense and the doctors had to sedate him again while they ran a gamut of tests on him to make sure nothing else was amiss.

I did this to him.

My question was the straw that broke the camel's back. I ignored his pallor, the sweat beading on his forehead, his rapid breathing, because I was consumed with the need to find out if Grace was related to me.

A chain binds around my lungs, restricting my breath, and my vision blackens.

The door to the room bursts open and I hear the sounds of my sisters running to the bedside.

"How is he?" Jess asks as she pulls my head to her side in comfort.

"How did this happen?" Emily clutches Father's hand in hers as Mother sniffles in the background.

"The doctors said he was overworked. They sedated him so he could get some rest." My words sound robotic in my ears.

I can't bring myself to tell them I did this to Father because I fell in love with my sister. I swallow as another bout of nausea hits.

I can't breathe.

I can't think.

Pushing back the chair, I stand up. "Doctor said he'll be fine. But I need to go back to New York. The FBI is waiting for me to meet with them over some additional inquiries for TransAmerica."

My pulse rings in my ears, and my feet move of their own accord toward the door. I can't talk to them and tell them the truth. I can't face Father after knowing how his mistake in the past has changed the course of my life in more ways than one.

I know I should stay behind and be with my family, but I. Just. Can't.

Ignoring their questions and Mother's pleas, I stagger out of the room, my body and mind not mine, my heart irrevocably broken.

A flight and several hours later, which included a long discussion with the Feds, I find myself swaying at the edge of a sidewalk, so close to being three sheets to the wind.

The skies are dark tonight. A brisk night breeze blows by, but I can barely feel the chill.

My mind is still reeling from the events of this morning, and after using the last of my willpower to answer the remaining questions the

Feds have on Voss, I needed to escape. Rational thought is a foreign language to me right now and all I feel is pain.

So. Much. Pain.

I wanted to call Grace. So many times, but I couldn't bring myself to do it. To blow her world up just as mine did. And like a coward, I'm burying myself under the haze of alcohol, trying to delay the inevitable.

I keep hoping this is all a dream, and when I wake up, perhaps everything will miraculously be a nightmare, a fevered hallucination.

The imagination of a sick, twisted mind.

"Give me the bottle," I lunge toward Ryland, who holds the top shelf whiskey above his head out of my reach.

Maxwell grabs onto my waist and holds me back. I should be honored. His Majesty is making an appearance from his Upper West Side mansion for me.

To witness the King of Wall Street bleeding on the ground, his crown in the sewers, his body flayed by a thousand whips, blood draining from every orifice.

My head is woozy. Heavy. The world spins around me in a tempest of darkness and dim lights. The smell of gasoline and screeching of tires skidding on asphalt reach my ears, but they sound faint. I wish the world would burn and take me with it.

I'm once again underwater, the hole in my chest cavernous, as if a shotgun blasted pellets at point blank repeatedly over my heart. Unlike a year ago, this time, everything hurts. The crippling agony robs me of my breath, strangling my lungs in a tight grip, squeezing, twisting, pulling.

"I can't let you drink anymore," Ryland murmurs, his voice sounding far away as I sway and topple sideways, and a flash of blond hair and light eyes appears in front of me, strong arms stopping my face-plant to the ground. Charles.

"How did you guys find him?" His voice is gravelly. Worried.

"I saw him at the race, attempting to get behind a car while looking like this. Fucking asshole has a death wish. He gave me a right hook as I dragged him out of the driver's seat." That was Maxwell...I think.

"Rex and the others are on their way," Ryland adds as he tucks his arm around my waist and, along with Maxwell, carry me to the sidewalk and slumps me against a building.

"Fuck, you're heavy," Maxwell mutters.

"He's dead weight right now. I doubt he even knows his name." Ryland lets out a ragged sigh.

I laugh at that, my shoulders shaking, tears streaming down my face. My cackles sound loud in the night. I grip my stomach, curling over my body as I bury my face between my knees.

"Fuck, what's wrong with him?" Maxwell sits down next to me.

My body trembles, my breathing coming out in heavy pants as my tears wet my trousers, my nose running, but I couldn't care less. "I-I'm Steven *fucking* Kingsley..." I laugh again, my voice delirious, sounding far, far away. "I wish I could forget my name. I wish I could forget me. I wish I was anyone else other than Steven Kingsley."

My sobs blend with my chuckles and I'm sure I look like a madman. Deranged. Someone who should be committed to a mental institution. I wrench the bottle of whiskey away from Maxwell and take a big swig—it's my second or third bottle for tonight; I lost count—the burn barely registering. It can be water for all I care.

It's not working. I'm still awake. I'm still here. I'm still living this farce of a life.

My phone buzzes once again.

Maxwell tears the bottle from my grip as I retrieve my phone, swiping it open, and stare at the text notifications.

Thirty missed calls from Jess, Emily, and Mother. I don't want to talk to Mother and hear her sad, pathetic attempts at consoling me after her and Father failed me in every way that matters. I don't want to face my sisters, who I know would cry alongside me when they put the pieces together.

Ten missed calls from Grace.

The remnants of my heart spasm in agony as I think about my beautiful girl with breathtaking eyes and the warmest soul. The person who brought me back to life.

I read through my darling's messages again, my chest heaving and clenching in pain. I'm a masochist, intent on snuffing out the last bits of life within me. There's no way out of this swirling madness, this pitiful existence.

I can never forget her. I can never live without her.

I can never *be* with her.

Grace

> I got a call from Emily. She got my number from Millie. She said your father is in the hospital and you didn't seem right when you left. But you aren't picking up her calls. I went to your apartment; the doorman said you weren't there. Please tell me what's going on. We're a team. I'm worried about you.

Grace

> Please answer my calls. Please talk to me. I saw the light on in your apartment. You're there. Please, just tell me what's going on.

Grace

> I love you so much, Steven. Something happened, didn't it? Please don't scare me. I'm terrified. Call me.

Grace

> Steven Kingsley, don't make me come over to The Orchid and find you. You're there, right?

Grace

> Whatever is going on, I'll always be by your side. I'm worried sick about you. Please let me in. Whatever it is, we'll get through this. I love you.

There are dozens more messages just like this one, each one angrier, more desperate, and terrified.

I want to reply so many times, want to pick up her call to hear her voice, want to go to her apartment and pull her into my arms.

And then want?

Sorry, darling, we can't be together because my father had an affair with your mother and we are half-siblings?

The world is one perverted joke and we are the punchline.

Tears blur my vision again as I laugh into the ruckus of the night, my shoulders trembling from gallows humor or from pain. I can't tell the difference anymore.

More footsteps pound nearby, and several fresh voices join the fray.

"Shit. He's been like this since you found him?" Rex sounds concerned, his jovial, teasing tones nowhere on display. "Look at him. He's fucking a mess. Hair all crazy, haven't shaved, cufflinks missing, shirt hanging out of his pants. What the fuck."

"Oh Steven, tell us what's going on." A whiff of feminine floral perfume hits my nostrils and the pain slices me once again. The scent is not jasmine, not my favorite smell in the world. The warmth next to me is not her. I don't need to look up to know.

Lana wraps her arms around my shoulders, her hand making smoothing motions on my back, but I barely notice.

"Come on, man. You're almost like a brother to us. You're an honorary Anderson. There's nothing you can't share with family. Tell us so we can help you," Ethan's quiet voice speaks from in front of me.

Slowly, I lift my head up, a pounding headache cleaving me in half. I get all the pain from the alcohol, but none of the benefits. No blackouts, no drunkenness, no forgetfulness.

Only the pain.

So much pain.

Ryland squats in front of me and places his hand on my shoulders, his slate eyes piercing. He squeezes. Maxwell sits silently next to me—he's a man of few words, but I can feel his support radiating from his body heat.

Charles paces, his lips thinning as he rakes his hand through his hair. Ethan and Rex stare at me from their standing positions a few feet away, blocking my vision of the road where the cars are flying by, speeding along the streets in an underground race for the rich and elite that The Orchid hosts once a quarter.

Lana sighs and wraps me around my shoulders to the best of her ability. "You can tell us. We won't judge. We're your family."

I heave out a breath and tilt my head up toward the heavens. The skies are a dark abyss—a stark, starless sky. The gods don't want to peer down between the frissons of worlds to see us. I want to stand up, scream on top of my lungs, and yell, *"Look what you made happen. What sick, twisted minds you have to do this to us!"*

"Grace and I are siblings," I whisper, but the five words pierce the intimate circle of the group. It might as well be the sound of a gunshot.

Maxwell sucks in a deep breath.

"What the fuck," Ryland mutters.

"What!" Rex exclaims, disbelief lacing his voice, as Lana, Ethan, and Charles echo the same sentiments.

My eyes glaze over as I recite the events to them, my voice monotonous, for the emotions have already rendered me into a ghost of my former self. I tell them about my memory of the rainy night, how Grace and I fell in love, how I finally found peace in my soul, and how Mother tore it apart when she revealed to me the truth of the past.

The group was quiet, the silence heavy when I finished telling them everything that transpired. A cheer sounds from far away, spectators no doubt enjoying the race of flashy cars and rich people with nothing better to do than to tempt death.

I grab the whiskey from Maxwell again, and this time, he hands it over freely. Taking a large swig, I flinch at the renewed pounding in my head.

"What are you going to do?" Ryland asks from in front of me. He gently takes the bottle from my hand.

I shake my head. "What can I do? I'll have to let her go. But I won't tell her why. It'll kill her. I'd rather be one of the rich assholes she's used to in the past. I'll disappear from her life. The past year has been nothing but a beautiful dream. And like every dream, we have to eventually wake up."

The words tear inside my chest, sinking their talons into the muscle and digging, but I barely feel the pain anymore.

Even in my drunken stupor, it doesn't feel right. I know she deserves the truth from me, but in this one selfish moment, I'm too obliterated from everything to think clearly.

Because everything inside me is scything agony. I can't even take a breath without feeling like I'll keel over from the heartbreak.

I guess I've now experienced the crippling blow of heartbreak cutting out my knees from under me.

I chuckle mirthlessly, thinking back to the thoughts I had a year ago when I was still an unemotional block of ice, saying farewell to Liesel in the Rose suite, not knowing my life was about to turn upside down.

My mind is filled with Grace. A rotating slideshow of soft smiles, brilliant eyes, of random factoids of the world, to her alluring smell of jasmine, her warmth, her touch, her intoxicating love.

She's the other half of my soul and now I'm dealing with it being torn away, fates ripping it apart seam by seam, tossing everything into the flames of hell.

If I get to do it all again, I'd stay away from her.

Anything to prevent this pain and agony, which I know will devastate her.

It'll hurt her and that's the one thing I can't bear.

Regret, my most hated emotion, cloaks over me like a plastic bag on my face, slowly suffocating me as the oxygen runs out.

"Don't you think you owe it to her to tell her the truth?" Ryland murmurs, his fingers fiddling with a pebble from the ground. "She deserves to know."

"I'm sick, you know." My words are slurring now. *Finally.* "I thought about being selfish. Before I told you guys, no one knew the truth. If I don't tell anyone, and my parents won't tell anyone of this shame, no one else has to know. She doesn't have to know. I could pretend nothing happened and still be with her."

The dark thoughts have haunted me ever since I found out the truth. Sick. Corrupted heart. Vile.

My mind spun with possibilities. We could adopt. We could move far away and leave this world behind us. We could change our names and hide our identities. She'd never have to know she's related to me. I could still love her and bask in her warmth, *and no one would know.*

It's sick and I'm disgusted with myself.

It's wrong.

And whenever I could fall asleep, whether on the plane or in my apartment earlier, my dreams would be filled with her—her kisses, our bodies coming together in a union so much more than the physical, her screams when she tremors in pleasure underneath me as I pound into her, chasing out my demons. Her laughter, the twinkle in her eyes.

The way she says I love you because she *does* love me, wholeheartedly, desperately, just like the way I love her.

When I'd wake up, I'd find my face wet with tears, my hands clutching the pillow she used before against me, my lungs drawing in the faint fragrance of jasmine, a smell that's fading away, just like my life is without her by my side.

Ryland creeps closer and clasps me on the shoulder. "Steven. Steven, look at me." His voice is terse. A command.

I glance up.

"Don't make any rash decisions. You're not in the right frame of mind right now. Talk to her. You owe her that. If you love her as much as you do, you owe her the truth."

"Some of us aren't allowed to tell the truth...I of all people, understand that," Maxwell begins, his words cryptic, "but in your case, I think you should tell her. She needs to hear it from you. Didn't you say she's looking for her father? Eventually, she'll find out. It's better for her to learn it from you."

I nod glumly. "I know that," I mutter under my breath. "I know that."

"And we'll be here for you afterward, Steven. All of us," Charles says softly as he crouches down, his face grim, and the others agree in unison.

She deserves to know.

We're a team. This is my last act of kindness to her as I stab her in the heart and cripple her in pain. My parting gift so she can receive the news with kid gloves, knowing I love her until the very end, until I'm not allowed to.

Because she's worth it. And I should let her know that. She's worth every wishing star in the skies, every factoid in the darkness of the night.

I'm not leaving her because she's lacking—she needs to know that.

And hopefully, one day, when the dust settles and her heart heals, and the scar has faded, she can find a good man to love her. Because she deserves the love. She deserves everything in the world.

Tears cloak my vision and my chest tightens in a vise, stealing me of breath at the idea of her with another man, of someone else kissing those beautiful lips, listening to those soft sighs, eating the damn hot dogs with her in Central Park, doing all the things I want to do.

The weight on my chest smothers me and acid churns in my gut, swirling, roiling like a ship in dark seas amidst a hurricane. Another flash of pain—a bolt of lightning—hits me in my heart.

My fingers tremble as I pick up my cell phone, hover over her name, and press the call button.

"Steven? Steven, are you there? Are you okay?" Her sweet, frantic voice filters through the line.

My kindhearted darling Grace. Her first words are not of censure, not of anger, but of concern. For me.

"Steven?"

I let out a ragged sigh and clear my throat. The Andersons and Charles have stepped away, no doubt to give me privacy as they hover a few feet in front of me, talking amongst themselves in hushed whispers.

"I'm here and I'm fine." *Liar.* My voice is hoarse and raw. "W-Where are you?"

"I'm with the girls. What happened?" I can hear the worry bleeding through her voice.

"Send me the address. I'm coming to you."

CHAPTER 33

Grace

I PACE AROUND THE colorful living room of Millie's and Belle's two-bedroom apartment in SoHo. Moments ago, the girls were consoling me as I was drowning my sorrows and worries in a pint of vanilla ice cream. After we won the war against Timothy Voss and Steven boarded his jet to bring the news of our victory to his father, he disappeared without a trace.

Normally, a day with no contact wouldn't worry me, but Emily's frantic voice when she called me on the phone was something I wouldn't forget for a long time.

His sister sounded desperate. Worried beyond measure.

If it weren't for the "read" notifications on my text messages and the lights turning on in his penthouse apartment on the Upper West Side, I would be afraid for his safety, thinking the worst had happened.

The memories of our last moments together haunt me. The tears in his eyes when he found me after his talk with Elias, when he held a bundle of documents in his shaky grip he said would win us the war. The soft, searing kiss he pressed on my lips before he got on his jet for LA that night, promising me he'd come back the next day and we'd be able to spend the rest of our days together in peace.

I was worried sick and when I found out something happened and he was back in the city, and the concern mixed with anger when he ignored my calls and texts, leaving those who love him to worry alone.

How could he do this to me? To his sisters? Doesn't he know we're worried?

And so, tonight, my mind mad with swirling emotions, we had our girls' night at Millie and Belle's apartment, where we watched *Sex and the City* the movie—the iconic scene where Charlotte curses the day Mr. Big was born on the day he was supposed to marry Carrie—our ceramic bowls filled with heaps of ice cream.

When men disappoint, my girls will always be here.

But my mind was still cluttered, my thoughts still full of Steven, and even the rich creaminess of ice cream couldn't stave the pain.

Then, my phone rang and my heart leaped to my throat as my fingers trembled as I answered. Suddenly, all thoughts of anger flew out the window and concern for him darted to the forefront.

One minute. That was how long the phone call lasted. But I had a distinct feeling it was the start of the end. A sixth sense. A harbinger of doom.

The world fades into the background as Steven's voice on the phone echoes in my mind.

He sounded like he was in pain. Like his knees were cut out from under him. I have never heard him this way before. The desolation. The hopelessness. The slurring, like alcohol was his newfound best friend.

It was not the King of Wall Street riding the chariot of victory on the phone. It was not the calm, collected, always in control man who hid behind his stoic veneer.

It was someone in crippling pain.

My pulse is chaotic in my ears, my heart slamming against my rib cage, desperate to escape. I feel queasy, like I'll relieve my stomach of the ice cream I was consuming on the couch moments ago.

The sixth sense is first mentioned by William Whitson in the eighteenth century in relation to one of the apostles in Christianity.

The factoid flitters in my mind—my body's defense mechanism because I know, deep in my gut, a sixth sense if you will, something is terribly, horribly wrong, and even without knowing what it is, my entire being is fighting it, is dreading it.

And for the first time, I don't want to see him. Steven. I miss him like I'd miss an amputated limb, but at this moment, I know he's the bearer of bad news. Somehow, my body and mind know the moment I see him, my world will change and nothing will ever be the same.

My eyes burn as I mourn an unknown loss which I'd bet my life would be devastating, cutting, obliterating to my soul.

I pant out heavy breaths as I walk back and forth in front of the lavender sectional of their art déco-inspired living room, where the girls are watching me, their mouths agape.

"What's did he say, Grace? You look like you've seen a ghost," Millie asks, her brows pinched.

Taylor snarls. "Did the bastard give an explanation? How could he make you worry like this!" My sister, the fierce honey badger, already leaping into battle mode for me.

"Tell us, we're here for you," Belle muses, her eyes piercing and sharp.

I shake my head repeatedly, my feet digging holes into the carpet as I pace in front of them. My body can't stop moving or else I'll go insane. "I don't know. He sounded bad. Devastated. He's coming over now."

I look up and moisture wells in my lips. I tremble. "I-I'm scared, girls. I don't want to know what's going on."

Millie's lips wobble as she takes in my expression and she hauls to her feet and wraps her arms around me. The other girls follow suit. I try to breathe but cold sweat is gathering on my body.

"We'll be here. Whatever happens, we'll be here," Millie whispers.

"Sisters forever," Taylor muffles into my hair.

"Maybe it isn't as bad as you think it is. Our imaginations can be wild." Belle is the voice of reason, but even she sounds unsure at the current moment. "The man is crazy in love with you. There has to be a logical reason for everything."

I swallow, my heart lodging in my throat. "And that's what I'm afraid of." For a calm, rational man to act completely out of the ordinary, it has to be something horrible.

"All I know is, Steven is a good man. He's not like one of the assholes in your life before." Millie nods, her eyes fierce. "He has to have a reason for his behavior."

Deep down, I believe her. The man I know would never knowingly hurt anyone without reason. He's tough. He's an asshole at times. But he has a conscience in that big heart of his, the one he claimed for the longest time not to have, only for me to unearth it beneath a pile of rubble that is his childhood trauma.

The clock ticks ominously in the background as we huddle on the sofa, as if waiting for our turn in front of the firing squad on death row. My eyes close and I sit in tensed silence, trying to calm myself and clear my thoughts.

Maybe it isn't as bad as you think it is.

Minutes later, a terse knock slices through the quiet and I nearly jump at the intrusion.

My legs tremble as I walk to the front door, the girls loitering behind in the living room as they whisper amongst themselves.

Looking back at them, I see Millie doling out a sweet smile, Taylor with a scowl on her face, ready to take on Steven if he breathes in the wrong direction, Belle giving me a calm, reassuring nod.

Millie makes a motion toward her bedroom with her hand and ushers the girls in the direction, no doubt to give us some privacy. I hear her door click shut.

Taking a death breath, I open the front door, and my heart drops to the floor. I feel as if someone punched me in the chest.

My beautiful man, rendered into this ghost of a living being.

Steven sways as he stands before me, supported by Ryland, whose tall frame shakes imperceptibly as he hoists Steven up to the best of his abilities.

"Grace," Ryland greets me, his voice somber, his slate eyes roving behind me, but I barely pay attention because I can barely believe my eyes.

Steven's beautiful hair is sticking out in all directions, like he hasn't seen a shower in days. His eyes are bloodshot and glazed over. His breath reeks of alcohol. His dark suit, if you can call it that, is wrinkled, with dirt on the jacket and the pants, the white shirt hanging out, untucked from his pants, a tie nowhere to be seen.

The sixth sense inside me rears to life and my hand flies to my mouth as a gasp escapes my lips.

"My sweet, darling G-Grace," he slurs before collapsing on top of me, wrapping his arms around me in a vise, like he's afraid I'll vanish. "I love you, so, so much."

"Steven, what's going on?" Moisture clouds my vision as I hear the anguish in his voice. It's as if I can feel his pain. He's drowning in it.

Shakily, he pulls back and curls his hand around my face, his thumb circling my cheek in reverence. Moisture mists his eyes as he stares at me with utter heartbreak. He looks at the living room behind me, his brows furrowing.

"The girls are inside the bedroom," I answer the question in his eyes.

He nods and sways on his feet. "Do you have somewhere p-private we can talk?"

I glance at Ryland, finding his somber gaze on us. Turning back to Steven, I reply, "I-I guess, they have a private rooftop garden."

"I'll be back, girls," I holler without tearing my gaze off Steven, my heart already cleaving into two at this powerful man being rendered into this person who seems to be only half alive.

Ryland grunts as he hoists Steven against his shoulder while I curl my arm around his waist. Steven grips me tightly against him as we stagger toward the elevators. Minutes later, we find ourselves in a dark, quiet garden and Ryland deposits Steven on a bench and steps away, no doubt to give us privacy.

The garden is normally one of my most favorite places in this building. There are colorful potted plants carefully tended to by Millie and small trees dotting the periphery, the space normally filled with fragrant blooms—a small, private oasis in the middle of the city. It's usually warm and inviting and gives me a sense of peace as soon as I step foot inside.

But tonight, it's cold. Stark. Barely illuminated as the moon and the stars are hidden by the thick storm clouds. Only a fraction of the normal light shines through the garden, with the twinkling lights of the adjacent buildings lending to visibility.

The wind is brisk, carrying a thick layer of humidity, and I shudder and rub the goosebumps pebbling my arms. The sounds of the city can be heard from far below—honking of cars, subway trains chugging over metal tracks, but everything fades into thick silence, with only the sound of my clamoring pulse in my ears as I take a seat next to the man I love.

A broken shell of his former self.

My hands grow clammy and I wipe them on my leggings before wrapping my arm around his waist and leaning my head on his chest. He clutches me against him, his heartbeats sure and strong, his warmth surrounding me.

My nose inhales his scent of safety. My home.

Suddenly, the anger from hours ago dissipates, and the rioting pulse inside me calms as we sit in stillness. He threads his hand with mine, and I notice his watch missing from his wrist, his most prized possession, the gift from his father I always see him handling with care. I trace the empty spot with my other hand, my fingers grazing at the tan lines in his muscular forearm.

"Where's your watch?"

He chuckles, his voice full of pain.

"Mind over matter," he whispers, and shakes his head. "It doesn't work. I can't mind over matter out of this. I can't lock my emotions away any more than I can stop breathing."

He clasps his other hand on top of mine. "I don't want to wear it anymore."

My heart breaks because I know this is significant. This is one of his father's rare gifts to him, a token of his affection, something Steven desperately wants but always feels he lacked.

"What happened? Is your father okay?"

"They had him sedated earlier before I left LA. The doctors said he needs rest and to avoid stress." Steven lets out a mirthless chuckle. "He'll be fine."

I frown. "What happened then? Why haven't you answered my texts? I was so worried!"

He doesn't look at me, but instead stares into the darkness ahead.

"Steven...you're scaring me. What happened?"

He stills, his muscles clenched. He tilts his head toward the sky. "A starless night," he breathes, "of course it'd be a starless night."

His words make no sense and yet, I sense the answer at the tip of his tongue, the puzzle pieces sifting, trying to combine into a whole.

The silence stretches into seconds, into minutes, his body tensing, muscles clenched, his frame so still, he would've blended into the background if I weren't sitting next to him and feeling his warmth against my body.

After what could've been ten or fifteen minutes of silence, he releases a loud exhale. A long, tortured sigh.

Slowly, he turns to me, his soulful eyes staring into mine. His hand trembles as he cradles my face once more. "Can I be selfish for one more time? Will you forgive me later? I promise you, I'll tell you everything."

My heart riots inside me, and my breathing quickens. *Of course I'd forgive him. I'd forgive him for anything.* It's a hopeless cause. I could never stay mad at him.

At my silence, he continues, "I'd like to cash in one of my days. Can I?" His thumb touches my lips, as if testing the texture. "One last day."

My mind flits back to our bet, which feels like a long time ago. The karaoke bet between a cold king of the realm and the intern who didn't know her place, two people who had no business being together and yet somehow found themselves mired in the same web, drinking the same poison, falling in love.

Intoxicating, desperate love.

My eyes mist, a heaviness sits atop of my chest, as I process his last words, "one last day."

It seems final. Like no matter what I say or do, I'd never be able to change his mind. The spark of anger begins in my gut, threatens to travel up to my chest.

How dare he decide for me?

His eyes falter, as if he knows what I'm thinking. "You'll understand after I tell you." He swallows, "B-But before then, can you give me one last day?"

I take a deep breath and quash the flames inside me. I'll convince him later once he tells me everything. I'll be the lifeboat in his turbulent seas, the calm within the madness.

But if somehow this all collapses later, I want this one last day with him.

I nod, my heart splintering, a lump forming in my throat. "You can have all my days."

Steven chokes and shudders, and he leans forward, pressing his forehead against mine. "Don't hate me afterward, Grace. I wouldn't be able to bear it."

I throw my arms around his shoulders and cling tightly.

I'll never be able to hate him.

He has my whole heart—all the broken pieces, all the raised scars and bloody seams. He has it all. If it were to be crushed, I wanted him to be the one to do it, because I knew, when this ended, I'd never open myself up to anyone again.

I'm not my mom. I'm not that brave. I recognize the love we have is once in a lifetime, and something I'll never, ever be able to recreate. The pain is too great, the cost is too high, and this is the end of the road for me.

I'm going to fight like hell to protect us.

CHAPTER 34

Grace

WORDLESSLY, HE STANDS UP, takes my hand, and pulls me upright. Ryland appears by our side and Steven tells him, "I'm fine. Go home. I'm calling a car."

"You sure?" Ryland's gaze skims to my face before returning to his. "Did you tell her?"

Steven shakes his head. "But I will."

Ryland clasps his hand on Steven's shoulder and wraps him in a one arm hug. He murmurs something in his ear before stepping back. With a terse nod, he strides away, leaving Steven and me in the darkness of the garden.

A few minutes later, Steven and I are in a black town car. The ride is quiet, a somber atmosphere cloaking us in silence. His hand clutches mine, his fingers gripping me in a firm clasp, as if he's afraid I'd pull away and bolt out the door.

He keeps his face turned toward the window, but I know he's not watching the city lights and cars blurring around us.

Steven is an intelligent man, someone who deals with chaos with ease. For him to be rendered into this shell of his former self, I know it isn't just because his father is in the hospital. It's something more. Something horrible. Devastating. Something he doesn't see us recovering from.

A lump lodges in my throat as my pulse riots in my ears.

I'm terrified.

Part of me doesn't want to know what has rendered the strong, formidable king into the drunken person next to me.

I'm afraid, whatever this is, it'll end us.

A suffocating weight sits on my chest, a burning behind my eyes, and I feel like I'm already mourning a devastating loss, but I don't know what it is, or what the cause of death is.

If I get to relive the last day before Mom's life was cut short by an intoxicated driver, I'd want to bask in her warmth, whisper how much I love her over and over again until she believes it to the marrow in her bones, so she'd fall asleep with a smile on her face.

The same feeling courses through me in this aching silence with our fingers intertwined. If this is the day before the loss, then every minute, every second of this day would be emblazoned in my mind forever. Every touch, smell, sound, and sensation would reappear in my mind during my waking hours and flutter across my dreams as I remember and mourn, wishing I could relive this day and say the words that are unsaid, to minimize my regrets.

Anger has receded into a dark corner in my mind now. My mind senses I'm standing at the edge of the cliff, my fingers gripping Steven's as he hangs on the precipice. But my hand is growing sweaty, my muscles are aching, the fibers tearing, and he's slowly slipping away.

The last grains of an hourglass.

And so, I'd live as if I'd already lost—a day of no regrets.

Bringing his hand up to my lips, I whisper, "I love you, Steven. I'm not giving up on us. Whatever you think has happened isn't as bad as you think it is. We can overcome this. But I want you to know I love you so, so much. No matter what happens, I want you to carry my heart with you always. And when you lie asleep in the middle of the night because a thunderstorm is raging outside, take my heart out and know my love will be with you always. Never forget that."

His body shakes as he tightens his grip on mine. A choked gasp, but he remains silent.

Minutes later, he's unlocking the door to his penthouse on the Upper West Side. He hasn't been to The Orchid as much in the recent weeks. I wonder if he was usually there previously because he was lonely.

He quietly leads me up to the solarium, which is darker than the last time I was here, when we made love as if we were among the stars in the galaxy.

Raindrops patter against the glass as the storm slowly unleashes its power. The world blurs around us as we're cloaked in our shelter from the elements.

He pulls me to a loveseat and hauls me on top of him.

Steven's eyes are intense swirls of darkness as they travel over my face, his fingers skimming over my eyelids, my nose, my cheeks, as if memorizing me by touch.

"I don't know how I could've forgotten," he whispers. "Your eyes...I should've known."

He heaves out a breath as he touches me, as he loves me with his caresses. "If I were him, I'd give my hug to you too. I'd love you. How could I not?"

His words make no sense, but something nags at me, like some truth is just out of my reach.

"I'm a vile man and I don't deserve you. If I got to do this all again, I'd stay away and let you live your life without me. Unsullied. But I'm selfish."

"No, don't say these things, Steven." I press my finger on his lips.

He kisses the tip, his tongue flicking out and swirling on it, sending a thousand pinpricks of sensations through me.

"My father once told me emotions are liabilities, and don't fall in love because when a woman leaves you, she'd inevitably take a piece of you with her, and you'd never get it back and you'd be bereft the rest of your life," he whispers ardently as he cradles my face with his hands.

"If I knew you'd leave this unscathed, I wouldn't regret a thing. Because I'd rather feel my heart break knowing I had your love at one time, knowing I was worthy of it. Even if you took a piece of me with you, I'd be comforted because I knew it'd be in your tender, loving care, that even though the rest of me were broken, bereft, and languishing away," he swallows, his voice thick, "one tiny piece of me would always be happy."

Wetness gathers in his eyes as he chokes on his words, and I swallow, trembling, my eyes clouding over with tears as well.

"I love you, Grace Felicity Peyton. More than you could possibly understand."

My eyes well with tears as I reach up and press my lips to his.

The raindrops fall harder, a pounding rumble against the glass, and nature rears its ugly head, blurring the windows in a swath of water, cloaking us in this one tender moment of intimacy, of privacy.

He freezes, his body falling still. I press harder, wanting to imprint ourselves onto each other's souls. My hands trail to his chest and try to unbutton his shirt.

With an anguished grunt, he pushes me away and instead wraps his arms tightly around me, burying his face in my hair.

"I love you," he gasps, "I just need you in my arms for tonight." His words are strained and hoarse. Thick with secrets.

He pulls me up and clasps my body to his. I can hear the steady thudding of his heartbeat as he sways in place with me.

"Baby, don't leave me in my personal version of hell, take me with you, even if it's not in this world but beyond..." he sings, his voice thick with tears. The heartbreaking lyrics of "You're My Stars."

I clutch his back tighter as we dance under the starless night with his heartbeat and husky voice as accompaniment.

We sway and sway and I inhale his unique scent of safety and comfort, even though my heart is heavy and tinged with sadness from the agony leaching out from his voice.

I shush him, sliding my hand over his back in comfort, and he presses another kiss into my hair as he guides me into a shaky rhythm.

Closing my eyes, I relish in the heat of his embrace, the love in his voice, even if everything feels so heavy. *I'll save you, Steven, from whatever is plaguing you.*

"Take me with you to the beyond...because you're the stars in my skies," he whispers as we stop.

Without another word, he carries me to the bedroom and tucks me under the covers before crawling in next to me and drawing me into his arms, wrapping me in his familiar scent of the ocean and leather, the feeling of love and safety.

Then I feel it, wetness dripping on my forehead.

He trembles but remains quiet. He's crying silent tears. The man who once said he has no emotions is broken into pieces before me and I'm helpless to stop it.

The tears I've been holding in for so long finally slide down my cheeks, wetting my pillow.

As the storm batters the city outside, a hurricane blows through our hearts and after long moments of silent tears and hidden anguish, we fall into a deep sleep.

I knew he left before my eyes flutter open. I can feel the emptiness in the apartment, the stark absence of him. I don't want to open my eyes, to face whatever reality awaits me because somehow, I know I won't like what I'll find there.

But I'm not a coward. I'm not one to shy away from problems. I'm Grace Peyton, the girl from the seediest part of the South Bronx who, despite all odds, graduated with honors and became a consultant for a top investment banking firm. I'm the person who did everything she could possibly do to keep her family together, to pay off the loan from the loan shark, to pay for her sister's tuition at ABTC. I'm the girl who dared to fall in love, despite vowing to myself never to step into Mom's shoes.

I'm brave and I won't shy away from this.

If I fall and break my legs, my heart and body battered and bloodied, I'll still get back up and survive.

I inhale deeply, his scent of the sea and worn leather filling my lungs, and I force my eyes open. Sunlight streams in from the windows, warm and bright, like the storm last night were figments of our imaginations.

Steven's side of the bed is empty, as I expected, but on top of his pillow lies an envelope with my name on it.

With shaking hands, I take out a folded sheet of paper and a photo. Setting the photo aside, I read the letter on top first.

My darling Grace,

Perhaps you're the brave one between the two of us. I don't know how to break the news to you in person. I don't know how to watch your world crumble, just like mine did in LA. I hope you can forgive me for telling you the truth on paper instead.

I know who your father is. He's much closer than I'd ever thought possible.

Grace, a long time ago, my father had an affair with your mother and you and your sister were born as a result. Remember the story I told you at dinner about that one stormy night when I saw my father's other family, when he gave them all his hugs and kisses? That night, I remembered seeing a little girl clinging to her mother in the pouring rain as they sobbed together. My father was crying along with the storm. My memory had holes in it, and I didn't realize until now, until my mother told me...

That little girl is you.

I gasp, my heart bolting to my throat, choking me, and a sudden wave of dizziness hits me. Quickly grasping the bed frame, I steady myself as old memories flood into my mind.

I had only been on a plane two times in my life. One time was the beautiful trip to Hawaii with Uncle Bobby, the only time I got a taste of what a family vacation would feel like. The other time also revolved around him. Taylor was at a weekend sleepover and Mom rushed me to the airport and we flew across the country.

I remembered the storm, the rain, the loud thunder, which terrified me every time it rumbled after the lightning flashed around us. I remembered Uncle Bobby kneeling in front of me, his eyes wet with tears, blending with the rain as he held out his arms.

I remembered hugging him and him hugging me back and kissing my hair. I remembered how, on the way back to the airport, Mom told me we wouldn't see Uncle Bobby again.

And now...I suddenly remember the shadow of a boy older than me, hiding behind the windows, who looked so heartbroken and sad. But he disappeared after Uncle Bobby gave me the last hug. I always thought it was a child's imagination, my psyche inventing a companion during one of the most heartbreaking nights of my life.

Someone to share my burden and pain with.

My lungs heave in pants of air as I quickly read the rest of the letter.

I'm your half-brother, Grace. I learned the truth after I went home to tell my parents about our triumph over Voss. Mother is devastated in a way I've never seen her behave before. Father fainted from the shock when I confronted him. It turns out the reason Mother was so against us wasn't because of your background. It's because you're my sister.

We can never be together. It's immoral. It's a disease.

Please forgive me for last night, for not telling you the moment I found out. I desperately wanted one last memory with you. Please forgive me for my behavior. Instead of dealing with the situation like a man, I chose to be a coward, to drink myself into hopes I'd never awaken and I can keep you with me always.

But all dreams have to end. Not all wishes come true, even the wishes made upon a wishing star.

My only regret is hurting you because I know you'll be crushed by this news, just like I was when I found out. But selfishly, I could never regret you.

I'm thankful you exist.

I'm thankful you got his hug and love when I got everything else from him.

I'm thankful you walked into the halls of Pietra and into my life.

I'm thankful I got to be the one to love you, to receive your love, even if it's only for a short while.

I'm thankful you've resurrected my heart, even though I'm dying of pain, but at least I have the memories of our time together with me always. At least I've loved and truly lived before.

I love you forever and always, even though we can never be together.

"You're the stars in my skies, the reason I breathe at night, how will I live now that you're not by my side?"

I understand these lyrics now, and I thank you for teaching me the power of love.

Forever yours,

Steven

P.S. Once you've had time to process this, if you want to find me, I'll be at my suite at The Orchid. I won't run away this time.

The letter falls from my hands onto the blankets, and I look at the photo on the bed. It's a faded one, but I recognize a slightly younger Steven, his mother, two women I presume are his sisters, and a man I haven't laid eyes in over fifteen years—Uncle Bobby, known to the world as the reclusive Robert Kingsley. He's thinner, his hair graying, but those kind eyes and regal bearing are very much him.

I let out a shuddering sob as tears stream down my face. Clutching Steven's pillow, still heavy with his scent to my chest, I cry as the reality of the situation finally catches up to me. That's why he pulled away last night when I kissed him. That's why he looked so broken, so haunted. That's why I was mourning a loss I couldn't identify until now. That's why he told me not to hate him.

I want to be angry; I want to feel disgusted and perhaps a part of me does, with the nausea joining in or the pounding pain in my chest, but at the end of the day, I could never bring myself to hate him.

How could I? He's very much a victim of the same circumstances as I am. Two broken people who, despite all odds, fell in love when they shouldn't have, because of the sins of our parents.

One doesn't fall out of love because something as inconvenient as the truth enters the picture. The heart doesn't care about common sense, rational thought, what's right or wrong.

They say the heart wants what it wants.

I always thought that was foolish, but now I realize I'm the fool, a fool still madly, desperately in love with a man she has no future with. With someone she isn't allowed to love romantically.

My heart splits apart into broken slivers, joining his tattered pieces as the vultures of reality feast on the scraps.

An unbearable pain scythes through my insides, cleaving me in half as my tears wet the pillow and guttural cries tear from my throat.

It can't be.

The denial is a constant chant, echoing in my mind. I shake my head. I refuse to believe it.

Taylor and I asked Mom if Uncle Bobby was our father and she always said no. She was vehement about it, and I never sensed deceit from her.

I fist the blankets as I rake in desperate gulps of air, my mind trying to hang on to the last vestiges of rational thought, of logic.

It can't be. There has to be a mistake. Mom would've told us. I'm sure of it. My father is someone else. He can't be Uncle Bobby.

The irony doesn't escape me—the person I longed to be my father when I was a kid is the one person I desperately hope isn't my father now.

The flames in my heart refuse to dim, my soul denying this twisted fate as the end.

An icy resolve fills my veins and I breathe in calming breaths of air and brush away the tears from my cheeks.

I'm going to get to the bottom of this. I'll find the truth, the answers, and until I see the DNA results in front of my eyes, I refuse to accept this is the end for us.

CHAPTER 35

Steven

MY PHONE BUZZES CONSTANTLY, but I ignore it. My head feels like it'll explode alongside my heart, the pain so eviscerating, I wish I were unconscious so I'd be out of this misery.

My mind keeps flashing to the way Mother kneeled with me in the mud and grass, soiling her couture dress. If the revelation came only from her, I might not have believed it. After all, she wasn't party to the affair. But then, Father's shock and how he whispered, *"Y-You found out? You know?"* I'd never forget the horror on his face and how he promptly collapsed in front of me. How I wish he'd tell me it isn't true.

I don't want to speak to anyone, not my family, not the Anderson siblings, who'd taken turns appearing at the door of my suite once someone spotted me back at The Orchid, not Charles, not my brothers-in-law, Adrian, Parker, or James.

I don't want to see anyone except Grace.

Despite everything, I still can't bring myself to admit she's my sister, that we're related by blood.

There's a rightness between us, the way her rough edges fit against mine, how our souls call out to each other, how our bodies connect and become greater than our individual selves, how everything in the world makes sense when she's by my side. Life is a sick, cruel joke if this feeling is an illusion.

It's a terrible nightmare, one I wish I could wake up from. I'd take a thousand nights of violent storms and howling winds over this.

Popping a few ibuprofens, I chase them down with a large sip of water before I stagger back to the sofa in the dark living room. The shades are mostly closed except for a small sliver of light peeping through. I told Jarvis to go home, but he insisted on leaving a sandwich on the counter for me to eat.

"The heart can't mend until the body has strength," he said.

But a huge part of me doesn't want to get over this, because if I accept this pain, I'm accepting reality and perhaps there's still a kernel of whimsical inside me, a piece of Grace I'm carrying in my chest, the hope somehow, there's a way out of this, and I can keep loving the only woman who's ensnared my whole heart and taken off with it.

I frankly don't think I can ever stop loving her.

I don't see a way out of this.

The pounding in my chest worsens as I lie on the sofa, staring into the blank ceiling above. Empty, like my soul.

By now, she should've woken up and read my letter. I didn't want to leave her this morning, when she curled up sweetly against my chest, her hand clutching my shoulders like I'd disappear. She had a beautiful bloom on her face. Her chocolate strands spread like a halo on her pillow, but she looked so happy with the small smile on her luscious lips.

She looked breathtaking.

She looked like she belonged there next to me.

She looked like mine.

I wanted to stay by her side as she read the letter, but my heart was too heavy and I couldn't bear to witness her pain, knowing there was absolutely nothing I could do to heal her, to fix the problem. And so, I ran away, back here to my suite at The Orchid, waiting for her to find me, waiting for her to end things with me, because I know I don't have the strength to.

I hope my letter brings her answers—at least she doesn't have to search for her father anymore. At least that hole inside her will be filled. Maybe in time, with distance, I'll be able to bring myself to see her at family reunions with a smile on my face, making conversation with the man she brings home with her, hiding the pain in my chest, the impulse to punch whoever claims Grace as hers, the clenching and fluttering of my heart in her presence.

Because I don't foresee myself ever falling out of love for her.

Buzz. Buzz.

As I mull about the dismal future, the doorbell buzzes to the suite.

I don't move to get off the sofa—it's probably another Anderson. Why the fuck are there so many of them? I throw my arm over my eyes to block out the sunlight filtering in through the gap between the curtains.

Buzz. Buzz. Buzz.

Nuisances, all of them. I groan and yell, "If your last name is Anderson, please go away. I'm alive."

"It's me, Grace."

Her sweet voice jolts me from my stupor, and I sit up, my head protesting at the sudden motion.

Grace. My sweet darling, Grace.

I clamor to my feet and lurch toward the door. My hands are clammy as sweat gathers on my forehead. My fingers tremble as I grab the doorknob and twist, pulling open the door.

Her thick hair is in disarray, her face bare of makeup, her body hidden by an oversized sweater reminiscent of the ones she used to wear when I first saw her at Pietra. The thought sends a small ember of warmth inside me.

She's still the most beautiful person I've ever seen.

Her lips are flattened, her eyes narrowing and with a huff of breath, she shoves me hard in the chest and I stagger back into the suite.

"How dare you, Steven Kingsley!"

The darkness enveloping me recedes briefly as confusion enters the picture. "Grace?"

"You think I'll just accept a letter and a photo from you and let you upend my life?" She stomps into the suite, all fire and blazing glory, determination lacing her voice.

I'm awed. Floored by her passionate anger.

"Darling, my mother told me the truth. My father collapsed when I confronted him. Trust me," my voice breaks, "this is the last thing I want to be true."

She whirls around, her hair flying behind her like a whip through the air. "And your mother is the end-all-be-all truth-holder now? The last I checked, it takes a man and a woman to make a baby and that woman *definitely* does not include the jilted wife. And your father...did he specifically say the words 'Grace is your sister?'"

My breath catches and I stay silent.

Grace charges forward, her finger wagging at me, and presses me against the door. "I asked Mom multiple times if Uncle Bobby is our father and she always said no. And forgive me, but I believe the woman who birthed me out of her vagina over your mom or whatever you thought your father said."

My pulse thrums in my ears as her words sink in. A kernel of hope, the one tiny piece of her left in my chest, wants to take root, to blossom inside me.

Can it be? Can this all be a misunderstanding?

"Grace, why would she lie? She was devastated. I've never seen her like that before. And Father...he looked at me with horror and shock when I confronted him."

She throws her hands up in the air. "I don't know! Mistakes happen. But I don't think my mom would lie to us either. You believe your parents and I believe mine."

Grace heaves out a frustrated breath, her small frame shaking, her face flushed, her body teeming with energy, with determination, with life. And I can't help but love her even more, even though that's the last thing I should be doing.

She's one of a kind. Amazing. I fucking love her to the ends of the earth.

She shakes her head. "I'm not going to believe anything unless I see the truth in front of me."

Suddenly, her frame stills, mere inches from my body as her eyes take on a sharp glint. I can practically see the gears turn in her head. I read the look in her eyes as the first logical thought in the last twenty-four hours lights up my mind.

"You thinking what I'm thinking?" I ask.

She dips her head in a nod.

"This is *so* stupid." She mutters other things under her breath before she takes out her phone from her purse and swipes on the screen, her brows furrowing in concentration.

The phone rings three times before a deep male voice answers.

"Emerson Clarke speaking."

Her investigator.

The breath lodges in my chest as I take in her furrowed brows, her eyes fierce and determined, because she refuses to give up, because she's running the facts to the ground, like the meticulous intern I met a year ago, the one person who never misses the details because it's the details that matter at the end.

"E-Emerson, this is Grace," she says breathlessly, nervousness in her voice.

"Perfect timing. I was just about to call you."

She grabs my hand and clutches it in a tight grip. I lace my fingers with her, telling her without words I'm with her every step of the way. "You were?"

"I just got the DNA results back. One of my candidates is indeed your father."

There are moments when the world stops spinning and time slows to a standstill, when I swear I could hear every second ticking by, feel every atom of air brushing against my body, my nose picking apart every component of her sweet fragrance—the heady notes of mint, followed by the middle notes of jasmine, and a lingering base note of sweet, summer grass, everything that makes up her intoxicating aroma.

My body freezes, my lungs cease to work, my heart clamoring inside my rib cage like summer rain—whether it becomes a much-needed reprieve from the heat or a hurricane is yet to be determined.

I squeeze her hand tightly as every auditory nerve focuses on the deep, smooth voice of Emerson Clarke.

"Tell me, please. Is it Robert Kingsley?" Grace's voice is shaky as she trembles before me.

A second passes by, but it feels like forever.

"He was one of our three candidates. I'd ask you how you knew that but I gather you probably don't want to satisfy my curiosity at the moment," Emerson begins, oblivious to the tension in the spacious foyer, which suddenly feels as small and claustrophobic as the trunk in the back of a car.

"And the answer is...no, he's not your father."

Grace lets out an audible sigh as she collapses on my chest, and oxygen, much needed oxygen, rushes into my lungs as I hold her against me.

Shell-shocked. Disbelief.

My body can't begin to respond, to process his words. It seems too good to be true.

I clutch her against me, feeling her warmth in my arms, something I thought I wasn't going to do again because there'd be no way I could hold her in my arms even as her brother because it would be the cruelest torture to do so.

"Your father is Linus Anderson."

The proverbial gong strikes, the sound echoing in the room.

"What!" Grace exclaims, the shock evident in her voice. She looks at me, her eyes wide.

"Linus Anderson, as in the Anderson family patriarch? The family owning Fleur Entertainment and The fucking Orchid?" I couldn't help but interject, suddenly finding my voice.

Emerson stays quiet at my intrusion as Grace stammers, "S-Sorry for not letting you know, but Steven Kingsley is here with me right now."

Another long pause before low chuckles filter through the line. "Ah, I see. You don't need to answer my question from earlier. Thank you for satisfying my curiosity."

The fucking bastard. Emerson Clarke is one of the best in the business—I've known other businessmen who use him for investigations, and they've always called him a sarcastic son-of-a-bitch, and I can see why he got that nickname now.

"And yes, the same Anderson of the Anderson family you both know."

"You're sure?" I push. Now instead of upending my life, it turns out we'll be upending my friends' lives instead.

"DNA doesn't lie."

Grace's mouth is slack as she gapes at me, her arms still around my waist.

"And my sister?" she asks.

"Still one hundred percent your sister. Same father. I tested his sample against hers too. And still the same answer as last time, don't bother asking me how I got your samples. I have my methods."

After a few more moments of shell-shocked silence, Emerson clears his throat. "I'll email you the test results. Do with it what you will. I hope this brings you closure, and I'll send you the rest of my bill. If you or your friends need my services later on, just call me."

I start shaking, my muscles relaxing as a delirious laugh rips out of my mouth. I'd pay him my entire net worth and give him all the fucking stars on Yelp for this news. The chuckles soon become laughter as I bowl over and clutch her waist tightly to keep me upright.

A thousand sensations filter through me—the zinger of shock, the heady intoxication of happiness, the sweetness of love—and it's as if my heart, which I thought was irrevocably broken, has suddenly been pieced back together by divine intervention and my body doesn't know how to behave or respond. I find myself laughing, crying, tears streaming down my face as sobs tear from my throat, all the while trembling, my head against her stomach as she cradles me in her arms.

"Steven? Steven!" Grace's voice is so sweet and so beautiful.

I rake in a few gasps of air as my body catches up to my mind and I straighten up, my blurry vision taking in her smiling face, her brilliant violet eyes also red and wet with tears.

"We're not related," I rasp out in between inhales. "We're not siblings."

I haul her into my arms and clasp her tightly against my chest, feeling her heart beat against mine.

"You're so *stupid*, Steven Kingsley. I could've told you that. There's no way life would be so cruel to us, to give us each other, only to keep us apart. There's no way. I refused to believe it and I was right," Grace mutters into my chest.

"You're always right, Grace. Always."

Tilting her face up, I lean down and claim her lips with mine once more.

This time, I'm definitely never letting go.

CHAPTER 36
Grace

OUR KISS TURNS FEVERED and passionate as my phone slips from my grip and onto the floor, but I barely notice. Steven spins me around and presses me against the door, his tongue delving into my mouth like he's desperate for air, like he's on the brink of drowning and I'm the oxygen tank thrown into the dark waters seconds before he loses consciousness. He nips my bottom lip as he hoists me higher against him, so that we're pressed to each other in all the ways that matter.

"Grace," he rasps against my lips. "My darling, I'm the luckiest man alive." His cheeks are still wet from tears, his eyes, oh my God, his eyes...

They're burning with so much love, the hazels iridescent, the green edges vibrant and teeming with life. It's like life has returned to his body and he has just been given a second chance. My lips tremble as I take in his emotions flitting across his face—shock, awe, happiness, and overflowing love.

"No, Steven," I whisper, our breaths ghosting over each other's lips, "I'm the luckiest person alive because I get to have you by my side."

He groans, his pupils darkening and dilating, and he swallows the rest of my words with his mouth again as he moves his body against me, his hard shaft grinding against the crook between my thighs.

Everything feels too sensitive, my skin aflame, the clothes chaffing my skin. The air turns thick with desperation as we claw at each other, trying to get closer, for nothing feels close enough. My breasts feel heavy and swollen, my nipples already beaded and saluting him, and I arch back, thrusting my chest at him as he trails kisses and nibbles along the column of my neck, scraping his teeth over my fluttering pulse, sending sparks straight to my clit.

"I need you, Steven," I moan as he thrusts harder against me, his hard cock hitting my swollen clit, but it's not enough. There are too many layers of clothes between us. I need them gone. I need nothing to separate us. I need to feel his body, his heat against mine.

He growls as he comes to the same conclusion and carries me to the bedroom. We grapple with each other's clothes along the way, my sweater falling to the floor first, followed by my leggings. I scratch at his body, my fingers trembling as I try to undo his buttons, to no avail. He tosses me on the bed and rips his shirt off, sending buttons pinging across the dark master room and he makes work of his pants.

Our harsh breathing fills the silence as I stare awestruck at him, all coiled energy and rippling muscles, a hard, intense gleam in his eyes, which are so dark I could barely see the tawny irises anymore. He looks hungry, desperate, his nostrils flaring as he slowly prowls toward me, the muscles in his body flexing with each movement.

With his unkempt appearance, the disheveled hair and rugged beard, he looks wild, like a caveman coming to stake his claim, like he's ready to fuck me in front of the world to tell everyone I belong to him.

My pussy pulses as my chest heaves under my thin shirt, which, along with the wet panties I have on, are the only barriers separating us. My eyes sweep down his body, taking in the corded muscles, which look even more defined and cut than I saw him last, and the beautiful, hard cock curled against his stomach, the veins on both sides pulsing, the tip dark red and angry, like it wants to obliterate anything in its path.

My empty core clenches and my mouth waters. I need him inside me, over me, next to me.

I tremble on the bed before my legs part of their own accord and he lets out an animalistic growl as he stares at my damp panties. I see the last restraints of the rational man snap free and the primitive beast takes front and center.

"Mine." His voice is rough. Possessive.

Wetness seeps out of me as my body vibrates in response.

"Yours," I whisper, watching the flush crawl up his body as he climbs onto the bed and braces himself on top of me, his muscles shaking from tension.

"We're never separating again." A vow. A command. A promise all rolled into one.

"Never aga—Steven!" My words end on a shriek as he rips my shirt in half with a strength I've never seen him unleash before and the woman in me melts at the violence. He could bend me over, twist me, tear into me and I wouldn't be able to stop him.

My mind shuts off as I relinquish my body to him.

Use me. Fuck me. Love me. I tell with my eyes as he lets out a guttural grunt before clamping his mouth on my breast, sucking the tip in, laving it with his tongue and tasting it like it's the best delicacy in the world. Sharp bolts of electricity shoot to my clit and I let out a moan. He pinches the other distended tip as I thrash against him.

"I've gone crazy for you. Mad with obsession." He turns his attention to the other breast as his hand snakes down my body and with one rough yank, tears the lace from between my legs. With no warming, he thrusts a finger inside me as his thumb rubs my clit.

I nearly careen off the bed, only for him to bear down on me, insert another finger inside me, and curl them to rub against my G-spot and I see stars.

"Steven!" I scream, my legs shake as he finger-fucks me in earnest.

The slick sounds of his fingers in my wet core echo in the room. The sparks turn into a wildfire in a matter of seconds and my entire body burns, the sensations all coalescing to my throbbing pussy.

He grunts, his breathing harsh against my ear, and he bites the lobe in a punishing nip as if to mark me from the outside as well. "You're so fucking wet. So fucking mine. I can feel you gripping my fingers like you're desperate for me, for my cock."

He leans in and rasps, "My fucking dirty, naughty girl, so good for me..."

His fingers move faster as my body tenses and my loud moans fill the air. "Are you going to come for me, give me all your cum, and tell me you're mine?"

I arch back as the pressure builds to an unbearable point and my body explodes into a million pieces under him. "I'm yours, Steven. Forever."

With a roar, he spreads my legs and thrusts into the hilt, sliding home, his cock filling me to the brim. He pins my hands over my head, his fingers lacing with mine, like he's desperate for this intimate connection as much as me and he pounds into me like someone possessed.

A claim. Ownership and merging of two souls.

His eyes are wild, his hips unrestrained as he slaps against me in a harsh rhythm, the pounding sounds loud in the room. Lurid. Wet. Hot.

Steven's control is obliterated, and he hoists my legs over his shoulders and climbs higher over me, completely dominating my petite frame with his large body and at this angle his cock hits deeper, harder, like he's trying to get to the deepest recess within me and never come out.

A rapid heat gathers where we're joined, where I'm so full of him, so full of love and lust, and he pins me in place, rendering me immobile.

"Take me," he grunts. "Take all of it. Fuck, you're taking it so well. I'm going to bury myself so deep inside you, you'll always have a piece of me with you."

A groan tears out of his voice as he throws his head back, sweat dripping over his face. "Fucking good girl for me, you're my fucking good girl."

Thrust. Thrust. Thrust.

My pussy burns as the friction inflames me and my eyes roll back and my body spasms underneath him.

"Yes, come again. Milk my cum with your tight pussy."

I let out another scream as I shudder against him, my legs shaking, wetness gushing out of me in torrents.

Before my orgasm subsides, he pulls out of me and tosses me face down on the bed. I'm limp, my body a rag doll for him to use, my core vibrating, throbbing, overly sensitized.

I moan as he presses my breasts to the sheets, and even the silk sheets feel rough against my distended nipples.

He hoists my ass up in the air and rasps, "Your body is mine. You are mine. From now on, I'll take care of you. Your problems are mine to solve, your pleasure is mine to give. You won't need to worry about anything anymore."

His words are a sharp heat wrapping around my heart and for the first time, I feel like I don't need to be in control. I don't need to shoulder everything in life because someone else is there to do it for me.

I'm cherished. Loved. Safe.

"You're mine, Steven Kingsley." The control goes both ways.

His breath puffs against my swollen pussy. "I've been yours since the day we met."

With that sentiment, he unleashes his tongue on my wet slit, licking away the juices trailing down my thighs, before spearing his tongue inside my still throbbing entrance.

I try to scamper away, the area too sensitive, but he growls and grips my hips tighter. "This pussy is mine. You don't get to leave until I'm done with you, and you don't get to come until I say you do."

With a punishing grip, he renders me immobile as he feasts on my pussy. "Fucking delicious, I'm addicted for life," he rasps between licks and suction as I mewl incoherently, my face pressed to the sheets, my body shaking, protesting, yet wanting his torment at the same time.

The pleasure gathers again, my core torn between wanting to fall over the cliff and wanting to escape from his torture. "Steven, oh my God, it's too sensitive, shit."

"Let go, darling. I'll take care of you."

My vision blurs again as my body caves to his pleasure, letting him use me, fuck me, do anything he wants with me, because as long as it's him, I don't care.

As I am about to fall into the abyss again, he pauses and I cry in protest. "I need to come. Make me come," I wail.

"No, darling. Not yet."

He climbs up behind me and uses a finger to swipe my wetness over the puckered rosebud and I nearly come right then from the foreign sensations.

"Next time, my cock will be in here, filling you up." His finger slides in and I clench against him. "Yes, baby, suck me in here too. My cock is much bigger."

I bite onto the bedsheets as two fingers spear into my pussy, moving in tandem with the one in my ass, and the throbbing sensations are tenfold as my hips gyrate back, eager to climb to the pinnacle again.

"You're doing so well, darling. Such a good girl for me."

His praises are arrows to my clit and my body burns once more and I feel like I can fly, my body poised at the brink of exploding—

Then he stops.

"Noooo!" I scream into the sheets.

He chuckles, his voice hoarse, and I shake my ass at him.

"Release your control to me, darling."

Steven lines his cock up at my entrance and finally thrusts inside, and we both groan from the sensations.

My body is on fire as he moves against me with my ass tilted in the air and face smashed against the bedsheets. His hips snap against mine, slamming his hard cock home in a punishing rhythm. His thumb replaces his finger in my ass, and his other hand wraps around my long hair and tugs.

The pain intensifies the pleasure and I tilt my face up, my lungs raking in desperate gulps of oxygen as my body burns into smithereens under his pleasurable onslaught.

I can't think. I can't speak. I can only feel and fuck, as there are too many feelings rioting inside me. My heart is filled to the brim as my mind blanks, handing over the reins of my body to him as he jackhammers inside me, the sounds of skin slapping skin loud in the room.

He curls his large body over mine, his hand still gripping my hair tightly, and he turns my face to the side before slamming his mouth with mine.

We feast on each other, melding our bodies and souls together, becoming one entity. His cock grows impossibly thicker and longer as his thrusts become more erratic. His eyes are obsidian as we break apart for a breath and the pleasure gathers sharply again, taking me higher and higher, and I'm rendered helpless underneath him.

"I can feel your walls clenching, darling. You're close. This time, you'll come," he grunts, and I feel his hips piston harder against my ass, his balls hitting my clit with each movement, his thumb spearing my rosebud as I'm filled to the brim with him.

The pleasure sharpens and breaks and I let out a keening cry as my vision whitens and I can feel myself pulverizing into a thousand pieces.

"Come. Come for me, Grace."

A loud scream tears from my throat as juices gush out of me and I topple into a supernova of white-hot bliss. He swallows my cries and continues to rut against me, his finger, cock, and tongue filling me and with a roar, he comes, his cock throbbing as it unleashes ropes and ropes of cum inside me.

Steven collapses on top of my body as his kiss turns gentler. The sweat is plastered to our skin and our bodies and limbs are intertwined, such that I can't tell where he ends and where I begin. Our heartbeats sync and pound in unison as we come back from the most excruciating high I've ever experienced, things I've read in my novels but have always thought were figments of an author's imagination.

"God, I love you, so, so much, Grace Peyton. Let's not let anything separate us again."

My eyes are heavy and I can barely move my arms but manage to press my hand to his chest, where I feel the thudding of his heart, so strong and sturdy.

I whisper, "I love you more, Steven Kingsley. We'll never be apart. We're a team."

Darkness overtakes me and I drift into a boneless, deep sleep, feeling completely content and safe within his arms.

CHAPTER 37
Steven

SMILING, I CARRY INTO the master bedroom two plates Jarvis procured from the kitchens of O'Hare's, the eponymous restaurant opened by renowned chef, Jefferson O'Hare, who is known for his artistry in the American fare—perfectly cooked steaks, ribs, burgers, and...hot dogs.

My beautiful darling is sprawled face down on blankets and thousand-thread-count bedsheets, her thick chocolate hair a tangled mess on the pillow, her skin glistening with a thin layer of sweat, and her smooth, round backside partially displayed.

My cock twitches in my sweatpants as I take in those luscious globes, pink palm prints on the side, courtesy of me as I gripped her and contorted her lithe little body into a thousand different positions the last few days where we washed off the pain and heartache in love and pleasure.

So much fucking love and pleasure.

We barely left the suite the entire weekend after the revelation, and I regained her after I almost lost her. The last few days breathed life back into my body.

Suddenly, my world is filled with color once again, and everything seems sharper than before—the warm sunlight streaming in from the windows after Grace pulled back the thick curtains to let in some much-needed light into the dark space. The apartment smells of an intoxicating mix of jasmine and leather, our scents intertwined like they belonged together all along. The carpet feels soft against my bare feet and my body is filled with bone-curling warmth.

I feel alive for the first time in almost thirty years.

I feel enough.

Setting the plates on the nightstand, I chuckle under my breath as Grace stirs awake after another bout of sex. This time, I edged her five times before I gave her an orgasm and she spewed out a thousand expletives in the process. Our clothes litter the floor, books and papers scattered all over the place as we fucked on every available surface, but I don't feel the urge to clean, to organize, to put everything in its proper place.

I just want to spend every waking minute with her next to me, teasing out her smiles, making her come against my fingers, my mouth, my cock, having whole-hearted discussions with her about everything from finances to why penguins are monogamous.

And apparently...eating hot dogs.

As much as she loves the fine dining I've taken her to before, she's still hung up on the Central Park hot dog we had almost a year ago. She claims it was a fluke that we got a stale hot dog from the wrong vendor that day, because a good street dog is a New York City staple and classic.

"Steven." She doles out a lazy smile as she stretches her arms over her head and sits up against the tufted headboard. She winces as she adjusts into position.

My eyes drift to her full tits peeking out of the covers and my cock twitches again. I'm fucking insatiable for her.

She notices my perusal and narrows her eyes. "We haven't gotten out of bed this entire weekend, Steven. This is getting ridiculous." She pretends to glare at me, but her lips curve up and an endearing pink flush crawls up her neck, settling on her face.

Laughing softly, I climb into bed with her and lean over, pressing a soft kiss on her plump lips and she melts against me as she always does. "I can't get enough of you."

She moans as I press down, letting her feel my hard cock over her pussy. She winces again and I ease off her. "Did I make you too sore, darling?"

"You beast."

"*Your* beast."

We smile at each other and she bites on the plump bottom lip, a teasing glint appearing in her eyes.

My heart can burst from all the heat and love inside me, an emotion I apparently have bottled up so long I didn't know it was there and now that it's been uncorked, I can't stem my feelings any more than I can stem my need for her.

"I got you proper hot dogs." I wink, pointing to our perfectly plated gourmet hot dogs. "The one on the left is Jefferson's famous umami hot dog. It's one hundred percent Angus beef and has caramelized onions, roasted seaweed, sesame mayonnaise. The one on the right is his interpretation of the Manhattan Street Dog, and has the Angus beef sausage, honey Dijon mustard, homemade ketchup, spiced relish, and caramelized onions."

She grins, her brows arched high on her forehead. "We'll see about that. Sometimes the simpler the food, the better they taste."

I bite back a smile as I put our plates in front of us and we dig in. She makes a cute moaning sound that makes my blood heat and I smirk. "Good, right?"

She nudges me and purses her lips. "You may be on to something here. I hate to admit it, but I may actually be wrong in this case."

I laugh, the sound echoing in the spacious room, and she stares at me with those beautiful gemstone eyes. She whispers, "I love that sound from your lips."

My face softens, and I dip my forehead against hers. "You gave me that gift. The gift of happiness. I'll spend the rest of my life repaying you."

Grace flushes as she ducks her face and returns her attention back to her food.

Suddenly, a tension fills her tiny frame, almost imperceptible, but I know her better than anyone else. A small twinge—a phantom ache—enters my chest. Perhaps after everything, our souls are indeed connected now because I know exactly what she's thinking.

"You're thinking about your father?"

She nods. "I'm scared about our meeting tomorrow."

Heaving out a sigh, I nod. "I'm the same way about my family."

Father called me the night we heard the truth from Emerson. After resting and taking it easy, he was given the all clear to go home. He told me Grace isn't my sister, and I misunderstood him, but he'll explain to us in person. Jess and Emily somehow rounded up the entire family last night and are now flying over in Adrian's private jet. They're probably due to arrive at any minute and we'll be meeting at The Menagerie within the building for afternoon drinks and a much overdue talk.

It's time to air out all the secrets, reveal all our scars, so we can put the past in the past and move on, because there are so many beautiful things waiting for us in the future now that I have Grace by my side.

"I'll be with you, Steven."

I smile and clasp her hand in mine, giving it a soft squeeze. "And I'll be a phone call away, but you have my support with you always."

Grace told me she wanted to talk to her father in private, just the two of them, before meeting her siblings, and I respect that.

She glances at me and leans her head against my shoulders. "We'll be fine. Things will work out the way they should."

"Yes. And if they don't, I'll be here because we're a team."

✦

Cracking the stiff joints in my neck, I clasp Grace's hand tightly in mine as we stroll into The Menagerie, an intimate wine and cocktail lounge within The Orchid. It's one of their hidden gems, which Sarah, Jack's girlfriend, once mentioned in passing. Emily made the reservations before they left LA.

She said, "This is in between a coffee and a full-on meal, since this conversation is more serious than a passing hello or idle pleasantries and I don't want you two to suffer through a few hours of stilted silence of a meal if things go south."

I bite back a grin as I think of my energetic sister, who has had her wars with our parents before she got to her happily-ever-after with Adrian.

"Wow, this place is beautiful. I didn't know it was here," Grace marvels as she takes in the elegantly decorated lounge, with its dark green and gold wallpaper of hand painted foliage and vines and glittering pendant lights shaped like twigs and tree branches, a nod to nature.

I tug her past the sunken velvet setting, where only one of the ten tables is currently occupied by patrons quietly enjoying a peaceful moment in one of the busiest cities in the world. My eyes skim my reflection as we pass by a wall of gold-trimmed mirrors. My hair is brushed and styled, jaw freshly shaven. I look normal in my navy suit with a white dress shirt and maroon tie. But even from a passing glance, I see the sharpness in my eyes, a brightness not there before.

I know I can only attribute the change to the beautiful woman next to me, Grace.

"There are a lot of hidden gems and nooks and crannies in The Orchid. It's almost like a city within a building," I murmur.

She looks breathtakingly radiant in a lavender wrap dress, which brings out her eyes and clings to her beautiful curves. Her hair is fashioned into some sort of updo, with wispy strands framing her face.

My queen.

We stop in front of one of the private rooms and she whispers, "You got this, Steven. Whatever happens, it's us against the world."

A burst of warmth hits my chest and I push open the door, finding the serious faces of my parents and the casual bearings of my siblings and their husbands already seated around a table, quietly chatting.

The conversation pauses as they take in our arrival. Mother looks regal, her hair swept up and pristine as always. Father appears shocked as his piercing gaze pins on Grace, his lips parted open in a soundless gasp.

James sits ramrod straight, his gaze sweeping over my face as if to check if I'm okay. I give him a nod as I turn my attention to his wife, my oldest sister Jess, who gives me a warm smile.

I clear my throat. "Where are Violet and Lucas?" My niece and nephew are the cutest little creatures in the world.

"They're with my parents. They're visiting," James answers as Grace and I take a seat next to Emily and Adrian.

Emily doles out an impish smile. She wiggles her brows as if to tell me, *I got this* as Adrian curls his arm around his wife and cocks his brow at me, a look I can only describe as sympathy because I knew he went through his own share of hell with my parents.

"So, Steven and Grace are here. Let's air out all this nonsense, shall we?" Emily clasps her hands together and looks around the room, waiting for someone to start.

My father lets out a heavy sigh, his eyes weary, like he hasn't slept in the last few days. "Before I share my story, I want to make it clear that Grace isn't my daughter, even though, for a few years, I treated her as one."

He gives us a sad smile. "Steven, that day, I was shocked you found out about the affair. That was what I was referring to before I fainted. I didn't know you saw the confrontation and kept it inside you for all these years."

I nod before sneaking a glance at Grace, finding her quirking a brow slightly at me, as if to say, *what did I tell you?* I give her hand a squeeze. *You're always right.*

Father continues, "I failed you all. I should've come clean a long time ago, but I was ashamed of myself. As someone who prided himself on adhering to morals and standards, I blew through one of the most important ones—fidelity."

Mother chokes on an anguished sob and blinks her eyes rapidly, clearly trying to stem any outward displays of emotions.

"You know our relationship was not based on love. For a lack of a better term, we started as a business arrangement. Your mother's family and financial influence to infuse money back to our family name and bring back TransAmerica to its glory days in exchange for the Kingsley name. I had a duty to my family as the only son to do this. It was ingrained in me growing up, especially since I was the only man in my family with your grandfather passing away when I was young."

His hands clench his tumbler in a tight grip, his knuckles stark white. An old ache resurfaces as I take in his solemn face. I know it must be hard for him to discard his pride and tell us his past, something that'd mar his character.

"I was content. Your mother and I had a respectable relationship and, I believe, even fondness. She loved to drive our social calendars and make friends, whereas I was content with my work. But in our circles, we needed to have good relationships with other families. So, we complemented each other. We fulfilled our duties and had three beautiful children."

Father sweeps his gaze at me, Jess, and Emily. I bite my lip and wait for him to continue.

"But I thought something was missing, and it didn't occur to me what it was until I met your mother, Grace, one time when I was in New York." He doles out a shaky smile at her. "Your mother was warm, a ray of sunlight. She always did the unexpected, singing while waiting for the subway, dancing in the middle of Central Park. She was fun, charming, everything I wasn't and had never experienced. I fell hopelessly in love with her—there wasn't even a contest at that point."

Mother lets out a ragged gasp as she stares at the drink in her hands, her eyes dipped low and away from our view. For the first time, my heart aches for her, at her heartbreak at hearing how the man she clearly loves has given that love to someone else. I'd die if this were to happen to Grace and me.

"Lisbeth was already pregnant when I met her, and you, Grace, were very little, a mere baby. Whenever I visited, Lisbeth would welcome me into her arms, into your lives, and even though we were eating from street vendors or riding on public transportation, I felt so much love and warmth. It was addictive. Intoxicating. Almost enough for me to want to abandon my morals and responsibilities and stay behind."

Grace shakes beside me and I sneak a glance at her, finding her eyes welling with tears. "Uncle Bobby," she whispers under her breath.

Father smiles, but the expression is laced with anguish. "Being your Uncle Bobby was my privilege, Grace. Then, your sister was born, and you two were so adorable, so sweet. It was hard to let you go. But I knew I had to, because I'm already a father to three beautiful children at home."

He swallows and heaves out an exhale. "The guilt was eating away at me. Spending months away from LA, away from my actual family, but I couldn't leave you three and the longer I stayed, the harder it was to leave. Eventually, I realized I couldn't keep this up, keep two families and two lives on opposite coasts. It wasn't right. Not for you, Taylor, and Lisbeth, and definitely not for my wife and my three children. And so, I broke it off."

Grace leans forward, a tear dripping down her cheek. "But Mom still took me to LA..."

Father nods as his own eyes mist. "She said she wanted to give it one last shot. To find me and see if she could convince me to leave with her. And I was a horrible man because at that moment, seeing her and you in tears, dripping wet from the rain, I wanted to. I wish I could turn back time and not make the mistake in the first place because I ended up hurting everyone around me. It wasn't fair to any of you."

He rakes in a ragged breath. "I'm so, so sorry, Steven. I know you think I don't love the three of you, but I do. Very much so. I just went about it the wrong way. I thought I was toughening you up because you are Kingsleys. You are born with silver spoons in your mouths. Your social circles are filled with sharks and other predators. We need to be strong to survive this cutthroat world where everyone wants a piece of us. I thought I was teaching you that by being strict and not to overindulge."

Father shakes his head, his eyes teeming with regret. "But I see now I was wrong. All of you, pieces of my heart, only wanted one thing from me—my love and affection. I just didn't realize. I didn't know..."

His voice trails off as he stares into space, his mind clearly thinking about the past and everything that occurred. Mother sits stiffly next to him, her own eyes moistened as she tries to discreetly blot away her tears.

Father slowly reaches over and clasps her hand in his—a rare display of public affection. "I'm sorry, Audrey. I'm sorry you thought I fathered two other kids for the past twenty-three years. It must have devastated you on top of the betrayal from the affair. I set everything in motion with my poor choices. Perhaps I pushed you too far, made you believe I wanted a perfect wife, perfect kids, in order to keep me here. That should never be the case. I should've done the right thing and not put you in this position. I take the blame. Regardless, thank you for sticking by me all these years."

Mother breaks down and sobs into her hands. My vision blurs as I glance at my sisters, finding Jess burying her head against James's chest as James whispers in her ear and Emily blinking her own tears away as Adrian kisses her hand in reassurance.

Grace links her fingers with mine and squeezes, her warmth traveling through the contact to my aching heart, which had a wound that never healed and finally, after almost nineteen years, I'm getting the answers I need, the medicine to dress the old wound, to stop it from festering for good.

"Steven," Father begins, his hand swiping his face, his voice thick, "I'm proud of the man you've become. You're smart, successful, but most importantly, you have a good heart. You may think you don't have one, but I've seen it over the years. How you'd lay your life down to protect your sisters even though the three of you squabbled growing up."

My lips twitch into a smile as I remember the way I pranked Emily, the way we played hide and seek, the way Jess and I would play Monopoly when we were kids, only to have Emily later ganging up on me. We'd keep each other in the loop of our lives, even when we were living far apart. Then there was the time when I wanted to smash Adrian's face when he broke Emily's heart.

"You're a good man, a wonderful son. I couldn't have asked for more. And I'm so proud of you for finding a good woman, a life partner worthy of you. And I should've said this more often. I love you, and I love your sisters."

I draw in a ragged inhale, my lungs suddenly flooding with air. A swift heat flushes through my insides, singeing everything in its path as my nose burns and my eyes prickle. I rub a hand over my mouth and jaw and swallow the growing lump in my throat. My nostrils flare and I look away, overcome with emotions.

I'm worthy. I've always been worthy. I'm loved.

I choke out a half-sob and stand up, turning my back toward everyone and I feel Grace's delicate arms wrapping around my waist, giving me the most tender, warmhearted hug.

Father speaks again, and I can feel Grace turning back, her hands still tight around me. "Little Grace, how you've flourished over the years. You were a sweetheart back then and a brilliant, wonderful young lady now. Lisbeth would be so proud of you." His voice shakes.

When I told my sisters what transpired, I also told them Grace's mother passed away not long ago. Clearly, by the thick timbre in his words, he still carries residual feelings for her. I rake in deep breaths—slow inhales followed by slower exhales and feel my pulse settle. I take a seat back in my chair and Grace follows suit.

"I hope she's finally at peace up there, looking down on you both. When I met her, her heart was broken into pieces already and I hoped I was able to put some of it together and give her some happy memories," he concludes and takes a sip of his drink, his shoulders slumped like all the tension has been leached out of him.

"Her heart was broken?" Grace questions, before glancing my way.

Father nods. "As much as we had a lot of good memories together, your mother's one true love wasn't me. It was your father. But that's not my story to tell."

Mother's eyes are red as she stares at us. "I'm sorry, children. The sins of our generation shouldn't fall on you, but they did. I never loved you the way I should've and while your father wants to take the blame, I know the bulk of it rests on me. Bitterness, resentment, and unhappiness have no place in your lives. But I failed you all as a mother and I only hope, with the years I have left, you'll find it in your hearts to forgive me and hopefully we can have a better relationship going forward."

My eyes sweep to Jess and Emily, finding their faces flushed, and I'm sure I'm faring no better. We stare at each other and our hearts finally begin to heal and I give them a nod.

"Let's leave the past in the past, Mother," I murmur, still holding their gazes.

Mother continues, "And I owe you and Grace an apology. I was unforgivably rude that night at the restaurant and it was inexcusable. For all of these years, I always assumed Grace and her sister were your father's daughters because of how much he doted on them. I should've verified. I'm so sorry."

Grace gets up, her fingers trailing over my shoulders as she strides to my parents, both sitting rigidly in their chairs. She walks behind them and clasps both of them in a light hug.

"Thank you for giving birth to a wonderful son," she says as she stares at me, her dazzling eyes shining with tears.

My kind-hearted Grace. My wish upon a shooting star.

Chuckling under my breath, I get up and Jess and Emily follow suit, and we walk to our parents and envelop them into a group hug.

Let bygones be bygones and tomorrow be a fresh start.

Moisture shine in our eyes once more, but this time, they're...

Tears of happiness.

CHAPTER 38
Grace

MY PULSE FLUTTERS IN my veins, nervousness threading its insidious waves inside me as I stare at the large, sprawling mansion on Riverside Drive on the Upper West Side. Everyone knows of the Anderson Estate, one of the rare standalone estates in the expensive land of the exclusive neighborhood, a stone's throw away from Columbia University and my temporary apartment in Morningside Heights.

With its white marble exterior, terracotta roof, copper cornices oxidized into the beautiful pale green of the Statue of Liberty, and two spires atop the distinct towers of the two wings, the impressive building is impossible to miss. I have passed by it to and from work and have admired the perfectly manicured landscapes and the stately appearance of the building, albeit a bit too Gothic for my taste. It's well known the affluent Anderson family has lived there for generations, with the house always occupied by the oldest living male and his immediate family.

I just never realized my hunt for my birth father would lead me here, mere blocks away from where I already live. Taylor wanted to go with me this morning, but I told her I wanted to meet him first, to verify if he is indeed our father, before she meets him. Deep down, I'm afraid of his reception toward us and if it's negative, I don't want to subject her to it.

I swallow the pins and needles in my throat as I make my way up the steps after the guards let me in at the gate. The door swings open before I press the bell and an old, regal man with white hair and kind eyes peers down at me. He looks ancient, like the building.

A butler. My father has a butler.

I stifle a snort and smile at the man, who says, "Welcome to the Anderson Estate, Ms. Peyton. I'm Morris, the butler. Mr. Anderson is expecting you in the back gardens. Allow me to show you the way."

He leads me inside the house, past an elegant marble foyer with a towering floral arrangement atop a round table, through a door leading to a long corridor that would be dim if it weren't lit up by elegant sconces. My heels tap on the hardwood floors as I keep my pace with him, my heart lodging in my throat as nervousness slithers through me at finally meeting the person I've been missing my entire life.

As much as our lives were happy with Mom and we weren't lacking, there has always been this clawing hunger inside me to know who my father is and who broke my mom's heart and made her the person she was before she passed away.

And now, I'm apparently moments away from meeting him in person.

I've read about him in school—the Anderson family is practically a case study in and of itself with the patriarch, Linus Anderson, and his eldest son, Maxwell, both equally famous for their reclusive personalities. They rarely, if ever, show their faces to the media. There may be one or two photos out there of them at the Christmas ball at The Orchid, the only time paparazzi are allowed inside those doors, but even those photos are their side profile or are blurry. The family is shrouded in mystery, but they are powerful as they own half of New York City.

Morris pushes open the French doors at the end of the corridor and makes a right at a tall hedge which resembles the entrance of a maze, and it's then I see him.

The man himself.

His nostrils flare and his mouth parts as he stands. He's a good-looking man for his age, what looks to be mid-sixties or so. The first thing I notice about him is his slate-color eyes. Beautiful and large. The same shape and color as Taylor's eyes. His hair is mostly gray but streaked with the dark hair I've seen on the Anderson siblings when I pass by them at The Orchid.

His shoulders straighten as his gaze bores into mine, as if he's trying to commit every detail to memory. My heart skips a beat as I realize, while I look nothing like him, the way he stands tall and how he seems to miss nothing in his gaze reminds me so much of myself. His brows pinch and he swallows, the shock from his face bleeding into sadness, and he rolls his lips inward and lets out a sigh.

"Grace." His voice is rumbly and rusty. "You're the spitting image of your mother."

His words are solemn and his hands tremble at his sides.

My mind flits to the inscription in the purse my mom treasured until her passing. *The number of stars in the skies pales in comparison to my regard for you.*

As I stare at my father and see his slate eyes darkening, and his hands fisted and white-knuckled, I can't help but feel overwhelmed, an ache appearing behind my rib cage.

There was love. Soul crushing love. Standing mere feet in front of my father, I can see that as clear as day.

"S-Sir." I don't know what to call him. Father would be too presumptuous. Mr. Anderson would be ridiculous.

He gestures to the chair in front of him, and I take a seat as he follows suit. A middle-aged lady with kind eyes walks over and pours tea into my cup and disappears again.

My fingers tremble as I bring the cup to my lips, taking a tentative sip of the citrus infused tea my mom loved. I glance up in shock, finding his eyes softening.

"Lisbeth's favorite."

I don't reply, my voice suddenly rendered mute. The birds chirp in the background as butterflies flit around on this comfortable day. Summer is drawing to a close and fall is making an appearance as the leaves show a telltale orange tinge at the edges.

He tugs the lapels of his casual gray suit and blows out an exhale. His voice is rough but cultured. "Thank you for reaching out to me. I never knew where she went after she left here and I didn't know she was pregnant with your sister then. I could've had her tracked and found, but it didn't seem right when I was the one who forced her away."

"Why did you?" The million-dollar question which has haunted me throughout my childhood, never too far away from my thoughts.

Pain laced his voice and his eyes stare into the distance as if reminiscing about bygone days. "You see, Grace, as you're one of us now, I can share this with you."

He stares at me and swallows, his face serious. "You see, our family is inflicted with a curse."

"A curse?" I sit up, my brows hiked to my forehead, disbelief drenching my voice.

He chuckles mirthlessly. "It sounds ridiculous, but it's true. The firstborn male in our family cannot marry for love because once they do, they doom their wives to a painful death."

I gape at him, my hand clutching my teacup. *What on earth?* My mind drifts to the times when we barely had enough money to pay the rent, when our cupboards were empty and we'd pretend not to be hungry. Then there was the heartbreak in her eyes whenever we mentioned our father and the way she'd lovingly caress the beautiful purse he got her. Outrage, which has been tethered so deep down inside me, threatens to unleash.

They broke up because of a curse? This makes no sense.

My incredulity and anger must be showing because he continues, "Grace, I know you don't believe me and you have the right to be upset. Someday, you'll know the entire story and you'll understand. But it's very true. It's why there's a distinct lack of females in the Anderson family, except for dear Lana, that is."

"What does this have anything to do with Mom and us?"

Father lets out a wistful sigh, so full of regret. "Your mother and I met when she was performing on Broadway. Our family, naturally, had a private box there, and I had a fondness for the theater. She'd outshine the main starlets on stage, much to everyone's chagrin."

His lips twitch up in a smile before continuing, "And I'm sure you know how beautiful she was, inside and out. My first wife died at that point and before then, I was like you, thinking this curse business was ridiculous, but when your one true love keels over in front of you, perspectives change."

He shifts in his seat before taking a sip of his tea. "I didn't want to fall in love again. It was too dangerous. It also felt impossible for lightning to strike twice. But then, your mom came barreling in and it was impossible not to love her. She was one of a kind. I thought if I didn't marry her, perhaps we could carry on, out of sight of my other children and relatives, living in our own little world of happiness. Perhaps that'd be enough. At that point, we had you. She was adamant unless I make an honest woman out of her, she wouldn't put my name on your birth certificate. Even so, you were our brightest star in the sky, and for a short while, we were happy. I thought I beat fate."

Father pauses and takes a deep breath. "But alas, she wanted more. She didn't want to be a kept woman in the dark. She wanted her happily-ever-after with her prince and to live with him in his castle, sitting next to him at the dining table, waking up next to him in bed, as she rightfully should want. And after what happened to my late wife, I couldn't risk that happening to her, and after so many arguments and fights, she had enough and gave me an ultimatum."

"You had to marry her or let her go," I whisper, because I know that's what I would do. That's what my mom would ask for. And she deserved to be more than someone's hidden mistress.

He nods. "It pained me, nearly broke me, but I had to make a choice."

He leans forward, his voice ardent, his eyes beseeching me to understand. "I had to do this to *save* her. I had to let her go. Before she left, I offered her some funds to help raise you, but she didn't want it. She said she didn't want my guilt to be assuaged by giving her money. I came back from a business trip one day and found both of you gone and a note from her asking me to leave you two be. But I never, *ever* forgot about you or her. And there was no other woman for me afterward."

My eyes burn. Now that I have Steven by my side, knowing how intoxicating and wonderful love is with the right man, how it devastated me and him when we almost lost each other, how I couldn't fathom a world without him, my heart aches for Mom.

Suddenly, her love sickness made sense, and why she always believed in true love. How could you not if you've actually experienced its soul wakening warmth? And Mom was always a positive person, even during the challenges we went through, whether it be men or finances, and for the first time, I truly understand why she wanted that hole in her heart filled. And she thought she did to some degree with Uncle Bobby, only for that to end in tragedy as well.

How I wish she were still here and I could tell her I finally understand her and the man she gave her heart to still very much loves her to this day.

"But I've always thought about you and wondered how you're faring. And now, I learn I have another daughter, someone else I also failed over the years." His tone is morose and regretful and he swallows as if the next words out of his mouth are too difficult for him. He reaches over and takes my hand in his cold, trembling ones.

"Grace, would you object to us getting to know each other better? And your sister as well?" He lets out a ragged sigh, a muscle twitching in his bristled cheeks. "I'd very much love that if you both are open to it. You're...family."

There were so many nights in my childhood when I was angry at him. When I laid in bed when the winds beat outside, haunted by the night in the rain with Uncle Bobby, and I wanted to throw things at my father, whoever he was, wherever he was. How could he leave us? Leave mom? Why couldn't I be the happy kid at school sitting atop my father's shoulders as he stopped by an ice cream parlor for a treat of my favorite vanilla ice cream before we head home? Why was it every Father's Day, when the teachers taught us to write letters or to draw cards or we'd make little crafts of paper ties for our fathers, I'd be sobbing in the back, knowing whatever I made wouldn't go to anyone?

But now, looking at the heartbroken man in front of me, who from outward appearances is dressed in the finest clothing, living in the most beautiful home, I can see the void inside him, the loneliness and sadness in his eyes.

The pain of the past haunting him still.

And I can't find it in myself to hate him anymore. Instead, I pity him. While Mom, Taylor, and I didn't have much in the past, our lives were filled with happiness, and our hearts were full. I'm not sure if I believe in this curse, but it's obviously very real to him. It clearly took a piece of him when Mom left with me in tow. A precious piece of him.

He's family. Other than Taylor, he, and by extension, the rest of the Andersons, are my only family of flesh and blood left in this world.

Do I want the regrets of the past to follow us into the future?

After everything I've experienced this past year—the internship, meeting and falling in love with Steven, losing Mom, almost losing the love of my life—I'm tired. Weary. My heart only wants to hold love and warmth, not bitterness and hate.

And so, I take a deep breath and murmur, "I'd love that, sir. I'm sure Taylor would feel the same way."

I chatted with my father for two hours, where he asked me about my upbringing, his face falling when he learned of our financial troubles, his jaw clenching when he deduced the assholes Mom dated in the past, including Carl, the shock registering when I told him about my brief stint at The Orchid.

It was inevitable our paths would eventually cross, even if I didn't search for him. It's like he's standing at the center of concentric circles and I'm slowly removing the larger circles one by one, whether it be my relationship with Steven, who would've brought me closer to the Andersons, or my friendship with Belle or Millie, who both have families and connections to The Orchid.

It was inevitable. Fated.

While our conversation was heavy, and the old ache resurfaces, something that was temporarily forgotten when I'm basking in Steven's love, it was also freeing. Cathartic. It's the final shackles around my heart breaking open.

And now, as I step on the street after I leave my father sitting in his garden, heartbreak shining in his slate-colored eyes, I glance back at the towering mansion, the tall spires and impressive silhouette blocking off most of the sunlight, casting a dark shadow on the front lawns. A chill sweeps through me from a sudden breeze, and I think of the lonely man in his garden, surrounded by his abundant wealth and yet seemingly bereft, and I let out a wistful sigh.

My heart lightens when I walk away, thinking of Steven, feeling thankful for the twist in fate letting us have our happy ending.

⸻

I take a deep inhale as I stroll on the grounds of Central Park, smelling the sweet scent of wildflowers, something I tended not to notice when I was here in the past, hurrying from one location to another, and I let out a ragged, restorative sigh.

A smile appears on my lips as I stroll toward the bench where Steven and I ate the infamous street dog, where he also asked me to meet him tonight.

The skies are clear tonight; the sunset washing the canvas in a swath of reds, golds, and oranges, with a deep, mesmerizing blue slowly creeping in. The prima donna of the evening sky. I can see the faint stars, the backup dancers to the setting sun, twinkling in the backdrop, eager to make an appearance once the starlet disappears, hoping for their place and time to shine.

I hum a melody under my breath, "You're My Stars," thinking how much my life has changed since I heard Steven sang this song all those months ago, and I twirl on the path, swaying past the street musician setting up his saxophone under the ornate stone bridge, past the small crowds of pedestrians strolling to their next destination.

My eyes close as I let my hands fly. I can feel the warm air against my face as I spin, spin, and spin, the night feeling as magical as the one on the High Line, which feels so long ago.

Magic is in the air. I can feel it.

I smile.

"It looks like the conversation with Linus went well," my favorite, sardonic voice speaks from behind me.

Steven.

My heart leaps and flutters as my feet slide in the dirt, which is still soft from the rain a few days ago. His hand reaches out, his arm curling me tight against him, as if he anticipated my wobble.

"You know, if you don't balance well, you probably shouldn't twirl in public." He unleashes a sexy grin, his eyes twinkling with laughter as he tilts me back and stares down at me, looking exactly like a hero from my newest regency romance novel I began last night.

Dark hair. Piercing eyes. Strong jaw. Dashing attire.

"You surprised me, that's all. As you know, I can be an accomplished dancer when I put my mind to it." I wink.

He laughs, the smile transforming his entire face, rendering him to a level of handsome I can't begin to describe.

My lungs seize and I gnaw on my bottom lip, the swarm of butterflies flapping their wings harder inside me, threatening to break free.

I think I'll never stop reacting to him this way. It's like—

"Every time we're apart, our hearts are seeking its other half, and when we're together, we're made whole again," he completes my thought, his gaze darkening, his voice gentle. I hadn't realized I spoke my sentiments aloud.

"And our bodies know." I breathe out, my hands clutching the lapels of his sleek, gray suit, the very one I saw him wearing on stage at Lunasia.

Sultry strains of music echo under the bridge, traveling to where we're standing, his arm still curling around me in a half dip. The soulful sounds of the saxophone fill the air.

A familiar melody, one that'll make me smile and cry at the same time.

"You're My Stars."

Steven laughs, his voice husky, and pulls me upright. He steps back before bowing, one hand extended toward me. "My darling, may I have this dance?"

My eyes flutter to his, finding a twinkle gleaming in his eyes.

He remembered. He noticed my wistful staring at the couples dancing with their partners the last time we were here, and now, he's gifting me that same experience.

A heat forms at the base of my spine and spreads to my chest and I smile, placing my hand in his. He tugs me flush against him, cradling my head against his muscular chest. I can hear the strong beats of his heart.

My heart.

Because his will beat alongside mine for all eternity. It may be whimsical, it may be too soon, but I have a feeling. A sixth sense.

We sway to the music, his familiar scent of the sea and leather, something I finally understand why it's so addictive, the tinge of leather being a scent his father wore, something my subconscious remembered—safety—if it has an actual smell.

"When I look at you," he sings, his voice deep and raspy, his lips touching the outer shell of my ear, "I see my future in your eyes..."

My eyes mist from the deep timbre of his voice as he serenades me under brilliant skies.

Because the voice, the language of our soul, reveals the truth in every husky rasp, every ragged edge, and every smooth vibration. And it's the voice that inevitably reveals part of your hidden soul, breathing life and meaning into the musical piece.

A year ago, at Lunasia, when he was singing this very song, I heard the strains of emptiness and longing inside him.

He croons, the vibrations caressing my ear, "You're my stars in the skies, my everlasting high...our souls intertwined..."

I press a kiss on his jaw, over his fluttering pulse, moisture welling in my eyes.

Now, I hear love and happiness radiating from those husky tones. The once cold King of Wall Street, who ruled his kingdom with a broken heart and haunted eyes, is now happy. Truly happy from deep inside. I can feel it in every rasp, every breath, every twirl under the night.

"Do you know?" he whispers as we sway to the music, my soul filled to the brim with happiness. "In Chinese mythology, the lunar matchmaker, *Yue Lao*, ties a red string between two soulmates before they even meet. The two people connected by the thread are destined to be together, regardless of time, place, or obstacles. The string may tangle, stretch, or shrink, but will never break." His voice is thick, and he tips my chin up to face him.

His soulful eyes are dark, the tiger stones waxing and waning like the phases of the moon, and he smiles softly down at me. "You and I are connected by that red string, long before a heartbroken little boy witnessed a sad little girl in the pouring rain. We are soulmates and everything is destiny, the fates slowly wrenching the string in, pulling me across the country, leading me back to you, where I belong. You are the only person who makes my heart ignite."

My lips part as I marvel at his beautiful words, a sentiment I feel deep inside me. I still remember when I first met him at Pietra, when his soul called out to me as if we had known each other for a long time, despite us being strangers.

An immediate tugging, a calling, a ship coming home after being lost at sea.

Fated.

I return his smile with a wobbly one of my own and I whisper, "I love you, Steven Kingsley."

He clutches my hands against his chest and presses his forehead against mine. "Not as much as I love you, Grace Peyton."

Just then, I see a bright light streaking across the purple sky and I shriek, grasping onto his arm and pointing toward the heavens.

"Steven! A wishing star! Hurry!" I tug him harder when he doesn't respond.

"Bossy," he murmurs.

He chuckles under his breath and slows our pace until we're standing, before closing his eyes, his strong profile angled toward the sky. My heart skips and flies into my rib cage as I bring my hands to my chest, my eyes fluttering shut, and I make a wish to the gods peering down from the gap between the cosmic spheres.

I wish for happiness and for our souls to fly.

Together. Always.

EPILOGUE
3 MONTHS LATER

Grace

"I'm so proud of you, darling," Steven whispers into my ear as we stand in front of the glass double doors to the rooftop bar at The Orchid, where the rest of my family and friends await us.

The deep timbre of his voice sends jolts of awareness to my core as he used the same tone on me this morning at the crack of dawn when he woke me up with his cock between my legs, his rumbly voice in my ear and my body already half-starved and throbbing around him. I bite my lip as the inconvenient images play like a slideshow in my mind.

"Good morning, darling," he rasps as my eyes flutter awake to the sharp sensations gathering on my clit and wetness leaking down my thighs. "You sleep so soundly. I was wondering when you'd wake up."

I gasp, my eyes fluttering open as my body arches up, my breasts already swollen and aching, my legs already wrapped tightly around his back as my hips are gyrating against him, his hard shaft buried deep inside me.

"Fuck," he grunts. "Your pussy needs me even when you sleep, my naughty girl. She wants to wring out all my cum."

His hips piston deeper as the fire builds and my mind, still woozy from sleep, is now drunk with pleasure and I claw his back, desperate to get him deeper inside me.

"You fuck me so good," I whimper, our pace quickening.

Steven hisses and smashes his mouth on mine as he reaches one hand between us and pinches my swollen clit. "Come for me, darling."

"Steven!" I cry as I burst into a million pieces, my legs trembling.

He lets out a tortured groan before he rasps, "Fuuuck," and floods my insides with his heat.

We lay satiated in bed, the soft glow of the morning light streaming through the windows. At this rate, I may as well move in with him since I spend most of my nights here instead of at the apartment.

"Good morning, Grace." He presses a kiss on the outer shell of my ear as he gathers me into his arms.

Steven chuckles like he's aware of my thoughts before kissing the sensitive spot where my ear meets my neck and a frustrated whimper escapes my lips.

"Why, I think you're insatiable for me," he murmurs, his arms curling around my waist as he hugs me from the back. I feel his hardening bulge pressing into the cleft of my ass through our clothing.

I elbow him softly. "Stop distracting me. How did you function the last thirty years?"

"I was asleep...until you."

A flood of warmth spreads from my heart to my fingers and toes, and I feel myself melting against him.

My fingers trace his arm, landing on his watch, and I smile. He's wearing his father's watch again. Their relationship has mended and has been improving in the last few months. I see more smiles on his face after he talks to his parents on the phone now.

Steven slowly unclasps his watch and turns it over. My eyes widen at the additional inscription there.

Mind over matter. Heart above all.

I look up at him, finding him smiling at me. "You taught me that. Take the leap, follow our hearts, even when times get tough."

Gnawing on my lip, I rise to my tiptoes and place a soft kiss on his jaw. I love this man so much.

"Come on," he whispers as he puts back on his watch. "Let's go inside. They're waiting for us."

I bite back a grin as I step into the double doors and see Taylor and Belle rushing up to me, their lips tilted up in bright smiles.

"You're here!" Tay pulls me into a hug and gives me a hearty slap on my back. "I'm so fucking proud of you, opening your own consulting business."

She pulls back and grins, her nose piercing, a red crystal heart today, glimmers from the waning sunlight and pendant lighting hanging from the enclosed glass ceiling.

A wet sheen appears in her eyes, but she blinks it away before whispering, "Mom would be so damn proud of you. I know she's looking down and watching you kick ass."

My heart squeezes and I nod, a burning sensation creeping behind my nose. Today marks the first day of Peyton-Anderson Financial Consulting opening its doors to the public. I'm the owner and sole employee right now, but between my experience in assisting Elias Kent with his investment analysis and working on the high-profile TransAmerica takeover case at Pietra Capital, calls and emails requesting consulting services have been coming in from others in the business community.

I'm sure the Anderson name on the header doesn't hurt either.

"Like I said, I'd hate you if I didn't love you." Belle arches her brow, her eyes taking on a teasing grin as she pulls me into a hug. "Why are you so smart?"

Laughing, I give her a nudge. "I'd say you're the smart one, Belle, when you sat next to me in criminal psychology and declared us to be the best of friends."

She takes a sip of her Long Island Iced Tea and grins. "Of course, I always have impeccable taste. I mean, did you see what your sister is wearing? I got her to actually dress up for this occasion."

My eyes swivel back to Taylor and find her face souring as she rolls her eyes. She's wearing a black sheath dress, which looks beautiful on her slender frame and...pearls. But of course, she kept her signature rebellious streaks in her outfit—the thick, black eyeliner, a dark mauve lipstick, her nails painted in the same color as her dress. She looks like the black swan in *Swan Lake*.

"Belle said they wouldn't let me in if I were to wear my usual getup," Taylor mutters under her breath.

"Where's Millie?" My eyes scan the space, not seeing my petite sweetheart of a friend.

"She's on her way. She's bringing a date today," Taylor replies, her eyes widening.

"What? She's bringing someone even though she has a crush on you-know-who?" My eyes dart around the room until they snag on the imposing figure of my second-eldest half-brother, Ryland, standing by the bar. Millie finally told us the other day why she was so morose lately, and it had everything to do with her professor, who, coincidentally, is Ryland.

Belle leans in and whispers, "I think she's trying to make him jealous."

Taylor's lips curl into a snarl. "If I didn't get to know Ryland in the last few weeks, and have found him to be a pretty cool person because he's one of the few men who haven't gotten on my nerves, I'd smack him for whatever is going on between Millie and him. Millie is the sweetest soul alive. How dare he make her feel bad?"

The same sentiments echo inside my mind as I think of the last few girls' hangouts at their apartment, when Millie would curl up in her chair, her hands hugging her bowl of ice cream, but a heaviness would cloak her frame. Whenever we'd ask, she would say it was nothing. Seeing our sweet, normally exuberant friend losing her glimmer is worrying all of us.

Just then, a whiff of faint roses wafts through the air, and a warm voice joins our group. "Congratulations, Grace. We're so proud of you."

I smile at Lana, who, along with the rest of her siblings, has taken Taylor and me under their wing, embracing us as part of their family. Like her older, or our older brothers, she's stunning, with her sleek russet strands tumbling in waves over her shoulders, her large eyes warm.

"You guys have outdone yourself." I gesture to what looks to be hundreds of sphere lights hanging from the glass ceiling of the large rooftop space, usually cordoned off in sections with tall hedges and perennial trees, is now rearranged such that there's a spacious central area for our gathering. The décor is in a swath of reds, orange, yellows, and golds, the space dripping in tall floral arrangements of chrysanthemums, marigolds, and snapdragons, with bright yellow goldenrods interspersed throughout. The beautiful colors of fall.

"We like to celebrate the big and the small and you're one of us now." Lana winks.

Loud masculine chuckles fill the air and I glance up, finding Steven laughing with the boys congregated by the large, backlit bar, his hand slapping Ryland's back as Rex guffaws in front of them with Ethan shaking his head, a smile tilting his lips. Charles gestures wildly and another roar of laughter fills the space.

The lingering warmth from moments ago flares up as I see how happy Steven is, a lightness never seen before in his frame. The dark eye circles have long disappeared, and he looks sharp and healthy in his double-breasted navy suit. The King of Wall Street is still very much there and from what I heard, he can still be an asshole in the office, but a true exuberance emanates from his being.

He no longer looks haunted and lonely.

He no longer looks like he's walking around with a hole in his chest.

I release a happy sigh as I stare at my soulmate, and as if he is aware of my perusal, he looks up and ensnares me with those molten eyes of his. His lips curve into a private smile, one that singes my insides, and he doles out a flirty wink.

My heart trips and tumbles and heat travels across my skin.

"You two are disgusting," Taylor comments as Lana and Belle laugh at her no-nonsense tone.

We walk toward the men and I whisper back, "One day it'll happen to you."

She snorts as the men step back and make room for us. "Ladies," the collective Anderson men greet us in unison and I quirk my brow. Those well-bred manners seem to be hammered into the Anderson blood.

Rex unleashes a shit-eating grin and pulls me in for a big hug. "I'm so glad you and Tay are part of the family now. That way, Lana doesn't have to tag along to all our hangouts."

"Hey! You enjoy having me around. Who picks up your messes and gets you home when you're drunk?" Lana glowers at her brother, but amusement laces her voice.

Rex smirks and throws his arms around Tay's and my shoulders. "You know, the clues were there all along. We should've known you were related to us."

I quirk a brow. "What do you mean?"

"The ABCDEs."

"Huh?" Tay looks as bewildered as me.

Ryland sighs, like he's used to his younger brother's antics. "Our parents gave us alphabetical middle names in order of age as a private joke. Apparently, there were too many of us. So, Maxell's middle name is Angus, and so on and so forth until Lana is Elise, and then..." He cocks a brow at me as my mouth parts in surprise.

"My middle name is Felicity and Tay's is Gianna," I finish as my sister and I trade glances. "Mom kept with the Anderson tradition."

Rex wags his brow. "So, I guess we are the ABCDEFGs now."

We chuckle before Ryland interjects. "Father and Maxwell apologize for not being able to make it today. They have a meeting with an important investor. And I'll only be here for a few hours because I have to run back to NYUC for a meeting with the dean. Unfortunately, he's only available today." He grimaces before reaching out and clasping my shoulder in a soft squeeze.

"I don't understand why you do this to yourself, bro." Rex is now munching on peanuts he seemingly procured out of thin air. "Aren't you busy enough already with Fleur? Why do you insist on being a fucking professor and corrupting our future youth, anyway?"

Ethan guffaws and slaps Rex on his shoulders.

Ryland pinches his nose as if he's exasperated. "Some of us want to contribute back to society with our privilege. It's something I've done for the past few years and thoroughly enjoy. So, fuck off." The men snort at Ryland's glower.

"Anyway, His Majesty did say to eat and drink to your heart's content tonight. There are suites here with your names on them, so you don't need to worry about getting home afterward," Ethan supplies, changing the subject and turning back to us.

Charles comes back with a tray of champagne and starts handing them out to each of us. "Some refreshments for everyone to toast this wonderful human being for finally, thank fuck, taking my friend off the market so the ladies can focus on me for once. You guys always say I look like Scandinavian royalty. Maybe it's high time the ladies go for blond hair and blue eyes instead of tall, dark, and handsome."

He unleashes a flirtatious smile, his blond hair gleaming under the pendant lights. Steven told me he's playfully bitter about how Jess, Liz, and Sarah didn't choose him but fell head over heels for the men in their lives.

Taylor snorts and rolls her eyes. "If people aren't going for you, maybe you need to look into yourself to see why."

Charles freezes and turns his attention to her, his light blue eyes narrowing, but Taylor shrugs as she takes a sip of her champagne and continues, "I mean, maybe it's your whole charming golden prince aura—life is not all sunshine and fucking sunflowers. Maybe women like substance, men who have seen darkness."

I nudge Taylor in the ribs and she winces. "What? Just telling the truth." Sometimes, her doom and gloom may be a party killer.

"I'm so sorry—" I begin, but Charles cut me off.

"Oh, you have no fucking clue what you're talking about, you brat."

My eyes bug out at the uncharacteristic growl from Charles's voice as he engages in a brief staring contest with Taylor, with neither backing down. Charles is normally the charming, charismatic one out of Steven's friend group, but it seems ever since the two of them met a few months ago, this hidden, angry side of him would make an appearance in her presence.

"And on that note, let us raise our glasses to toast the first Anderson female entrepreneur. May she take New York City by storm." Charles smiles again, as if the last few seconds didn't occur.

Steven curls his arm around me and clinks our glasses together before we do the same with the others in the group.

Ryland steps forward and clears his throat, his champagne flute still raised in the air. "We don't tell you enough, but we are thrilled to have you and Taylor be part of our family. Father seems so much happier since he reunited with you both and I know Maxell, if he were here, would say the same. We're proud to have you two as our sisters."

I beam at him and his normally cool slate eyes soften, a muscle feathering his jaw. From what I've seen so far, Maxwell and Ryland are the least emotional of the Andersons and this is a rare display of affection from him.

"Thank you, Ryland."

He nods and brings the flute to his lips, but pauses midway, a chill befalling his features. His nostrils flare and jaw clenches as he straightens up, his eyes staring at something behind me. His eyes flash with something fierce—an angry spark burning within coal.

Frowning, I turn around, seeing Millie and an unassuming guy her age—the clean-cut boy next door type with blond hair and a friendly smile—standing there, with Millie's lips trembling for a second before curving in the fakest smile I've seen from her.

"Professor Anderson, nice to see you here," the boy next to her says before gulping visibly, fear flashing in his eyes.

Ryland doesn't answer him and the boy's complexion pales and I can almost see the sweat beading on his forehead.

Millie strides forward, tugging her companion behind her, and wraps me in a hug. "Sorry, I'm late. Fred and I had a study session because our asshole professor gave us a ridiculous project," she spits out, her eyes flashing to Ryland again, the venom in her voice absolutely unheard of.

She then links her hand with her date and leans on his shoulder, batting her eyelashes at the poor guy, who looks like he wants to kiss her and also flee Ryland's thunderclouds at the same time.

Ryland emits something sounding suspiciously like a growl, the vein in his forehead throbbing. His hand curls into a fist as he steps forward, his tall frame practically vibrating with rage. "Millie Callahan, if you don't detach yourself from him at this moment, I'll—"

"You'll want? Flunk me in class? Run away and pretend I don't exist like you did before?"

My mouth drops open as I take in this intense quarrel between a professor and his student—no, something definitely more than that. Millie's jealousy warfare may be working after all.

Charles clears his throat and nudges forward, handing Millie and her date two flutes of champagne. Ryland seethes in the background, his face flushed, and Millie turns away and smooths her expression into another fake smile.

Steven cocks a questioning brow at me, and I shrug. I won't be the one to disclose Millie's secrets, girl code and all.

He steps up to Millie and wraps her in a brotherly hug. "So, does Adrian know about this friend of yours?" He nods toward her date.

Millie laughs and shoves him playfully. "I already have one brother. I don't need another one, but I love you all the same for being a bonus brother." She gives a quick peck on his cheek and I swear I can hear another growl from Ryland.

Steven cocks a brow at his friend and the two of them seem to have this strange stare down, silent communication. Steven chuckles and steps back from Millie.

He pulls me against him and lifts his glass up once more. "Thank you all of you for being in our lives."

He turns to me, his eyes intent on mine, and adds, "I'm so proud of you, Grace. For everything you've accomplished. Thank you for making my wish under a star come true every single day."

A chorus of "aww" and "don't make me puke" sounds around us, the strange tension from earlier disappearing.

I turn into a mush as I lean forward and press my lips softly on his, our family and friends cheering in the background.

We finally take the sip of champagne, the bubbles washing down my throat to the pitter pattering of my heart and Steven retrieves an envelope from the inner pocket of his suit jacket.

Turning to me, he bites his plush bottom lip. "Grace, I'm here to cash in on that second day," he says, referring to the second "official" day I gave to him when he agreed to spend his birthday a year ago with me at Central Park. He hands me the envelope.

My fingers tremble as I open the seal, pulling out a travel itinerary. Gasping, my eyes widening, I exclaim, "Paris? For Thanksgiving?"

He grins. "It's your dream to go and it'll be my honor to take you to the City of Love for the first time."

Squealing, I launch myself into his arms, curling my hands around his neck. "Yes, the answer is yes!"

The room dissolves into laughter and more cheers as I cling to him, the man who has given me everything I could possibly want.

"Yes, Steven, I'd love to go to Paris with you," I murmur as he presses soft kisses on my hair, his warmth transferring to my body through our clothes, his familiar scent filling my nostrils and I close my eyes and sigh in contentment.

The answer is always yes with him.

Thank you for reading WHEN HEARTS IGNITE. Hope you've enjoyed Steven and Grace's story as much as I did writing it.

Bonus Epilogues: Want to experience Thanksgiving in Paris with Steven and Grace? There may be a *sparkly* surprise in there! These are the bonus epilogues you don't want to miss! Sign up for my newsletter to get **THREE EXTRA BONUS CHAPTERS**, new release alerts, exclusive bonus material, and more. Just click on the "When Hearts Ignite Bonus Epilogues" on the website: https://www.victorialum.com/bonus

Read Ryland's Story Next: Do you know Ryland and Millie's story is next? This is one hot professor, student, age-gap billionaire romance with angst, steam, and did I mention primal kink? Don't miss WHEN HEARTS COLLIDE. Read it here: https://geni.us/whenheartscollide

Please Review: Please consider leaving a review on the retailer website and Goodreads https://www.goodreads.com/book/show/200420 226-when-hearts-ignite. Your reviews will really help this author out and will allow for more readers to find this book.

THANK YOU

WHEN STEVEN'S CHARACTER FIRST came to my mind in my debut novel, *The Sweetest Agony*, I knew he had a tragic backstory to tell. After all, why would he be so unemotional and disbelieving in love? Grace's character came to my mind around the second or the third book of the *LA Hearts* series and interestingly enough, my first scenes of her were of her dancing at the burlesque club within The Orchid. She's a strong woman facing tough circumstances and serves as the perfect foil for our hero. After all, he deserves the best. They have become one of my favorite couples to write about. Steven's character arc is remarkable, evolving from someone emotionally stunted to someone who realizes the depth of the emotions. I hope you've enjoyed their story as much as I've loved writing it.

As always, thank you to everyone who has supported me, in no particular order:

My family: To my husband and my children, my biggest cheerleaders as I'm the tiny fish swimming upstream these days.

My editors: Theresa Leigh and Amy Briggs, thank you for your insightful feedback as always.

Proofreader: Thank you to Virginia Tesi Carey for catching all those little typos and errors and being a sounding board for my grammar questions.

My PA: Thank you to Nikki Johnson all of your help!

Cover designer: To the awesome LK Farlow of Y'All That Graphic, these covers are gorgeous! I can't stop staring at the discreet covers!

Beta readers: Malia, Jenn, Jess, Fiona, and Isha, thank you so much for your prompt feedback and suggestions! My stories have improved because of you!

My ilLUMinati girls: you know who you are! Thank you for everything! And this blurb would not be awesome without your feedback!

Fellow authors: So many authors have helped me on this journey—it is impossible to name everyone, but I appreciate each and every one of you.

PR Firms: Thank you to Greys Promo and Literally Yours PR for your promotional efforts and helping me get the word out!

My Fellow Readers: I love you all and thank you so much for reading my stories! I've enjoyed every DM, post, comment you've left for me and love chatting about books with you.

With love,

Victoria

ALSO BY
VICTORIA LUM

CATCH UP ON VICTORIA's backlist! Don't miss these swoony, romantic stories with all the sizzling spice and angst. All stories are standalones and can be read out of order.

LA Hearts:
The Sweetest Agony (James and Jess)
The Coldest Passion (Parker and Liz)
The Harshest Hope (Adrian and Emily)
The Brightest Spark (Jack and Sarah)

The Orchid:
When Hearts Ignite (Steven and Grace)
When Hearts Collide (Ryland and Millie)

ABOUT THE AUTHOR

VICTORIA IS A LOVER of all things romance, including movies, books, and television shows. A hopeless romantic since childhood, she is always dreaming up stories and happily ever afters. Caramel lattes are her fuel in the morning and she can usually be found reading anything she can get her hands on. She lives with her family and a beautiful Siberian husky in sunny California.

Keep in touch!

Sign up for her newsletter:

https://www.victorialum.com/sign-up

Follow Victoria on social media:

Victoria Lum's Luminaries Facebook Group
https://www.facebook.com/groups/576423100572205

Facebook Page
https://www.facebook.com/AuthorVictoriaLum

Instagram
https://www.instagram.com/authorvictorialum/

Tiktok

https://www.tiktok.com/@victorialumwriter

Bookbub

https://www.bookbub.com/authors/victoria-lum

Amazon

https://www.amazon.com/stores/Victoria-Lum/author/B0BSGCSH-
NY

Goodreads

https://www.goodreads.com/author/show/23933618.Victoria_Lum

Scan the QR code below for all the links!

Made in the USA
Columbia, SC
16 February 2024

31654413R00255